ALSO BY HOWARD FRANK MOSHER

A Stranger in the Kingdom

Marie Blythe

Where the Rivers Flow North

Disappearances

NORTHERN
BORDERS

DOUBLEDAY

New York   London   Toronto

Sydney   Auckland

NORTHERN
BORDERS

HOWARD FRANK MOSHER

PUBLISHED BY DOUBLEDAY
a division of
Bantam Doubleday Dell
Publishing Group, Inc.
1540 Broadway, New York, New York 10036

DOUBLEDAY and the portrayal of an anchor
with a dolphin are trademarks of Doubleday,
a division of Bantam Doubleday Dell
Publishing Group, Inc.

Portions of *Northern Borders* have previously appeared
elsewhere as follows: "Upland Game," "The Snow Owl,"
and "Down the Coat" appeared in *Yankee Magazine.*
"Hannibal Rex" appeared in *Vermont Magazine.*

Book design by Marysarah Quinn

Library of Congress Cataloging-in-Publication Data

Mosher, Howard Frank.
Northern borders / Howard Frank Mosher. — 1st ed.
p.   cm.
1. Family—Vermont—Fiction.   I. Title.
PS3563.08844N6   1994
813'.54—dc20   94-6443
                                                      CIP

ISBN 0-385-47337-0
Copyright © 1994 by Howard Frank Mosher
All Rights Reserved
Printed in the United States of America
September 1994
First Edition

1 3 5 7 9 10 8 6 4 2

To Phillis

CONTENTS

CONTENTS

We have advanced by leaps to the Pacific, and left many a lesser Oregon and California unexplored behind us.

—*The Maine Woods*
Henry David Thoreau

A LESSER OREGON

Even today Kingdom County is an out-of-the-way and little-known fragment of a much earlier rural America. Forty years ago, when I was a boy growing up there on my grandparents' farm, it was still something of a true frontier. Sequestered from the rest of New England by the Green Mountains to the west and the White Mountains to the east, and further isolated by its notorious seven-month winters and poor dirt roads, the Kingdom during the late 1940s and well on into the 1950s was just the sort of remote, unspoiled enclave Thoreau must have had in mind one hundred years before, when he characterized interior northern Maine and other tracts of overlooked territory east of the Rockies as lesser Oregons.

From my grandparents' place at the end of Lost Nation Hollow, you could strike out ten miles and more through big woods in three directions without crossing a single road, other than a few disused old logging traces. Their farmhouse was situated less than a mile south of the Line, as everyone in the Kingdom called the international boundary between Vermont and Canada. Unguarded and for the most part unvisited, the Line north of our place passed through some of the last authentically wild and undeveloped terrain in the state. And with its two-hundred-year history as the site of countless skirmishes between the Abenaki, French, and English, its tradition of whiskey smuggling and legends of huge yellow panthers and savage gray wolves, and its vast stands of tall timber made nearly inaccessible by still vaster cedar bogs, the border imparted an additional frontier atmosphere to Kingdom County.

Yet it was not just the wild and mountainous terrain or the Canadian Line or the myths of marauding catamounts that defined the Kingdom of my boyhood as a frontier. It was also the terrifically independent-minded people who still lived there, enjoying, as they did, the essential elbowroom not only from outsiders but from each other as well, to develop unique styles of thinking and living.

Moreover, although the Great Depression had officially ended several years before I was born, few Kingdom natives seemed to realize it, any more than the Kingdom had ever acknowledged the Depression when it arrived. The fact of the matter is that Kingdom County had always been poor. During the Depression and its long, lingering aftermath throughout rural northern New England, my grandparents and their neighbor had, perhaps, somewhat less ready cash than usual—which is to say, next to none at all.

Still, with the passing of my boyhood, the era that had distinguished the Kingdom as a lesser Oregon was rapidly coming to a close, along with the lives of the generation, my grandparents' generation, that sustained that era into the middle of the twentieth century. In fact, much of the drama and conflict inherent in the lives of the last traditional hill farmers derived from the sheer impossibility of preserving their special way of life in the face of inexorable progress and changes, such as Vermont's bulk tank law prohibiting the shipping of milk in cans, the arrival of electricity, improved roads and cars and easier accessibility both to and from the outside world in general.

Fortunately for me, the world of my grandparents remained intact a little longer in the Kingdom than elsewhere. Long enough, at least, for me to live through its final years, as recorded in the following remembrances. All date from my boyhood with my Kittredge grandparents, from 1948, when I turned six, to 1960, when I was eighteen and my grandfather astounded me and the rest of the family by doing something so totally marvelous and unpredictable, even for him, that in a very real sense you could say that he put an end to the era of which I am writing himself. For the most part, I have selected recollections designed to record that world that no longer exists and I have arranged them more or less chronologically. Some describe single events during the twelve years I spent with my grandparents; others are more general; still others concentrate on one or more family members since this is, first and foremost, a family memoir.

These are the events and people that have stayed with me, undiminished in clarity, over the past four decades. They are as vivid in my mind and imagination today as the old family photographs in the albums in my grandparents' attic, which as a boy I pored over for hours on end, and which I still keep on the shelves of my study. Often at night, just before falling asleep, they appear unbidden, image after image, photographs never taken, of my great and little aunts, my Uncle Rob, my cousins, and mutual ancestors whom I never knew but seemed to live with, through family stories, like near neighbors. Yet always my thoughts return to my grandparents themselves, whose fierce pride and diligence, not to mention sheer Kittredge cussedness, seemed to embody the spirit of Lost Nation Hollow and the Kingdom.

For twelve years, they were at the center of everything for me. They remain now, forty years later, at the center of that vanished world, that lesser Oregon, whose like will not be seen again, in Kingdom County or elsewhere.

Austen Kittredge III
Lost Nation Hollow, 1994

1

THE FARM
IN LOST NATION

When I was a boy living on
my grandparents' Kingdom
County farm, I sometimes
amused myself by looking
through an ancient family Bible in
the farmhouse attic. This ponder-
ous tome was a gloomy-looking affair if one ever existed. It weighed
a good fifteen pounds, and it was bound tightly shut by a tarnished
metal clasp which snapped open with the report of a pistol and
never failed to startle me, alone in the remote, dim attic of my
grandparents' vast old house.

Once this formidable mechanism had been breached, the Bible's
contents were intriguing. Besides the Old and New Testaments, it
contained a Kittredge family birth register illuminated in gilt; a
death register edged in sable; a table of standard weights and measures from which I gleaned the invaluable information—it must
have been invaluable because I still remember it today, some four
decades later—that one country furlong is the equivalent of forty

rods; a dozen or so remarkably well-preserved wildflowers collected by a distant aunt said to have died at eighteen of a broken heart; and several pages of genealogical charts inscribed with the biblical-sounding names of more ancestors than I'd ever dreamed one boy could lay claim to, beginning with my great-great-great-great-great-grandfather: the first Kittredge to venture up into the trackless mountain fastness that would become Kingdom County.

His name, aptly enough, was Sojourner Kittredge, and he was a Loyalist schoolteacher and part-time log sawyer who fled Connecticut and the American Revolution for Canada in the summer of 1775 with a lone red ox and a high-sided cart containing all his worldly possessions. Two arduous months later, my ancestor stopped for good on the headwaters of a small, fast, icy river, which he promptly named the Kingdom, in honor of his beloved mother empire. Unfortunately, there was one small difficulty with Sojourner's choice of a homestead. As my grandfather, who disliked all schoolteachers in general and those in our own family in particular, loved to tell me nearly two centuries later, the old Tory had put down stakes here as the result of a minute but fateful miscalculation. Since the Kingdom River drains north, toward the St. Lawrence, though by a circuitous and at times even contradictory route, he erroneously assumed that he had already reached Canada and sanctuary when in fact he'd fetched up instead in northern Vermont.

Not, you understand, that such a trifling technicality as a line on a map mattered a whit to the old expeditionary once he'd made up his mind to stay put. By the time Sojourner finally figured out where he actually was, the Revolution had been over for several years. He'd already established the first grammar school and sawmill in Lost Nation, as he wryly named our township. And by then he did not have the slightest intention of lighting out again for Canada or anyplace else, though for three generations afterward his descendants marched in the Independence Day parades in Kingdom Common wearing bright scarlet coats and carrying the Union Jack.

This is nearly all I know about my great-great-great-great-great-grandfather—except that in 1790 he astonished his neighbors and outraged his heirs by ceding the title to a ten-thousand-acre tract of woodland just south of the Canadian border to the state whose authority to govern any other part of the Kingdom he refused to acknowledge to his dying day. Sojourner's intention was for Vermont to use the donated property as the site of a college to educate the youth of its white settlers and native Abenakis alike. In exchange, he neither demanded nor received a single shilling. He requested only a written guarantee that every qualified graduate of the Lost Nation Atheneum, as he rather grandiosely called his one-room country school, be entitled to attend the proposed state college free of charge, for as long as the grammar school and college should both exist.

Of course the University of Vermont never did take advantage of my ancestor's offer. Instead it situated itself one hundred miles across the Green Mountains to the southwest, on the considerably more clement and accessible shores of Lake Champlain. Yet even after the university sold off its Kingdom real estate holdings to pay debts incurred during the Civil War, it continued to honor the agreement between Sojourner Kittredge and the state that he otherwise declined to recognize. All duly prepared graduates of Lost Nation Atheneum were entitled to attend the university at no expense to themselves; and it was partly as a result of this ancient pact that a Kittredge family decision was reached that I would receive the first eight years of my education at the tiny country schoolhouse established one hundred and seventy years ago by my forward-looking ancestor, and live during those years with my Kittredge grandparents on their farm in Lost Nation Hollow, spending some of my school vacations with my father in White River Junction, eighty miles to the south.

Other considerations influenced my father's decision to send me north to Kingdom County, however. No doubt the first, and most weighty, was that my mother had been dead for nearly a year at the time, and my father had concerns about raising me entirely on his own. As a child and teenager, my mother had waged a protracted and costly battle with tuberculosis, and throughout her brief adult life she continued to have periodic relapses. Several times since marrying my father and having me she had been forced to return to the famous Trudeau Institute at Saranac Lake, where she'd spent much of her youth; and for several months when I was two, she convalesced at a sanatorium in Tucson, Arizona, while my Grandmother Kittredge kept house for my father and took care of me in White River. I don't remember that my mother ever said much about her illness to me. I'm sure she made every effort not to. But from my grandmother and my two little aunts, Dad's sisters, I received at a very early age the alarming impression that Mom was much more sickly than she ever revealed. "Your mother is a poor frail soul if one ever existed," my grandmother told me frequently; and although it was terribly difficult for me to lose her when I was just five years old, I must say that even at that tender age, it came as more of a surprise than an outright shock.

From those early years, I vividly recall two things about my mother. Unlike most of the Kittredges, including my father and both of my grandparents, she laughed easily and frequently. And she loved to read to me, so that one of my very earliest and strongest childhood recollections is of sitting beside her on a rather battered green living room couch and looking at the pictures in the storybooks we went through together by the dozens, especially the marvelous old tales of the Brothers Grimm and Hans Christian Andersen, whose brilliantly-colored illustrations of the most hideous scenes and creatures imaginable I found deeply fascinating.

Because of my mother's huge medical bills, the opportunity to send me to college free someday must have been unusually appealing to my father. And a further factor in his decision to send me up to my grandparents' farm in Lost Nation was that as headmaster of the White River Academy, my father, wisely enough, did not want me to be stigmatized, possibly for the next twelve years, as the principal's son. Also I believe that Dad may have had a secret motivation in sending me north—one he did not mention to anyone.

For many years my grandfather and my father had not, as my little aunts put it, seen eye to eye with each other. Dad had left home at eighteen for the state university and returned only for brief visits. The division had deepened when, to my grandfather's utter disgust, my father had chosen to become a schoolteacher. But time and distance have a way of softening even the most acrimonious of family feuds; and although I have no real evidence that this was the case, I strongly suspect that I was sent to Kingdom County partly as a peace offering from my father to my grandfather.

What I know for certain is my father decided that to become acclimated to the Farm, as we called my grandparents' place, and to my grandparents themselves, who to this day remain two of the most unusual people I have ever met, it would be helpful for me to spend the summer before I entered the first grade with them in Lost Nation. We would try a one-month stint at first and see how it went. Dad would then visit me in Lost Nation, and if all was going well, I would stay on at least for the rest of the summer.

And this is how, one sunny June afternoon a few days after my sixth birthday, I came to be waving good-bye to my father from the grimy window of a Boston to Montreal passenger car carrying me north toward the wild border country of Kingdom County and, though I had no way to know it, some of the most memorable years of my life.

What do I remember from that long-ago train trip up the Connecticut River to the little-known territory that might well become my new home for the next eight years or more? Fleeting impressions, mainly. Backward-rushing glimpses of the river, with cows and barns spread out at intervals along it. Small villages with tall white church steeples. A few bridges. For some reason I also recall that the seat material was of a fuzzy, worn felt, which set my teeth on edge when I ran my fingernails over it, and made me shiver. What a solemn, daydreaming, standoffish little fellow I must have been, with an entire seat to myself and my suitcases, which to the annoyance of the conductor I had insisted on carrying aboard with me. In one were my clothes. The other contained my favorite storybooks.

Of course I was sad to be leaving home, and somewhat apprehensive about my first solo train ride. But there have been few times in my life when I have not been able to achieve a degree of serenity by immersing myself in a book—in part, no doubt, because my books provided me with a certain tangible connection with my mother even after her death. Shortly after leaving White River I dug a copy of *Heidi* out of my suitcase-library, and soon I was far off in the Swiss Alps, though whether I was absorbed mainly by the book's gorgeous color plates of the mountains, or my recollections of the tale as read to me by my mother, or the actual words themselves, I don't know. I do remember being especially interested in Heidi's old hermit-grandfather, since not long before her death my mother had confided to me that he had always reminded her of my own grandfather, who could be "rather gruff" himself at times. To which my father had bluntly replied, "*Gruff!* Good God, the man's a bona fide misanthrope." I didn't know what a misanthrope was, bona fide or otherwise. But it sounded forbidding and I must say that I looked forward to meeting my grandfather for the first time with some trepidation.

As we rolled north on the local passenger train, or Buntliner, as it was called—the entire train consisted of a silver-and-blue engine that looked more like a passenger car than a locomotive, and four silver-and-blue coaches—the hills became steeper and shaggier. The farms began to look shabbier. The spanking white houses and fire-engine red barns gave way to unpainted houses connected by sway-backed sheds and ells to listing barns. In the farm dooryards, lilacs were just coming into blossom though back in White River the lilacs had gone by two weeks ago.

At one riverside town a fearsome-looking old man with long gray hair and black whiskers and a greasy slouch hat got on my coach and sat down in the seat opposite me. When the Buntliner pulled out of the station, he produced a flat, amber-colored glass flask from his lumber jacket pocket and took two or three swigs of a very vile-looking dark liquid. As he wiped off his mouth with the back of the hand holding the flask, he darted a severe look out from under his drooping hat brim straight at me. I looked away fast. But when I glanced back at him a moment later he was still staring at me. And in a single, bonechilling moment, it became irrefutably clear to me that this bewhiskered apparition was in fact my grandfather.

The conductor who'd been annoyed with me for bringing my bags into the car was coming down the aisle checking tickets. "Have you been drinking, mister?" he said to the old man.

"No, sir!" he declared.

The conductor knew better. "There's no drinking permitted in the day coaches," he said. "I've had to speak to you about it before, haven't I?"

"I don't believe so," said my grandfather in a very loud and very indignant voice.

The conductor gave him a hard look. "Well," he said, "I mean business. If I catch you drinking, I'll put you off at the next station without a second thought."

He moved on down the aisle, swaying to the motion of the train like a veteran trick-rider at the circus. There were only five or six other passengers in our coach, including a large woman in a small blue hat and a minister with a white patch of collar showing. After punching their tickets with an odd little silver apparatus, the conductor swayed gracefully back up the aisle, and passed on into the next car.

In the meantime, the whiskery man was shooting me many covert, fierce looks. He knew very well that I'd seen him drinking from the amber flask. I had no idea what was in it, of course, or why drinking was not permitted in the day coaches. But the old fellow now seemed to feel that he owed me some sort of explanation for the very palpable falsehood he'd told the conductor. For without the slightest warning he lunged halfway out of his seat across the aisle toward me and growled, "I suppose you're a-wondering why I ain't drinking when it appears otherwise, be you, be you?"

Not having the faintest idea how to respond to this query, I didn't.

"Aha!" he said, and took another quick pull at his bottle. "Cat's got his tongue, I see."

He made another start in my direction, seizing the armrest of my seat for support. With his flushed face very close to mine he said, "Speaking of cats, which you wasn't but I was, I've got a cat up home to Lost Nation that weighs twenty pounds. It weighs as much as a wheel of cheese."

He raised his tangled gray eyebrows as though to better impress me with this disclosure. Then he said, "This cat of mine can kill five full-growed rats in a grain barrel in sixty seconds flat. Do you believe that?"

"Yes," I said. Although I was not quite sure how we had gotten so rapidly from the matter of his drinking or not drinking to cats, I was very eager to accommodate this rough old cob, if only to forestall another ferocious lunge in my direction. Also, his mentioning Lost Nation Hollow confirmed for me that this was indeed my grandfather and namesake, Austen Kittredge, in what I fervently hoped was some sort of raffish disguise designed to help him assess me unobserved.

"Besides rats," he continued, "this cat that weighs as much as a cheese cannot abide dogs, other cats, or spying young boys. Neither as a rule can I."

The topic of the rat-fighting cat had evidently made my traveling companion thirsty. He sneaked another long drink. Then he made as if to offer me one. Before I could decide what to do he whipped the flask back out of sight and chuckled and nodded his head knowingly.

"Now," he said to the entire passenger car in an altogether different, remarkably businesslike tone, "why ain't I a-drinking? I shall tell you why. I ain't a-drinking for that I ain't a drinker."

This revelation was received by the rest of the car with stunned disbelief. By now everyone had seen the bottle, which he had all along made a great show of displaying and then hiding. But an explanation was forthcoming.

Giving me a look of the deepest significance, he announced, "Why ain't I a drinker? Because I'm a sipper. Do you understand that?"

I said I did, whereupon he fetched out the bottle again and knocked back two or three of the longest sips in the history of the world.

"Ain't I an awful old whore, though?" he said with a smirk of his whiskers, and both the big woman in the small hat and the minister gasped.

Whereupon the gentleman who was my grandfather tipped me a sly wink and ripped out loudly, "Ain't you and I *both* a pair of old whores, though."

I readily agreed that we were. This seemed to please him a good deal. So much so, in fact, that he entrusted me with a grave charge. "My boy," he said, "I want you to watch sharp. Watch sharp, and notify me immediately if you spot that train fella coming through again.''

So saying he repaired to the far corner of his seat to nurse his bottle, sipping away to beat the band, while I kept an eye out for the conductor, and wondered what an old whore was and, for that matter, what a young whore was, and just what sort of country this Lost Nation that I was traveling to might be.

"What's in them two valises?" the sipping man barked out suddenly a few minutes later, pointing with the neck of the flask at my suitcases. "Your duds?"

"Yes. And books."

"Books!" he said in an outraged voice. "What sort of books?"

I shrugged. "Boys' and girls' books, I guess."

"I'll show you a book that ain't no boys' book nor girls' book, neither," he said. From the hip pocket of his wool pants he extracted a well-worn paper-covered volume. He tipped my way precariously and flashed me a glimpse of the cover. To my amazement it depicted a smiling young woman, stark naked from the waist up.

"What sort of speller be you?" the man said.

I told him I believed I was a fair speller.

"Well, then. Do you care to know what I call these books?"

He flashed the naked young woman at me again. Good heavens, she had brown eyes and dark auburn hair, the exact color of my Sunday School teacher's, Miss Irene Proctor's. Could it possibly be Miss Proctor?

"Yes," I said with great interest. "What do you call them?"

"I call them F·U·C·K Books," he said loudly, laying the most precise emphasis on each letter, like a finalist in a championship spelling bee.

Three or four gasps could be heard this time; but all he said was, "Do you know why I call them that?"

"No," I said, truthfully enough.

"It's because someone usually always gets F·U·C·K·D on every page," he roared out for the benefit of the whole Buntliner.

This time a general gasp went up. "See here, there are women on this conveyance," the minister said.

I, for my part, could hardly wait for another glimpse of the

F·U·C·K Book. But the old scholar across the aisle slipped it back into his hip pocket with a sneering chuckle, had another long sip and leaned over to confide to me that he had once "tooken twenty dollars off a seed salesman in a railway car" by winning a bet that he could "hurinate fifty yards at one whack."

I had never witnessed a grown-up misbehaving publicly before, and was terribly delighted by the spectacle. But the minister had heard enough.

"Here now," he said. "You, lad. I want you to come back here and sit with me."

"Don't you move a muscle, young boy," the old man said. "Do you see that soft maple over yonder?" He jabbed with the neck of the flask out the window at a tree on the riverbank. "Such a distance as that is mere child's play for me."

Abruptly, he stood up, gripping the tops of the seats on either side of the aisle to steady himself. "Who in this coach will lay twenty dollars I can't make water fifty yards from a dead standstill with no running start?" he demanded. He frowned at the woman in the blue hat. "Are you game, madam?"

"I'm going to ring for the conductor," the minister said. "This has gone too far."

"If you tech that cord, preacher, I'll tear it off the wall and throttle you with it," my whiskered friend said, and took half a dozen long swinging strides to the rear of the car and out onto the small railed rear platform of the Buntliner.

We all swiveled around in our seats, even the fat woman and the minister. I was afraid that the old man would fall off the rear of the train. But evidently he had performed this operation successfully enough more than once before; for after turning his back and groping around in his pants for a minute, he cut loose a great jetting stream that arched out over a prodigious distance of track behind the speeding train. After fumbling with his pants some more he returned to his seat.

"That's how I won my bet with that flatlander seed salesman," he said, and promptly fell asleep.

The old man woke up again just once, shortly after we left St. Johnsbury. Starting bolt upright like a man frightened out of a

nightmare, he stared over at me with his eyes all fiery red and said
very clearly in a booming official voice: "Now comes the State of
Vermont against WJ Kittredge in the Eighth District Court of Kingdom County, on this the twelfth day of June, nineteen hundred and
forty-eight."

Immediately after making this announcement he seemed to
come to his senses. "What's your name, boy?" he demanded.

"Austen Kittredge," I said.

"The hell!" he shot back. "I may be sipping drunk and I may be
piss-whistle drunk but I ain't blind drunk. Austen Kittredge is my
neighbor and blooded cousin and you ain't him by about fifty
years."

"I was named for him," I said with mixed relief and disappointment now that I knew that the mischief-making old devil across the
aisle was only a cousin. For clarification I added, "He's my grandfather."

"You don't have no grandfather," he said, and fell back against
the felt seat dead to the world.

It did not take the Boston to Montreal Buntliner long to cover the
sixty miles from White River to Kingdom Common. It was still
only late afternoon when we pulled into the station and I struggled
down the aisle with my two suitcases.

I was hoping that my grandfather's cousin, Mr. WJ Kittredge,
would wait with me on the platform. His company, I reasoned,
would be better than no company. But I had little hope from him in
this regard. Without a word to me, he cut across a long central green
toward a large white building at the far end. I could see the dark red
top of Miss Irene Proctor's close likeness on the F·U·C·K Book
sticking out of his pocket, and I reminded myself to ask my grandfather what under the sun such a book was about and how I could get
hold of some—assuming that my grandfather ever showed up.

From where I stood on the platform I could see most of the
village. Farther up the street, on the same side of the green as the
railroad station, were three large stone buildings. Facing them on the
opposite side of the green was a three-story brick building contain-

ing several stores on the ground floor. A baseball diamond was laid out on the green, which interested me considerably.

As the short silver train pulled out of the station, gathering speed for the last leg north before the Canadian border, a harsh voice behind me said, "I wouldn't mind being aboard her, would you? Headed north for Labrador."

I whirled around to see a tall man wearing a red-and-black-checked flannel shirt and neatly-creased green work pants. He had short white hair, and when he shifted his gaze from the departing train to me, I was struck by his eyes, which were pale blue and critical-looking. I do not mean that my grandfather's eyes—for this was my real grandfather, I had no doubt—were cold or unkind. But they were the sharpest pair of eyes I had ever seen, the kind that miss nothing at all. And when he spoke to me again I was struck by how harshly his voice grated, and how well it matched those assessing blue eyes.

"Be you Austen?"

"Yes."

"Then I'm your grandfather." He picked up my bags as easily as if they were empty. "Get in the truck," he said.

My grandfather's truck had a rounded, dark green cab and a long flat bed. It rode as rough as a lumber wagon, which is exactly what it turned out to be: a lumber wagon, with trailer wheels, welded onto the cab of a 1934 Ford pickup.

As we drove out of town my grandfather lit a cigar. Then he informed me that, besides lumber, he transported milk to the cheese factory on the edge of the village three times a week. Although his voice was very hard and sharp, he spoke to me without condescension, the way he might speak to another man. And both he and the truck cab smelled very strongly of tobacco and Christmas trees since, as I would discover, he was an inveterate cigar smoker and he also carried with him at all times the aromatic evergreen scent of the timber he worked with, which my grandmother could not wash out of his pants and shirts.

We drove along a fast river, up into a jumble of abrupt, green hills, past woods and dilapidated farm buildings. Some of the farms were abandoned, and my grandfather told me who lived at the others. In two or three instances he added a brief, critical commentary. "They say Ben Currier's a prosperous farmer. I'd be a prosperous man myself if I had half the money Ben Currier owes . . . That man who lives there abuses his horses. I'll tell you one thing. He won't soon do it again whilst I'm driving past."

I told my grandfather about the whiskery man on the train, and how I'd originally mistaken the fellow for him. He made a rasping sound in his throat, not a laugh exactly, and said that would have been his cousin, all right, Whiskeyjack Kittredge. "He's a poacher and a moonshiner and a general all-purpose outlaw," my grandfather said. "How did you like him?"

"I liked him all right," I said. "He told me he's got a rat-fighting cat that weighs twenty pounds. And he peed off the end of the train and reads F·U·C·K Books where someone gets F·U·C·K·D on every page."

My grandfather made that singular, sharp noise in his throat again. "How old did you say you were?"

"Six."

"Yes, sir," he said.

"What does it mean?" I said. " 'F·U·C·K·D on every page'?"

"I'll tell you when you turn twenty-one."

Then, quickly, as though to indicate that he had said all he intended to on the subject of his bewhiskered cousin with the outlandish name and the arcane reading matter, he informed me that he'd heard I intended to go to work for him that summer, and to stay on and attend the Lost Nation School in the fall if I was satisfied with my situation. I was surprised. This was the first I'd heard about working for my grandfather. A troubling thought crossed my mind. What if, at the end of this probationary period, my grandparents weren't satisfied with me? In point of fact, my grandfather looked as though he might be a hard man to please.

As we turned off the paved road onto a one-lane dirt track my grandfather said, "Do you like fairs?"

"Fairs?"

"Yes. County fairs."

My father had taken me to the county fair near White River last summer, and I'd loved it. "Yes!" I said enthusiastically.

"Well," my grandfather said, "I'm not by any means a wealthy man. I can't afford to pay regular wages to a fella. But if you work hard and learn your job and pan out, I'll stake you to a full day at Kingdom Fair come August. How does that sound to you?"

I said it sounded fine, and after that a lull fell over our conversation and we traveled on up the dirt road in silence for a few minutes. It was obvious that this was a much more remote part of Vermont than any I had ever visited. The stream we'd been following was smaller and quicker, the heavily-wooded hills came crowding down close to the narrow valley on both sides. Many of the farms seemed disused. Those still in operation looked even poorer than the farms closer to the village. In the dooryards I began to notice what looked like covered trash barrels with darkish smoke curling out. "Smokers," my grandfather explained. "Burning softwood to keep the black flies down. It's buggy up here this time of year."

At the top of a long hill my grandfather jerked his thumb at a weathered building, one entire wall of which seemed to consist of small square windows. "That's where you'll be going to school. If you decide to stay on in the fall."

The school looked abandoned too, with buttercups and daisies blossoming in the yard; still, there was something both exciting and unsettling to me about the place, which I would forever afterward connect with the idea of school and going to school.

"I went there for a spell myself," my grandfather said. "I left when I was twelve to go on a log drive. The truth of the matter is, I didn't agree with school and school didn't agree with me."

My grandfather paused a moment to let this announcement sink in. Then he said, "Your father went there too. I'm sorry to say he turned out to be a schoolteacher."

My grandfather stated this fact as though my father had committed armed robbery and been caught, tried and convicted, and sent to state prison. But having been warned ahead of time about his views on schoolteachers and my father, I knew better than to pursue the subject.

From the next hilltop I could look off in three directions at mountain ranges. Some of the peaks were still white on top. I could scarcely believe that we were looking at snow in mid-June, but my grandfather assured me that we were. He showed me Jay Peak and Mount Washington. He pointed to a rugged heap of mountains straight ahead. "Canada," he said.

Higher up the Hollow we passed an elderly woman out in a hayfield with two horses and a wagon. My grandfather lifted his hand to her and said, "That would be your Big Aunt Rose. She hates to admit it but she's my sister. That's my place up there. The last one up the Hollow."

Just ahead, in a kind of scooped-out bowl at the base of a high, forested ridge, the dirt track ended in the dooryard of a very large two-story house, weathered to a pearly gray, with a much larger faded red barn linked to it by an ell consisting of a hodgepodge of connected sheds. On a steep slope between the rear of the barn and the edge of the woods were a dozen or so red and white cows, all facing the same way. Across a meadow from the house, just below a small pond where the river had been dammed, slouched a long low building, open on one side, which my grandfather identified to me as his sawmill.

My grandfather stopped his truck in the road and surveyed his buildings critically. Suddenly he looked straight at me and inquired in that perpetually harsh tone if I were afraid of him.

"No," I said promptly.

I think my answer pleased him. But all he said was, "Do you know who lives there?"

He was pointing at the gray house.

"You do," I said.

He shook his head. "I'll tell you who lives there. The meanest old bastard in Kingdom County, that's who. Remember that you heard it first from me."

I did. And I was so delighted by the phrase that, from then on, each time my grandfather and I approached the Farm in his home-made lumber truck, I would, with great innocence, inquire who lived there. Whereupon he would respond, "The meanest old bas-tard in Kingdom County."

After which he would look at me with a kind of grim satisfaction and say to my complete puzzlement, "Remember that you heard it first from me."

Although I had never laid eyes on my grandfather until that day, my grandmother and I first met the day I was born, June 8th, 1942. She and my little aunts, Little Aunt Freddi and Little Aunt Klee, had been visiting our home in White River to assist with what my grandmother was pleased to call my mother's "laying-in." I was born at the local hospital around six a.m.—a propitious hour, according to my grandmother, who believed that children born before eight o'clock in the morning would never have a lazy bone in their bodies—and my grandmother first viewed me around seven. My mother was holding me in her arms at the time.

According to my little aunts, no sooner did my grandmother clap eyes on me than she nodded with grave approval and announced, to the absolute astonishment of the attending nurse, "Ah! He looks exactly like the doomed young pharaoh, King Tutankhamen. What have you named him, Sarah?"

"Austen," my mother replied. "After his father and grandfather."

My grandmother nodded again. "Austen he'll be then. But I'll call him Tut. If he lives, he'll forever be Tut to me."

For the next six years, my grandmother visited us regularly twice a year: at Christmas, and on my birthday, as well as during that period of several months when my mother was recuperating in Tucson. I cannot recall a great deal about her from those early times: a dark-haired, dark-eyed, tiny and intense woman, dressed entirely in black, who when she spoke to me at all called me by the name of an Egyptian king, and who seemed always to be watching me with a kind of determined approbation. It was my grandmother who, when I was four or five, coined the phrase "a famous reader" to describe me, and concluded that such a prodigy would someday "be heard from." But mainly I remember her as that small woman in black, who came to our home punctually twice a year, evidently for the sole purpose of observing me—as she was doing this instant from the porch of the huge, rambling farmhouse while my grandfather and I continued up the lane in his lumber truck.

"There they are," he said.

"They?" I said.

"Your grandmother. Spying on us with those glasses."

My grandfather was right. As we drove closer I saw that not only was my grandmother watching us, she was watching through a small pair of binoculars or opera glasses, and I very distinctly recall that tatters of dark gray smoke from the smoker barrel in the dooryard were drifting between her and us, so that she looked a little like a mirage. When we came into the barnyard she lowered the glasses but did not lift her hand or speak, even when I got out of the truck and went shyly up to her, which made her seem more like a mirage than ever.

My grandmother neither hugged nor kissed me. I had not expected her to. But as I climbed up the wooden porch steps she reached out and seized my wrist in her tiny, strong hand, an action she would repeat over and over again in the future. "Welcome home, Tut," she said. "Come inside for supper."

Before we ate, my grandmother gave me a quick tour of the farmhouse and barn. The current house, she told me, had been built in the early nineteenth century to replace the log-framed home Sojourner had thrown up in the wilderness soon after his flight from the Revolution. Originally, it was a simple eight- or nine-room structure of two stories. Over the decades, as the Kittredge family had grown, extending itself far beyond mere bloodlines, so had the farmhouse. By degrees, it had linked itself to the barn, North Country-fashion, by means of an ell stretching due west more than one hundred and fifty feet. Through this labyrinth of connected sheds you could pass all the way from my grandmother's kitchen to my grandfather's milking parlor without once setting foot outdoors. At the same time, the house proper had expanded correspondingly in the opposite direction. I may be forgetting a back upper chamber or two, or some obscure jerry-built shed slung onto the rear of the summer kitchen as an afterthought; but to the best of my recollections, the architectural camelopard known to all Kittredges for the past hundred years simply as the Farm contained—including the subdivisions of the ell and barn—a grand total of thirty-eight distinct rooms. I didn't visit them all that first evening, but the impression I received was one of vastness.

I don't remember all that my grandmother said on our tour, but I do recall that on her apron belt she wore a great ring of weighty old iron keys, and that as she walked the keys jingled loudly. In the best parlor she pointed out an elaborate coat of arms made decades ago from the hair of twenty or more family members, and framed in glass, which I found unsettling and fascinating, in equal parts. My bedroom was to be in the small loft-chamber over the kitchen, which was a relief to me. I definitely did not want to be stuck off in one of the remote, isolated second-story rooms far out of earshot from my grandparents.

Supper, which we ate in the kitchen at a plain white table, was a quiet affair. I don't recall what we ate; noon dinner was the main meal in Kingdom County in those days. I was aware of a certain strained atmosphere, which I attributed to the unaccustomed presence of a boy at the table but in fact, as I would soon discover, had much more to do with the strained relationship of my grandparents in general. I sat next to my grandfather, with my grandmother across from me; and on the rare occasions when they addressed each other at all, they referred to one another as "Mrs. Kittredge" and "Mr. Kittredge" with grim irony detectable even to a small boy.

"Austen, ask Mrs. Kittredge to pass the butter along if it isn't too much trouble."

"Perhaps Mr. Kittredge would like to put the newspaper down, Tut, until we're finished eating. It might occur to him that reading at the table is a very bad example to set for a boy."

At the end of the meal, my grandfather silently rose and left the table with his paper.

"You're welcome, Mr. Kittredge," my grandmother said. At the same time she looked at me significantly, just as my grandfather himself had done once or twice during the meal. The true import of these glances would dawn on me only gradually. At the time, I had no way of knowing that each of my grandparents regarded me as a potential ally in their Forty Years' Domestic War.

"Come, Tut. I want to show you something wonderful," my grandmother said as soon as the dishes were done. My grandfather had settled into a large wooden rocker by the south kitchen window with the latest issue of the *National Geographic*. He shot a brief, meaningful look at me over the top of his reading spectacles as my grandmother and I headed down the short hallway connecting the kitchen with the large dining room used only on Sundays and special occasions.

Just before entering the dining room, my grandmother veered off into a small sitting room-bedroom she hadn't shown me on our tour before supper. It was growing dusky outside, and she lighted a lamp on a sort of worktable by the window. As the wick flared up, the strangest room I had ever laid eyes on came into view. Except for a small bed hardly larger than a child's trundle bed, and the table with the lamp, it was a perfect museum of a room, full of the most astonishing items.

"Egypt, Tut," my grandmother said solemnly.

On the wall opposite the doorway was a poster-sized picture of a creature unlike any I had ever seen before: a vast winged individual with the body of a lion and the head of a woman, who seemed, in the protean light of the kerosene lamp, to be staring straight at me.

"That's the Great Sphinx," my grandmother said. "You didn't want to get on his bad side, I'll assure you. But don't worry, they've been extinct for thousands of years.

"That's Lord Ra," my grandmother continued, indicating a foot-high wooden fellow with a jaunty hawk's head in a flowing yellow and blue headdress. "You can bet he knew what the score was."

In frames here and there on the walls were black and white photographs—later I learned that my grandmother had cut them out of my grandfather's *National Geographic* and *Life* magazines—of pyramids and temples. Other photographs, my grandmother explained, recorded the celebrated discovery of King Tutankhamen's—my king's—tomb in the Valley of the Kings.

"That's Howard Carter," my grandmother said, pointing to a man in short pants and a light-colored helmet. "Listen to this, Tut."

My grandmother stood up on her toes and read the caption beneath the picture aloud: " 'When asked by his excited assistants what he saw when he broke through the final seal and played his electric torch over the contents of the innermost chamber, the intrepid archaeologist exclaimed, "Wonderful things! I see wonderful things!" ' "

My grandmother looked at me earnestly, as if to appraise my reaction to Egypt. "I have an important question to ask you, Tut. Would you like someday to be a great archaeologist, like Mr. Howard Carter?"

I nodded.

"Then it's settled," said my grandmother with great finality. "You'll continue with your famous reading and studying, and someday long after I'm gone you'll be heard from for some discovery like Mr. Carter's. You too, Tut, will see wonderful things."

We did not tarry much longer in Egypt that evening. Yet as I stood gazing at the extinct Sphinx and Lord Ra and the marvelous photographs of King Tut's tomb, it seemed to me that they were all, like my grandmother herself, watching me: quite benignly, yet with a certain note of expectation, too, as if they shared my grandmother's belief that I would certainly be heard from someday, and become a famous archaeologist—whatever that might be—and see wonderful things.

That first month on the Farm with my grandparents was a veritable geography lesson for me. "Idaho," I discovered, was the big woods upriver, where my grandfather cut timber for his sawmill. For some unaccountable reason my grandparents referred to the outside latrine behind the farmhouse as "South America." And the morning after I arrived, my grandfather took me to "Labrador," high up on the wooded ridge behind the house.

We set off immediately after chores, in a warm, fine drizzle, up through the steep cow pasture behind the barn, past my grandfather's red and white Ayrshire cows, and into the dripping evergreen woods on a narrow path. In spots I could look back through small clearings and catch a glimpse of the farm buildings below, growing smaller and smaller.

I recall how quickly and easily my grandfather seemed to swing along up the trail, despite his raspy breathing. It seemed to me that there was an angry determination in his long strides. Once we stopped and he stooped to part the branches of an evergreen tree containing a neat small nest with four speckled blue eggs. "Thrush," he said.

The trail grew steeper. It wound up around outcroppings of ledge. Twice my grandfather paused to catch his breath, leaning his long arm against a tree. "Someday this ticker's going to stop altogether and they'll come and put me in a pine box," he announced the second time he stopped. "Don't be surprised when it happens."

After this declaration my grandfather lit out for the top of the ridge again with a vengeance. I supposed that he must be figuring that the sooner he got there, the less chance there was that his ticker would stop altogether.

Suddenly the ridge leveled off into a clearing containing a low log building with a stovepipe jutting out of the roof. In the light June rain, the place looked forlorn and empty.

"This is it," my grandfather said, pointing at the camp. "Labrador."

I was surprised that Labrador was so close to home, but happy to have arrived. We went inside, where even with the door open it was quite dim. I looked around the large single room. There were two bunks, a wooden table, three or four chairs, and a good-sized black iron cookstove. Three of the four log walls were decorated with old maps and photographs, mostly of men with hunting rifles standing by very big deer hanging from trees; but when I looked at the rear wall I was astonished to see, just under the slanted ceiling, a row of a dozen or so bucks, with huge racks, which appeared to be looking down at us. I had never seen such tall deer before, and for just a moment, before I realized that these were mounted heads, I thought that they were standing outside the rear of the camp looking in at us through holes in the wall.

"Well, Austen," my grandfather said, "what do you say?"

I had no idea what to say, but I must have looked as impressed as I felt because my grandfather nodded and said, "If you decide to stay on here, we'll see to it that you shoot one too. I'll have the head set up on the wall beside these. Would you like that?"

Yes, I would like that, and said so. I would like that more than anything I could think of.

"Your father, the schoolteacher, hasn't hunted deer with me for ten years," my grandfather said. "Evidently he'd rather be shut up in a dusty schoolroom showing little sissy boys and girls how to cipher.''

This, I knew for a fact, was totally inaccurate. Whatever my father's feelings might be about hunting with my grandfather, Dad was an expert woodsman himself. I was beginning to worry about the upshot of the big family dinner planned for next month, when my father would visit the Farm to see how I was getting along. But immediately my grandfather changed the subject, showing me on the blue and green topographical maps of Kingdom County where he had shot each of the mounted deer. He showed me other maps of the far-flung territory along the U.S.-Canadian border, where he had traveled many years ago as a young surveyor, and finally, on a large map of Labrador, he showed me where he had gone surveying when he was twenty-one.

"There," my grandfather said, placing his thumb on a twisting blue line through the middle of the Labrador map. "Right there, Austen. You and I and a canoe. The summer you turn eighteen. If you decide to stay on here, that is. You and I and a canoe, in Labrador, for an entire summer of fishing and exploring. Just us. No one else.''

I was pleased but perplexed. When my grandfather said that he and I would spend the summer I turned eighteen fishing and exploring in Labrador, I assumed that he meant his camp here on the ridge and its immediate environs. The point, however, seemed to be that he and I would do this fishing and exploring alone together. And although I believed I knew exactly whom he meant by no one else, I was very happy to think that he wanted to take me with him. Still, at the age of six it seemed next to impossible to me that I would ever be eighteen. For the time being, it was enough to have come here on this rainy June morning, to see the deer and see Labrador with my grandfather and namesake, Austen Kittredge.

As we approached the farm buildings at the base of the ridge twenty minutes later, he stopped to point at the house and dooryard. "Who lives there, Austen?''

"The meanest old bastard in Kingdom County," I said promptly.

He nodded. "That's right," he said. "Remember that you heard it first from me.''

ike all hill farmers in Kingdom County during the late 1940s, my
grandfather had what seemed to me like an infinite number of
skills; and he had several sources of income, all of which were
equally uncertain, dependent on the caprices of the weather, the
current agricultural market, and the precarious durability of his antiquated second- and third-hand machinery. He kept a dozen Ayrshire dairy cows, which he milked by hand at five in the morning
and five in the afternoon; electricity didn't arrive in Lost Nation
until 1952. And though he detested barn chores, which tied him to
the farm morning and night, seven days a week, he did like each of
his Ayrshires, as he liked nearly all animals.

In addition to his dairy, my grandfather operated a water-powered sawmill situated on the river just across the pasture from his
barn. Sawmill work, by contrast with milking, he liked very much.
But since the mill was a dangerous place, with its huge whirring log
saw and shrieking ripsaw and planer, at six I was not allowed to
work there with him.

In the spring my grandfather tapped eleven hundred maple
trees. He raised a few pigs and a steer for beef, and cut all his own
firewood as well as ten cords for his sister, my Big Aunt Rose. In the
fall and winter he worked in the woods cutting timber for his mill,
sometimes with the help of his two elderly cousins, Preacher John
Wesleyan Kittredge, the part-time minister of the small Methodist
church at the junction of the Lost Nation Hollow road and the
county road, and WJ Whiskeyjack Kittredge, my sipping acquain-
tance from the train.

Except for light barn chores, much of the work I did for my
grandfather that first month consisted of tagging around the Farm
after him and listening to his stories. I had arrived at the peak of
haying time, and as we hayed together in the hot afternoons—my
job was to drive the horses, which was a joke, because they plodded
up and down the windrows of raked hay entirely at my grandfather's
voice commands—he told me story after story about his life and
travels.

The spring he was twelve, my grandfather had run away from

home and school to join the annual Connecticut River log drive, all the way from the Canadian border to Long Island Sound, a total of nearly four hundred miles. Later he had worked in Manitoba, driving a twelve-horse grain combine; and as a chainman on a survey crew establishing the American-Canadian Line between Montana and Saskatchewan, where he had learned the basic techniques of surveying and mapping. Over the next half dozen years he surveyed sections of the Line from Maine to the Yukon; and during the summer of 1909, he'd journeyed to the Far North to survey the Ungava-Labrador boundary, where, to my immense admiration, he had stayed on for a year to live with a nomadic group of Barren Grounds Indians.

Eventually my grandfather had come home to Kingdom County and married my grandmother, an event that coincided with the end of his traveling or, as she liked to put it, his "sashaying about the countryside." He kept his hand in the surveying profession by doing local jobs for farmers and timber companies. But it was generally agreed in the Kittredge family that much of my grandfather's misanthropy dated from the time of his marriage and was accounted for, at least in part, by his resentment over giving up his sashaying about the countryside to become a homebody.

My grandfather had a number of distinguishing idiosyncrasies. He smoked nothing but White Owl cigars, and when he was in the barn and the sawmill, where he never lighted a match for fear of fire, he simply chewed his White Owls down to the end, spitting out the shredded tobacco. He averaged about forty-five minutes per cigar, and I never ceased to marvel at the mysterious process by which a fresh unlighted cigar in his mouth vanished by degrees into what seemed like thin air.

His highest form of praise was to say that a man was "a good fella to go down the river with." No doubt this locution derived from his early days on the big log drives; and while on rare occasions he might mention to me that one of his neighbors fell into this category, he far more frequently informed me that such and such a man—quite often a relative—was decidedly *not* a fella he would go down the river with. From his days on the log drives he also retained the lifelong habit of carrying his paper money buttoned in his shirt pocket, instead of inside a wallet in his hip pocket, where it might get wet.

My grandfather had a number of sayings. When he was absolutely sure of something, he liked to say that it was "as certain as the sun coming up over the White Mountains of New Hampshire in the morning and setting behind the Green Mountains of Vermont at night." If a tool did not work properly, my grandfather often wished it "up Mike's ass." After one of the horrendous runs of bad luck endemic to operating a hill farm, he would announce with harsh irony bordering on genuine satisfaction, "Well, Austen, we can't have good luck all the time." And when everything went completely to smash, he might say, in reference to old Sojourner Kittredge's original geographical miscalculation, "That's what I'd expect in a township settled by mistake to start out with. Everything else has just followed suit."

He kept Ayrshire cows, he told me, because like Holsteins they gave a large quantity of milk, but with a fairly high butter-fat content, like Jersey milk. In fact, I believe that my grandfather favored Ayrshires primarily because most other farmers in the Kingdom preferred Jerseys or Holsteins; regardless of his rationale, however, his preferences and dislikes in all matters great and small were fixed and intense.

"I like a basswood tree, Austen," he said to me one noon a week or so after my arrival on the Farm, while we were eating our dinner up in the Idaho woods under a big basswood. "A partly hollow basswood tree like this one makes the best bee tree in the world. A maple is a serviceable tree, and beeches are good for bears to climb up for the nuts, and lovely to look at. But I'll tell you something and don't you forget it. I hate a gray birch above any other tree in the woods. Gray birches are good for absolutely nothing. I wish every gray birch in Vermont were up Mike's ass."

My grandfather never wished animals up Mike's ass. Besides his cows, his pigs, and his two all-purpose Morgan horses, which actually belonged to my Big Aunt Maiden Rose, he had a partially tamed raven, which he called out of the evergreen woods across the river and fed corn to each morning and evening. To my delight he had taught this bird to announce, in the most strident tones imaginable,

"I hate school"—following which the saucy raven, as my grand-mother liked to call it, never failed to give two short, derisive croaks. My grandfather also had a semi-trained raccoon named Fred, who hibernated in the hayloft; and a huge pet skunk, which shared the same saucer used by the barn cats.

In the evenings my grandfather read for hours on end. Besides a vast collection of westerns that included every tale Zane Grey had ever written, he had amassed an impressive collection of popular travel and adventure nonfiction by or about such indefatigable globe-trotters as Osa and Martin Johnson, Richard Halliburton, Clyde Beatty, Frank Buck, and the famous African ivory hunter Frederick Courtney-Selous—not to mention anyone and everyone who had ever ventured up into his beloved Far North and survived to write about it.

Also my grandfather enjoyed reading biographies of historical figures who had played a part in the settling and establishment of Vermont, and debunking them at every turn. Besides being a mili-tant autodidact, he was a bold, iconoclastic, muckraking historical revisionist before his time, who loved to look up from his books and inform me, out of the blue, that Ethan Allen was nothing more than a "land-grabbing, rum-guzzling scoundrel," Robert Rogers and his Rangers "cold-blooded murderers."

He read each issue of the *National Geographic* cover to cover; and despite my grandmother's muttered injunctions against sashay-ing, or perhaps in part because of them, he read many *Geographic* articles aloud to us, looking up at me each time my grandmother shook her head and sighed loudly over the pernicious folly of such gallivanters.

As for my grandmother, when I think back to my first weeks on the Farm, I connect her in my mind first with Egypt and then with relentless work. With the exception of my morning and eve-ning barn chores, I did not work for my grandfather so much as I kept him company and provided an audience for him. My grand-mother and I were good companions too; but for her, from the outset, I worked, and worked pretty hard.

Feeding and watering her laying hens on my way in from barn chores was simple. Gathering the eggs each afternoon was actually fun. But weeding my grandmother's mammoth garden was not only tiresome but nerve-wracking to boot. My grandfather also kept a large garden, immediately across the lane from hers. And though he didn't make me work in his, he and my grandmother competed with each other fiercely to grow the earliest and biggest tomatoes, squash, ears of corn, pumpkins, potatoes, and twenty other varieties of vegetables. Moreover, as I would soon learn, they each entered all of the same categories in the horticultural contests at Kingdom Fair, where each year they vied for the most blue ribbons.

Drying the dishes and putting them away was less onerous than weeding, but I didn't much like doing it. By far the worst household chore, though, was winding my grandmother's clocks. It would not be accurate to say that my grandmother kept a clock in every room in the house. My loft chamber over the kitchen had none. Neither, come to think of it, did her sitting room, Egypt. Some rooms, however, had two, including the dining room and the long upstairs hallway; and the best downstairs parlor was adorned with three timepieces. I don't believe that I ever counted, but at the time that I moved to the Farm, my grandmother must have had at least twenty working seven-day clocks; and it immediately fell to me to wind the infernal things with her great set of keys, first under her supervision, and then alone.

These clocks kept their own time and struck when they were so moved. For many days, until I was accustomed to them, I was unfailingly startled by their sudden, unpredictable banging and clanging, their shrill and brassy tolling of some vague approximation of the actual time. My grandmother's clocks were nothing special, you understand, though a number of them were embellished with painted scenes of an old-fashioned, bucolic nature. She had acquired them from here and there, one at a time over the years. None was particularly valuable. In fact, the ritual of winding the clocks seemed far more important to her than the time they kept. Years later I would come to the conclusion that, for my grandmother, the clocks did not mark regular daily time anyway, so much as the minute, inexorable progress from some antediluvian event known only to her—the erection of Tutankhamen's pyramid, perhaps—toward some equally private, and quite possibly apocalyptic, event in the future. This much was certain: she rarely heard their dreadful cacophony without scowling briefly toward my grandfather, if he was within scowling range, as though all that chaotic hammering somehow signified that the poor man was doomed to a final and unspeakable retribution for his youthful transgressions as a sashayer, or heaven knew what other offenses, real or imagined, during their years together in Lost Nation.

People seemed to read more in those days than they do today; and my grandmother herself read for an hour or two each day. She read the Bible carefully, yet with a critical eye, particularly for those passages dealing with the alleged treacheries of the Egyptians, which she discounted as sheer propaganda. What about the evil pharaoh who enslaved the Children of Israel, I wondered? Well, my grandmother acknowledged that there might be one bad apple in every barrel. But she had little good to say about Moses, Aaron, or Joseph, who, she confided to me some years later, she had always suspected of casting eyes upon Potiphar's wife instead of the other way around. What other harm was reported of poor Mrs. Potiphar? "None, Tut. None." Yet my grandmother was a very sincere churchgoer, whose severely charitable works extended to everyone in Lost Nation, though her unwavering belief in an inclusive and egalitarian afterlife transcended any single religious doctrine. As far as she was concerned everyone—Egyptians, Hebrews, Christians, you name it —was eligible for advancement, so to speak. Everyone, that is, but my grandfather for whom she seemed to have slim hopes in that regard.

"When I fell afoul of Mr. Kittredge," she frequently stated, in reference to their nuptials. "Well, never mind, Tut. The time will come when he'll meet his Waterloo."

I had no idea what my grandmother meant by this assurance. But it sounded like a very dire fate indeed, and for some years in my early boyhood, I pitied my grandfather his apparently inevitable appointment with Waterloo, and hoped it would not transpire for a long time to come.

Before straying too far from the subject of reading, I should report that one rainy afternoon about two weeks after my arrival at the Farm I discovered a great literary treasure in the far regions of the attic. In a corner under the high, dusty west window overlooking a hundred miles of mountains, I came upon crate after crate of books: more than I could begin to read in an entire summer of rainy afternoons. Besides a complete set of Dickens—this was a spare, there was a set in better condition downstairs in the parlor bookcase —and a pirated edition of Poe's tales with which, at about the age of nine, I would begin scaring the living daylights out of myself, there were boxes stacked full of my grandfather's back issues of the *National Geographic,* no doubt spirited away to this lofty redoubt by my grandmother lest their very presence in the house below reactivate in the old man that evil urge to go sashaying. There were trunkfuls of my father's and my Uncle Rob Roy's boyhood books, including a couple of dozen dog-eared volumes chronicling the spectacular feats of a veritable young Edison named Tom Swift, given to inventing, totally from scratch and at the drop of a hat, every conceivable machine from futuristic racing cars to airplanes— spelled "aeroplanes." Another set of books recorded the glorious saga of one Baseball Joe's meteoric career on the diamond, from some prep school whose name I have blissfully long since forgotten through Yale and the New York Giants. There were the less fascinating—to me—but undoubtedly better written stories of Anne of Green Gables and Louisa May Alcott's tireless little women, only recently relegated to the attic by my little aunts, Freddi and Klee; an old Encyclopedia Britannica; the immense family Bible containing the genealogy I mentioned earlier; several random volumes of the legislative proceedings of Vermont spanning the period 1874–1886; and a badly-worn copy of Bulfinch's *Greek and Roman Myths,* with some illustrations of mostly unpleasant moments in the lives of ancient mortals, gods, and goddesses. I conducted a pretty vigorous impromptu search for one or two of WJ Kittredge's F·U·C·K Books; but I cannot say that I was much surprised not to find any represented in my grandparents' attic library.

I don't know how long I stayed up there on that first visit. Maybe forty-five minutes. I recall bringing a very old children's book back downstairs with me and asking my grandmother to read it to me that evening. It was an ancient cloth picture book entitled, unpromisingly enough, *Cautionary Tales for the Young.* One illustration in particular leaps into my mind. It depicted two boys in a forest clearing, squaring off with doubled fists. At least I think they were boys, though all of the children in the book had, besides oddly oversized heads, an androgynous aspect sharply at variance with their features, which were those of case-hardened forty-year-old men. In the background, evidently as yet undetected by the children, were two gigantic bull moose with their great antlers hopelessly intertangled in combat. Obviously, the poor animals were fated to die a terrible death, but the creator of this cheery woodland tableau wasted little sympathy for them. The caption below read: "Boys given to QUARRELING should TAKE NOTE of the fate of TWO DOOMED MOOSE and MEND their ways." My grandmother read this aloud to me in her precise way, then gave me a long look to see if the lesson had sunk in.

My grandfather, however, glanced over at the illustration and inquired whether I believed I could "hold my own in a go-round with the pair of 'maphrodites" in the picture. I assured him that I believed I could, which seemed to satisfy him. But the fact is that I was not much given to quarreling with other boys, that summer or later, for the simple reason that there were no other boys, or girls either, to quarrel with within three miles of my grandparents' place.

When it came to quarreling, my grandparents themselves walked away with the cake. Never in my life have I known two people to disagree on so many issues, large and small, day in and day out. Of course our entire family, along with everyone in Lost Nation and half of all Kingdom County, knew about Ab and Austen Kittredges' Forty Years' War—which, like most wars, had caught up neighbors and other family members alike, and had resulted in deep rifts and alienations, such as my father's defection from the Farm at the age of eighteen. But I think that very few persons knew how implicit constant rivalry was to the very existence of my grandmother and grandfather.

One morning following an argument between them over whether I was to be allowed to fish alone, without supervision, in the millpond behind the sawmill dam, my grandmother called me into Egypt. She gestured toward two exotic houseplants: a velvety purple African violet and an especially unamiable form of primitive vegetation called, by my grandmother, an Egyptian asp vine. The asp vine, it seemed, had of late aggressively latched onto the violet with one of its hairy tentacles, and was bidding fair to strangle the very life out of it. From this belligerent action my grandmother extracted an exemplum. "See, Tut," she said very earnestly, "even the plants of the earth strive to achieve ascendancy one over the other." Adding, "It's only a matter of time now before Mr. Kittredge will meet his Waterloo."

Well! At six I had no idea what to make of this Darwinian demonstration. I was further puzzled to hear my grandparents routinely refer to each other in the third person as "Mr. Kittredge" and "Mrs. Kittredge," usually with the most sardonic irony. And why did they sleep not only in separate beds but in separate bedchambers? I wondered but didn't know. A more sensible question might be how two such individuals as my grandparents ever got together in the first place, and that I learned only much later. For the time being, since I seemed to get along capitally with them both, I decided not to worry about their feuding. That was the way matters stood between them, and there wasn't a blessed thing I or anyone else could do about it.

In Egypt, on a special shelf under the picture of the extinct Sphinx, my grandmother kept a large scrapbook. It contained hundreds of newspaper clippings and photographs, chiefly of local disasters, which she had begun to compile from *The Kingdom County Monitor* soon after coming to Lost Nation and falling afoul of my grandfather. My little aunts had coined a name for this grisly compilation. They called it the Doomsday Book, because it chronicled all of the most violent deaths and accidents, maimings, poisonings, and other human and natural catastrophes recorded in the county over most of the past half century.

Sometimes in the evenings my grandmother ushered me into Egypt and read to me from her Doomsday Book. I was both delighted and horrified by these seminars, from which I acquired a good deal of esoteric local history. I learned, for example, that 1927 was the year of the Great Kingdom Flood, and that 1936 was the summer of the Great Fire that gutted the entire three-story brick business block in Kingdom Common. Much later, in school, I would study the Crash of 1929 and the end of Prohibition. Neither of these signal events in the annals of American history impressed themselves on my imagination so vividly as the articles that my grandmother read to me from the Doomsday Book chronicling the discovery, in 1929, behind Orin Hopper's orchard, of five shallow graves containing his entire family; or the sacking of the nearby railroad town of Pond in the Sky by "a desperate gang of tramps and hoboes off the Canadian National Railroad, estimated at 250 strong," on the day of F.D.R.'s first inauguration.

In late December of 1941, the front page of the *Monitor* had been printed edged in black. But the infamy of Pearl Harbor was eclipsed for my grandmother and me by the nearly simultaneous advent in Kingdom County of two far more innocuous wayfarers from the Orient: a "Hong Kong Chinaman" and his young daughter, who were picked up trying to slip over the Line from Canada. And it is an odd fact that, along with fire and moving water, my otherwise intrepid grandmother harbored a great fear of "Hong Kong Chinamen" all her life, and never failed to give a small shudder each time she read me the account of the apprehension of the benign-appearing Mr. Wing and his pretty daughter Li, on the border just north of our place.

So my first full month in Lost Nation passed in this happy, strange way. Tomorrow my father was coming for Sunday dinner, to determine how I was getting along and whether I wanted to stay on with my grandparents for the remainder of the summer and the coming year. I knew what my decision would be. Just how to disclose it without hurting anyone's feelings was another matter. For the first time since my visit to my grandparents began, I went to bed worried about what the following day would bring.

Sunday had rolled around at last, as all days must, dreaded or otherwise. After chores my grandfather washed up and, as usual on Sunday morning, put on a white shirt and a necktie. The first time this had happened I thought it very strange. Both he and my grandmother had given me to understand that he never attended church. When he pulled on his hip waders I was doubly surprised. I struggled into my Sunday clothes, my grandmother brushed down my cowlick, and we three paraded out to the truck, my grandfather now in full Sunday regalia—and his waders. I could scarcely believe he was going to fish while we attended the service, but that is exactly what he did, then and each Sunday afterward.

The interior of the tiny Methodist church at the foot of the Hollow was as stark as the beliefs of its congregation. The stovepipe hung from the ceiling on long wires, and ran horizontally all the way from the stove, in the middle of the room, to the rear wall. Besides my grandmother and me, there were never more than a dozen other worshippers in attendance. The presiding minister was Whiskeyjack Kittredge's old ramrod-straight brother, John Wesleyan (JW) Kittredge, who was a kind of lay clergyman.

JW's text on the Sunday of my father's scheduled arrival was "Spare the Rod," with many lurid examples of how children whose misdemeanors were allowed to go unchastened turned out very badly indeed. He suggested that the most infamous malefactors in the Bible from Cain to King Herod had all been spoiled as boys, a misfortune to which their subsequent villainy was directly attributable. I had no idea what my grandmother thought of this strange message, but the lay minister frowned in my direction several times during the sermon and once pointed his finger directly at me and shook it menacingly.

At the end of his tirade, John Wesleyan said we could all say a silent prayer now, and though mainly we should pray for others, particularly our minister, we could all ask for one thing for ourselves. All I could think of to pray for was that I'd never have to attend church again; but this didn't seem right to do under the circumstances, so I didn't get in a personal request in time, and the next thing I knew we were singing again.

The service was longer rather than shorter, and afterward my grandfather, who had just come up from the river, got me aside on the pretext of showing me a one-pound brook trout in his wicker fishing basket and asked me very earnestly, as he always did, if

Cousin John Wesleyan had preached against him. I assured him that
he had not.

"Did my name come up at all in the sermon?" my grandfather
asked. No, it hadn't. My grandfather looked at me, then shut his
basket lid abruptly. "You report to me when and if it does," he said.
"And that'll be the last time it happens."

On the way back up the Hollow my grandfather asked me
whether I'd prefer to attend church again next Sunday or go fishing
with him. My grandmother answered for me. "Church," she said.
"That's what civilized people do on Sunday, Tut."

As we approached the farmhouse I waited for my grandfather to
initiate our meanest-old-bastard-in-Kingdom-County ritual. When
he did not, I nudged him and said, "Who lives there?"

"What's that?" he said.

I poked him again with my elbow. "Who lives there?"

"Never mind that foolishness now," he growled, shooting a look
at my grandmother.

"Who does live there?" she said. "What's Mr. Kittredge been
telling you, Tut?"

"Nothing," my grandfather said. "It's nothing to do with you.
They're here, I see."

"Who's here?"

"The schoolteacher."

Parked in the dooryard beside a battered red pickup truck was
my father's Chevy sedan.

"Do you mean your elder son?" my grandmother said sharply.

"I mean the schoolteacher," my grandfather repeated, slamming
to a stop.

Evidently my father had been here for some time because just
then I spotted Dad and Uncle Rob—the owner of the pickup—
coming up through the meadow from the river with their fly rods.
They waved. But although my grandfather had known about my
father's visit all month, he suddenly appeared to be very angry. "No
doubt they've come to fetch Austen back downcountry," he said as
he got out of the truck. "Well, take him and be damned!"

Then he stalked off toward the house with his fish basket, without another word. Dad had already entered the dooryard and I was
pretty sure he'd heard my grandfather's remark. All he said, though,

was, "Well, Mom, I see things haven't changed around here since the last time I came up."

"Surely you hadn't expected them to," my grandmother said, taking hold of my father's wrist and looking up at him with pleasure.

Uncle Rob laughed and asked me how I'd liked church. "Did that old mossback JW Kittredge denounce your grandfather from the pulpit again?"

"No," I said. "I think he denounced me."

Rob and my father both laughed.

"Hi, Buddy," Dad said. "Tell me one good thing about your month."

"I went to Labrador with Gramp and saw Gram's Sphinx," I said. "It's extinct now."

Although I wasn't sure why, Dad smiled and Uncle Rob laughed hard. On the way inside, they jostled each other and joked about who could pin whom. My grandfather stood with his back to us at the sink, cleaning his trout; but I heard him declare that he could by God pin them both with one hand tied behind his back. "A school-teacher and a kid!" he said to the trout he was cleaning.

Just then Little Aunt Freddi and Little Aunt Klee, who'd come up from the village with Rob, appeared from the dining room, where they'd been setting the table for the big Sunday dinner. After hugging me, they went over to the sink to admire Gramp's fish. Klee had heard what he'd said about Dad and Rob, and she put her arm around him and said in her best Bogart imitation, "Lay off my brothers, old man. They just might have to take you out back and shoot you."

Gramp grunted. Although he paid little attention to my little aunts, his daughters, referring to them mainly as the flibbertigibbets, Klee and Freddi were the only members of the family who could get away with teasing him. I was excited about seeing Dad's pretty young sisters, known as my little aunts to distinguish them from several great or big aunts.

Freddi and Klee had visited us in White River several times a year, and like Uncle Rob, they always made a great fuss over me. Freddi called me Old Toad and Mole and Ratty after the animals in *The Wind in the Willows* and Klee talked to me in a mock tough-guy accent, like a character from the Dashiell Hammett and Raymond Chandler novels she was forever reading. I thought the world of both of them and of Uncle Rob as well.

Freddi's and Klee's real names were Nefertiti and Cleopatra. My grandmother had named them after the fabled Egyptian queens, and as far as I was concerned they were every bit as beautiful. Klee was small and slender, with ivory skin, my grandmother's dark hair, my grandfather's pale blue eyes, and a sharp tongue inherited from both of them—though she never spoke sharply to me. Freddi was tall and statuesque, with a reputation for being overly sensitive. She had lovely huge brown eyes, long, honey-colored hair and a tawny, golden complexion. At twenty-one and nineteen, Klee and Freddi were attending the state university on full scholarships, courtesy of our old ancestor Sojourner. During the summer they worked on the assembly line varnishing chairs at the American Heritage mill in Kingdom Common, where they boarded with a local family.

Besides reading to me from *The Wind in the Willows* and my other favorite storybooks, my little aunts loved to whisk me off to the cupola atop the old farmhouse for what they were pleased to call Sunday School lessons. In fact, these lessons consisted of the wildest tales of spirit rappings, the sorrowful wanderings over the face of the earth of the dispossessed Russian princess Anastasia, the dreadful curse of King Tut's tomb and, best of all, the many tragic secrets and hidden scandals from our own family history.

In addition to being beautiful, high-strung, and full of the most fanciful tales, both Freddi and Klee were terribly independent-minded. No doubt they could have had nearly any boyfriends they'd wanted in all northern Vermont; but for some years they had sustained tumultuous off-again on-again relationships with, respectively, Pooch and Artie Pike, two hard-drinking local roughnecks Uncle Rob had ironically dubbed the Marvelous Wonderful Pike Brothers, like some sort of circus aerial act. My little aunts were also given to all kinds of theatrical demonstrations, particularly in front of me, whom they esteemed very highly as a most appreciative and sympathetic one-boy audience. In much the same way that my grandfather harked back to Sojourner Kittredge's geographical misapprehension to explain all of the subsequent blunders and misfortunes of the Kittredge family right up to the present, Little Aunt

Freddi and Little Aunt Klee loved to conclude their horror tales in the cupola by sadly extending their hands, which were stained red from the chair varnish at the mill, and announcing, to my great delight and their own, "Behold, Austen! Look at these poor mitts. These tell the whole story"—as though, somehow, the red stain on their hands proved all of their most fatalistic theses and notions about the Kittredge family.

Rob Roy had just graduated from high school and was as wild as a yellow bumblebee, as my little aunts put it. They called him the anointed because as the baby of the Kittredge family he could do no wrong in the eyes of either of my grandparents. He worked in the mill too, and did some stringing evenings and weekends for *The Kingdom County Monitor*. Rob aspired to be an outdoor columnist for a newspaper large enough to send him to Alaska and Africa, and claimed to be doing field research for a treatise-in-progress called *Angling and Shooting in Eastern North America*—which Freddi and Klee said was no more than an excuse to spend every spare minute of his time hunting and fishing and riding the roads drinking Budweiser beer with the like-minded Marvelous Wonderful Pike Brothers.

"Well, buddy," my father said to me, "what do you think? You like it up here in Siberia?"

Suddenly I was overcome by tongue-tied shyness. I'd never been away from home for more than a night or two before. Now I was about to betray my father altogether by announcing that I wanted to defect from our home in White River and remain with my grandparents.

I think Dad understood my dilemma. He gave me an affectionate hug and suggested that we take a quick tour of the Farm before dinner. This was just the ticket to get us back on our old confidential footing, and a minute later we were joking together.

We visited the chickens and the barn and walked down through the pasture to the river where Gramp and I fished together evenings after supper. Then my grandmother was ringing the dinner bell. It was time to eat.

Like most countrywomen of her generation, my grandmother was an excellent cook. Her fried chicken and mashed potatoes with chicken gravy, fresh peas, homebaked bread and homemade butter were never less than superb; but today every eye was on my father and grandfather, who were separated from each other only by me.

My grandmother sat at the foot of the long dining room table, at the opposite end from my grandfather. For a moment the room was totally silent. Then she said, "Go ahead, Tut."

This was my cue to say Sunday grace, which I detested, the more so because, instead of bowing his head, my grandfather watched me the entire time. He knew that I was squirming and he delighted in my mortification. For a panicky moment I drew a complete blank.

" 'Our Father,' " Aunt Freddi prompted softly, " 'bless this . . .' "

In one great gulp, the words barely distinguishable from each other, I gasped: "Our-Father-bless-this-food-to-our-use-and-us-to-thy-service-amen."

"Amen," said my grandmother and father and little aunts.

But before the word was out of their mouths, and before I had the faintest notion that I was going to do it, I'd finally thought of the one personal request Preacher John Wesleyan Kittredge said I could make if I wanted to, and blurted out: "And help Dad and Gramp see eye to eye!"

"Amen!" Uncle Rob said, and burst out laughing.

"Brother!" my father said.

"Amen!" Little Aunt Klee said out of the side of her mouth.

"Je-sus!" my grandfather said. "Did they put you up to saying that?" He pointed his fork at my grandmother.

Even Freddi was smiling behind her napkin.

But my grandfather was genuinely mad. He was mad at them, meaning my grandmother, since he imagined that she had been responsible for my pathetic little supplication for family harmony.

"Pass the chicken down this way," he growled at her. "Some of us around here work for a living and don't have time to spend all day praying and jabbering."

"Austen works," Little Aunt Klee said, nodding at my father, her eyes shining with mischief.

"Austen!" my grandfather said indignantly, as though he'd never heard my father's name, though it was his and mine as well. "Austen's a schoolteacher. Schoolteachers don't know what it is to put in a day's work."

"Stop inciting trouble, Klee," my grandmother said sharply, to which my little aunt replied, in a crisp offended voice, "Very well," and got up from the table, as straight and regal as her haughty Egyptian namesake, and disappeared into the kitchen not to return.

Across the table from me Rob mouthed a word or two, I couldn't tell what. Freddi leaned over and whispered, "Don't worry, Old Toad. Klee does this at every family dinner."

My grandmother sighed. She looked down the table at my grandfather and said, "Mr. Kittredge, your son is not a school-teacher. He's a headmaster. What's more, he's the headmaster of one of the finest schools in New England."

My grandfather had paid no attention to Klee's outraged depar-ture. Very deliberately, he put down his fork. Staring straight at my grandmother, he said: "Saying a headmaster isn't a schoolteacher is like saying a trout isn't a fish. A fish may be a trout. But all trout are still fish and all headmasters are still schoolteachers. That's as cer-tain as the sun coming up over the White Mountains of New Hamp-shire in the morning and setting behind the Green Mountains of Vermont at night."

My grandmother, who had not served herself a morsel yet, glared back at my grandfather. "That," she said, "is one of the most peculiar declarations I've ever heard in my life."

"I'll tell you what's peculiar," my grandfather said, pointing a long arm toward my grandmother's sitting room-bedroom, Egypt. "That, by God, is peculiar."

My father set down his drumstick. "Okay, I can't stand any more of this," he said, and took his plate out to the kitchen. He was immediately followed by Little Aunt Freddi, who burst into tears on her way out of the room.

Rob kicked me under the table. This time I caught what he mouthed at me. "Three down."

"Now even you must be satisfied, Mr. Kittredge," my grand-mother said. "You've driven three of your four children away from their Sunday dinner."

"By Jesus Christ, I haven't driven anybody anywhere!" my grandfather barked out. "The next time you hear from me, I'll be in Labrador."

And he, too, was up and gone.

My grandmother nodded grimly. "Once a sashayer, always a sashayer," she said. "His Waterloo looms nearer, Tut."

Across the table Uncle Rob was holding up four fingers.

At exactly the same time, as though to immortalize this awful moment in my memory, the dining room clock began to strike twelve, in a wild, frenetic manner, followed at irregular intervals by all of the other clocks in the house both near and far.

Rob grinned. "Well, Buddy," he said, helping me to another piece of chicken, "dig in."

When I looked up from my plate again, I just caught out of the tail of my eye the dark swish of my grandmother's skirt, retreating into Egypt.

"That's five," Rob said cheerfully. "Welcome to the Kittredge family, kiddo. Hope you like chicken."

After dinner, Rob and Dad and I played flies and grounders in the cut hayfield beside the house while the women washed those few dishes that needed washing. Then while my father visited with my grandmother in Egypt, Little Aunt Klee and Little Aunt Freddi spirited me up to the cupola for a Sunday School lesson. They had just finished washing their hair with the soft rainwater from the big cistern outside the kitchen door, and they wanted to dry it in the sunshine and breeze coming in the cupola windows. Aunt Klee appeared to have gotten over her peeve and Freddi was as enthusiastic as ever. In fact, it seemed to me that with the exception of my grandfather, off in Labrador, nobody in the family acted as though anything much out of the ordinary had happened.

No sooner were we ensconced in the cupola than Klee and Freddi confirmed my impression that such domestic brush-ups were not at all unusual. "That was a wonderful grace that you said, Old Mole," Freddi said. "I'm sure it made all of us Kittredges stop and think how much we really love each other."

It occurred to me that if Freddi was right about the effect of my prayer, the Kittredges had a strange way of showing their affection; but I said nothing.

"That's how nearly all our Sunday dinners break up," Klee said with a certain note of pride. "Should the Sunday School lesson today deal with Dad and poor Austen, Freddi?"

"Mother certainly wouldn't want it to," Freddi said. "On the other hand, if Mole's going to be heard from, won't he need to know?"

Klee nodded. "The sooner the better, I think. Listen closely, now, Austen. The reason your grandfather and your father don't see eye to eye has nothing at all to do with the fact that your father is a schoolteacher. It's that secretly, way down deep, he and your grandfather are too much alike."

"In other words, proud," Freddi said.

"Yes," Klee agreed. "They are both very, very proud."

"And very, very stubborn," Klee said.

"Oh, yes," Freddi said happily. "Which accounts for the feud."

"You see," Klee said, "your father is fifteen years older than I am, and I'm the next oldest. So for years and years he had to bear the brunt of your grandparents' quarreling all by himself."

"That's why he can't stand an argument of any kind to this day," Freddi said. "He heard so much arguing growing up."

"He tended to side with Gram," Klee said. "Not that we blame him. Your grandfather can be a regular Tartar when he wants to be."

"Grief, Klee, not a Tartar. The old boy isn't that bad. Don't make him out to be Attila the Hun. Imagine what it must be like to be lawfully married to a woman with an official paper forbidding you to touch her."

"There wasn't any such paper until years later, Fred. Not until after Uncle Rob nearly killed Mom being born."

"At any rate, Austen, your father never said much to your grandfather, but when it came time for him to go to the university—" Here Freddi's voice began to quaver.

"Do you want to have a good long cry, Fred?" Klee said savagely. "Go ahead. I'll wait while you have your bawl."

"I'm not going to cry, Klee. It's just all so sad. You know it is. What happened, Old Mole, is that—"

"—off he went and didn't come back for four years!" Klee ended triumphantly.

"Kittredge pride," Freddi said.

"And Kittredge stubbornness," Klee said in a fatalistic, delighted voice.

"Hey, you up there, Buddy?" It was Uncle Rob, calling from the foot of the attic stairs. "You're wanted down here, kid. Your dad's getting ready to go back down the line."

"Ah," Klee said. "The moment of truth has arrived. Flee while you can, Old Toad. Flee before you become consumed by Kittredge pride and stubbornness, like the rest of us."

"That's silly, Klee. How can you tell him such drivel? He's just a boy visiting his grandparents."

"Fly away, fly away!" Klee cried melodramatically, though I had the distinct impression that she did not want me to leave the Farm, any more than I wanted to.

Just how I would tell this to my father, however, was more than I knew. I wasn't at all sure I could tell him, and I dreaded the awful moment when I would have to announce my decision more than I had ever dreaded anything in my life.

They were waiting for me in the kitchen. Dad, Rob, and my grandmother. "Well, Bud," Dad said, "what do you say? How do you like it here?"

"I love it," I said, "but I miss you."

He grinned. "That's natural. I miss you, too."

Everyone was looking at me: my father, Rob, my little aunts, who'd followed me down from the cupola to be on hand for my big decision. Most of all, though, I was aware of my grandmother's presence. She was standing at the table putting the best silver back in its chest, and she was watching me intently with those sharp, dark, kind, and eternally expectant eyes. Yet if it was my grandmother I was most aware of, it was my father who best understood my predicament and how to make this momentous decision easy for me.

"Austen, would you like to stay on with your grandparents for a while longer this summer?"

You bet I would! Staying on for *a while*. That was the operative phrase. Now when my grandfather returned from Labrador he would find me here. I could atone for my terrible blunder after the grace. But the fact of the matter is that I desperately wanted to stay on at the Farm with my grandparents. I knew I would see Dad frequently in any case.

After arranging to come back in a couple of weeks, and to have me spend a few days at home with him later in August, Dad left for White River. Soon afterward my little aunts rode back to the village with Uncle Rob. My grandfather appeared for evening chores and seemed neither surprised nor particularly pleased to discover that I was still there. He said nothing to me while I grained the cows, and returned to Labrador again as soon as he finished milking.

During supper my grandmother sighed frequently, and spoke very little herself. But after the dishes were done and dried and put up, and she'd swept and mopped the floor, she looked at me earnestly and said, "Today was one of the most mortifying days of my life, Tut."

"I know, Gram," I said. "I'm sorry about the grace."

"You, Tut, have nothing to be sorry for. Your grace was very fine, very fine indeed. If you weren't destined to become a great archaeologist, I'd say you were cut out to be a renowned clergyman like Mr. John Wesleyan Kittredge. No, all the blame for today can be laid directly at your grandfather's doorstep."

I scarcely knew how to respond to this assertion. Fortunately, though, neither my grandmother nor my grandfather ever seemed to expect much response from me at such times. And after spending the remainder of the evening reading with my grandmother in the kitchen, I went up to bed feeling that the day had been pretty successful despite all the turmoil.

Still, I lay awake for a time, turning over in my mind some of the ineluctable mysteries of the dynasty that Sojourner Kittredge, my forward-looking ancestor, had founded in Lost Nation so many years ago. Even at six, I sensed that there must be more to my father and grandfather not seeing eye to eye than Aunt Klee and Aunt Freddi had told me. Nor was I any closer to understanding why my grandparents themselves didn't see eye to eye. How had Uncle Rob nearly killed my grandmother, and what was this mysterious paper in my grandmother's possession? And why was my grandfather so insistent on reminding me that he was the meanest old bastard in Kingdom County and that I had heard this first from him?

Although I was not very sleepy, I was dog-tired. I shut my eyes and imagined that I was descending into a dark Egyptian tomb, down and down, until I fell into a restless sleep. But the unpredictable events of that unpredictable day were still not quite over.

Sometime later, I had no way of knowing exactly when, the kitchen door slammed. I heard someone walking beneath me, and the sink pump working. Then the steps retreated toward the dining room.

"Tut," my grandmother called up the steps of my loft a minute later. "That was your grandfather, back from Labrador. We're all here where we belong now. You can go to sleep."

So I did, knowing with a certainty that would remain with me for many years that the Farm at the end of Lost Nation was where I too belonged, and that for as much time to come as I could now foresee, my grandparents, for all their singularities, would be at the center of everything for me.

2

HANNIBAL REX

The end of my first summer in Lost Nation was fast approaching, and I was becoming happily ensconced in my new life with my grandparents. For a six-year-old who had led a rather sheltered town existence until now, every day on the Farm seemed to hold several fresh surprises; and my grandparents themselves continued to be endless sources of fascination for me, with their ongoing rivalry and strange ways of incorporating me into it.

Recently everything they did around the Farm in their spare time seemed calculated to prepare for Kingdom Fair, which fell on Labor Day weekend, just before I would start school. They spent hours out in their respective gardens, earmarking the choicest vegetables for their individual displays at the horticultural exhibit. Never one to put away her work for the day and retire before eleven or midnight, my grandmother was now working nearly round-the-clock, putting up preserves for the canned produce competition, dispatching me on forays for blueberries and long blackberries to go into jams and jellies, baking pie shells for the pastry displays sponsored by the local Grange.

My grandfather was busy on fronts of his own. Now instead of reading in the big kitchen rocker after supper or taking me fishing, he washed and groomed the four Ayrshire milkers he'd selected to show at the cattle exhibit, selected some beautiful maple and fir boards for the lumber display, and circled his work horses around and around the barnyard, pulling a small buckboard wagon in preparation for the two-horse hitch driving competition.

My grandmother had a summer kitchen off the regular year-round kitchen. This was a large, unfinished room with a dry sink, a long wooden counter, and an old-fashioned kerosene range where she did much of the cooking in the summertime in order to keep the regular kitchen cool to eat in. The walls of the summer kitchen were emblazoned with blue ribbons from forty years of my grandmother's triumphs at the fair. My grandfather's ribbons hung over the milking stanchions in the barn.

It is hard to convey exactly how determined each one of my grandparents was to win the greatest number of ribbons. Suffice it to say that never since then have I witnessed such single-minded rivalry between two people. For weeks it infected the entire household.

As Labor Day and the fair drew nearer, a special anticipation hung in the air all up and down Lost Nation Hollow and throughout Kingdom County. One day on our way into the village to deliver our milk to the cheese factory, my grandfather and I spotted many bright red-and-yellow posters on the sides of barns and sheds, in store windows, plastered to roadside trees and telephone poles. They depicted a performing elephant rearing up on its massive hind legs with its trunk raised majestically. Of course I had seen pictures of elephants before, but compared to the Elephant Child in my Kipling storybook, or even the gigantic beasts in the caravan of elephants in *The Arabian Nights*, the elephant on the posters was huge almost beyond belief, dwarfing the midway Ferris wheel sketched in the background. Covering its back was a vast tapestry of many brilliant colors. Its headdress glittered with rubies and emeralds, and its alabaster tusks were long and curved, and as lethal-looking as twin ivory scimitars. "See Hannibal Rex, King of the Big Top, the Third Largest Elephant in Captivity," the posters announced.

Even now, I vividly remember the thrill of that gaudy scene repeated a hundred times all over the county. I hoped my grandfather hadn't forgotten the promise he'd made to stake me to a day at the fair, but was too shy to remind him of it.

Fair day arrived at last. Lately my greatest fear had been that it would rain, but today was cloudless. My grandfather had put the high sideboards on his truck and taken his four show cows and two horses into the fairgrounds the evening before. Uncle Rob had carted in my grandmother's displays.

While my grandfather and I did barn chores, my grandmother packed our lunches since like most farm families at the time, they deemed it wasteful to purchase lunch at the fair. Immediately after breakfast we headed down the hollow in the mist.

The fairgrounds weren't crowded this early on opening day. Except for the carousel, most of the midway rides and game booths weren't set up yet. But the freshly painted dairy barns sparkled white in the sunshine, the stalls had been draped with colored bunting and decorated with cedar boughs and wildflowers in sap pails, and as the farmers moved quietly along the aisles with hay and grain and wheelbarrows carrying out manure, there was an anticipatory, festive air about the scene that reminded me of Christmas.

In the lower end of the Ayrshire barn, a boy of eight or nine was helping his father milk cows. He had a peashooter, and every once in a while he'd ping a pea in our direction. One drilled me in the forehead and smarted like a bee sting. "Who's that?" I asked my grandfather.

He waited until the man and kid went outside for sawdust. Then he said, "That's Preston T. Hill and his boy Hermie from down on the county road. Preston's the town poundkeeper. He rounds up stray animals and such. His boy's a young pissant if you want the truth. You let me know if he hits my cows with that peashooter. I'll kick his ass over the grandstand."

"Elephant's coming! Elephant! Elephant!"

Hermie Hill was rushing past the open end of the barn, shouting as he ran. Several other boys came charging along behind him. They were chasing a boxy, round-shouldered old truck with slatted openings in the sides. In faded letters on the back were the words "Hannibal Rex, King of the Big Top." Without a moment's hesitation I joined the gang of boys running behind the truck as it coughed and bounced its way across the racetrack toward the infield in front of the grandstand. Through the slats I caught a glimpse of something gray and enormous. As the battered vehicle jolted and rocked along with its enormous weight, I was breathless with anticipation.

The truck lurched to a halt and a spry, undersized, unshaven man in a dirty blue T-shirt and jeans, scuffed red cowboy boots, and a wide-brimmed big-game hunter's hat jumped out with a scowl on his face. He made a short dash toward the gaggle of us kids behind the truck, then pulled up short and stamped one red boot. "Scat!" he yelled.

Just the way you would to a cat.

"Scat!" he shouted again. "No kids yet. This elephant's a man-killer until he's been fed and watered. No elephant rides until noon."

The little man in the big hat could have devised no more enticing come-on for us. We'd stopped in our tracks when he'd rushed at us. Now we surged forward again, determined to see this man-killing elephant, this Hannibal Rex, the third largest elephant in captivity.

In the meantime, out of the passenger side of the cab stepped the skinniest, slinkiest woman I'd ever seen. She wore a spangled blue costume, like a cowgirl, and appeared to be much younger than the man in the big-game hat and boots. She stretched out her arms as though they'd been riding all night and she'd gotten very stiff. Then suddenly she was standing on one leg with the other leg folded flat up against her back, like a stork's leg. She reached up over her shoulder and scratched the ankle of the lifted foot.

"Double-Jointed Woman, Freaks of the World Show," the man said to us over his shoulder. "Also the wife, name of Mrs. Twist. Step back away now. I'm about to let Hannibal out of this truck. He's a rogue, he's a man-killer and a child-killer, back, back, back.

You, rube!" He whirled and pointed straight at me. "Fetch me a bale of hay. Hannibal ain't quite so apt to tromp you to mush if you hay him a little now and then. Hurry, hurry, hurry!"

I ran for the cow barn, tremendously proud to be singled out to fetch hay for Hannibal. My grandfather was still milking, and Mr. Preston T. Hill was talking vehemently to him about school taxes. Gramp listened to me without comment, then finished his milking unhurriedly while I shifted from foot to foot and Mr. Hill ran on about taxes. Finally my grandfather picked up a hay bale and headed out of the barn toward the infield, with Mr. Hill and me beside him.

We arrived just as the elephant man was unchaining the massive rear door of the truck. It dropped down onto the grass with a resounding thump, converting itself into a makeshift ramp. Out of the dim interior of the truck drifted a nearly overpowering odor of old straw and manure and a musty, ineffable presence of elephant.

Hannibal looked leviathan as he backed out of the truck down the ramp. Until that moment, the largest animals I'd ever seen were our team of workhorses. Hannibal would have made half a dozen of them. I simply could not believe how big he was. He was taller than our milk house at home, and nearly as wide. At six, I could scarcely have been more incredulous if the showman had produced a Tyrannosaurus Rex.

Hannibal felt cautiously, almost daintily, for the ground with each hind foot, then lumbered around to face us as the elephant man jabbed at his legs with a long pole ending in a sharp hook.

Mrs. Twist was now sitting on the grass with her back against the front truck tire and her legs crossed behind her head.

"Christ Jesus!" Mr. Preston T. Hill said to her. "Who the hang are you?"

"Freaks of the World Show," she said.

"Freaks is right," Mr. Hill said.

"Stand back, he's a rogue, he's a child-killer and a baby-killer!" the elephant man said, feinting another dash at us boys.

"Oh, pipe down, Show," Mrs. Twist said in a bored voice. "Han never hurt nobody in his life."

"Yes, he did too," the little man she'd called Show shouted.

"You there, rube," he said to my grandfather, "break that bale open and scatter it out here for Hannibal. Same as you would for a cow."

My grandfather set the hay bale down. "What did you call me?" he said.

"Nothing," Show said. He was in perpetual motion. Now he was driving an iron stake into the ground, now fastening the elephant's leg chain to it, now jabbing at the animal again with his hook.

"He could yank that stake clean out of the ground with one quick jerk. Be on the rampage seconds later," Show said to my grandfather. "Annihilate half the midway crowd, the way he done down in Arkansas a few years back." He brandished his hook. "This keeps him in line, you better believe."

"Did you call me rube?" my grandfather said.

"No, I was talking to them infernal kids," Show said. "Hannibal don't take to kids at all. He killed a young scamp was teasing at him with a water pistol over in Albany two years ago this past June."

My grandfather gave Show a skeptical look. Then he cut the baling twine and spread out the hay for Hannibal. "That'll be fifty cents," he said.

"Put it on my tab," Show said. "I don't have fifty cents or five cents and won't until after I commence giving rides this afternoon. I coasted in here with the fuel needle on empty the last five miles."

"That's the Jesus truth, mister," Mrs. Twist said, her legs comfortably folded behind her back. "That's the plain sad Jesus truth. Show don't have one thin dime to his name and neither do I."

"Yah!" Hermie Hill called out suddenly. "I ain't a-scart your stupid old elephant." He whipped out his peashooter and zinged one at Hannibal. It bounced off his massive shoulder. If the elephant noticed at all, he gave no sign of it. But Show saw what Hermie had done.

He made a sprint at Hermie, who ran around the truck, laughing. "Hannibal made boy-soup out of a young fella in Macon for doing less than that!" Show yelled. "All he done was poke Han with a little stick. Boy looked like smashed shortcake afterward."

"Hear him, won't you?" Mrs. Twist said amiably.

"Listen, mister," Mr. Preston T. Hill piped up, "I'm here to tell you to keep your critter hitched and under control. I don't care how big he is. If he gets loose and does any damage, I'll have him impounded before you can say Jack Robinson.''

Very cautiously, I edged several steps closer. Hannibal had short yellow tusks and saggy, smooth-looking skin, all variations of gray. His massive ears hung halfway to his knees, and he was swinging his great head and trunk back and forth in time to the distant strains of calliope music from the midway. He did not seem interested in any of us boys so I inched closer.

The showman ran two buckets of water from a hose stretching from the grandstand, and Hannibal drank both immediately, one right after the other. Until now I'd had no earthly idea how an elephant drank. I was delighted to see Hannibal suck the water up into his trunk and then squirt it back into his low-slung mouth. He ate most of the hay, swinging it into his mouth with his trunk in small neat bunches. Suddenly Mrs. Twist flipped me a peanut to give him. My heart beat faster as I stepped closer and held it out. Very delicately, the gigantic beast removed the peanut from the palm of my hand with the moist end of his trunk. It tickled, and I jumped back, but Hannibal paid no attention to me at all. He did not look in the slightest way dangerous.

"This elephant's getting on in years," my grandfather remarked to me. "He's not very well taken care of for an old elephant. See these hook marks on his legs?"

Now Hannibal was swaying to the distant carousel music and tossing wisps of loose hay and dust onto his back with his trunk. As I peered up at the raw-looking gashes Show had made with the hook on the elephant's legs, Hermie Hill suddenly dodged out from behind the back of the truck and let him have it again with the peashooter. This time the missile struck the inside of the huge animal's ear. Hannibal gave a snort and stamped his back foot once.

"By the Jesus!" Show shouted, and took off after Hermie at a bandy-legged gait.

"You ought to take that kid to the woodshed, Preston," my grandfather said to Mr. Hill. "That's a mean boy you've got there if I do say so."

"He don't like elephants," Mr. Hill said. "Neither do I. They're too damn big if you ask me."

I reached out and touched Hannibal's side. His skin was dusty, and rougher than it looked.

"Come here, Austen," my grandfather said when we were back in the cattle barn. He took a bill out of his shirt pocket. "Your work this summer was satisfactory. Here's your pay."

He handed me the bill. To my astonished delight it was ten dollars. Ten whole dollars to spend at the fair. I was rich beyond my dreams.

"It's yours to do as you please with. You can husband it along or you can binge it away like a drunken lumberjack. I don't care which. I'll tell you just one thing. Keep your money safe. The midway's full of pickpockets. I worked for a traveling fair one summer when I was a kid and I know."

Terrifically happy, I headed for the midway while my grandfather got ready to take his Ayrshires to the judging ring and rack up some ribbons against my grandmother. The grass was still wet, and the thick red and black wires snaking out to the rides from the humming generators glistened with dew in the early-morning sunshine. The food booths were still serving breakfast, and the air was laden with the sharp, exciting aromas of cooking bacon and sausage, strong coffee, gasoline fumes, and cigar smoke. Some of the rides were in full swing. The lilting calliope music led me to a huge old-fashioned carousel with a menagerie of carved wooden circus animals painted every color in the rainbow: pink zebras, orange hippos, blue giraffes, yellow-and-green tigers, and a bright red elephant, which I regarded with scorn now that I had seen and fed a peanut to Hannibal Rex, the real McCoy. There were pony rides, and little boats and cars on rails, but I wanted no part of these kiddie rides, either.

Farther down the midway, rough-looking roustabouts with iron bars and outsized wrenches were setting up the big-kid rides: the Octopus, with its long steel arms extended like a huge Tinkertoy construction; the blue-and-silver Tilt-a-whirl, slanted skyward like the deck of a ship in a storm. From somewhere nearby, the recorded music of a brass band blared out over the midway. The Ferris wheel didn't have its seats fitted on yet but it looked as tall as my grandfather's barn. Just gazing up at it made my head swim, and I wondered if I'd have courage enough to ride it later on.

Here on the midway was where all the color and music and excitement of the fair seemed to be concentrated. There were games where you covered a red circle with three silver disks, threw a ball as soft as a pincushion at wooden Kewpie dolls, pitched dimes onto colored plates and glassware. There were shooting galleries, horse race games, basketball throws. A barker with a motorcycle hat and a black leather vest over a gargantuan bare belly urged me to try his hammer-and-bell, where you used a sledgehammer to drive an iron weight up to a bell for a cigar. I grinned and moved on down the midway.

A whistle blasted out nearby. "Step right up and give her a try, can't win nothing walking by."

I turned and was startled to see that the man with the whistle had a big blue-and-yellow snake with a green head coiled around his naked upper body. It was a huge tropical snake. Some of the coils drooped down over the man's bare ribs and some were thrown over his shoulders. The snake's long neck spiraled down his arm. Suddenly its bright green head shot out at me and hissed loudly.

I jumped back and the man laughed. To my humiliation, I realized that it was not a snake at all, but an amazing tattoo following the contours of his body in the uncanny likeness of a snake. The thing's green head was tattooed on the back of the man's hand. Its split black tongue was represented by his darkly-inked middle and index fingers.

The strange individual with the snake tattoo laughed again, not pleasantly. He was standing in front of a baseball-throwing booth, where the idea was to knock down a pyramid of three brown milk bottles with one throw. "Come on, kid," he said to me in a voice like a snake's hiss. "Give it a try. Knock 'em down, you get the clown."

He pointed at a stuffed circus clown hanging over the front of the booth in a row with many other brightly-colored stuffed creatures. "Dime a throw and here we go," he said, thrusting a baseball out toward me.

I stood stock-still, staring at the stuffed prizes. Next to the clown was a pink crocodile. What a treasure that crocodile would be for my grandmother. I imagined it in Egypt, next to the extinct Sphinx, imagined my grandmother looking at it with satisfaction, then looking approvingly at me.

"That's Lyle the Pink Crockingdile, kid," the Snake Man hissed. "Want it? All you got to do is knock down the bottles. Dime a go."

I hated to break my ten-dollar bill, but I had to have that crocodile for my grandmother. I held out the bill.

"Hey, we got a player," the Snake Man said. He blew his whistle. "Take his money, Satan." He whipped out his hand, and it was exactly as if a big green-headed snake was taking my money with its fangs. At the same time he made a hideous reptilian hiss through his teeth.

My ten-dollar bill disappeared. The barker tossed me the baseball. It felt punky compared to the one Rob and I played catch with in the dooryard at home, but I started to wind up the way Rob and my father had taught me.

"Hey, hey, we got a regular Babe Root here," the Snake Man chanted, and gave a blast on the whistle just as I released the ball, which whizzed two feet over the top milk bottle, missing everything. "Got to hit 'em to knock 'em down, kid. Want your change?"

In the embarrassment of missing by a country mile, I'd started to walk off without my money. I turned back and the snake hand lashed out and slapped a handful of coins into my palm. I retreated fast, nearly dropping my money.

Immediately the whistle blasted out again and he was chanting, "Step right up, give her a whirl, win a panda for your pretty little girl."

Already I knew that something was not right, though I was unsure what. The midway music roared in my ears. The noon sun seemed too bright, too hot. I looked at the money in my hand: three quarters, a dime, and a tarnished buffalo nickel.

I ran back to the baseball throw booth. "Mister," I said. "Mister. You didn't give me the right change."

"A dime a throw and it's a go," the Snake Man chanted as though he hadn't heard me. "Hey, hey, hey."

"You didn't give me the right change," I repeated. "For my ten-dollar bill."

"I don't know what you're talking about, kid," the Snake Man said.

Again I wailed out something about change for my ten dollars. By now a crowd was gathering around us.

"Listen, bub," the Snake Man said in a weary voice, "you give Satan here a one and Satan give you back ninety cents. Satan's honest as the day is long. Ain't you, you old devil?"

He held the snake-hand up to his head, and it nodded vigorously and let out an angry hiss in my direction.

Long and loud, the Snake Man blasted his whistle, as though to blast me from the face of the earth. I turned away, the tears starting now, and bumped smack into my grandfather. "What's all the ruckus about?" he growled.

Even as I poured out my story, I knew that my grandfather would get my money back for me. He would never let the Snake Man get away with this.

My grandfather stepped up to the baseball throw booth.

"Hey, Gramps, win a stuffed animal for old Grandma? Step right up—"

"This boy handed you a ten," my grandfather said, cutting the Snake Man off. "I gave it to him not twenty minutes ago. You gave him change for a one."

"Like hell he handed me a ten," the Snake Man said. He reached for the money pouch on his big studded belt. He fanned a large number of bills out in his snake-head hand, like playing cards. There were a couple of dozen ones, a few fives, a two, and a twenty.

"See?" he said, holding the flapping handful of bills up to the crowd. "No tens. You find a ten, you can have it, Gramps. Otherwise, move along."

"You'd best produce it," my grandfather said. It did not sound like a threat. It sounded like a statement of fact.

"Look, Clyde," the Snake Man said. "See this whistle? All I got to do is blow one long, two shorts, one long, and yell 'Hey, rube!' There'll be twenty carnies here before you can fart twice. There ain't no ten dollars. Now shove along."

"You go ahead and tootle your whistle," my grandfather said. "I'll take the boy's correct change myself."

As my grandfather reached toward the fanned-out bills, the barker jerked them back and blasted the S.O.S. signal on his whistle. "HEY, RUBE!" he yelled. "HEY, RUBE!"

Instantly other carnies up and down the midway took up the age-old war cry: "HEY, RUBE!" Within seconds the grassy aisle between the game booths and rides was swarming with men running toward us. The Snake Man continued to blast his whistle as they rushed up to his booth. Some carried short chains, others had iron bars. One man wielded a pipe wrench. He menaced with it like a short baseball bat. *He could kill somebody with that*, I thought. *He could kill my grandfather.*

The barker held up the green snake-head like a rearing cobra. "Back off, Gramps," he hissed. "Satan says back off or meet him in hell today."

My grandfather looked around himself unhurriedly. I recognized a man with a stocking cap on his head from the Ferris wheel, and an eye-patch man from the dime toss. The hammer-and-bell man with the motorcycle cap and vest and the big belly had a blackjack.

My grandfather towered over most of the carnies by a head or more, but there must have been fifteen of them, all armed.

He shook his head slightly. "All right, gentlemen," he said. "I could still maybe take two or three of you. I can't take a dozen of you."

"This seems to be your lucky day, Gramps," the Snake Man hissed. "Come back and play the game. You might win."

My grandfather looked at him carefully. "All right," he said. "I will."

But the barker never heard him. "Step right up, give her a try," he chanted, lashing Satan out at passersby and hissing as though my grandfather and I and my ten dollars were the furthest things from his mind.

I fought back my tears. In a matter of minutes, the best day of my life had turned into one of the worst. Everything about the midway now seemed to mock me. The brassy, carefree music, the delicious smells of fried food, the colors and the crowd and the excitement. Everything was a cruel reminder of my carelessness and gullibility.

Back at the cattle barns the judges had been through with the awards. Four large shiny blue ribbons, one for each of our show Ayrshires, hung above our stalls. But my grandfather barely glanced at them. He'd fully expected to win the cattle judging division all along.

Not knowing what else to do, I wandered out of the barn and over to Horticultural Hall, where I found my black-clad grandmother standing off to one side of the exhibits, frowning at three women judges sampling the baked goods. She seemed as self-possessed and inscrutable here as in our farmhouse kitchen. How could the judges dream of not conferring blue ribbons upon her raspberry tarts, strawberry rhubarb pie, yeasty-smelling salt-rising bread? The stony and impassive stare of her friend the Great Sphinx himself could hardly have been more intimidating than her gaze.

"Well, Tut," Gram said, "how many blue ribbons does your grandfather have? What's the tally thus far?"

"Four," I said.

"Ah," she said. "Only four?"

I nodded.

"Sample my miniature angel food cake, ladies," my grandmother called out sharply to the cowed judges.

She glanced at me, her eyes watchful and appraising. "Winning is all, Tut. Remember that, now and later. Winning is all. Do you think failure of any kind ever once entered the mind of the great archaeologist Mr. Howard Carter? No, it did not. Achieving your goal, be it a blue ribbon or the discovery of a new tomb, is all."

My grandmother moved off down the aisle after the triumvirate of timorous judges as they headed for the preserves section, having duly placed a blue ribbon on her miniature angel food cake. Penniless and defeated, I drifted back outside, unable to tell my grandmother how I had let myself be cheated.

Suddenly there was an unearthly shriek from the infield in front of the grandstand. It was followed immediately by another blast, even louder than the first.

I ran down across the racetrack toward the infield, where Hannibal was trumpeting steadily, his trunk lifted high above his head. I had never heard such a piercing, angry roar in my life. As I approached, the elephant reared up onto his hind legs, screaming to high heaven. Little Show was trying to get his hook over the animal's head to pull him down.

"Hut, hut, hut!" Show shouted.

The elephant dropped onto his front feet and reared right back up again. As he towered above us, I saw the crumpled figure of a man lying beside Show's truck. No, not a man. A boy. Hermie Hill!

Now Hannibal was dragging Show all over the lot. Show was swinging from his hook, being tossed from side to side like a doll. Again the elephant raised onto his hind legs, shaking Show off like a child. For a terrible moment, Hannibal was poised directly above Hermie. He let out a long furious blast and just as he was about to come down on his victim, my grandfather appeared from nowhere, scooped Hermie up and rushed him around the truck. It all happened so fast that for a few moments I didn't fully understand what I'd seen. The elephant gave one last inhuman cry. Then he dropped down onto all fours again and stood there quietly.

My grandfather had laid Hermie on the ground beside the Double-Jointed Woman, Mrs. Twist. Hermie was bleeding from the nose and moaning. "Fetch the ambulance, quick!" Gramp said.

Somebody ran to call the ambulance. Mrs. Twist hurried to the truck cab and came back with a blanket to put over Hermie. "It weren't Hannibal's fault, mister!" she shouted to my grandfather. "Han ain't to blame."

By now Show had gotten Hannibal safely inside the back of the truck. He ran up and pointed an accusatory finger at Hermie, moaning on the ground. "I tol' him to stop it with that bean shooter," he yelled. "He hit Han smack in the eye with it. I swear to God he did. Hit him right smack in the eye, and when the kid come near him, Han snatched him up and throwed him. Oh, Jesus!"

Siren wailing, the ambulance came tearing across the infield from the first aid station. Volunteer attendants in red jackets with gold lettering that said "Kingdom County Fire Department" leaped out and loaded Hermie's crumpled body onto a stretcher and into the back. The injured boy looked totally helpless. In my heart I secretly rejoiced over the bully's fate, and was enormously proud of my grandfather's heroism.

"You saved the kid's life, mister," Mrs. Twist said as the ambulance went racing out of the fairgrounds.

"It's barely worth saving," my grandfather said. He rounded on Show. "You ought to control your animal."

"He never done nothing like this before," Show cried. "I swear it."

By now Sheriff White had arrived with Mr. Preston T. Hill. Mr. Hill was already hollering about Hermie, the elephant, hospital and undertaking bills. He kept trying to get at Show. Sheriff White had to hold him back.

"What a circus," my grandfather said. "Let's get out of here, Austen."

On the way back to the cattle barn Gramp told me that he believed that one and possibly both of Hermie's legs had been broken. He didn't know what other injuries Hermie might have sustained but he didn't think the boy would die. He said if he knew Preston Hill, he was far more concerned about losing Hermie's free help around the farm than losing Hermie, anyway.

"Now, Austen," my grandfather said to me in a tone indicating that the subject of Hermie Hill and the elephant was closed, "I intend to visit some people this afternoon. I want you to come with me."

I was sharply disappointed. Although I was always happy to go anywhere with my grandfather, I had counted on spending the afternoon on the midway even though my money was gone. A few minutes later when my grandfather and I drove out of the grounds together in the blazing noon sun, it seemed to me that I had lost my day at the fair forever. As the midway music receded behind us, so did all my hopes.

M y grandfather said nothing more to me that afternoon about the fair. We spent the next several hours driving the back roads of the county visiting people he knew, mostly in remote mountain hollows and far up country lanes. He did not stay long in any one place. Some of the people he wanted to see were at the fair themselves. He said that was all right; he'd catch them there this evening. He did not invite me up into the barnyards and dooryards with him or tell me what he said to the men he spoke with. When I asked him who the people were, he said only, "Neighbors."

The Farm seemed preternaturally quiet when we arrived around five o'clock. Just knowing that my grandmother wasn't there made me uneasy as I rounded up the remaining Ayrshires and drove them down through the pasture to the barn to be milked. We headed back to town as soon as chores were over, not bothering to fix supper; we'd snacked on crackers and cheese and soft drinks that afternoon during our long ride up and down the hollows.

By the time we reached the fairgrounds it was growing dusky. The sky above the grounds was a rich indigo. Beneath it the midway lights gave off an alluring glow in the early fall twilight. I wanted to ask my grandfather if we could go back to the midway, but King-dom Fair seemed destined to be a place of turmoil for us that day. No sooner had we finished milking the four prize-winning Ayrshires at the cattle barn than my Uncle Rob Roy ran in with alarming news. "Dad, quick!" he shouted. "They're going to shoot Hanni-bal!"

"What are you talking about?" my grandfather said. "Who's go-ing to shoot Hannibal?"

"Preston Hill, the old son of a bitch."

"What, did Hermie die?"

"No, Hermie's got a fractured leg and arm, maybe a ruptured spleen, they aren't sure. He's going to be all right, more's the pity. But Old Man Hill bulled right ahead and hauled that little moron they call Show up in front of Kip Pierce, and Kip fined him a hun-dred dollars for not keeping Hannibal properly confined. Show doesn't have one hundred dollars. Now Kip's saying the elephant has to be destroyed according to some town ordinance . . . I don't know, just *hurry*."

My grandfather swore savagely. But he headed fast for the in-field. Already a good-sized crowd had gathered around the elephant, which was staked out behind the truck again. Sheriff White was there, looking very uneasy. With him were Justice of the Peace Kip Pierce, Mr. Preston T. Hill, and Show. Mr. Hill was toting his deer rifle, and Show was pleading with Justice Pierce and Sheriff White, begging for just three days to raise the fine money from his elephant rides. Backlighted by the glowing midway, it was a nightmarish scene.

"What's the trouble here?" my grandfather said.

"Nothing at all to do with you, Austen," Justice Pierce said.

"I'll tell you what the trouble is," Mr. Hill shouted. "This beast broke one of my boy's legs and one of his arms and now he's laid up in the horsepittle. He won't be able to work for two months, never mind putting me in the poorhouse with doctor's bills."

Mr. Hill was so mad that flecks of saliva were flying out of his mouth. "That animal's been declared a public menace, Austen Kittredge. I've got authorization to destroy it. Right, Kip?"

"That's true, Austen," Justice Kip Pierce said, not happily. "We can't have an animal like that running loose on the rampage. The law on such matters plainly stipulates a fine not to exceed the value of the damages, which I estimate as no more than one hundred dollars medical bills, or forfeiture of the animal if it's dangerous to public safety or private property, or both. I told this fella here if he'd pay the fine and clear out of town we wouldn't destroy his elephant. I was as reasonable about it as I could be. But he says he rolled in flat broke. In view of that I've authorized Preston here, as poundkeeper, to shoot it."

"You men would shoot an elephant?" my grandfather said in an incredulous voice. "You'd do that? In cold blood?"

"It's a what-you-call-it—a rogue," Sheriff White said. "It's dangerous to the public safety, Austen."

"Clear out of the way now," Mr. Hill said to the growing crowd. He began putting shells in his rifle. I noticed that his hands were shaking.

"You fellas listen to me now," my grandfather said. "Hermie asked for what he got. He provoked the animal, nearly put out its eye."

"A fine not exceeding the damages incurred or forfeiture of the animal or both. That's the written law," Mr. Pierce intoned.

"Give me three days," Show implored. "I'll raise the money from elephant rides."

"Who's going to ride your elephant after what he did to young

Hermie?" Sheriff White said. "You won't be any closer to raising that money three days from now than you are today. You didn't have a single customer this afternoon once word about Hermie got out."

More fairgoers were pouring in from the midway. News of the elephant's impending execution had evidently spread to the entire grounds and everyone seemed eager to be present. Mr. Hill was still fumbling to get his shells into his gun. Sheriff White was directing the crowd away from the line of fire. I felt as though I was about to witness a murder I was helpless to prevent. Show was frantic, running here, there, everywhere.

"Simmer down," my grandfather told Show. "Can't you get your carny cronies down on the lot to pony up that hundred dollars for you?"

"They ain't my cronies," Show said. "They hate my guts. I'm circus, they're carnival."

"That's the Jesus truth, mister," Mrs. Twist said. "For once in his life the runt's told the truth. Carnies ain't like circus folks. With carnies, it's dog eat dog, except maybe they gang up on some rubes with their billies and such."

"Preston," my grandfather said, "you seem to be having some trouble loading that gun. You sure you want to go big-game hunting here tonight? You hit old Hannibal in the wrong place, he's going to trample you before you can shoot again."

Mr. Hill hesitated. He looked warily at Hannibal. "Put him back in the truck," he said to Show. "We'll shoot him through the slats."

"God Almighty," Sheriff White said. "I don't know about that. Shooting a helpless animal inside a truck?"

"Come on," a man in the crowd said. "Shoot him. We footed it clear up here from the girlie shows to see an elephant shot. Now blast him, goddamn it."

"Austen's right," Kip Pierce said with all the magisterial deliberation of a Supreme Court justice. "Do you good folks have any idea what mayhem this animal is capable of wreaking if Preston here don't put the first bullet in its brain? Do you want a wounded rogue bull elephant loose on the midway? I don't believe so. We'll put him in the truck and drive it out to the town gravel pit on the river road and fill it full of holes."

"Yes!" Preston said. "Now you're talking."

"Let's get to it, then," a drunk yelled, and some other men growled in assent. In the dusky glare from the midway the faces of the nighttime fairgoers were hard and unyielding. Mrs. Twist sobbed and ran to Hannibal and put her arms around his trunk.

In that moment a sense of collective hesitation seemed to fall over the entire fairgrounds, broken only by the faraway noise of the midway and the creaking of the truck springs as Hannibal, oblivious to his fate, once again began to rock to the distant music.

Then my grandfather spoke, breaking the spell. "Kip, I'll pay your one-hundred-dollar fine and take personal responsibility for the elephant. I'll guarantee the public safety if that's what you're worried about."

"How can you do that, Austen?"

"I'll take him up on my farm. I've got plenty of work he can do up there. We can keep each other company when the boy's off at school. An elephant's the best company there is for a fella who understands them and doesn't abuse them."

"No one can prove I ever abused that animal," Show said. "It cannot be proved."

My grandfather made a harsh sound in his throat, a sardonic approximation of a laugh. But I was thunderstruck by his announcement that he would take Hannibal home with us. I wanted to shout out loud. An elephant! An elephant on the Farm in Lost Nation. Through my mind flashed a wildly improbable montage of Hannibal plowing our cornfields, Hannibal hauling logs out of the woods to my grandfather's sawmill, Hannibal pulling our hay wagon and myself high on the load of hay, driving him. Then almost as quickly I was overcome by a great wave of despair. Surely such a marvel as this could never come to pass, except maybe in one of my storybooks.

"I'll pay the fine and take the elephant," my grandfather repeated.

"Like hell you will!" Mr. Hill said. "I intend to haul that animal out to the gravel pit and shoot it, Austen Kittredge. He half-killed my boy."

"You've nearly killed him yourself a dozen times over," my grandfather said. "But you aren't going to harm that elephant. No

one is. I said I'll pay the hundred dollars. I'll pay it by ten o'clock
tonight. In the meantime, Kip, you better stand guard over Hannibal so nobody gets an itchy trigger finger. Mason, you might want to
escort these people''—nodding at Show and Mrs. Twist—''to the
county line. The quicker they get out of here the better. Is that
fair?''

"I guess it is," Justice Pierce said after a pause. "But where are
you going to get a hundred dollars between now and ten o'clock,
Austen?''

"Yes, how do I know I'll get my money?" Mr. Hill said.

My grandfather looked at him. "Did I say you'd get it, Preston?"

"Well," Preston T. Hill said.

"You wouldn't be questioning my word?" my grandfather said
softly.

"The written law says forfeit the animal or pay the fine or both,"
Justice Pierce said. "If Austen can pay the fine and guarantee the
public safety, as he says . . .''

"Can you keep the last of the great ivory hunters here off Hannibal until ten o'clock?" my grandfather said. He jerked his head at
Mr. Hill.

"Nobody," Kip said, "but nobody, will touch one hair on this
elephant's hide until ten tonight.''

"If you ain't here at ten sharp with the money, I intend to shoot
him," Mr. Hill said.

"Well," my grandfather said, "I intend to be here, Preston. With
the money. If only to deprive you of the great satisfaction of slaugh-
tering an elephant shut up in a truck.''

"Are you folks all set to skedaddle on out of here?" Sheriff
White said to Show.

"I don't know," Show said slowly. "One hundred dollars is a
mighty cheap price to pay for the third largest land animal in captivity. Especially when I'm not getting nothing out of it.''

"You're getting out of having the elephant shot, damn it," Kip
said. "I thought you didn't want the elephant shot.''

"He's old anyway," Show said. "I don't know as I want this fella
to have the benefit of him.''

"Mister," Kip said, "I am giving you one last chance to get out of
this mess and this county scot-free, with a safe-conduct escort from

Sheriff White. Or would you rather go to jail for a hundred days? Because you are one half step away from there this minute."

"Get in the truck," Show said to Mrs. Twist. "We'll go back down to Albany and hire a lawyer."

"Good luck," Kip said. "To you and your Albany lawyer."

Mrs. Twist ran up to my grandfather. "You really going to buy Han, mister? You promise you won't let nobody shoot him?"

"Nobody's going to shoot him," my grandfather said. "Best get going now."

Mrs. Twist gave Hannibal's trunk one last hug, then got in the truck with Show, who leaned out the window and called to my grandfather, "Hey, you, pops. You're such a free spender. You got a loose five-spot on you? Gas tank on empty, and I wouldn't want to run out on the road in this forsaken state. Probably get lynched."

My grandfather thrust a few bills in through the window and Show grabbed them and without a word of thanks drove off across the infield toward the nearest exit. Halfway to the gate Sheriff White passed him and flicked on his blue light to lead the way.

"That'll take care of him for an hour," my grandfather murmured.

"Show?" I said, surprised.

"No. Mason White."

My grandfather looked at me and shook his head slightly as if all the furor over Hannibal was nothing more than a momentary nuisance. "You and I have some unfinished business, Austen. Come on."

My grandfather started toward the cattle barn with me at his heels. Inside the barn, in the dim light of the few bare overhead bulbs, I spotted a shadowy group of men near the far entranceway. These men were not loud and fast-moving and half-drunk like the raucous gang of townies who'd come rushing like sharks to a kill to see Mr. Hill shoot Hannibal. They were standing quietly in the weak light, dressed in checked shirts and wool pants or overalls. Most of them were tall and lean and wore slouch hats or caps embossed with the names of feed brands and tractors. Some carried log peaveys and pulp hooks. Others carried shotguns nearly as tall as I was.

As we approached, I recognized half a dozen of the men from the hollow farms my grandfather and I had visited that afternoon.

Neighbors, he had called them then. That is what he called them again now, tilting his head toward them and saying to me quietly, "Neighbors, Austen. Being good neighbors."

There could not have been fewer than thirty armed neighbors in the entranceway of the barn.

"All right, gentlemen," my grandfather said, "if you'll just follow along about ten paces behind me and my grandson here, and only step forward should I give the word."

My grandfather looked soberly at his neighbors: men from the far mountain hollows, the last full-time hunters and trappers and six-cow farmers in Kingdom County. They looked soberly back at him. No doubt some of these men had been on the big river drives with him long ago. They were men he'd helped in haying and sugaring time, as they'd helped him. They had helped each other milk in times of sickness. Some of them had eaten and slept in his deer camp.

"Just one thing more," my grandfather said to his neighbors. "Earlier I told you this would take about five minutes. I miscalculated. I've got a friend who's in bad trouble. I've got to bail him out and that will take closer to an hour."

One or two of the men nodded. The rest just waited silently. No one objected.

My grandfather had not often taken my hand that summer, except maybe to cross fast water in the river when we went trout fishing. Now he took my hand and led me up to the midway. Our neighbors drifted along some distance behind us, shadowy in the night. The dew-soaked grass under our feet smelled fresh as morning and the scent of fried food was pungent and mouthwatering on the damp night air. The strings of Christmas lights adorning the rides and booths, the hurdy-gurdy music and snapping cracks from the shooting gallery and crescendoing shrieks of kids on the fair rides were a thousand times more exciting tonight.

My grandfather made a beeline to the baseball throw booth. There was the Snake Man, right where he'd been that morning. "Step on up, give her a whirl, win a prize for your pretty little girl."

My grandfather shouldered his way to the front of the crowd. "We're back," he said.

The Snake Man glanced at my grandfather. He gave a short laugh of recognition. "Hey!" he exclaimed. "It's Old Gramps. Old Gramps and Babe Root, the kid who can't throw and can't count change. Sic 'em, Satan."

The blue-and-yellow snake-arm with the frightful green head struck at me. I jumped back and the crowd laughed. But my grandfather calmly took a dollar bill out of his shirt pocket and handed it to me. "Play the game, Austen."

I gave the bill to the barker, who held it up in Satan's mouth and shouted, "See, folks. It's a one. Not a ten or a twenty or a hundred. A one."

He tossed me the punky, lopsided baseball and this time I threw quickly, with no windup. The ball grazed the rim of the top bottle. It teetered momentarily but didn't fall. I was disappointed. More than anything I still wanted to win that stuffed pink crocodile for my grandmother. It, or one identical to it, was still hanging above the booth with the other stuffed prizes.

"Got to hit 'em to knock 'em down, kid. Play again?"

"Give the boy his change," my grandfather said.

"Sure, Gramps. Whatever you say. Make change, Satan." The green snake-head spit the change out into my hand. In a loud, hissing, mocking voice, the Snake Man said, "Twenty-five, fifty, seventy-five, eighty-five, ninety-five, one dollar, rube."

Satan reared up his head and hissed at me in derision, and as fast as chain lightning my grandfather reached out and seized the barker's wrist just behind the tattooed snake-head, as he might grab a real snake that was threatening to strike me.

"Hold it," my grandfather said. "The boy gave you a ten."

"Like hell he did!" the Snake Man yelped. "He give me a one."

"He tendered you a ten-dollar bill," my grandfather said, not loudly. "You owe him nine dollars."

"Where are your witnesses, old man? I'll blow one long, two short, one long and yell, 'Hey, rube!' In thirty seconds flat you'll be— Hey! Hey!"

The Snake Man yelled hey, all right. But he did not yell 'Hey, rube.' My grandfather had yanked the whistle out of his mouth and tossed it high over his shoulder into the swirling confusion of the midway. Just the way my grandmother might deadhead a rusty blossom on her moss rose in the dooryard at home—with no more thought than that.

"Boys," my grandfather called over his shoulder. Out of the shadows along the edge of the midway came our neighbors, the one-horse loggers, the eighty-acre hill farmers, the poachers and moonshiners and mountain men from the wild northern hollows along the Canadian frontier.

"How much did I give this fella, boys?"

"I see you hand him a ten-spot, Austen," Henry Coville from Lord Hollow said. "I'll swear to it in any court in the land."

"You handed him a ten outen your shirt pocket."

"You give him ten dollars, Austen Kittredge."

"It would have been that, all right. Ten."

The Snake Man's eyes were furious as an angry serpent's. But he said nothing. My grandfather released his grip.

"You want to yell 'Hey, rube!' go ahead. Yell away."

The Snake Man looked at the armed men crowded around his booth. Then he shrugged and shook his head. "Okay, Gramps," he said. "You win." He counted nine dollars out into my grandfather's hand, a five and four ones.

My grandfather gave it to me. "This belongs to you, Austen. Keep better track of it this time."

But he wasn't through with the Snake Man yet. He got a dime out of his pocket. "I want to play your game," he said. "Toss that ball here."

To my surprise, my grandfather stepped off to the side and threw low and hard, knocking one of the two weighted lower bottles sideways into the other and upsetting all three.

"Remember what I told you about working for a fair one summer?" he said to me. "I learned a thing or two. Pick your prize."

"I want that crocodile," I shouted. "Lyle the Pink Crocodile!"

The Snake Man wordlessly took down the stuffed pink crocodile and shoved it at me with Satan, who no longer frightened me in the least.

"Now, gentlemen," my grandfather told the men behind him, "we'll bail out my friend."

I clutched Lyle tightly to my chest as we moved a short distance down the midway to the coin toss glassware booth, diagonally across from the baseball throw. The red, green, and blue ice-cream plates, the decorated tea sets and cut glass pitchers and matched dinnerware sparkled beautifully under the overhead lights.

The barker with the eye patch was busy handing out change and prizes, though most of the coins people threw just bounced off the glassware onto a dirty sheet spread out on the ground below them. Again my grandfather handed me a dollar and told me to play.

The eye-patch man took my dollar and handed me back a dime to toss. I flipped it out toward the glittering array of glass and china, and it landed on the far edge of a turkey platter and slid off onto a plain white crockery tea saucer.

"Winner here," the barker rasped out as he handed me the saucer. "We got a winner. Play again?"

I looked at my grandfather, who shook his head. "Give the boy his change," he told the barker.

The eye-patch man spilled the remaining ninety cents he'd hoped to con me into spending into my hand, and started along the counter toward an old woman throwing dimes the way some people play a slot machine, one after another after another.

"Carnival man!" my grandfather called out.

Patch squinted at him with his one eye. "This young fella here gave you a ten," my grandfather said. "You owe him nine more dollars."

"Bull!" Patch growled. "He gave me a one."

"Boys," my grandfather said, and on cue, his neighbors materialized again.

"I won't stand for this," Patch shouted. "I'm going for the sheriff, by Jesus."

"The sheriff's tied up just now," my grandfather said. "He's escorting a man out of town."

"Look," Patch said. "Whatever trouble you had earlier with Snake, it don't have nothing to do with me and my booth."

"Why'd you come rushing to his defense with a billy, then?" my grandfather said.

"He yelled 'Hey, rube!' damn it. We got to come a-running when a carny hollers 'Hey, rube!' "

"No, you don't," my grandfather said. "You've got to fork over the correct change or I'll invite this man to take target practice on your wares."

My grandfather jerked his head toward Cousin WJ Kittredge, who was squinting down the barrels of his shotgun to be sure they were clear.

"I'm real scart," Patch said defiantly.

My grandfather shrugged. WJ inserted two large red shells in the barrels of his gun and snapped it shut. He looked up, just two coal-black eyes between his tangled black beard and slouch hat. Patch's face turned pale. WJ lifted his shotgun and pulled back one of the hammers and Patch hollered, "All right. All right."

He gave my grandfather nine dollars, and Cousin Whiskeyjack lowered the shotgun and vanished into the crowd.

My grandfather passed the adjacent booth, the Kewpie doll throw, without stopping. The barker there was a girl I didn't recognize.

As we approached the hammer-and-bell, near the Ferris wheel, I saw Patch run up to confer with the shirtless man with the black vest. This looked like trouble.

"What the hell do you want?" the big-bellied man growled at my grandfather. He was already tapping a blackjack against his bare stomach. It made a hard smack each time it sprang forward and hit.

"The boy wants to play," my grandfather said, and handed him a dollar.

The hammer-and-bell man held out the change, which my grandfather ignored. "Try it, Austen."

I picked up the sledgehammer, then put it down. I couldn't even lift it to my waist.

"Let me give you a hand," my grandfather said, and took the hammer and with an easy-looking swing rang the bell.

"Okay," the man with the blackjack said. "Here's your cigar and here's your change."

"I gave you a ten," my grandfather said.

"Did you now, rube?" Before I had any idea that he intended to do it, the blackjack man was yelling, "HEY, RUBE! HEY, RUBE!" at the top of his lungs.

From up and down the midway, for the second time that day,

the carnies came swarming with their billy clubs and blackjacks and iron bars. One man was holding a broken bottle. Another palmed a knife. This time my grandfather didn't need to speak to his neighbors. Instantly they appeared from the shadows, forming a loose phalanx around him, their peaveys and long pick poles and guns at the ready, waiting for the onrushing carnival men, who stopped in their tracks as a shotgun blast rang out over the midway, accompanied by a clangorous gong from the top of the hammer-and-bell.

Beside my grandfather, Cousin WJ Kittredge was drawing another bead on the bell, which now resembled a badly dented hubcap. This time when he fired it flew completely off the post.

"Jesus Christ Almighty, the rubes got guns!" a carny in a dirty white sailor's hat yelled.

The mountain men stood silently around my grandfather, who was watching the hammer-and-bell man carefully. "You owe me nine dollars," he said in his harsh voice, not loud. "I want it."

Without a word the man handed him the money. My grandfather put it in his billfold and moved off with me in tow. The carnies gave way before us.

On down the midway we went, in a euphoric cloud of hazy colored light. We stopped at the rifle shoot, the basketball throw, the booth where you covered a red circle with three silver disks—all places where the barker had responded to the Snake Man's "Hey, rube!" that morning. At each game my grandfather handed the barker a one and extracted change for a ten. At most of the booths my grandfather played the game after me and won a prize, which he let me pick out. Soon my arms were overflowing with stuffed animals, painted china figurines, framed pictures of baseball players and movie stars, and afterward, while my grandfather went up to the infield to purchase Hannibal, I rode on the big Ferris wheel, wedged into the swinging seat laden with my spoils from the midway. Up and up and up it went, and then stopped, swinging like a cradle, high above the midway in the cool night air.

I hugged Lyle and looked out over the seat bar. The booths below looked small and insignificant, the colored lights glowed eerily through the evening mist creeping up over the fields from the Kingdom River. The music, even the shrieks from the Octopus, sounded far, far away. Horticultural Hall gave off a warm glow, and the cattle barns glimmered like barns early in the morning before daylight when lantern lights have just come on inside. In the distance, beyond the rosy haze of the midway lights reflecting off the fog, I could see the fainter lights of the village of Kingdom Common, where not three months ago I'd stood alone on the station platform, waiting for my grandfather to take me up to Lost Nation.

"Hey, rube!" I said. Then I shouted it: "HEY, RUBE!

"HEY, RUBE!" I yelled, as the Ferris wheel started with a jolt and revolved on into the night, and on and on, until I thought it might never stop.

My grandfather did purchase Hannibal Rex. To the mortification of my otherwise triumphant grandmother—it was obvious that once again she was going to walk away from Kingdom Fair with more blue ribbons than my grandfather or anyone else—we brought the elephant home in the back of the lumber truck that very night and quartered him in the upper hay barn. That fall, after I started school, my grandfather used Han for a number of jobs around the Farm: hauling logs down out of Idaho, yanking some recalcitrant stumps out of a high pasture he was reclaiming northwest of the house, and, on more than one occasion just before winter and again in spring mudtime, pulling the lumber truck out of the quagmire our dirt road turned into whenever it rained hard. By degrees, Hannibal went from a wonder to a curiosity to a fixture on the Farm in Lost Nation.

I rode him off and on, and sometimes kids from the village came up to see him with their folks, but my grandfather discouraged this. As for the newspaper reporters who wanted to photograph him, he summarily put the first two who showed up off our premises. Apparently word spread because they were the last reporters we saw.

Sometimes one or two of the mountain people who'd helped my grandfather earn the money to bail Hannibal out and save his life came by to see him, usually just appearing in the dooryard as though they'd dropped out of the sky. These men my grandfather was always happy enough to see. I thought that Show and Mrs.

Twist might appear someday themselves and try to buy the elephant back, but my grandfather told me he wouldn't return Han to Show to be abused with that hook for any amount of money in the world. The showman never did contact us, and neither did his Albany lawyer.

My grandmother, for her part, rarely alluded to Hannibal at all. Most of the time she simply ignored his presence as if he didn't exist. She did cut the article about Hermie Hill's hospitalization out of the local paper and paste it in her Doomsday Book; and on especially cold winter nights, when the temperature fell to forty and forty-five below, she'd look up from her sewing and say to me, "You and your grandfather had better check on that animal before you go to bed, Tut."

And we always did.

The times I remember best with Hannibal were three or four frigid nights in deep winter when my grandfather hitched him to a flat-bed sleigh and he and Han and I took hay up to the deer yarded in the deep evergreen woods of Idaho. After unloading the sled, we'd wait on the edge of the trees under the cold starlight, with Hannibal's breath billowing up through the branches like steam from an open spot on the river. First singly, then in pairs and small family groups, the winter-thin deer came out of the woods to feed, unafraid of us or of Hannibal. Those were fine times for my grandfather and me, and I think Hannibal enjoyed them too.

But besides being a prodigious hayburner, Hannibal Rex was an old elephant when my grandfather acquired him. The long border-country winter was tough on him, even after Gramp moved him from the hayloft to a stall at the far end of the milking parlor, which was much warmer.

One afternoon the following spring, a few days after we'd turned Hannibal in with the cows in the upper pasture, he vanished. My grandfather followed his tracks into the Idaho woods and found him lying on his side, big as a gray granite outcropping, near where he'd helped us take hay to the deer the previous winter. Apparently he'd gone off to die there alone, peaceably, the way old elephants are said to do. I cried some, but my grandfather shook his head and reminded me that Han's last year was a good one, semi-retired on a

Vermont hill farm with a man and a boy who understood elephants. He rented Bumper Stevens's bulldozer for half a day and buried him there, overlooking half the county. That summer he put up a cedar marker that said: "Here Lies Hannibal Rex, the Third Largest Elephant in Captivity. He Was a Good Elephant." The marker is there to this day, though the inscription has faded to illegibility during the forty-five summers and winters since.

3

THE SNOW OWL

Early on during my first winter in Lost Nation, I discovered that just getting by from one day to the next at that time of year was a nearly full-time job for everyone in the Hollow. Three times a day, starting in mid-October, I brought in several armloads of wood apiece for the kitchen and parlor stoves. Each morning before school, and again as soon as I got home, I helped my grandfather with his barnwork. On Saturdays I worked with him in the woods or swept up at his one-man sawmill by the river. Of course I continued to help my grandmother, too: drying and putting away the supper dishes, winding the clocks, shoveling a path through the snow to her birdfeeder in the pin cherry tree behind the summer kitchen.

As I grew older, my tasks increased. At eight I was helping Gramp clean out the gutters in the milking parlor and feeding and watering Gram's laying hens. And by the winter I was nine, I was

tailing a saw on weekends for my grandfather, and I had full charge
of my grandmother's chickens, a job that included collecting each
day's eggs on my way in from afternoon barn chores.

Not counting One Eye Jack, her rooster, my grandmother kept
twenty Buff Orpington laying hens. They were large birds of an
unusual color between orange and cinnamon, and they were quartered in a henhouse converted from an old grain room at the far
end of the long ell connecting the farmhouse and the barn. All up
and down Lost Nation Hollow, my grandmother's Orpingtons had
a reputation as famous layers; and three times a week, when
my grandfather trucked his milk out to the cheese factory, he took
along several cartons of fresh eggs to sell at Cousin Clarence Kittredge's general store at the junction of the Hollow and the county
road.

As anyone who has ever kept them can tell you, chickens are
notoriously foolish and dirty creatures. So I will state at the outset
that neither my grandfather nor I had any use at all for the Buff
Orpingtons, especially after our annual hoeing out and white-
washing of their premises. Yet the flock of laying hens was of great
importance to my grandmother, who, since my first week on the
farm, had set aside a portion of her egg money each month to de-
fray the future costs of my college books and other incidental ex-
penses.

Even in the dead of winter the Orpingtons were remarkably
steady layers, a fact my grandmother attributed to their daily outdoor feeding and exercise in a barnyard pen adjacent to the
henhouse. But in March of the year I turned nine, in the middle of a
long stretch of unseasonably frigid weather, even for Kingdom
County, there was a sharp decline in the productivity of her twenty
laying hens, from an average of sixteen or eighteen eggs a day to
fewer than a dozen.

At first my grandmother blamed the drop-off on the cold spell.
But on the afternoon that I reported to her that the best nest in the
henhouse had turned up empty again for the third day in a row, she
told me to go back out and count the chickens themselves.

It was nearly five o'clock and already quite dark inside the
henhouse. The chickens were lined up asleep on their roosting pole

and easy to count, even by lantern light. I counted twice, carefully, and came up with only eighteen both times.

To make sure that I hadn't overlooked any, I checked outside in the exercise pen. Nothing. Sometimes in the summertime a wayward hen fluttered up through a chute in the ceiling dating back to the era when the henhouse had been a grain room, and established a hidden brood nest in the haymow overhead. Not in the winter, though. In the winter the laying hens never strayed far from the vigilant single eye of Jack the rooster, venturing outside the henhouse only with him, and then just to eat and peck around in the snowy pen for a few minutes each day.

When I reported to my grandmother that two chickens were missing, she frowned and gave a long audible sigh. "Those hens are your ticket to college, Tut," she said. "You can't go to college without the wherewithal to buy your books."

My grandmother threw her black shawl over her shoulders, took the lantern, and went out through the ell to the henhouse to count for herself. But to her dismay and my secret satisfaction, she came up with the same result I had: eighteen, plus the rooster.

There was no longer any doubt about it. Somehow, two of her prize laying hens seemed to have vanished into thin air. The rest were laying erratically at best. And from my grandmother's grim silence during supper and throughout the evening, you might have supposed that my entire college education was in imminent jeopardy.

The following morning before school, the most probable culprit in the case of the missing chickens came to light. Just as I was bringing in my last armload of stove wood, a white weasel with a black tip on its tail ran out into the kitchen from under the cupboard beneath the sink. It stopped no more than four feet away from my grandmother, who was standing at the stove stirring a double boiler of oatmeal. The weasel stood up on its short hind legs and looked around at its surroundings with the fearless curiosity of a tame cat.

I was so surprised that I nearly dropped the wood. Now the

weasel seemed to be staring at my grandmother, and she was staring directly back at it. Both the weasel's eyes and my grandmother's were as shiny and round and black as the side buttons of my grandmother's black shoes, though Gram's eyes were somewhat bigger. Only when she set down the oatmeal ladle and reached for her broom did the creature drop onto all fours again and slink back under the sink.

"There's the sneak thief that's been carrying off my hens," my grandmother said. "Go tell your grandfather a winter weasel has taken up residence under my sink. I want him to come in here and dispatch it straightaway."

I dumped the wood in the woodbox with a clatter and took off through the connected woodshed, toolshed, henhouse, and horse stable to the cow barn. I found my grandfather in the milk house, slamming milkcans into his wheelbarrow and cursing under his breath.

"Guess what just came out from under the sink into Gram's kitchen," I shouted.

My grandfather straightened up to his full height and looked at me critically with his pale blue eyes and said in his harsh voice, "A winter weasel, no doubt."

For the second time that morning I was astonished. How had my grandfather possibly guessed this? For a moment it occurred to me that he might have caught a weasel and released it under the kitchen sink to frighten my grandmother.

Then he explained. "Sometimes in the winter your wild white weasels will venture into farmhouses for mice."

"Gram and the weasel stared at each other for quite a long while," I said.

My grandfather made a rasping noise in his throat, like his big log saw striking a knot in the butt-end of a hemlock log. "I imagine they did," he said.

"For its size," he continued, "your white winter weasel is probably the fiercest customer in these parts. It's totally fearless."

"Gram wants you to come in and dispatch it."

My grandfather picked up the handles of his wheelbarrow. "Open that outside door and shut it tight after me, Austen," he said. "It's thirty below out there if it's a degree under freezing."

The wind had blown hard the night before, and on our way down the Hollow to school that morning, my grandfather's lumber truck bucked through one high snowdrift after another. Each time the truck shuddered through another drift, my grandfather cursed, and his white breath hung in the unheated cab between us like smoke from his fiery expletives. Above the dozen remaining occupied farmhouses in the Hollow, woodsmoke rose eight or ten feet, then flattened out into tattered horizontal ribbons, unable to climb higher in the overarching cold.

The schoolroom never warmed up that day. We huddled as close to the tall, cracked stove as we could get, scalding our faces and freezing our backs. The boys' felt boots steamed faintly, giving off a powerful barn odor as we shivered and burned our way through the day's lessons. It was hard for me to concentrate. All day long I wondered what my grandfather would do about the thieving weasel.

When Gramp picked me up after school that afternoon, he informed me that the weasel was dead. He had trapped it in a number-four muskrat trap, and nailed the carcass up on the inside of the woodshed door. As soon as we got home I ran out in the shed to see it. It looked much smaller than it had that morning, standing on its hind legs and staring defiantly at my grandmother. Now I supposed that the chickens would begin to lay again.

But that afternoon only three eggs appeared in the henhouse nesting boxes and yet another chicken was missing.

That night the northern wind brought more snow and cold down out of Canada. The temperature fell to forty-five degrees below zero. The millrace at the foot of my grandfather's sawmill dam froze solid for the first time since I'd moved up to Lost Nation. My grandmother had to keep a steady trickle of water running out of the kitchen faucet to prevent the line from the spring from freezing.

Again I wondered if the terrible cold could possibly be keeping the chickens from laying. Perhaps so. Yet when a fourth hen turned up missing later that week, and then a fifth, the remaining chickens began to panic. Day and night they huddled together on their roost,

as close to One Eye Jack as they could get. My grandfather kept the
muskrat trap set and baited under the sink, but there was no sign of
a second weasel.

One sub-zero morning in the middle of March when I opened
the henhouse door to let the Orpingtons outside to eat, they refused
to come off their roost. As usual, I dumped a large pan of chicken
feed onto the packed snow inside their pen. But only with great
difficulty was I able to harry them out. Instead of going inside the
barn to start chores, I waited behind the milk house door to see
what would happen next.

Now the hens were fluttering frantically around Jack, now piling
up against the shut henhouse door. Jack let out a long, quavering
crow, then hunkered down on the packed snow with his panicked
flock.

I was so intent on watching the hens that I didn't see the huge
white bird until it was halfway across the pasture from the river. It
seemed to materialize from the sky, advancing swiftly over the
snowy contours of the pasture with its wings impossibly white and
wide. For a moment it hovered on rapidly beating wings directly
over the chicken pen. The hens below were frozen in terror. Even
Jack couldn't muster another warning.

The great white bird plummeted with its talons extended. It
struck a hen in the back of the neck, swooped up out of the pen at a
steep angle, and bore the bundle of tawny orange feathers back
across the pasture. But instead of carrying its prey into the ever-
greens beyond the river, the bird landed in a soft maple tree not far
below the frozen spillway of my grandfather's dam.

Just behind me in the milk house doorway, a harsh voice spoke.
"I was wrong if I do say so, Austen," my grandfather said. "However fierce your winter weasel is for its size, it can't hold a candle to
a white snow owl. Now there is a fierce customer. I haven't seen a
snow owl in this neck of the woods for years."

Except on the covers of my grandfather's cigar boxes, I'd never
seen a snow owl before. I hadn't even recognized this one as an owl
until my grandfather told me what it was.

The bird was perched on a low limb of the soft maple, facing
away from us toward the river and woods. Maybe it heard my grand-

father speak because abruptly it swiveled its head around in our direction. It was as if the owl's head was on a separate mechanism from its body, like a toy of some sort. But this bird was no toy. It was an alien-looking creature a full two feet tall, and except for its amber eyes and the faintest gray cross-hatchings on its back, it was totally white. Even its talons were covered with thick white foot feathers.

For what seemed like a long time my grandfather and I stood in the milk house doorway, watching the snow owl watch us. Finally, for no apparent reason, the bird rotated its head forward in a single clockwork motion, glided off the tree branch, and disappeared into the fir trees across the river, with the limp hen in its claws.

"Put the chickens back inside and feed them in there," my grandfather told me. "Don't mention any of this to your grand-mother. This afternoon we'll rig up something that'll make Mr. Owl think twice before he carries off another hen."

That afternoon when my grandfather picked me up at school he had with him in the back of his lumber truck a brand-new roll of fine black netting, the kind my grandmother draped over her ripen-ing strawberry beds and raspberry bushes to discourage blackbirds. On the seat beside him sat a small brown paper sack of metal staples.

"Can't he tear right through that net?" I said.

"No doubt," my grandfather said. "But he doesn't know that. He'll be afraid of getting his feet tangled up in it."

As we approached the pasture across from our barnyard, I spot-ted the owl. It was perched on the low branch of the soft maple tree where it had landed with the dead hen the day before, and it was staring straight at the chicken pen. The bird made no move to fly when my grandfather and I got out of the truck and unrolled the black netting on the snow. It continued to watch us as we stretched the net over the top of the pen and stapled it to the four cedar corner posts. Now the pen was totally enclosed, top and sides.

Just as we finished I happened to look up and see my grand-mother at the kitchen window. Caught between the bold gaze of the snow owl and my grandmother's silent presence, I felt an intense discomfort.

"There's Gram," I said. "At the window."

"Let Gram be at the window," my grandfather said without looking toward the house. "That's a good place for her. You go shoo those chickens out here, Austen. We'll see what Mr. Snow Owl makes of this setup."

The chickens began to flutter frantically around the henhouse as soon as I entered. Two or three nearly escaped through the chute in the ceiling, but with feet and arms flying, I drove them out into the pen, under the protective netting.

Immediately they began to rush around like frying pullets in butchering time. They cackled wildly and Jack gave several alarmed outcries. Then they huddled in an orange mass against the door, just as they had that morning.

But the owl, sitting huge and spectral on the maple limb, apparently wanted no part of that net. My grandfather nodded, and told me to go change my clothes and meet him in the barn for chores.

Inside the kitchen I pulled off my felt boots and started upstairs to put on my barn clothes. "Come over here, Tut," my grandmother said.

As we stood side by side at the window, my grandmother grasped my left wrist with her right hand, and her fingers on my wrist felt as strong as the talons of the owl.

"Gram, Gramp said to meet—"

"Hark," she said.

Far to the southwest, the setting sun was resting on the shoulder of Mount Mansfield. The mountains to the east were a deep purple. Overhead the sky was an icy blue, and the snowy pasture and the frozen river beyond it had acquired a sympathetic blue tint. Even the owl's feathers had a bluish cast.

As my grandmother continued to grip my wrist, the owl suddenly launched itself into a flat trajectory. It came soaring toward our buildings no more than ten feet off the ground and its bluish wings seemed to brush the lavender-tinged snow on the higher knolls of the pasture. This time it did not hover above the pen. It dropped straight onto the flimsy berry netting with terrific force, bearing it down onto the massed chickens and pinning them to the snow beneath like so many flopping fish.

Without a second's hesitation the owl took off again with a dead bird and the netting in its talons. I thought it would rip the entire net loose. But the ascending owl simply yanked the dead hen through the small rent in the net made by its claws, like a feather duster being yanked backward through a keyhole. Once again it flew straight to the soft maple tree, where it began to devour the Buff Orpington, feathers, feet, beak and all.

"There," my grandmother said, releasing my wrist. "Now we know."

That evening my grandfather got out his *Birds of North America* book with its gorgeous colored plates and studied the section on great snowy owls. Occasionally he looked up over his reading glasses to provide us with a short commentary. "Your white snow owl usually stays up in the Arctic year-round," he said. "It eats mice, mainly. Mice and lemmings. Every few winters when the lemming population drops off, it ventures down below the tree line for food. The snow owl is actually a most beneficial bird. It can eat its own weight in rodents every two days."

"This one eats one of my chickens every day," my grandmother said. "I want you to shoot it first thing in the morning."

"Shoot it! That bird is legally protected by the federal government," my grandfather said angrily, though on most occasions he had little good to say about any governmental entity. "It's strictly against the law to harm one. There's a penalty of one hundred dollars for shooting a snow owl."

"Not up here in Siberia, there isn't," my grandmother said. "Or if there is, it isn't enforced. You get your gun and shoot it first thing tomorrow morning."

I was amazed. My little aunts had confided to me in a Sunday School lesson that when my Grandmother Kittredge was a small girl growing up in Scotland, her older brother had been killed in a hunting accident. Since then she had been terrified of guns; and although she did not interfere with my grandfather's hunting, or forbid me to go hunting with him, I knew that she worried herself sick whenever we went to the woods with a gun.

"As soon as the weather breaks, that bird will fly back north," my grandfather said. "In the meantime the chickens can eat inside, like normal chickens in the wintertime."

"And let that white demon lay siege to them? Why, they'll never lay again, Mr. Kittredge."

"I won't be a party to shooting a protected animal," my grandfather nearly shouted. "I might go so far as to scare him off, but that's all. He'll be gone by sugaring season anyway. Shoot him I will not, Mrs. Kittredge. That's final."

The next afternoon when I got home from school the owl was sitting in the maple tree again, waiting for the chickens to come outside. Before starting chores my grandfather went down in the meadow with his double-barreled twelve-gauge shotgun and fired twice over the bird's head. It flew back into the woods across the river, and to my great relief, we didn't see it again for the rest of the winter.

April came, and with it mud season. Overnight the Hollow road turned from white to brown. Everything smelled like mud. The maple sap ran hard and early that year, and we were busy night and day, gathering sap and boiling it. As usual, school closed for a week so that Hollow kids could help out at home with the sugaring.

Throughout sugaring season my grandmother insisted that we continue to keep the chickens inside. Even so, they refused to lay more than five or six eggs a day. When I went into the henhouse to feed them, they crowded together on the roosting pole, clucking in alarm.

"They know," my grandmother said. "They know it's still out there, lurking in the woods."

"It's gone back north," my grandfather said. "To Labrador. I'm of half a mind to go myself come spring, and take Austen with me."

"It's there," my grandmother said. "And I don't mean Labrador."

But as the days continued to lengthen, and the soft spring light illuminated the greening hillsides, One Eye Jack's confidence began to revive. He crowed earlier each morning, trying to encourage his harem. Breeding time was approaching. Jack was a fine, brave rooster, who had lost his right eye defending the henhouse from an egg-sucking rat two years ago. For three summers in succession he'd been named Grand Fowl of the Show at Kingdom Fair. But the rooster's efforts to rally the traumatized hens were futile. They could not be induced to go outside to eat, and they laid so few eggs now that my grandmother said we might as well let them brood their nests and replenish the dwindled flock with new chicks.

"I suppose we're fortunate to still have Jack," she remarked after supper one Friday evening in early May as she went to the kitchen window to check the temperature.

The evening before, the spring frogs across the pasture near the river had sung for the first time, though tonight was cold again, threatening snow. "Twenty-eight and dropping fast," my grandmother said.

The words were hardly out of her mouth when a terrific commotion broke out in the ell.

My grandfather jumped up from his chair and grabbed the lantern off the table. With my grandmother and me close at his heels, he rushed through the woodshed into the henhouse. The chickens were shrieking from their roosts like so many banshees, and on the floor directly under the chute in the ceiling the huge white owl was mantling its outspread wings over the limp body of One Eye Jack.

My grandfather grabbed a long forked support pole out from under the central roost and jabbed it at the snow owl, which reared up and spread its wings like an eagle and hissed at us fearlessly.

"Destroy it!" my grandmother cried. "Kill it with that stick or I will."

I don't know whether my grandfather would or wouldn't have killed the owl. He was still holding the lighted kerosene lantern in one hand, and if he'd dropped that our entire place could very well have gone up in flames. Before he could decide what to do, the owl flew straight up in the air through the opening in the ceiling with the lifeless remains of my grandmother's prizewinning rooster in his talons.

"Quick, get your gun," my grandmother said. "He's trapped in the hayloft."

"He isn't trapped," my grandfather shouted. "He'll get out the same way he got in. Through the cupola window."

Sure enough, when I ran outside into the barnyard there was the owl, just visible on top of the cupola against the night sky, devouring the rooster my grandmother had been counting on to reestablish her laying flock.

"He doesn't allow much to go to waste," my grandfather said a minute later as all three of us stood in the barnyard, looking up at the owl. "We have to give him that, at least."

"No, we don't," my grandmother said. "All we have to give him is a double load of buckshot. Fetch your shotgun this instant."

Without replying my grandfather went inside and got a hammer and some nails. He disappeared into the ell, and a few minutes later we could hear him hammering.

When he came into the kitchen from boarding up the chute in the henhouse ceiling, he went to the window and looked out into the dark barnyard for a long time. I thought he might be about to change his mind. Maybe he would shoot the owl after all.

Finally he turned away from the window. "It's commencing to snow again," he said to no one in particular. "Big flakes. Sugar snow."

"What did I say, Tut?" my grandmother said to me. "Snow in May and white Arctic owls. Siberia. You and I will deal with that creature tomorrow morning if your grandfather won't."

It was still dark when we got up the next morning for chores. When it was light enough in the barn to extinguish our lanterns, my grandfather went to the milk house door and looked out. After a minute he beckoned for me to join him there. It had snowed six or eight inches overnight. Once again the barnyard and the road, the pasture and the evergreen woods beyond the river were white. It was bitterly cold and the wind was gusting hard out of the north.

"In the soft maple," my grandfather said.

There was the owl, staring across the road at our buildings. Neither one of us spoke again. Yet I had the feeling that my grandfather and I and the owl were somehow linked together, though I could not say how.

The sun came up as we ate breakfast. From where I was sitting I could look out the window over the pasture and see the snow owl in the tree. Neither one of my grandparents so much as glanced at it, but I knew that they could not have been more aware of its presence if it had been sitting on the kitchen table beside the chipped blue enamel coffeepot.

Immediately after breakfast my grandfather headed across the road to his sawmill. He had to pass quite near the snow owl and I hoped he would try to scare it away again. He did not, though. He never looked in its direction.

My grandmother washed the breakfast dishes and swept the kitchen floor while I brought in the morning's wood and checked the henhouse. A few orange feathers lay on the floor under the nailed-up ceiling chute. They were the only sign of the owl's assault the night before.

Back in the kitchen, my grandmother was waiting in her boots and long black coat. She had put her black shawl over her head and fastened it under her chin like a huge scarf, and she was peering into my grandfather's gun cabinet by the hall to the dining room. "Which one of these does he use for birds, Austen?"

I pointed to the double-barreled twelve-gauge, and my grandmother opened the cabinet and lifted it out. I had never before seen her touch a gun of any kind. This one was nearly as long as she was tall, and delivered a kick like a logging horse.

"Do you know how to operate this weapon?" she asked.

I was more alarmed than ever. Apparently my grandmother intended to order me to shoot the owl, which would infuriate my grandfather.

A desperate idea sprang into my mind. I would deliberately fire over the bird's head, as my grandfather had done, to scare it away. Last night's snowstorm was certainly the winter's final one, and any day now the owl would fly back to his home in the Far North. But my own light twenty-gauge would be far better for this purpose than my grandfather's old cannon.

"Look, Gram. This single-barreled gun's a lot safer. This is the one I use."

"Get some bullets," my grandmother said quietly. "For the double-barreled gun. Then put your warm wraps on. You and your grandmother have a job to do this morning, Tut."

It was terrifically cold outside, with a cutting wind, more like a wind in January or February than May. The shadow of the wood-smoke blowing from the kitchen chimney writhed over the snow in the dooryard like something alive. Miniature snow spouts whirled across the road, though high overhead the sky was blue and once again the snowy pasture had acquired a temporary azure hue.

I was hoping against hope that the sight of my grandmother advancing across the barnyard with the shotgun would scare the owl away. Instead, he watched fearlessly as we crossed the road and headed into the pasture through the swirling snow twisters. Gram marched ahead of me. The wind blew her coat away from her boots and tugged at her black shawl. I had the strongest impression that if she hadn't been weighted down by the shotgun, she would have been blown right off her feet.

When we were halfway across the pasture the big saw from my grandfather's mill shrieked out, causing me to jump. It rose to an angry crescendo as it ripped through a log. Then the sound of the saw seemed to blow away on the wind.

Still the owl held its perch, motionless as an alabaster bird in a china cabinet. When we were about twenty feet away my grandmother stopped and looked at it steadily. Then in her own odd way, I believe that she gave it one last chance to leave our lives forever.

"You, Satan," she said in a sharp, unafraid voice.

The great bird swiveled its head around and looked at the snowy woods across the river, as though considering a retreat. Then the bluntly-rounded white head with its tremendous amber eyes swung back toward us, and I realized at last what my grandmother had known from the start: that the owl had absolutely no intention of leaving our farm until it had killed every last one of the hens.

Gram turned to me and held out the twelve-gauge. "Load the weapon, Tut."

The moment I had dreaded was here. I no longer had any faith at all that I could fool my grandmother by deliberately missing the bird, or that it would fly away if I did. Nor did I see how I could betray my grandfather by shooting the owl.

"Load the gun."

As reluctantly as I had ever done anything in my life, I broke open my grandfather's shotgun, shoved two number-four shells inside the twin dark chambers, and closed it back up with a hollow *thunk*. At the same time I was vaguely aware of my grandfather's log saw, shrieking out again in the background.

"Now tell me, Tut," my grandmother said. "How does it fire?"

I looked at her dumbly. Surely my diminutive grandmother did not intend to fire my grandfather's huge old twelve-gauge herself? Yet that is exactly what she planned to do, despite her great fear of guns.

What choice did I have? I had to demonstrate how to cock back the hammers and which trigger went with which barrel; how to hold the gun in tight to her shoulder to absorb as much of the recoil as possible.

"I understand," she said. "Hand me the weapon."

She took the gun from me, brought it up to her shoulder, pulled back the hammers, aimed in the general direction of the bird, and fired both barrels.

There was a crashing roar and the snow owl gave a hard jerk and toppled over like a painted tin duck at the shooting gallery at Kingdom Fair. Beyond all doubt it was dead. But its feathered talons still gripped the branch of the maple tree, from which it now hung upside down, swaying slightly in the wind, defiant and fierce, even in death.

The impact of the shotgun's kick had driven my grandmother back two or three steps. She tottered briefly, then sat down in the snow. It would be inaccurate to report that the gun knocked her off her feet. Rather, she seemed to sit down almost as an afterthought. The roar of the gun had echoed off the ridge behind the farmhouse and dispersed over the snowy landscape in the wind. Except for the ringing in my ears the morning was now silent again.

My grandmother dropped the gun and extended her left hand. "Help your grandmother up, Tut."

As I pulled her to her feet, her right arm hung straight down at her side. "Pick up the weapon," she said.

I picked up the gun and brushed off the snow. My grandmother walked over to the maple tree, her right arm limp at her side. She peered up at the owl, hanging upside down from the limb. A steady trickle of blood dripped onto the snow at her feet.

"Finished," she pronounced. "He won't be carrying off any more chickens, Tut. Or keeping boys out of college."

With my ears still ringing from the gun blast, I walked back across the pasture with my grandmother. My eyes stung from the fine blowing snow. Or maybe I was crying. I did not know or care which.

Suddenly I saw my grandfather. He was standing in the entrance-way of his mill, watching our progress toward the house. I wanted to shout to him that I hadn't killed the owl, but a second later he was gone. Before we reached the road the angry scream of his saw ripped out over the pasture again.

We went quickly across the barnyard. I opened the woodshed door with the weasel pelt nailed to the inside, and held it against the gusting wind for my grandmother. But she grasped the handle in her good hand and told me to go inside first. For a second or two she stood in the half-open doorway, looking back across the barnyard and pasture. I waited just inside the woodshed, and in that fleeting moment beheld the tableau of the snow owl, the white weasel, and my grandmother, her profile grim and fierce and triumphant against the morning sky.

4

THE GREEN
MOUNTAIN WHALE

 In the beginning, my grandfather
told me soon after I came to
Lost Nation, there was only the
river. There were no farms, no
sawmills, no towns. Icy and amber-colored, it seeped out of an
impenetrable cedar bog high on the northernmost ridge of the
height of land dividing the present-day Connecticut and St. Lawrence River watersheds, and ran southwest through hills heavily forested with fir and spruce and white pine. It flowed past the future
site of my grandparents' farm, and wound down through the narrow
valley that my ancestor, Sojourner Kittredge, would name Lost Nation Hollow in ironical commemoration of his geographical miscalculation. At the foot of the Hollow it joined the Main Branch of the
Kingdom River to run due west for ten miles, to the spot where the
county seat of Kingdom Common sits today. There it dropped over
a long, steep cataract later known as the High Falls.

Below the falls, the Kingdom passed through a flat where willow trees grew thick on both sides. Then, having already transformed from a lacy network of hidden rills into a swift brook and from a brook into a small river, it metamorphosed in character once again. It broadened out, deepened, slowed to a crawl, and entered a marshy wetlands full of ducks and snapping turtles, muskrats and minks and otters and moose. Leisurely, almost unnoticeably, it twisted north through the swamp another ten miles, to the south bay of Lake Memphremagog, "Beautiful Waters," in Abenaki, which stretched twenty-five miles into Canada between tall mountains before emptying into yet another river that headed out to the great St. Lawrence.

At one time, according to my grandfather, glaciers crept down into our hills from northern Canada, inching their way south by their own immense weight. That was ten thousand years ago. Then the mile-high mass of ice had retreated, leaving an inland sea extending from the wide valley of the St. Lawrence to the southernmost boundary of what would become Kingdom County. This was a saltwater sea, connected directly to the ocean by a vast tidal arm five hundred miles long, and my grandfather told me that in those ancient times, salmon and seals and occasionally even whales swam all the way up this inlet. The whales passed icebergs hundreds of feet high, broken off from the retreating glacier, and swam between the soaring mountain peaks on each side of Lake Memphremagog, and on up the drowned-out valley of the Kingdom River into the flooded hollows, high over the future site of the Farm in Lost Nation. My grandfather referred to these whales as Green Mountain whales, and said that the original Abenaki Indians who had roamed through these parts had hunted them from kayaks. Still, all this seemed as fantastic to me as Aladdin's treasure caves and genies in my *Arabian Nights* storybook.

"There's one now, Austen," he said, and pointed to a cloud shaped vaguely like a whale, high overhead in the summery Vermont sky.

I was seven at the time, and we were taking a short break from haying. During the past year, I had learned that my grandfather frequently liked to pull my leg, and could do so with a perfectly expressionless face. I looked at him, and he looked back at me with his pale blue eyes. Then he winked.

I had no idea whether to believe what he said about the glaciers, the inland sea, and the long-ago Green Mountain whales. For all I knew my grandfather was kidding about those, too. With him, it was hard to tell.

The East Branch—our branch—of the Upper Kingdom River was by no means wide. By the time I was eight I could easily wing a stone across it from bank to bank. But it was very quick, very cold, and full of colorful, hard-fighting native brook trout. For two or three weeks in the early spring it was strong enough to drive a moderate quantity of logs; and in my Great-Great-Great-Great-Great-Grandfather Sojourner Kittredge's time, when it ran through mile upon mile of dense, uncut forest, its flow was steadier still.

The river is one of my earliest memories from the time I first went to live with my grandparents. For years it was the last sound I heard out of the narrow, slanted window of my upper bedchamber before going to sleep at night, and the first sound I heard when I woke up the next morning. And like the Canadian border just north of our place, and the Boston and Montreal Railroad through the village of Kingdom Common, the river was a tangible geographical link, for both my grandfather and me, to the world beyond Kingdom County.

For my tenth birthday—I had lived in Lost Nation four years by then, and it had become as much my home as anyone else's, and my grandparents were now as much my parents as my grandparents, though I remained on the best of terms with my father and saw him quite frequently—Gramp got me a Hammond's World Atlas. I distinctly recall his opening it on the kitchen table and showing me how a chip of wood from his sawmill could ride merrily down the Kingdom River to Lake Memphremagog and thence all the way to the St. Lawrence and Quebec City. Possibly, that hypothetical woodchip might even wind up off the barren coast of Labrador, where my grandfather had gone as a young surveyor and to which he had promised to return, with me, when I turned eighteen.

"There," he said, planting his blunt, rough forefinger in the middle of the blank white interior of that little-known, boreal wilderness on the two-page map of Canada in the birthday atlas. "Right there, Austen. You and I and a canoe. You'll see rivers there that'll make the East Branch look like a meadow brook in August."

Yet my grandfather liked the East Branch, too. It powered his sawmill; he trapped along its banks in the winter; in the spring and summer he and I fished it together every chance we had; and he still drove logs down it from the big Idaho woods northeast of our farmhouse, to the horseshoe-shaped oxbow bend just above the mill-pond—where, more often than not, his logs jammed together in the tight U of the curve, in monumental pileups that took days and sometimes weeks to untangle.

The year I turned ten, which also happened to be the year when the first electrical line was run up into Lost Nation Hollow, was an especially bad one for logjams in the oxbow. By the middle of May, my grandfather had fifty thousand feet of thirty-two-foot-long logs hopelessly piled up in the crook of the elbow, and nothing he contrived to do with his pick pole or peavey budged them an inch.

One afternoon when my grandmother's apple orchard in the meadow adjacent to the jammed-up oxbow was just blossoming out, my grandfather was waiting for me in his lumber truck when I got out of school. A hefty coil of new fence wire lay on the floorboards. On the seat beside my grandfather was a long wooden crate with the words "Granite State Blasting Company" stenciled in black letters on the top. Packed inside the box in sawdust, Gramp informed me, were thirty-six sticks of dynamite. The box sat lengthwise on the seat, and stretched all the way from my grandfather, behind the wheel, to the passenger door of the cab.

"Hop up on top," my grandfather said. "It's stable."

Winter frost was still thawing out of the Hollow road in sheltered places through the woods. It was full of potholes and washouts, and as bumpy as a road can be and still be passable. All the way home I stole glances at the case of dynamite beneath me, though my grandfather assured me that it couldn't possibly explode until it was lighted or detonated with an electrical current. I was far from persuaded. As we jounced up the Hollow, he told me harrowing stories of his days as a shooter, or dynamite man, on the last big Connecticut River log drives. When we finally pulled into our barnyard, I was so relieved I forgot to ask him, in accordance with our ritual, who lived there. "The meanest old bastard in Kingdom

County," he said, anyway. "Remember that you heard it first from me."

Although there was still plenty of snow back in the woods, it was a warm and sunny spring afternoon. Bright yellow cowslips were in blossom near the steep limestone bank of the oxbow, where the logs were jammed up. My grandfather seemed very confident as he walked out onto the ledge in a jaunty, lumberjack gait. With him he had three dark red sticks of the Granite State dynamite, which he lighted from his cigar and tossed into the jumble of logs. He hurried back into my grandmother's orchard as the dynamite went off with three terrific reports, one right after the other. The air was filled with smoke and a gunpowder odor, but the jam didn't shift a foot.

Next Gramp cut a long pole from a brown ash sapling growing near the river. To one end he lashed half a dozen sticks of dynamite. Standing on the ledge, he ignited a fuse and thrust the business end of the pole deep into the tangled logs. He scrambled back up onto the bank, and I hunkered down behind an apple tree full of fragrant blossoms and put my hands over my ears. A second later a tremendous explosion shook the ground under my feet. Chunks of bark and woodchips rose twenty feet in the air. I was sure the jam had broken apart. But as the acrid smoke began to clear, I saw that the towering pile of logs was exactly where it had been for the past week.

My grandfather nodded grimly. He seemed quite satisfied by this turn of events. "It's that limestone ledge, Austen," he said. "That's what's hanging the logs. It runs out underwater from the bank halfway across the river and blocks off the channel."

My grandfather tied all but one of the remaining sticks of dynamite together in a single tight bundle, and hitched the free end of the new coil of wire to a detonating cap attached to the explosives. He wedged the package of dynamite down into a crevice in the riverside ledge, and instructed me to unroll the coil of wire back through the apple trees in the meadow, toward the road, while he went to get his truck. In the meantime, I'd spotted my grandmother, watching us from the farmhouse porch through her opera glasses. Their brass fittings gleamed in the mild spring sunshine, somehow accentuating her disapproval.

My grandfather drove the truck partway down the muddy lane

into the apple orchard, shut it off and opened the hood. I handed him the ends of the wire, which he wrapped around the starter coil. "Get inside and start her up," he told me.

Under my grandfather's supervision, I'd been driving his farm truck around the barnyard and fields for nearly a year. But it was always a great thrill for me to slide in under the big rubber-coated steering wheel with the smooth wooden knob for a handle. I turned on the key and reached for the starter with my foot, stretching as far as I could. It ground twice, and the engine coughed, turned over, and caught. At the same instant, an immense detonation ripped into the spring afternoon. From the oxbow, chunks of ledge rose higher than the barn cupola and came raining out of the sky all over the blossoming orchard. Several hit in the muddy lane near my grandfather, who paid no more attention to them than to a summer hailstorm. Then I was out of the truck and running through the apple trees behind my grandfather.

Ahead of us, beneath a great cloud of smoke, the jam was moving. In a solid mass, it progressed about thirty feet—only to come to a stop in the lower curve of the bow, just above the millpond. Then in the cleared bend above them, a great slab of the limestone ledge where my grandfather had stood to place the dynamite charges suddenly toppled outward into the river, leaving a sheer rock wall plunging from the top of the bank down into the water.

"Yes, sir," my grandfather said, an expression which, in the Kingdom County of my youth, could signify anything from an amiable salutation to a sarcastic disclaimer to an acknowledgment of the bleak lot of all farmers and loggers everywhere.

I was astonished by the way that huge chunk of rock had leisurely toppled over into the river. It must have weighed several tons, and it looked as if more of the ledge had been dislodged underwater, where we couldn't see it. But no matter. Just downstream, the logs were packed tightly from bank to bank again, in a solid, interlocked, immovable mass.

My grandfather got out the last stick of dynamite and tapped it thoughtfully against his palm. Then he stuck the dynamite stick in his back pocket and headed up the lane toward the barn.

For the next few days my grandfather was busy with spring work around the farm. There were fences to repair, sap buckets to collect and rinse out, two fields to plow and harrow and plant. As for the logs, I suspected that he was hoping for a big spring rain to bring up the river and move them along into his millpond. But no big rain came and as the middle of May approached, the logs were still snarled up in the lower bend of the oxbow above the mill, where they were as useless to us as though still standing in the woods upriver.

One evening after supper I wandered down to the sawmill dam, where my grandfather was fishing. It was a simple dam, built by Sojourner Kittredge and replaced twice since, at a spot where the river narrowed to less than twenty yards across. Just above, in the small millpond, was an island about the size of our farmhouse kitchen. The troublesome oxbow was situated one hundred feet or so above the island.

My grandfather, who never fished with anything but flies, and used only one fly, a number ten red-and-white Royal Coachman, made a short, precise cast up beside the island. "What I really ought to do, Austen, is raise this so-called pond another three, four feet and flood out the whole shebang, island and oxbow and all. Back this little puddle clear up to the Idaho woods above and float that Christly jam right on out of there."

My grandfather stripped in line and cast again. He made that distinctive rasping sound in his throat. "That would show them," he said.

By "them," of course, he meant my grandmother. But what did she have to do with this? Nothing, so far as I could see—until I happened to glance up at the towering logjam and the blooming apple trees beside it, scenting the entire meadow all the way down to the dam with their spicy pink and white blossoms.

"Wouldn't that flood out Gram's orchard?" I asked.

My grandfather frowned. "We'd never have a jam there again, Austen. Our problems would be over."

My grandmother's apple orchard was full of rare, old-fashioned varieties whose names were nearly as alluring as their fruit: Duchess of Oldenburg, Snow Apple, Cox Orange Pippin, Red Astrachan, Summer St. Lawrence, and twenty others. Along with her Buff Orpington laying hens, the old-fashioned apples were Gram's pride and joy. Besides being an important source of her private household income, the early-ripening varieties were blue-ribbon shoo-ins at the fruit and vegetable exhibit at Kingdom Fair.

"What about Gram?" I said again.

My grandfather rounded on me. "Gram!" he said as though referring to some distant interfering relative. "This is between you and me. Not them. Do you understand that?"

I said I did, and he handed me the fly rod. "There's a pretty fair trout just off the right side of that island, Austen. I can't seem to interest him tonight. See if you can get him to take a look."

My grandfather got out a cigar and lit it and watched me cast for the trout. I couldn't tell whether he approved of my technique or not. After a while he shook his head. "Gram," he muttered.

The next morning was Saturday. Immediately after barn chores and breakfast, my grandfather began work on his new project. According to his calculations, raising the level of the pond just four feet would dislodge the logs. This could be accomplished easily enough by lowering the gate of the dam and decreasing the flow of water through the penstock containing the waterwheel that powered his mill saws. With the additional pressure of the expanded millpond, however, my grandfather would first need to reinforce some of the old dam timbers. Cutting the new timbers was his first order of business.

"Tut, what are you and grandfather sashaying around that dam for?" my grandmother said to me when I went up to the house for a mid-morning snack.

To avoid telling her a direct lie I said, "Gramp says we're doing some repair work."

My grandmother looked at me with her sharp black eyes. "He said that? Repair work?"

I nodded.

She reached out and gripped my wrist. "Do you know where your grandfather's going to be sashaying next if he drowns out my apple trees, Tut?"

I shook my head, thereby inadvertently acknowledging my grandfather's intention to flood the orchard.

"I shall tell you where," my grandmother said. "He'll sashay straight to state prison, that's where. I'll send him there, for destroying my property and depriving me of the income from those apples."

She released my wrist and picked up her brass-bound opera glasses and trained them in on the dam. "Don't stray out of hailing distance, Tut. I'll want you to run a letter down to the mailbox shortly."

My grandmother finished her letter in ten minutes flat. I was far from surprised to see that it was addressed to Mr. Zachariah Barrows, Esquire, in Kingdom Common; old Zack Barrows was my grandmother's personal attorney and close ally in her ongoing battle for ascendancy over my grandfather.

Our mailbox was located half a mile down the Hollow, next to the one belonging to my Big Aunt Rose, at the mouth of the lane leading up to her place, which was as far as the RFD mail carrier could get up the Hollow road in mud season and bad winter weather. After I returned from posting the letter, I drifted over to the dam again to see how my grandfather was coming. He was still hard at work in his sawmill, cutting out dam braces. Without interrupting his work, he jerked his head down the Hollow in the direction of the mailbox. "Barrows?"

I nodded, and my grandfather continued working and said nothing more.

Over the course of the following week, the Farm became a domestic battleground. On Sunday my grandfather moved up to Labrador to sleep and take his meals. Then for the next several days he spent every spare hour reinforcing and repairing his dam. On Wednesday my grandmother wrote again to Attorney Barrows. By then she and my grandfather had ceased speaking to each other entirely, though occasionally one of them would send the other a terse and ominous message through me. I had long ago learned that when the chips were down, neither of my grandparents had the slightest compunction about recruiting me to their own camp. The newfangled notion put forward by various self-declared experts on family harmony that children should not be drawn into the disputes of their elders would have astonished and outraged them both. It was a cardinal precept of child rearing in the Kittredge household that I, like my little aunts, my Uncle Rob, and my father before me, should be indoctrinated in the divine correctness of all of their respective positions, beliefs, and opinions, large and small, and enlisted on the side of Right.

Thursday evening, as my grandmother and I were eating a grim and silent supper, Gramp having returned to Labrador to eat out of cans, as my grandmother put it, I glanced out the window and saw Sheriff Mason White coming up the Hollow road in his patrol car. My grandmother had been expecting him for two days, and I knew why. Before she had a chance to tell me not to, I ran outside and raced up the ridge to warn my grandfather. Beyond doubt, Sheriff White was here with a court order to prevent Gramp from raising the level of the pond and flooding my grandmother's apple trees.

My grandfather was sitting at the camp table in his red-and-black-checked lumber jacket, smoking a cigar and reading an old *National Geographic*. He glanced up at me over the reading spectacles he'd selected from the eyeglasses bin at the five-and-dime in Kingdom Common, then returned to his magazine.

"Mason White's on his way with a court order!" I blurted out. "I saw him coming up the Hollow."

"That's all?" my grandfather said. "I thought at the very least you were going to report that the house was afire."

My grandfather got up and went over to his bunk. He pulled a locker out from underneath it, and got something out of it, I didn't see what clearly. He stuck whatever it was in his lumber jacket pocket. Then he returned to the table and resumed reading.

In the meantime I looked around the camp. It was growing dusky and my grandfather had already lit the kerosene lamp on the table. The antlers of the deer heads mounted on the back wall shone softly in the lamplight. In other circumstances it would have been pleasant to flop down on the rear seat from an old 1938 Packard that my grandfather used as a camp sofa and get him to tell me about going down the Connecticut with big log drives or going to Labrador and out West with the surveying crews. This evening there was no time for such tales. Even now the gangling apparition of Kingdom County's chief lawman, Sheriff Mason White, was heaving into sight in the camp dooryard.

The sheriff came up to the open doorway and knocked on the outside wall of the camp. "Evening, Austen," he said in his high squeaky voice.

"Yes, sir, Mason," my grandfather said without looking up from his *Geographic* or inviting the sheriff inside.

"Very nice evening, Austen."

My grandfather continued reading.

"Evening there, young fella," the sheriff greeted me.

Following my grandfather's cue, I said nothing.

Sheriff White shifted his weight. He cleared his throat. "Well," he said, "maybe it ain't such an all-fire fine evening after all."

My grandfather wet his thumb and turned a page. He took a puff of his cigar, and read on.

The sheriff shifted again, before taking an official-looking document out of his coat pocket. "Now, Austen," he said in a shaky voice, "this ain't nothing personal. But I have been charged with delivering you this court summons to appear at the courthouse tomorrow morning at ten in the a. of m. for a civil proceeding in the case of"—he glanced at the document, which was shaking in his hand—"in the case of Kittredge vs. Kittredge."

Sheriff White held the court order through the open camp doorway. When my grandfather did not look up from his magazine, the frightened sheriff set down the paper on the floor and backed two or three steps into the dooryard. "It ain't nothing personal," he said again.

"Neither is this," said my grandfather, and he reached into the side pocket of his lumber jacket, took out the last remaining stick of Granite State Blasting Company dynamite, lit the fuse with his burning cigar, and with a sudden flick of his wrist tossed the lighted dynamite stick end over end out the doorway to Sheriff Mason White.

Sheriff White caught the dynamite stick reflexively. A look of terror came over his face. With the lighted dynamite clutched in his fist, he whirled around in the dooryard twice, like a man on fire. As he came out of the second revolution he heaved the dynamite far into the woods. It flared through the twilight like a skyrocket. Just before it dropped out of sight into the dusky softwoods, an explosion accompanied by a bright orange flash split the quiet.

"Good thundering Jehovah!" Sheriff White roared out. "You Kittredges aren't only outlaws, you're lunatics!"

In his confusion he whirled around yet again, then took off at a dead run back down the trail toward the Farm.

My grandfather continued to read for a minute or so. Then he jerked his head toward the shelf behind the camp woodstove, where he kept his provisions. "I could go for a number ten can of peaches, Austen. I'm getting sick of Campbell beans and jelly sandwiches on store bread that pulls apart in your hands."

I brought him the peaches and he took out his hunting knife and jabbed the point into the top of the can and haggled it open. He impaled a couple of peach halves and ate them off the knife, which he politely drove upright into the tabletop next to the open can for me to use. I ate some peaches with my grandfather, and neither of us spoke for a while. I looked over at the two bunks along the back wall, remembering how I'd awakened here one morning in deer season to find snow on my quilt, blown in through the chinks in the logs. Even before the border-country winter set in in earnest, the wood cookstove didn't keep the camp very warm. But if Labrador wasn't always comfortable, it was never less than a comforting place.

When we finished the peaches, my grandfather poured some kerosene on a few sticks of kindling in the stove and lit a small fire to take the chill off the evening. The wood flared up fast, reminding me of the lighted dynamite stick soaring through the dusk. I caught a whiff of that distinctive evergreen redolence my grandfather carried with him everywhere, imbued in his woolen pants and jacket, and remembered the first time I smelled that wonderful scent, on our way from the village to Lost Nation when I was just six years old. That seemed a long time ago now.

It occurred to me that I should get back to the house before my grandmother started to worry about me.

"So you're not going to the court tomorrow?" I said, getting up.

"Certainly I'm going to court," my grandfather said. "We're all going to court. You, too. Blowing up a two-bit sheriff is one thing, Austen. But a man can't be ignoring a summons to court. Tell them we'll be leaving shortly after nine o'clock.

"Kittredge vs. Kittredge," he called after me as I headed out the door. "That should be a court to remember."

I had next to no hope that my grandmother would allow me to miss school the next day to attend the court hearing, but for once she let me off the hook. Like my grandfather, she seemed to believe that witnessing this ultimate confrontation between them was actually more important than my precious education. I was delighted to hear her tell me that I could come with them.

We left at nine sharp in my grandfather's truck. I rode in the middle. My grandmother wore her most funereal black dress and a plain black hat with a tiny gold crocodile stickpin. My grandfather wore a clean red flannel shirt, neatly-creased khaki pants, and his steel-toed work boots. As always, he was freshly shaven and his short white hair was neatly brushed.

It was a fine day in late May. Under the clear northern Vermont sky, the hills were as green as any hills in the world. In another week it would be haying time in Kingdom County.

On the way down the Hollow neither one of my grandparents mentioned the impending hearing. My grandmother sat silently with her hands folded in her lap and a determined look on her face, which could have been carved from granite. My grandfather mentioned that a traveling circus was coming to town soon, and that he would take me to see it. "How would you like to go off to work for the circus, Austen?" he said. "Or a traveling fair?"

I said I would.

My grandmother gave a long sigh, and I heard her mutter the word sashaying. But I envied my grandfather his sashaying days, and yearned to see for myself someday what lay on the far side of the hills and mountains.

My grandfather slowed down to a crawl about halfway to the village so that I could get a good look at the crew running the new electrical line up to the Hollow. I knew that my grandparents disagreed over the power line, as they did about nearly everything else.

Gramp was looking forward to having electricity in the sawmill, where he now had to rely on our water-powered paddle wheel to operate his machinery. But my grandmother had stated flatly that she would never have electricity in the house; too many Vermont farmhouses had caught fire from faulty wiring over the years, and she did not intend to run that risk.

· We arrived in the village at nine-fifty by the courthouse clock. The following Monday was Memorial Day, and flags were already waving from house porches and in front of the stores. But the main excitement this morning seemed to be the hearing. A dozen or so curiosity-seekers were already standing on the long stone steps in front of the courthouse.

"Yes, sir, Mr. Kittredge," said Bumper Stevens, the commission sales auctioneer. "Who's that young fella with you? Your attorney?"

"He's as much attorney as I'll ever require."

Now that we'd reached the courthouse, I was afraid that they wouldn't let me in. But my grandparents marched right through the big front door as though they owned the place, and up a set of wide wooden stairs with me at their heels.

The courtroom was about the size of our double haymow at home. It had tall windows on three sides and smelled like a church. My grandmother sat with Lawyer Barrows at a shiny table below the judge's bench. My grandfather and I sat in two wooden chairs on the opposite side of the central aisle, about three rows back. A minute later I saw my Uncle Rob and my little aunts, Freddi and Klee, who were just out of college for the summer, come in and sit in the back of the room, opposite the curiosity-seekers, who by now numbered twenty or so. They waved to me and I lifted my hand.

The courtroom was very still. On the front wall, a large clock with a very white face and very black hands said nine fifty-five. At the table down in front, my grandmother and old Zack were conferring intently over a paper my grandmother had produced from her pocketbook.

My grandfather nudged me. "What sort of wood are the tables and benches up front made out of, Austen?"

"Rock maple," I said.

My grandfather gave me a curt nod. "What's the floor made of?"

"Red oak."

This time my grandfather didn't even bother to nod; it was enough that I knew.

A minute or two before ten, a man in a suit and tie came in and filled a water glass on the judge's bench. He nodded pleasantly to Zack and my grandmother, and to my grandfather. "That's the bailiff," my grandfather said. "He keeps order in— There's the old judge now."

A tall, rugged-looking man of about sixty came in through a door at the front of the room. He too smiled at us.

"All rise, please, the Superior Court of Kingdom County is now in session," the bailiff said in a solemn voice. "Judge Forrest Allen presiding, in the case of Kittredge vs. Kittredge."

The judge waved his hand. "Sit down, folks," he said. "Please sit down. We'll dispense with most of the usual formalities this morning. After all, we're all friends."

Beside me, my grandfather made that rasping sound in his throat, and glared in my grandmother's direction.

"Well," Judge Allen said good-humoredly, "most of us are friends."

A suppressed snicker or two broke out from the loafers at the rear of the courtroom. Then it was quiet again. Everyone present was eager to see the forty-year-old running feud between my grandparents come to a head in a public spectacle. I glanced over at my grandmother to see how mortified she looked, but this morning she did not seem discomfited at all. She looked severe and triumphant, as though she had won her case already.

I realized that the judge was smiling at me. "Hello, young man. You must be Abiah and Austen's grandson."

I nodded.

"How's the trout fishing up in the East Branch this year?"

Thinking that this might be some sort of trick question designed to get me to take sides, I looked at my grandfather. "Tell him," he said.

I told the judge that the trout fishing had been good, and he nodded and said he'd have to get up and try it some evening soon, assuming that he'd still be welcome on my grandparents' property after the hearing. Some of the spectators laughed out loud. But neither my grandfather nor my grandmother cracked a smile.

So far, all of the judge's good-natured efforts to break the ice had failed.

"Now, then, folks," Judge Allen said in a more businesslike voice, "the matter before the court today is a civil proceeding. This isn't a criminal case. Nobody's broken any laws or been accused of breaking any laws. Two people have had a misunderstanding and they've come here to iron it out in the fairest way. That's the long and the short of it. The fact that the two litigants in disagreement are married is interesting, but it isn't really relevant to the case."

I glanced back at my young uncle and two little aunts. All three were rolling their eyes. My entire family knew very well that the fact that the litigants were married, and couldn't stand each other, had everything to do with this case.

The judge picked up a sheaf of papers and fanned the air casually with them. He seemed determined to maintain a friendly air. "To put all this in the simplest terms," he said, "the plaintiff in this case, Mrs. Abiah Kittredge of Lost Nation Township, has requested a permanent injunction to prevent the defendant, Mr. Austen Kittredge, from raising the level of his millpond. Mrs. Kittredge has alleged that raising the pond would flood out her apple orchard. Does that fairly represent your client's contention, Mr. Barrows?"

Old Zack shoved himself partway to his feet. "Yes, Your Honor. It does."

The judge nodded. "How many apple trees do you have in your orchard, Abiah?"

"Thirty-six," my grandmother said. "Here's the list."

She walked up to the judge's bench and slapped her written list of apple trees down in front of him.

Judge Allen read through the list, mentioning some of the names aloud. "Tetofsky, Fameuse, Smokehouse . . . I haven't encountered these fine old varieties since I was a young rapscallion robbing Old Man Quimby's orchard up on Anderson Hill on my way home from school in the fall."

The judge looked at me and winked. I winked back. I liked him very much because he seemed to like both of my grandparents. Surely this amicable man could work things out between them if anyone could.

"So, Abiah, raising the level of the pond would destroy your old-fashioned apple trees?"

"It would."

The judge looked at my grandfather. "Is this the case, Austen? You intend to flood out your wife's apple trees, do you?"

"I intend to conduct my sawmill and lumbering operation without interference," my grandfather said. "I'm not a rich man. If I'm to proceed with my business and keep my own head above water, I need to enlarge my pond."

"Why is that?" the judge said with what appeared to be genuine curiosity.

"Because I've got fifty thousand feet of softwood logs jammed in the bend just upriver, and I need to float them free, that's why. It happens every spring. I've tried every other way in the world to get that timber out of there, including dynamite."

"So we hear," the judge said dryly. "But what about your wife's claim? Would the enlarged pond drown out her apple trees?"

"I suspect it would," my grandfather said. "What of it? Why should her apples be any more important than my logs?"

"I didn't say they were," the judge said mildly. "Or, for that matter, that they weren't."

Judge Allen frowned slightly. He tapped the list of old-fashioned apple trees with a long finger. Then he said, "Well, I can plainly see that there's only one way for me to get a complete picture of this situation. That's to drive up to Lost Nation Hollow and see for myself."

He stood up. "This hearing will recess for the time being and reconvene this afternoon at two o'clock sharp at the Kittredge farm. That's it for this morning, folks."

By one-thirty that afternoon, cars and farm trucks lined the Hollow road all the way from our barnyard down to my Big Aunt Rose's place.

"Your grandfather has continued to make a spectacle out of this matter," my grandmother said to me.

Although I couldn't see how my grandfather was to blame for it, my grandmother was right about the spectacle. Half of the village seemed to be in Lost Nation Hollow that afternoon.

Judge Allen arrived in his black Lincoln Continental at one forty-five. He was wearing ordinary clothes and a Red Sox cap, and seemed to be in a holiday mood himself. He sauntered around my grandparents' place, complimenting my grandfather on his handsome red-and-white Ayrshires, spread out on the hillside behind the house and all facing south toward the river as if they too were curious about the feud between my grandparents. Next Judge Allen admired my grandmother's Buff Orpington laying hens. He toured my grandfather's vegetable garden on the north side of the road and my grandmother's vegetable garden directly across from it. He was especially impressed by my grandmother's Harrison yellow rose in the dooryard, and the Seven Sisters rosebush beside the back stoop.

"And I see you have a moss rose, too, Abiah," the judge said graciously. "My Grandmother Allen had a moss rose up at the home place that was said to be over one hundred years old."

"Are you going to permit him to flood my orchard or not?" my grandmother said.

The judge announced that he was headed for the orchard that minute, and asked my grandmother if she'd do him the honor of accompanying him. Naturally, I tagged along. On the way down through the meadow he asked if she sold the apples commercially. She told him most certainly yes, and the cider she made from them. She pointed out that the enlarged millpond would no doubt flood her vegetable garden and raspberry beds as well as her trees.

The judge looked up and down the rows of apple trees my grandmother had planted in the meadow over the past forty years. Many she'd ordered from upstate New York and Wisconsin and even Idaho—wherever cold-climate fruit trees were cultivated. The judge shook his head. "That's a splendid sight, Abiah."

Next Judge Allen and my grandfather and I viewed the logjam stuck in the lower bend of the oxbow. We stood on the blasted-away ledge in the inner bend of the bow, where the huge chunk of limestone tilted out into the river. Downstream a hundred yards, black water ran out around the sides of the jam, gurgling like a subterranean river.

"Can't you twitch some of those logs free with your horses, Austen?" the judge asked.

"No, I can't," my grandfather said. "I wouldn't put my team anywhere near that death trap."

"How much timber did you say was tied up in there?"

"Fifty thousand feet."

"Flooding this meadow is the only way to come at it?"

"We could wait for the fall rains and hope. In the meantime, I could go bankrupt."

The judge nodded thoughtfully, and headed downstream, past the jam and the small pond above the sawmill dam. By now upward of one hundred spectators were gathered around the dam and mill. Greeting people right and left, Judge Allen seemed as much at home here as he'd been in his courtroom that morning. He strolled out onto the walkway of the dam, looked up and down the river, asked me about the best fishing holes. Were the riffles below the spillway good for brook trout? Did any big rainbow or brown trout live year-round in the pond above? He was especially interested in the small island in the middle of the pond. Was it, he wondered, ever under water? How deep was the pond off the island's head and foot?

The crowd along the bank continued to swell. Of course Bumper Stevens was there, and old Plug Johnson and his Folding Chair Club, who had all been at the hearing earlier, and Rob Roy and my two little aunts. Only Sheriff White was conspicuously absent.

Finally the judge cleared his throat and announced loudly enough for the entire crowd to hear, "Austen, I'll give you and Abiah a detailed written ruling in a day or two. But I know that this is a pressing matter to both of you so I don't intend to make you wait any longer for my decision. I've decided to let you raise your millpond."

A murmur ran through the crowd. Obviously, this wasn't what they'd anticipated at all.

"For how long?" my grandfather said suspiciously. "Two days? Three? It may take a month to get that mess all out of there, even with the extra water to help do it. It may take two months. I don't know."

"For as long as you deem necessary," the judge said. "Forever, if you want. That's entirely up to you."

A gasp went up from the crowd now. Knowing Judge Forrest Allen, they'd been expecting some sort of Solomon-like ruling, Kingdom County style: some brilliantly original compromise—permission for my grandfather to raise the pond level temporarily, say, long enough to float free at least some of the logs, without permanently harming my grandmother's apple trees.

There had to be a catch. But where? The judge's expression and voice were as amiable as always, his manner all the more magisterial in its casualness.

"All right," my grandfather said. "How high then? How high can I raise the water?"

The judge shrugged. "As high as you please. Five feet, ten feet. Twenty feet if you want to."

Now the crowd sucked in their breath in a sharp high whistle. Raising the level of the pond so much as two feet would flood out my grandmother's orchard, not to mention her garden and raspberries. People were beginning to exclaim out loud to each other when the judge lifted his hand.

He waited for the crowd to fall silent. Then he pointed up at the island above the dam and said, "Raise your pond as high as the Tower of Babel if you've a mind to, Austen—on one side, and one side only, of that island. Which side is up to you."

For about five seconds, the only noise was the low hush of the pond water dropping through the open gate in the dam. Then a sigh ran through the crowd, a collective suspiration of deep satisfaction, like the sigh of a circus crowd when the flying trapeze artist makes a death-defying catch. Judge Allen hadn't disappointed anyone after all. As even I could now see, raising the level of the pond on one side of the island, and not the other, was an absolutely impossible feat.

Someone laughed. Then two or three others. Seconds later all the men were laughing and hooting and shaking hands with the judge and with each other, until my grandfather barked out in his sharp voice, "Hold on here, now. You fellas look as though you could use a job to keep you out of trouble. I'll supply every manjack of you that shows up here with a pick and shovel tomorrow fore-noon at six o'clock all the white mule whiskey you can drink. Until then go on back to whatever job you don't have in the village. I want these premises cleared in five minutes."

Now the murmuring of the crowd grew even louder. But my grandfather ripped out in a voice that meant business, "Get moving, boys. Shove!"

As the people dispersed, he jerked his head for me to follow him into the sawmill. He went straight to his office, unlocked a tall wall locker, and got out the cases containing his surveying tools: the same collapsible transit and measuring chains and metal pins that he had used years ago in Labrador and along the Canadian-American Line out West. He handed me a bundle of pins and a sixty-foot surveying chain, and went back outside with the transit, through the thinning crowd headed for their vehicles. I was half-running to keep up with him, though as yet I had no idea what under the sun he intended to do.

It was evening on the river. From where my grandfather and I stood, placidly fishing off the mill dam, we could see the line of survey stakes we'd set late that afternoon, marching across the closed-off neck of land at the mouth of the oxbow: the place where, for years, my grandfather had counted on the river cutting a new, straight channel some spring.

The fishing was slow. We figured that the commotion along the bank earlier in the day had put the trout down. After a while, when the bugs started to get thick, my grandfather went up to Labrador for the night and I went inside the house to read.

As the mountain dusk settled over the Farm at the end of Lost Nation Hollow, and my grandmother went about her after-supper tasks in the kitchen, she seemed more solemn and thoughtful than triumphant. Although I have no doubt at all that she equated nor-mal human weariness with sloth—never once do I recall that she ever admitted to being tired—her dark face and eyes showed the strain of the strenuous day now coming to a close. Soon after sweep-ing and mopping the floor, she went into Egypt and sat quietly at her sewing table, looking at the black-and-white pictures of the pyramids and the Great Sphinx in her old magazines.

After a while I joined her there.

"Gram," I said, "would you like to go to Egypt sometime?"

"This is Egypt," she said. "Here."

She made a small gesture with her hands, turning the palms up in her lap to encompass the room with its artifacts.

"I mean the real Egypt. You know. See the Nile, visit the pyramids?"

I thought of the trip my grandfather and I had planned to Labrador, in the Far North, and that gave me an idea. "Maybe we could go together," I said.

My grandmother did not answer immediately. She sat quietly, abstracted by her own thoughts, her hands folded on her lap. Her jet-black hair shone in the lantern light. On the table next to the lantern, the Egyptian god with a hawk's head stared at me more severely than usual, as if he suspected that I was allied with my grandfather. My grandmother reached out and touched the hawk-god, Lord Ra, as you might touch a sleeping cat or dog, and for just a moment, her features looked entirely otherworldly to me.

"Provisions have been made," she said in a somber voice, more to the hawk than to me, "for going to Egypt."

She paused, then said, "For afterward."

A chill came over me, I did not quite know why. "For afterward?"

She nodded. "There will be a journey, Austen. There will be a destination. It's all been carefully arranged."

Without warning my grandmother reached out and seized my wrist. "When the time comes, I don't want my wishes thwarted. However outlandish they may seem to the family. Do you understand that?"

"Yes," I said, though I did not, entirely. Yet it was clear that my grandmother was charging me with something of enormous importance, compared to which my grandfather's plans for the following day were insignificant to her.

Throughout the house the twenty clocks began to strike. I was so used to them that I barely heard the cacophony of chimes, bells, bongs, and cuckoos. But my grandmother listened attentively as always, though this time with a new intensity in her expression, as though the clocks now marked her own inexorable progress toward the beginning of that chilling journey that I was somehow to safeguard when the dreadful time came.

"Bedtime, Austen," she said when the last faint peal from the most remote second-story chamber faded into the silence of the big, dark, empty farmhouse.

I woke up the next morning, Saturday, not to clocks chiming but to an irregular clinking sound coming through my open bedroom window. It was just getting light. I jumped into my pants and did not stop to button my shirt before running downstairs, past my grandmother at the stove, out the kitchen door and across the barnyard.

The cows were already out in the pasture so I knew that Gramp must have come down from Labrador to milk them in the dark before dawn. I raced down through the orchard to the river above the millpond. There I found my grandfather, a lone, stark figure against the pale eastern sky, raising his pickax and lowering it, striking a stone every three or four blows—at the lower end of the row of survey pins we'd set the afternoon before.

There was no longer the slightest doubt in my mind that he intended to cut a new channel for the river, and eliminate the troublesome oxbow forever.

"What's the old devil up to now?" Bumper Stevens said. He was selling cold drinks and hot dogs out of a food stand converted from a horse trailer, which he hauled around to horse pulls, fairs, and farm auctions.

"Goddamn old fool," said Plug Johnson, who was safely out of my grandfather's earshot. "I reckon he's digging Ab's grave."

"More likely he's digging his own," Bumper said. "Whether he knows it or not."

It was nine o'clock, and by now my grandfather had about thirty men helping him cut the channel. My grandmother, in the meantime, was watching through her opera glasses from the kitchen window, with a grim and resigned expression, as though she had made up her mind to let my grandfather make a fool out of himself if he was determined to. Uncle Rob had driven out from the village with my two little aunts, and when I went up to the house for a snack they were all standing around my grandmother at the window, drinking coffee.

"Your grandfather has made a Roman circus out of these proceedings," my grandmother said to me.

"Oh, Mom, don't be so melodramatic," Little Aunt Klee said. "Why not just a plain circus? Why does it have to be a Roman circus?"

"I wonder if Artie and Pooch Pike will be up?" Little Aunt Freddi said.

Uncle Rob snorted. "Not if they know there are picks and shovels involved, they won't be. Picks and shovels haven't ever been the strong suit of the Marvelous Wonderful Pike Brothers."

"If that isn't a case of the pot and the kettle," Freddi said as I went back out the door.

At the upper edge of the pond, Cousin Whiskeyjack Kittredge had set a gigantic hogshead of his white mule moonshine up on sawhorses, and was doling out free drinks in empty Coke bottles. Meanwhile my grandfather had the men divided into two crews. One was working their way up from the bottom of the row of survey pins toward the middle; the other had begun digging at the midway point of the neck of land and was working toward the top. The ground was sandy at first. Then they hit hard blue clay that had to be broken up with pickaxes. Furthermore, the two crews seemed to be engaged in a race. I overheard someone remark that in addition to the free moonshine dispensed by Cousin Whiskeyjack, each member of the winning crew would receive a quart of white mule to take home. I noticed, however, that my grandfather drank nothing at all, though I knew that he occasionally liked a small glass of brandy in the evening at Labrador.

By early afternoon the canalers were roaring and laughing and falling all over each other. Bumper Stevens and Plug Johnson were going back and forth from one crew to the other, asking to be notified when the diggers hit China, and inquiring just where they expected to hook up with the Erie Canal. My little aunts were as delighted as I was by all the excitement, and Rob said the scene begged for the brush of a Brueghel or the pen of Boccaccio, and hailed my grandfather as another Disraeli.

Only my grandmother seemed unmoved by the extraordinary events of the day. Except for watching the spectacle impassively through her opera glasses for a minute or two every now and then, she simply went about her household routines as usual until, about two o'clock, she suddenly decided to post me on the edge of a row of recently-grafted young apple trees with the strictest instructions to notify her if any of my grandfather's intoxicants came within fifty feet of her sacred plantation; and I really believed, now that Gram knew how to shoot Gramp's shotgun, that she would not hesitate to use it to defend her orchard if necessary.

As the day wore on it became apparent that the new channel would be completed by nightfall. It was only four feet across, and about three feet deep. But my grandfather assured me that the rerouted river rushing through would immediately enlarge its own bed. He looked off toward the west, where for the past half hour or so a bank of purple thunderheads had been building above Jay Peak. "Let's hope that storm misses us, Austen. I don't know if these stumblebums are quite drunk enough yet to work right through it."

Soon the entire sky had darkened. On the slope behind the house our Ayrshires were huddled around a big elm tree. I didn't wait to be told to run up and drive them into the barn. Every summer in Kingdom County farmers had cows killed by lightning. I could smell the rain coming as I trotted down the hill behind the Ayrshires, and they flared their nostrils and tossed their horns like western cattle about to stampede as they came into the barnyard. My grandmother was out shooing her laying hens into their house. As the cows ran past her she looked up with that same worn expression I'd noticed the night before. By the time I got the cows in their stanchions and joined my grandmother and little aunts on the porch, the first big spattering raindrops were hitting the barnyard.

A sudden gust of wind swooped in from the west, bearing the

powerful fresh aroma of a summer thunderstorm. On the edge of the woods across the river the poplar leaves turned up their white undersides in the onrushing wind. A few onlookers ran for their vehicles, but my grandfather's diggers toiled on, oblivious to the impending deluge. A vivid yellow jag of lightning flashed directly overhead. It was followed instantly by an ear-splitting explosion. Then the mountain storm struck Upper Lost Nation Hollow with a furious intensity. Sheets of lightning raced down the sky from zenith to horizon. Off to the west jagged tongues of fire leaped from peak to peak, illuminating the northern Green Mountain range all the way from Mount Mansfield deep into Canada.

Still the men dug feverishly on, as though their lives depended on it. Not even my Cousin Whiskeyjack's white mule could possibly have accounted for their frenzy. Rob said it was sheer curiosity to see what would happen when they connected the two ditches and broke through to the river at the top end. Despite the blinding rain, now pouring out of the sky with tropical prodigality, I could see my grandfather each time the lightning flashed, his pick rising and falling steadily, at the head of the upper crew. They were less than twenty feet from the top bend in the oxbow.

As usual during a hard storm, the rain came through the farmhouse roof in a dozen different places, and my little aunts and I had to run from room to room, under my grandmother's direction, with various domestic vessels to catch the leaks: roasting pans, chamber pots, ancient porcelain washbasins, soup tureens and gravy boats from Gram's best china.

By five o'clock the rain had stopped. The sky was a deep, washed turquoise as I ran down through the sopping orchard grass to see how much progress the diggers had made. The two ditches had been linked in the middle, and there was just a single barrier of earth, six or eight feet in width, separating the top of the uppermost section from the river.

I was standing a few feet back from the new channel, in the wedge of meadow looped by the oxbow, when I heard a new sound. To the degree that this noise resembled any other natural noise at all, it sounded something like the big hard wind that had immediately preceded the thunderstorm being sucked whooshing back to the mountains it had come from.

At the same time, I was astonished to see the towering logjam start to rearrange itself. The water around the logs seemed to be running out of the bend into the millpond, and no more water was flowing into the oxbow. Yet the current had not yet broken through that last earthen barrier between the river and the new channel, where my grandfather and his inebriated crew were still toiling like madmen. I could not imagine where the river had gone.

Then the backward-whooshing sound was replaced by a grumbling gurgle. The throng of men in the ditch had ceased working and were looking up with an inquisitive, listening expression on their faces. Days later, after all the excitement had quieted down and my grandfather could look back dispassionately on what happened next, he said that never before in his life had he seen a gang of men go from falling-down drunk to stone-cold sober in so short a time. One moment they were listening, with that odd, faraway expression on their flushed faces, and the hard blue clay under their boots barely moist. The next thing they knew they were ankle-deep, calf-deep, knee-deep in a churning quagmire.

"Jump, boys!" my grandfather shouted. "Jump for dry land and the devil take the shovels. Quick, for your lives. The water's coming up below us."

He leaped out of the ditch like a man of twenty, and snatched two or three of the slower men to safety. The others came clambering out of the rushing, waist-deep water in a mad general scramble. The earth barrier was still intact, but my grandfather was right; somehow the river was cutting under it and coming up from beneath the ditch.

The grumbling sound intensified and the remaining few feet of earth between the channel and the river collapsed inward upon itself. My grandfather yanked me backward just as the grassy bank I'd been standing on gave way into the new riverbed. In seconds the narrow ditch had become a thirty-foot-wide river, whose banks continued to shear off into the brown water in chunks that must have weighed a ton apiece. Downstream, the small pond above the mill had become part of the raging river.

"Good Christ, Austen!" my grandfather shouted. "There goes my waterwheel."

It was true. The force of the pent-up water unleashed down the new channel and on through the little pond had torn the paddle wheel that ran my grandfather's saws loose from its moorings. I could see the thing bobbing downriver on the furious brown flood. Part of the dam was missing as well. The section where Judge Allen had stood the day before, along with a large section of the sawmill foundation, had vanished. The unsupported corner of the building now hung out into midair over the boiling penstock.

As the gigantic waterwheel approached the first bend below the mill, bobbing slowly just above the surface, I happened to glance up toward the farmhouse. My grandmother stood on the porch, her opera glasses trained downriver on the fleeing wheel, her black-clad figure diminutive and apocalyptic in the unearthly lavender light that had settled over Lost Nation in the wake of the thunderstorm. But my grandfather just nodded and made that low sardonic sound in his throat that was as close as I ever heard him come to laughing.

"It can float clear to Labrador for all I care," he said.

That is when Uncle Rob Roy called to us. He was standing beside the bend in the oxbow, fifty or sixty feet away, and waving excitedly. At first I thought he just wanted us to see that the water had all emptied out of the marooned oxbow, and the logjam was hung high and dry. Then another man ran up beside him and shouted something about a fish. For all I knew they had discovered a record trout stranded in the old riverbed. Whatever it was, I wanted to see it before it got away.

By the time my grandfather and I arrived at the bend, half a dozen men were gathered around Uncle Rob, near the mammoth chunk of limestone Gramp had blasted loose from the ledge earlier that spring. Imbedded in the rock wall of the curve exposed by the draining water, where the chunk of ledge had toppled into the river, were the whitish bones of a gigantic fish, eighteen or twenty feet long. At first I could hardly believe my own eyes. This must be some optical trick, I thought, some illusion. A petrified tree trunk, maybe, shaped something like a fish. But as I stood gazing at this wondrous sight, I realized that it was no illusion. This was indeed the skeleton of a fish, huge beyond any fish I'd ever seen. What's more, it was in perfect condition. It looked as though it had been swimming upstream when somehow it had been instantly frozen in time.

"Look at the Christly shark!" Bumper Stevens yelled.

"It's not a shark, it's a *whale*," Uncle Rob shouted. "It's a fossil-ized whale, thousands of years old. From when this was all an inland sea. Good God, boys, look at the thing. There isn't a bone missing."

Uncle Rob was right. As I examined this marvel more closely, I noted that every bone stood out distinctly, etched in the exposed wall of the bend. I was speechless, and could only stare at the great creature. It was longer than my grandfather's farm truck, longer than the farmhouse porch, and perfect in every detail. Even the delicate white bones of its fin-like flukes were clearly etched into the limestone wall, and its long, streamlined skull, though it bore little resemblance to a human skull, looked remarkably intelligent, giving it an aspect both familiar and alien.

"It's a whale, Dad!" Uncle Rob shouted to my grandfather.

My grandfather frowned. "I can see that," he said. "What do you want me to do? Harpoon it?"

My grandfather looked at me. "I told you these customers used to venture up into this neck of the woods, Austen."

By this time twenty-five or thirty men were crowded around the drained oxbow, gaping at the exposed remains of the whale. I had a nearly overpowering desire to run for my grandmother, to show her this wonder as if I'd discovered it myself. But even in the first flush of my terrific excitement, I sensed that like my grandfather, Abiah Kittredge was not one to be impressed by the old bones of a whale, especially during a major public standoff with her husband.

"By the water-walking Jesus, now, Austen," Bumper Stevens said to my grandfather, "you can charge city fellas a dollar a throw to come here and have a gander at this gentleman. He's a better draw than your old paddle wheel any day of the week. You're going to make big money up here, mister man."

"I imagine it would put up quite a little tussle on a number twelve dry fly," my grandfather said. "How'd you like to hook into one of these Green Mountain whales some evening, Austen?"

I allowed as how I would. Yet as more and more people crowded around the oxbow to look at the Green Mountain whale, an unac-countable sadness came over me. In the aftermath of all the excite-ment—the river rerouting itself, the waterwheel floating away, the discovery of the whale—I felt strangely let down. Suddenly the whale looked lonely and vulnerable to me. It looked tragically out of place, trapped in the rocky bank of our little northern river, hundreds of miles from the sea. And I believe that something about it bothered my grandfather too, because so far from trying to make a profit from the whale, he donated it a few days later to the local historical society. They hired a geology professor from the state university to come up to the Farm with a group of students and remove it intact to their small museum on the second floor of the village library; and there it remained, encased in a custom-built twenty-foot glass cabinet. The last reference my grandfather made to it was the day it was taken into the village; he remarked to me that he'd seen far bigger whales in the Gulf of St. Lawrence on his way to Labrador, and I would too, when I turned eighteen and he took me there.

My grandmother displayed what to me was an equally unfathomable indifference toward both the whale and its ultimate removal. As far as she seemed to be concerned, it could stay or go. I don't even recall that she ever troubled herself to walk down through the orchard to view it. Her precious fruit trees had been preserved from harm, my grandfather had sustained a sort of preliminary Waterloo when his paddle wheel washed away, and she was satisfied. Once more, she had emerged victorious in a major battle in their famous Forty Years' War.

A few weeks later, the new power line from the village reached our farm. This was an exciting event since my grandfather would now be able to run his saws with electricity, though for some years afterward my grandmother continued not to allow electricity in the farmhouse. I personally missed the big waterwheel; but there is no doubt that the advent of electrical power in the other houses and barns up and down the Hollow made life easier in a hundred ways, at the same time that it marked a milestone in the closing of the lingering frontier era of Lost Nation.

"You can't predict the future, Tut," my grandmother told me many times, "but times change. That much we can count on."

At the time, of course, I had no idea of the changes that lay ahead, for Lost Nation or myself. On the day we discovered the

whale, after the crowd had all left, and my grandfather had finished
his barn chores and gone back up to Labrador, my grandmother read
me the story of the great flood from Genesis, then repaired to Egypt
to commune with her beloved relics. I sat out in the kitchen, reading until I was sleepy. But once again, I did not fall asleep immediately that night.

Outside the slanted window of my bedroom I could hear the
river running hard from the afternoon cloudburst, rushing through
its new channel, bypassing the oxbow and the fossilized whale. I
thought of the great waterwheel, by this time undoubtedly broken
into a hundred pieces and riding north on the swollen river for Lake
Memphremagog and the St. Lawrence. Semi-awake and drifting like
the fragments of that wheel, drifting into and out of sleep to the
sound of the river, I saw myself fishing a vast Labrador river with my
grandfather, as he had promised we would when I turned eighteen.

Yet the reality that I would ever be eighteen, like the reality that
my grandparents would ever grow older and die, or that I would not
live on the Farm with them forever, was impossible for me to grasp.
I fell asleep dreaming of seals and silvery salmon, and a lone Green
Mountain whale, swimming through the sunny June sky over Lost
Nation Hollow, with the river and fields and my grandparents'
house and barn lying unchanged and unchangeable beneath its
swiftly passing shadow.

5

DOWN THE COAT

The Lost Nation Atheneum, founded in 1780 by my great-great-great-great-great-grandfather, the fleeing Tory, was located three miles south of my grandparents' place and about the same distance north of the county road leading into the village. An unpainted building with cedar shingles on the sides and roof, it sat at the crest of a steep hill, with a hairpin bend halfway to the bottom, known locally as the Fiddler's Elbow. Here, surrounded by wooded hills, played-out farms, and miles of trackless mountains, I received the first eight years of my formal education.

The school proper consisted of one large room, with twenty desks. When there were more students than desks, we shared them, two kids to one desk. In the middle of the room stood a tall Round Oak stove whose most distinctive feature was a foot-long crack in its side. Ages ago someone had chunked a frozen log up against the red-hot metal, causing it to split apart like a butternut husk in a sharp fall frost, so that depending on which side of the main aisle we sat on, we could look in at the roaring flames.

Like most other country schools in those days, the Atheneum had two doors, one for boys and one for girls. Two privies squatted just inside the woods on opposite sides of the road one hundred yards or so down the hill, not far above the elbow of that imaginary fiddler. A good, steady spring ran out of a dark granite outcropping in a beech stand just behind the building, which was probably the reason my ancestor had chosen this location. In the schoolyard grew a horse chestnut tree whose leaves turned a deep umber-orange in late September. Mixed hardwoods and softwoods crowded right down to the woodshed at the back of the school.

The best feature of the schoolhouse was its southeast wall, which consisted mainly of three large windows made up of sixteen small panes apiece. Through these poured an enormous flood of light, even in the winter—which was a very good thing because, as I have already mentioned, electricity did not come to Lost Nation Hollow until 1952, when I turned ten, and the school was not electrified until 1955.

Centered over the double doors of the Lost Nation Atheneum was a plaque from Montpelier, the state capital, that said: "Superior School, 1937." My grandfather said 1937 was probably the last time anyone from Away had ventured up into Lost Nation to inspect the Atheneum, though Kingdom County's Superintendent of Schools, Prof Newt Chadburn, dropped by once a month or so—to make sure the roof was still on the building, my grandfather said.

During the course of any given school year, the Atheneum's enrollment varied dramatically. Sometimes I attended school with as many as thirty other pupils. At other times, such as during potato harvesting and maple sugaring, the number of kids in attendance dropped to as few as half a dozen. Of course chores at home were never an excuse for me to stay out of school. Neither was the most severe weather. No day, however bad, was ever deemed too inclement for a Kittredge to attend school. Nor were minor childhood ailments regarded as a valid excuse to stay home. "None of my children has ever been sick a day in their lives," my grandmother periodically announced in a way that made me strongly suspect that it would not fare well with a grandson who broke that rugged tradition. In fact, I missed only one day of school during my eight years at the Atheneum, and that was to attend the court hearing in Kingdom Common over the matter of my grandfather's dam and my grandmother's apple orchard.

How much I learned at the Atheneum is another matter. By the end of my sixth-grade year I'd raced through the entire curriculum, including Vermont history and elementary algebra. For the next two years I was pretty much allowed to read at random in a set of the Harvard Classics donated to the school by my Big Aunt Maiden Rose, who had taught there for fifty years, and to roam around in the eleventh edition of the Encyclopaedia Britannica, also presented to the school some years ago by my great-aunt. Prof Chadburn was kind enough to lend me books from his own extensive library, and my father, my Uncle Rob Roy, and my little aunts were forever presenting me with favorite books of their own. Certainly there are worse ways to spend one's seventh- and eighth-grade years than by reading Dickens and Twain and accounts in the celebrated Britannica of the far-flung and exotic places I hoped someday to visit.

But I do not want to make my years at the Lost Nation Atheneum sound idyllic. They were far from it. Even during the late 1940s and on into the 1950s, most of the outlying country schools in Kingdom County still had reputations as very rough places, where the code of behavior among the pupils was quite literally a tooth for a tooth. Our school was no exception. With the prickly outer shells that fell off the horse chestnut tree in late September, we played a primitive and brutal kind of dodge ball. In the winter we fired ice balls at each other, hard and from a close range. We slid down the Fiddler's Elbow on sheets of cardboard and, when it was crusty, on our own bottoms, sailing off the hairpin bend into a great tangle of barberry bushes with the tiny bright red berries still clinging to their thorny branches. There were quarrels and fist fights and several feuds lasting for years; and all of these activities were presided over by three entrenched bullies: Hermie Hill, Pit Santaw, and Big Bob Thompkins, who lorded over us kids in the schoolyard the way, years later, he was reported to lord over his fellow prisoners in the exercise yard of Windsor State Penitentiary.

True, some of the older students occasionally helped the younger ones with their lessons. Yet at Lost Nation there was much less of this admirable cooperative learning than I have since heard cited as one of the great merits of the one-room school—another being a close-knit family atmosphere. Maybe under the tutelage of my Big Aunt Rose such an atmosphere had existed. But if Hermie, Pit, Big Bob, and the rest of the outfit I went to school with resembled a family in any way at all, they did so only insofar as they fought tooth and nail with each other at every available opportunity.

The Atheneum could be rough on teachers as well. After my Aunt Rose retired in 1945, the school went through a long string of them, and none lasted for more than a year. I personally recall several unsuspecting young women fresh out of school themselves, and barely out of their teens, whose faces have long since blended together in my memory into a generic expression of terror. It was as if Kingdom County's long-standing reputation as a last New England frontier and a bastion for outlawry had devolved to a few bad schoolboys, who were determined to establish their notoriety by driving Lost Nation teachers "down the road"—as we said—before they had a chance to teach us anything.

Two or three young men brought in by Prof Chadburn and the local school directors fared no better. In the late winter of my sixth-grade year, the year I was eleven, a man imported from New York State was beaten so badly by Hermie Hill and his cronies that he not only lost several teeth but the sight in his left eye as well. His successor, another of those hapless young women, was nailed up inside the girls' privy late one April afternoon. No one discovered her until we came to school the following morning.

After Miss Fennel spent the night in the privy, the Lost Nation school directors and Prof Chadburn advertised all over the state for a teacher who could keep order. In the meantime Prof himself taught us, an arrangement very much to our liking. Prof was a vigorous man in his early sixties, and a born teacher. Every afternoon after we'd finished our recitations for the day he read to us from his own favorite authors: Charles Dudley Warner, George Peck, Booth Tarkington, Francis Parkman. He had us memorize poetry, which we actually enjoyed. At recess time Prof rolled up his sleeves and played ball with us in the schoolyard. He was a well-set-up man who had "been in the war"—which war was never clear to me at the time, though I now assume it must have been the World War I. No one sassed Prof Chadburn, not even Hermie. Prof "knew ju-jitsu," and could pin the biggest boy on his back in five seconds flat.

Prof introduced friendly competition to the classroom. He conducted elaborate spelling and geography bees, with presents for the winners in every grade: boxes of Good 'n Plenties from the five-and-dime in the Common; a slightly scuffed baseball; brand-new quarters and fifty-cent pieces. Sometimes, in order to make time to visit the other eighteen schools in his district, he would let us out for the day at noon. Suddenly school had become fun. We hoped the directors would come up empty-handed in their search for a new teacher so that we could have Prof for the few remaining weeks of the school year.

One warm afternoon in early May, when the maple trees were just putting out and the hills above Lost Nation Hollow were light gold with tiny new leaves, a battered old Ford rattletrap coughed and sputtered its way up the Fiddler's Elbow. It pulled into the schoolyard and came to a stop with a shudder beside Prof's Buick Roadmaster. Mr. Francis Dubois, Theresa Dubois's father and the chairman of the school board, got out. With him was a big, beefy, red-faced woman of about forty—the driver of the rattletrap.

Prof, who liked to tailor his lessons to the cycle of the seasons, happened to be helping us memorize Robert Frost's short poem "Nothing Gold Can Stay." He had just gotten us through the first two lines—"Nature's first green is gold, / Her hardest hue to hold"—when Mr. Francis Dubois and the husky woman came through the door. She was wearing a bright green dress decorated with large purple flowers. She walked with a slight limp and carried a thick, green-handled cattle cane. In her other hand she held a very large, black metal lunch box.

"This is Mrs. Earla Armstrong," Mr. Dubois said to us. "She's your new teacher."

He added, "We hired Mrs. Armstrong just this morning, Prof. I didn't want to let her get away from us so I rode right up with her."

Mrs. Armstrong slammed her huge lunch box down on the

teacher's desk. "I'll take the reins from here," she said in a deep, angry voice. "You two boys can skedaddle."

Prof looked somewhat discomposed. But he shut up his Robert Frost book, and after a few hasty words of farewell to us, and a brief welcome to Mrs. Armstrong, he drove Mr. Dubois back off down the Hollow in his Buick. Mrs. Armstrong watched them out the window, her hands on her hips, a look of disgust on her face.

"What was that fella reading when I walked in?" she demanded after Prof and Mr. Dubois disappeared around the bend halfway down the hill.

"He was reading us a poem," somebody said.

She nodded grimly. "I suspected as much. Well, that will be the last poetry recitation in this school for as long as I'm teacher here."

And it is a fact that not only was that the last poetry read aloud in the Atheneum for the next two years, it was the last time anyone read us anything.

Mrs. Armstrong wrote her name on the chalkboard in large, intimidating capital letters. She turned back to face us. "My name is Armstrong," she said. "And you'll find that I have a strong arm."

She surveyed the class with marked disfavor. Very deliberately, she began to roll up the sleeve of her purple-flowered dress, revealing to us an arm that resembled nothing so much as that Herculean limb depicted on the outside of the red-and-yellow baking soda box in my grandmother's kitchen cupboard.

"So," Mrs. Armstrong said. "Reports have it that you young rapscallions up here in the Nation put out your teachers' eyes. Who proposes to put out my eye this morning?"

She pointed her cow cane straight at beautiful, blond, sweet-tempered Theresa Dubois. "You, girl. What's your name?"

Theresa told her in a small, terrified voice.

"Speak up! I won't have mumbling in my classroom."

"Theresa Dubois, ma'am."

"Well, Theresa Dubois. Do you propose to put out my eye?"

"No, ma'am."

"Good. Because if you do, you'll *feel the arm*. You," she said, swinging around faster than you would suppose a woman of such bulk could move. The green-handled cane was pointed straight at

Johnny Pray, an undergrown little first-grader. "Do *you* propose to put out my eye?"

Johnny promptly burst into tears. Within seconds he was joined by most of the rest of the first- and second-graders.

"Hush!" Mrs. Armstrong commanded. "There'll be no bawling in my schoolroom—or you'll feel the arm."

The crying subsided into a few stifled sobs.

"Now then," Mrs. Armstrong said. "Report has it that you hoodlums lock up your teachers in privies. You, Kittredge . . . Where's Kittredge?"

I was almost too astonished to raise my hand. How had she learned my name?

She peered at me out of her reddish eyes. "You're the famous reader I've been told about," she said with a sneer. "Don't look so surprised, boy. Word travels. Reports travel. Do *you* intend to lock me up in the privy?"

"No, ma'am."

"No, ma'am is right," she said. "Or you'll feel the arm. There'll be no favorites and no famous readers in this classroom from this minute on. My own children wouldn't be allowed to put on such airs and you won't, either. Not in my classroom."

She glared around the room until her gaze came to rest on Hermie Hill. Hermie was guffawing behind his hand over my comeuppance.

To this day I do not know whether Mr. Francis Dubois had warned Mrs. Armstrong about Hermie. Allegedly, he was the boy who had put out the man teacher's eye, and the ringleader of the kids who locked Miss Fennel in the privy. Obviously Mr. Dubois had boasted to Mrs. Armstrong about my being a famous reader. He may very well also have cautioned Mrs. Armstrong about Hermie. But there is no doubt in my mind that our new teacher must have planned something drastic from the moment she laid eyes on the bully.

Without a word she descended from the teacher's platform and limped down the aisle to Hermie's desk.

"Stand up," she said.

Hermie got to his feet, still snickering. Although Hermie Hill was as tall as most men, Earla Armstrong stood eye to eye with him and outweighed him by more than fifty pounds. Total silence had fallen over the classroom.

Mrs. Armstrong slowly lifted her cane to about shoulder level. "Do you propose to lock me in the privy?" she said.

"No, ma'am," Hermie said boldly.

"Then why are you laughing?"

"Because," Hermie sang out loudly for the benefit of the entire class, "I misdoubt you'd fit inside it."

Instantly Earla Armstrong struck Hermie Hill. But not with the lifted cane. The cane was a ruse to distract his attention. She struck him with her other fist, full in the face, as hard as I had ever seen anyone hit, and this in a place and at a time when fist fights were common occurrences.

Hermie went over backward. Mrs. Armstrong was on him like a cat on a mouse. She grabbed him by the shirt collar and one leg and lugged him to the boys' door and heaved him bodily out into the schoolyard. "Don't you ever come back here!" she shouted.

And that was the last Lost Nation Atheneum saw of Hermie Hill, and the way Mrs. Earla Armstrong established order in our school.

Who was this woman I was destined to go to school to for the next two years? By degrees, her story filtered down to us. In plainest terms, she was a hardworking widow from the neighboring township of Pond in the Sky, who had taught several terms of school years ago, before she was married. Her husband, Nort Armstrong, had died last year, leaving Earla with an impoverished hill farm and six kids. My Uncle Rob Roy mentioned at a Sunday dinner at the Farm that it was rumored that old Nort had succumbed to husband-beatings, but my grandfather said that more probably Nort just faded out of the picture.

It was evident to all of us from the day Mrs. Armstrong arrived with Mr. Francis Dubois, sailing into the classroom in that bright green dress overrun with big poisonous-looking purple flowers, that the school directors had not hired her for her pedagogical qualifications. It was not just that she had never graduated from high school. Many capable country teachers in those days had never attended high school a day in their lives. Earla Armstrong, however, was profoundly and militantly ignorant. More than once she boasted—with me in mind, I am sure—that she had never read a book through for pleasure in her entire life.

Mrs. Armstrong's teaching techniques were rudimentary. She claimed to believe in the basics. What this meant is that we worked in our books for hours on end while she sat enthroned at her desk, sipping from her gigantic black thermos, which, we quickly surmised, contained something much stronger than coffee. At unpredictable intervals she descended to prowl the aisle with her cattle cane, with which she did not hesitate to thwack us, hard and repeatedly, for real or imagined offenses.

When her cane wasn't handy, Mrs. Armstrong administered a series of esoteric lesser punishments of obscure nationalistic origin, which she claimed to have learned from watching "the Saturday night wrastling" on television during a stint as a waitress at the notorious Hapwell House in Pond in the Sky. (A bouncer was more like it, Uncle Rob said.) There was the Indian wrist burn, a corrective measure that necessitated her grasping our wrists in both her hands and rubbing them raw and red with a corrosive pipe-wrench motion. A somewhat similar operation known as the Dutch rub involved scouring her clenched fist over the sensitive spot at the crown of our heads for two or three minutes while holding us fast in a headlock and suffusing our olfactory senses with the redolence of sweat, chalkdust, and, if it was past ten o'clock, the sweetish fumes of the gin with which she laced her coffee.

"Now we will take up world geography," Mrs. Armstrong would rip out on days when she'd had frequent recourse to the black thermos; and we would fall victim to the Chinese armlock, the Hindu neck stretch, and the Borneo thumb splint.

The most painful of these torments was the Hungarian dead finger. I have no idea where Mrs. Armstrong picked this up, but she resorted to the dead finger frequently, and with great effectiveness, particularly on the younger pupils.

"Hungarian dead finger!" she would announce, and start to

shake her left wrist and fingers like a southpaw pitcher performing some sort of outlandish warm-up exercise. When her fingers were flapping loose and fast, she gripped the first two digits under her thumb, and tucked in her pinky, leaving her ring finger vibrating at a furious rate. Then she would raise her arm, turn her wrist over and outward, and deliver a vicious crack on the head to the nearest malefactor. The blow was all the more anguishing because of the hard, shiny wedding band she wore on her vibrating dead finger.

All I can say on Mrs. Armstrong's behalf is that, her additional farm chores at home considered, she was indeed a hard worker; and that although she picked on some of us more than others, she had no favorites. Sooner or later during the course of any given week, we all came in for a dose of her sadistic brand of discipline.

"She keeps good order," my grandfather said when I complained to him. "You have to give her that."

His assessment more or less summarized the entire township's attitude toward Earla Armstrong. She'd been hired to keep order and keep order she did. Hers was a roughshod, Draconian brand of government; it was tyrannical and arbitrary and often cruel. But she kept order and in the Lost Nation of my youth, that, like being a hard worker, excused a great many other shortcomings, including a teacher's total unfitness to teach anything but fear and hatred. As I look back now on our two years under her tutelage, I believe that we pupils were a sort of Lost Nation ourselves. We were lost in a wilderness of ignorance, with no Moses to lead us out. Only Earla Armstrong.

One hot afternoon in the early fall of my eighth-grade year, when both of the doors of the school stood wide open, I happened to look around and see a strange boy standing in the girls' entranceway. I put up my hand, and finally got Mrs. Armstrong's attention. "Somebody's at the door," I said.

"Somebody's at the door!" barked Mrs. Armstrong, who had a habit of repeating any announcement that surprised her, however slightly. "What do you mean, somebody's at the door?"

"Somebody's at the door," I said.

The entire class's attention was now on the strange boy. He was tall and rail-thin, with a lanky shock of coal-black hair over his forehead. Although it was exceptionally hot for September in Kingdom County, he wore a man's suitcoat with an old-fashioned herringbone pattern. Under the coat he had on a faded blue flannel shirt and a baggy pair of suit pants with dark stripes that looked as though they'd once belonged to an undertaker. On his feet was a pair of shapeless brogans, laced with baling twine, and his pants were held up not with a belt but with a longer hank of twine. He looked to be two or three years older than me, around fifteen or sixteen. He had already started a wispy black mustache.

This was our first close look at Louis-Hippolyte LaFlamme: standing in the girls' entrance of the Lost Nation Atheneum, like a hobo on the Boston and Montreal Railroad tracks in Kingdom Common.

"Well," Mrs. Armstrong said finally, pointing her cattle cane at the new arrival. "Just what do you think you want?"

The boy hesitated. Then in a heavy French Canadian accent he said, "I come go school, me."

Mrs. Armstrong sighted at him over her cane like a hunter sighting in a buck deer. "Well now, Frenchy. *Where* do you propose to come go school, you?"

The boy shrugged. "To school," he said. "To . . ."

Here his meager English failed him altogether. All he could do was repeat, "To school."

"Well," Mrs. Armstrong announced to the class. "He wants to go school."

She heaved herself to her feet, came lurching off the teacher's platform, and clumped down the aisle with the assistance of the ever-present cow cane. "Do you know where you're standing?" she demanded of the boy. She thumped the floor at his feet with the tip of her cane. "You're standing in the girls' entryway. What are you, a boy or a girl?"

The boy shrugged again, and said something in a soft voice.

"What?" Mrs. Armstrong yelled. "What did you say to me?"

This time I heard him quite distinctly. He said, "Yes, sister."

"Sister!" she bellowed. "Who do you think you're calling sister, mister man? I'll sister you."

Mrs. Armstrong gave the strange boy in the herringbone coat a terrific shove in the chest. He backed up, but only a step or two. Mrs. Armstrong gave him another shove, pushing him out through the girls' door. "You stay right there, *sister*," she shouted. "Or go home. Stay there or go home. Until you learn you're a boy and how to address your teacher."

Mrs. Armstrong hitched back to her platform, slamming her cane onto the floor with each stiff step. As usual after one of her outbursts, she took a long pull from her black thermos. But even as she rammed the thermos bottle back into that leviathan of a lunch box, the strange boy was watching from the girls' doorway.

He continued to stand there for the rest of the afternoon. Two or three times Mrs. Armstrong interrupted her recitations to say, to no one in particular, "He can wait until doomsday for all I care. Until he knows he's a boy."

Once, just before three-thirty dismissal, I turned around and caught the boy's eye. And despite his outlandish appearance and the fact that he did not know fifty words of English, I sensed, then and there, the stubbornness about him that would make his subjugation the battle of Earla Armstrong's teaching career.

The next day it rained hard. I slogged the three miles down the Hollow road in my long India rubber coat and rubber barn boots. When I arrived at school, there was the French boy, waiting by the girls' entranceway. He was dressed just the same as the day before, but today the herringbone jacket was sopping wet and his hair was dripping steadily into his eyes. As I went through the boys' entrance I quickly pointed at it, then at him.

Mrs. Armstrong was ensconced at her desk, eating a meat sandwich with ketchup on it. I didn't know if this was her breakfast or just an early snack. No one knew such things about Mrs. Armstrong. Her ways were as different from ours as the ways of the French Canadian boy turned out to be.

"It's you, is it?" she said. "Early again."

In fact, I was nearly always the first to arrive at the Atheneum. Of course my grandmother packed me off to school a good half hour earlier than necessary, but also I was invariably eager to find out what happened next in whatever book I happened to be reading at school. Yet for more than a year, Mrs. Armstrong had greeted me this way, with sneering, mild incredulity: "It's you, is it? Early again."

She scowled at me over her sandwich. "Did you see Mr. Sister?" she said. "Right smack where he was yesterday. He can stand there until the cows come home, Sis can, if he don't learn he's a boy."

I wanted to go back and tell the French boy that he was in the wrong doorway. But with Mrs. Armstrong watching every move I made, I couldn't figure how to do it. Nor was I at all certain I could make him understand me. I slid into my seat and opened *David Copperfield*. David had just decided to run away from London, to his Aunt Betsy's in Dover, and soon I was thousands of miles from Lost Nation Hollow, adrift with my young hero on the merciless high roads of nineteenth-century England.

Although it continued to rain hard, many of the arriving students preferred to wait outside in their rain gear, under the horse chestnut tree, until Mrs. Armstrong went to the vestibule and rang the bell for morning classes. I glanced back and noticed that the strange boy watched carefully as the kids filed in through separate entranceways. Mrs. Armstrong, however, slammed the doors shut behind them with a cruel finality.

In view of the driving rain, I knew that we would not have our usual outdoor nine-thirty recess. But on the pretext of getting a drink from the water bucket in the vestibule, I got up from my seat at about nine o'clock and went to the rear of the room. When I opened the boys' door, I was not greatly surprised to discover that the French kid was standing in the entranceway.

Instantly I returned to my desk and shot up my hand. Mrs. Armstrong, in the meantime, had rooted a pickle sandwich out of her lunch box. She was preoccupied with that for some minutes and either didn't see my hand or pretended not to. Finally she snapped out, "What is it now, Kittredge?"

"That new kid's at the boys' door," I said. "The one you call Sis."

"What of it?"

"You said when he went to the right door you'd let him in."

"I said no such thing, Mr. District Attorney. I said when he knows he's a boy."

A year ago I would have been cowed. At thirteen, I stared at her hatefully, the way I had seen my grandfather stare with his pale blue eyes at his enemies in the village. Mrs. Armstrong returned to her pickle sandwich. When she looked up again I was still staring at her.

"All right, Mr. D. A.," she told me. "Go tell Sis she can come in. She can sit with you, seeing as how you've appointed yourself her attorney. Find out if she can read—you're the famous reader."

And she gave one of the little kids standing at her desk, waiting to recite, the Hungarian dead finger on the head and returned to her sandwich.

I knew that my grandfather was going to town that afternoon to deliver a load of lumber from his sawmill. Shortly after school let out, he stopped for me on his way home, and we headed back up the Hollow in the driving rain. On the way we passed Sis. He was trotting along on my side of the road in his herringbone coat, hatless in the rain.

"There's that French kid," I said. "The kid Old Lady Armstrong calls Sis. Let's give him a ride."

My grandfather slammed on the brakes. I opened my door and started to shove over but the boy waved and jumped onto the back of the truck like a kid jumping onto a hay wagon.

My grandfather shook his head. "Dumb Frenchman," he said. "He doesn't even know enough to come in out of the rain."

But it seemed to me that there was in my grandfather's tone a kind of grudging admiration, as though, being a proud and stubborn man himself, he admired the stubbornness and pride in Sis's refusal to ride up in the cab with us.

As we approached the long lane leading up to the abandoned Kerwin place, the boy banged with his hand on the top of the cab to let us know he wanted to get off. Instead of stopping, my grandfather veered off the Hollow road and rammed up the lane through deep ruts. In places the lane was under several inches of water from the flooding alder brook beside it. Water splashed high on both sides of the truck, drenching Sis as he clung to the rattling sideboards. My grandfather cursed all the way up the flooded lane, as though he were being forced at gunpoint to deliver the boy at his doorstep.

What was left of the Kerwin buildings sat on a knoll at the foot of the same ridge that curved up behind my grandparents' farm. At one time a pasture had been cleared on the lower slope of the ridge above the barn for cows or sheep. In the years since the Kerwins had left, more than a decade ago, it had grown back up to cedars and barberry bushes, wild roses and steeplebush. Near the woods someone had recently made an effort to hack away the encroaching brush.

The barn was partly collapsed, and the farmhouse had fallen into its cellar hole. Hunkered down on the knoll, alone in the rain, the ruins looked as desolate as any of twenty or so other abandoned places up and down Lost Nation Hollow. The only sign of habitation was some dark smoke coming out of a piece of stovepipe sticking up through a shed attached to the dilapidated barn.

"Christ, Austen," my grandfather said, "they're living in the milk house."

The boy jumped down and ran to my grandfather's window to thank him. In the meantime I noticed a woman driving a black-and-white cow down off the overgrown ridge behind the barn. She wore men's barn boots, a man's long denim coat, and a plain gray shawl. The cow had a horse collar around its neck and was pulling what looked for all the world like the inverted hood of an antique car. As they drew closer I saw that the old car hood had been converted into a stoneboat and was loaded with rocks. The woman waved and called something to the boy. He grinned. "You come me," he told us. "See *ma mère*, by da Jimminy Joe."

"Yes, sir," my grandfather said grimly, reaching for the truck door.

My grandfather got out, tall and stern-faced in his mackinaw jacket. I followed him and Sis across the old barnyard through the rain.

The milk house was the same size as ours at home, about twelve feet by eight feet. The air inside was smoky from a small, rusty stove like the one in the office of my grandfather's sawmill. There were two wooden chairs, a battered wooden table, and two cots. On the table sat a loaf of dark bread and a pot of boiled potatoes. Apart from the potatoes and bread, I saw nothing at all to eat. Some old clothes were drying on a rope strung near the stove.

Overhead, the rain leaked steadily through the rotten wooden shingles of the milk house roof. It hissed on the stovetop and chimney, which was the strangest chimney I'd ever seen. It was constructed from old milk cans with the bottoms hacked off and fitted together like stovepipe joints. Yet the cracked concrete floor of the room had been swept clean, the cots were neatly made and covered with bright quilts, and at the single small window hung a pair of makeshift curtains cut out of feedsack material.

From beyond the doorway leading into the barn, someone coughed. The woman who had been driving the cow appeared. Her wet hair was as gray as her shawl. She looked nearly as old as my grandmother, and she was coughing steadily, a deep, wracking chest cough.

"*Ma mère*," Sis said proudly. "Madame LaFlamme."

"Austen Kittredge," my grandfather said to Mrs. LaFlamme. "Your neighbor up the road. This young fella is my grandson. He goes to school with your boy."

"School!" the woman said. "We come States so Louis go school. Me Madame LaFlamme."

Madame LaFlamme coughed hard. I wondered if it was the smoke from the stove that made her hack that way. It stung my eyes and caused them to water. I didn't see how people could live inside that smoke-filled milk house.

"Sit, you," Madame LaFlamme said. "Sit."

My grandfather shook his head and said we had to get home to chores. Then he said something in French. I knew he was uncomfortable, standing in this smoky milk house converted into a French Canadian kitchen-bedroom, trying to talk with two persons who spoke less English than he did French.

Madame LaFlamme was not about to let go of us so easily, however. She began talking in French to my grandfather with great volubility. I thought I heard her mention the words Canada and farm, and the name Stevens. My grandfather nodded once or twice. When she finally stopped, he said something in French to the boy, who nodded vigorously. Then we left.

I was very curious to learn what Madame LaFlamme had told my grandfather. Where in Canada were they from? Where was Sis's father? And what had my grandfather told Sis? I knew better than to ask, though. I realized that my grandfather was concerned for these people; but at thirteen, I also knew him well enough to realize that his concern would very probably take the form of anger.

"How old do you think that boy is?" he finally asked me.

I shrugged. "Fifteen?"

"He's nineteen," my grandfather said. "Nineteen Christly years old. If he hasn't gotten his schooling by now, I guess he isn't about to get it. I told him to come up and see me about a job. He might better help me get up next winter's woodpile and earn a little money before they run out of potatoes and starve."

Immediately after we arrived home, my grandfather went striding into the barn to start chores, as angry as I'd seen him in a long time.

I said nothing to my grandmother about our visit to the LaFlammes, but after supper my grandfather brought up the subject himself. As nearly as he'd been able to determine from Mrs. LaFlamme's rapid-fire French, she and her son had moved down to the Kingdom from somewhere not far across the border about a month ago, with the assistance of Bumper Stevens. I knew the lowdown on Bumper from previous conversations between my grandparents. He was a local cattle and livestock dealer, who ran the commission sales auction barn in Kingdom Common. Over the past fifteen or so years, Bumper had bought a number of abandoned farms along the border, mostly overgrown and run-down old places he'd picked up for a song, and then placed French Canadian tenants on them. Sometimes, according to my grandfather, Bumper would sell a place outright to a Canadian family, for a small down payment, and hold the mortgage himself. Then he'd extend further credit to the family to buy cows and used machinery from his own auction barn. For Bumper, at least, these arrangements usually turned out to be lucrative. The immigrant family would reclaim the land for farming or grazing, and improve the buildings. Some who were willing to live for years on next to nothing, and maybe hold a full-time second job at the furniture mill in the Common while they built up their farms, eventually paid off their mortgages. The prosperous Ben Currier family down on the county road had gotten started in Vermont just this way. So had Francis Dubois's family here in Lost Nation. Other Canadians imported by Bumper Stevens had been unable to meet their payments after a few years. In these instances, Bumper had not hesitated to foreclose, though rarely until the farms had been cleared and put back into operation, after which he could resell them at a tidy profit. Throughout Kingdom County, Bumper Stevens was both grudgingly admired as a shrewd businessman and widely distrusted as a man whose success derived from sharp practice.

As far as the LaFlammes went, my grandfather said that Madame LaFlamme's husband had died two years ago. Since then they had been living with relatives. Sis was the youngest of eight children, seven of whom were grown-up girls, married or working on their own in Canada. He and his mother were trying to clear the place with the help of the lone, dried-up, black-and-white cow Bumper had supplied them with.

"What are they living on, Mr. Kittredge?" my grandmother said. "What are they eating?"

My grandfather snorted. "Spuds! Bumper sent a fella up there this past summer to put in a plot of potatoes and lure just such a brainless outfit as them down over the Line. They're living on potatoes."

"Potatoes!"

"Yes, damn them. Potatoes and black bread. How even a couple of dumb Frenchies believe they can get through the winter on black bread and a few sacks of potatoes is beyond me. The old woman seems to have contracted consumption. I doubt she'll make it to December."

"It isn't those poor French people you should be inveighing against, it's that double-dealing devil Stevens."

"Stevens is a hard man, Mrs. Kittredge. I don't deny it. But he's fair."

"Stevens is not fair. He's the devil's own agent in Kingdom County. What do you propose to do to help those folks?"

"Nothing," my grandfather said flatly, looking at me. "Nothing at all. If I run onto a dying animal out in the woods, I don't prolong its suffering. I won't prolong theirs."

I wanted to tell my grandmother that my grandfather had already offered Sis LaFlamme work, but I thought better of it.

"I intend to assist that family," my grandmother said. "One way or another."

"Assist away," said my grandfather angrily. "Assistance or no assistance, they won't last until Christmas. That's as certain as the sun coming up over the White Mountains of New Hampshire in the morning and setting behind the Green Mountains of Vermont at night."

Somehow the LaFlammes hung on at the old Kerwin place that fall. And somehow Sis continued to attend school. He did not come every day. But three or four times a week he'd show up, often late in the morning or early in the afternoon, and when he did, he always went at his lessons the way he and his mother went at clearing that old farm of rocks and brush: energetically, cheerfully, with the eternal hope of the absolutely hopeless.

The first day Mrs. Armstrong admitted Sis to the school he wrote his name in bold letters on his desk slate: LOUIS-HIP-POLYTE LAFLAMME. "Look," he told me proudly. "Look here, by da Jimminy Joe."

I believe that Sis could in fact read and write a little French. But English might as well have been Greek to him. He never did get a handle on it. Of course Mrs. Armstrong made him recite at her desk with the little kids, above whom he towered in his herringbone coat like a golem. "By da Jimminy Joe" was his favorite exclamation and Mrs. Armstrong took it up and hectored him with it mercilessly, as she hectored him about his mispronunciations and fantastical ragamuffin appearance. But Sis wasn't much perturbed. He stayed at it, plugging away harder than any of us.

For my part, I now had a project apart from my reading. I spent an hour tutoring Sis in the morning and another in the afternoon, and discovered that he was quick with numbers, if not with their English names. Perhaps when it came to reading he had what today would be called a learning disability. I don't know. He had a quick memory and memorized the first four reading books in the school word for word within a few weeks. But he was saying the words from rote, not reading. He was good at some of our schoolyard games, especially those that involved running. Sis never did learn to hit a baseball, though. We used to pitch to him by the hour just to watch his comic attempts to make contact.

He was unfailingly good-natured. "How's the bearded lady today?" Mrs. Armstrong would greet him, and he would nod and smile and say *très bon*, by da Jimminy Joe. Each time he handed in a paper with his name written in those big letters at the top, LOUIS-HIPPOLYTE LAFLAMME, she'd cross it out and write SIS in its place. He smiled gamely through it all.

Sis had some spirit. One morning a week after he started at the Lost Nation Atheneum he inadvertently called Mrs. Armstrong "Sister" again—a habit he'd no doubt picked up in Canada, at the parochial school where he'd received his early education. Without warning she struck him in the arm with her cow cane. Instantly he jumped up and stepped toward her, his black eyes flashing. He said something in French, and for a moment I thought and hoped that he might knock her down. He was the one student in the school who I believe could have: a lean, hard, strong young man, toughened by years of working outdoors. Somehow he got hold of himself. And although Mrs. Armstrong had looked momentarily alarmed, she steamed right ahead with her bullying.

At thirteen, I was much more confident than I'd been even a year ago. In the absence of Hermie Hill, I'd begun to emerge as a schoolyard leader and spokesman for some of the other students. The next time Prof Chadburn dropped by, I got him aside and complained to him about Mrs. Armstrong's treatment of Sis. He nodded sympathetically. "I know, Austen. I've spoken to her about it. I will again. But she keeps good order, and remember, that's why she's here."

"She isn't teaching us a damn thing, Prof, and you and I both know it," I said hotly. "You ought to send her down the road."

"It isn't that simple, son. When you're a little older, you'll understand." He went over to his Buick and got out a copy of John

Burroughs's *Winter Sunshine* and handed it to me. Prof Chadburn was a good man and a great teacher. But he was not going to rock the boat at Lost Nation Atheneum now that he finally had a teacher who could keep order. If Louis-Hippolyte LaFlamme fell by the wayside, well, that was unfortunate.

Despite my grandfather's vow to my grandmother that he would do nothing to prolong the misery of the LaFlammes, he did hire Sis to help him get up our woodpile and sugaring wood for the following year. Immediately it became apparent that Sis knew how to handle a bucksaw. My grandfather said he was as good with it as most men. I don't know how much Gramp paid him. But he'd promised to give the LaFlammes a steer to butcher for the winter once cold weather set in, and I had the idea that this was to be the main part of Sis's remuneration. My grandmother presented Sis with an old mackinaw that had belonged to my Uncle Rob Roy, and a pair of winter boots Rob had outgrown. She gave Mrs. LaFlamme two laying hens from our flock of Buff Orpingtons.

By mid-November Sis had bucked up all the wood we'd need for the following year. Just as he'd promised, my grandfather trucked a yearling Ayrshire steer down to the Kerwin place. He helped Sis and Madame LaFlamme stake it out on a chain behind the collapsing barn. Later that month he would come down and help them butcher it. The LaFlammes could keep half of the beef to eat through the winter, and sell half for cash to pay their rent to Bumper. Madame LaFlamme was so grateful she wept, which set off a terrible coughing spell.

My grandfather waved off their thanks and said Sis had earned the animal and then some. But as we drove back home together he shook his head and told me that all the dumb Frenchman jokes he'd ever heard must have been made up with the LaFlammes in mind, and reiterated his conviction that they would not make it through until Christmas.

Everything came to a head on the day before Thanksgiving. It was a gray morning, very cold, with a yellowish cast in the sky over the Canadian mountains to the north that usually meant a storm was approaching. As usual on Wednesdays, my grandfather took me to school on his way to the cheese factory with his milk. The day before, he had shot two big snow geese and hung them in the woodshed. One was for our Thanksgiving meal and the other he intended to drop off for the LaFlammes on his way back from the village. Of course he did not tell my grandmother this.

Oddly enough, Sis was waiting for us that morning at the foot of his lane. I thought he wanted a ride to school. But he began to wave his arms frantically, and he was shouting even before we stopped. Gesticulating wildly, he shouted something about the red-and-white he-cow my grandfather had given him, the chain he'd staked it with. Shouting *mal, mal*, he pointed up the lane and jumped onto the back of the truck, as he had that rainy afternoon two months ago when we first took him home from school. My grandfather cursed viciously as we jounced up the lane in the lumber truck. He had already begun to figure out what had happened though I was still in the dark. *Mal* was the word Sis used to describe his mother's condition. Had Mrs. LaFlamme somehow been accidentally trampled by the steer? I imagined the worst.

We skidded to a stop in the dooryard, which hadn't changed since the last time we'd been here. There were the sunken-in house and barn, the milk house with dark smoke coming out of its jury-rigged chimney. Descending the knoll above the house were Sis's mother and the angular black-and-white cow, just where we'd first seen them, dragging the makeshift stoneboat.

On the stoneboat was something reddish-colored, with patches of white. Even before I jumped out of the truck, I recognized it. It was the Ayrshire steer my grandfather had given Sis, and it was as dead as a doornail.

The steer's head was twisted off at an unnatural angle to its body, and one of its horns had dug a little groove partway down the hillside behind the stoneboat. As we drew near, Madame LaFlamme broke into a torrent of French. Although I did not understand a word, I gathered that somehow the steer had broken its neck.

Sis and his mother wanted my grandfather to butcher the animal on the spot, but as he angrily pointed out, it had already started to bloat. The meat was spoiled, he said. All he could do was send

Bumper Stevens up with his rending truck. The dead steer was good only for dog food.

"By da Jimminy Joe!" Sis kept exclaiming. "By da Jimminy Joe!"

"By the Jimminy Joe, what do you people intend to eat this winter?" my grandfather said. "How are you going to pay your rent? This is a fine morning's work. Go get in the truck, Austen. We have to get you to school."

My grandfather was so mad he flung the snow goose by its big webbed feet up toward the milk house and took off without another word.

On our way down the lane it started to snow. The flakes were huge at first and there were not too many. Sis and his mother stood by the dead and bloating steer, watching us out of sight in the lightly-falling snow.

All the way down the road to school my grandfather cursed the LaFlammes. He interrupted himself only to tell me that the steer had not, as I'd supposed, pulled up its stake and bolted, then tripped on the chain. Oh, no. It was worse than that. Sis had decided the previous day to double the length of the chain in order to give the steer more grazing room. At some point during the night, after eating its fill, the animal had evidently assumed that it was free. It had begun to run and been snubbed up short by the tightened chain, no doubt breaking its neck instantly. Within an hour or so, it had started to bloat from the fresh grass in its stomach.

"Do you see what I mean now?" my grandfather said as I got out in the schoolyard. "About prolonging their misery? I hope they have a pleasant Thanksgiving. They can eat tainted beef and rotten potatoes."

"What about the goose?" I said.

"I doubt they know enough to pluck it," my grandfather said. "I've never encountered such a misbegotten outfit in all my born days, Austen. I hope you and your grandmother are satisfied at last."

By now I was mad that my grandfather seemed to be mad at me. I hadn't told him to help the LaFlammes, or not to help them for that matter. Fortunately, Prof Chadburn's big black Roadmaster Buick was parked under the horse chestnut tree beside Mrs. Armstrong's old junker. This meant that Prof was here for his monthly visit, a couple of days early because of the Thanksgiving holiday, and we would have a good morning. In the excitement of Prof's appearance and the impending snowstorm, I'd forgotten all about the LaFlammes by the time I was inside the school building.

Prof was going over Mrs. Armstrong's attendance and midterm pupil progress reports, which I believe he all but had to write for her. When he finished those, he listened to the little kids recite. I was engrossed in Richard Henry Dana's *Two Years Before the Mast*. Each time I looked up from my book, it was snowing harder. The yellow cast I'd noticed in the sky that morning seemed to have seeped into the school. The classroom was illuminated by an eerie yellow snow-light in which the black-printed letters of my pages stood out sharp and dark. Surrounded by falling snow, the schoolhouse seemed unusually quiet. The only sounds were the scratching of chalk on our desk slates, the low hiss of the woodstove, and the reciting kids.

At recess we tried to slide down the Fiddler's Elbow on our cardboard sleds. It was snowing too hard, however, to keep a good trail packed down, so two or three other boys and I helped Prof put on his tire chains. Then we pestered him for a geography bee.

Geography bees were exciting events for us; and because it was the day before a holiday, Prof announced that this morning he would offer something special for a grand prize. From his vest pocket he produced a silver dollar: a big, heavy cartwheel, which he'd polished to a brilliant shine.

We divided into two teams and lined up on each side of the room and Prof began asking us questions out of his head. For the little kids the questions were easy at first. How many states in the Union? Name the five oceans. For us older students, the questions were much tougher, partly because Prof shared the delight of the little shavers in seeing us sit down first. Winnowing out the chaff, he called this process, and stumped me on my first try with the capital of Outer Mongolia.

"You're such a famous reader, Kittredge," Mrs. Armstrong piped up from her desk. "Evidently you'd best read up on your geography."

Prof grinned at me wickedly and spun the silver dollar in his fingers like a magician.

Finally only two students remained standing: Theresa Dubois and a sixth-grade girl named Craft, with a large head inclined slightly to one side. As Theresa and the Craft girl were dueling it out, the boys' door opened and a tall snow figure came in. It was Sis LaFlamme, and he was covered with snow from head to foot, so that he had to broom himself off in the vestibule and then stand by the stove, steaming, to warm up.

I was astonished. I couldn't believe that Sis would come to school after the tragedy of the Ayrshire steer. I had doubted that we'd ever see him set foot in Lost Nation Atheneum again. Yet here he was, standing by the stove in that weird yellow snow-light coming through the big schoolhouse windows, in my uncle's cast-off mackinaw that my grandmother had given him.

A minute later he slid in next to me and grinned and shrugged. It was the most eloquent shrug I'd ever seen. Life goes on, I supposed he was saying. Life goes on, by the Jimminy Joe. His sheer hope in the infinite promise of the day at hand was phenomenal, like his hope each time he picked up the Fifth Grade Reader or our splintered old Adirondack baseball bat. Dead steer or no dead steer, there wasn't an ounce of quit to Louis-Hippolyte LaFlamme.

Prof was holding up the bright silver dollar, revolving it slowly in the dull saffron light. "The capital of New Zealand," he said.

"Wellington," Theresa said promptly.

Prof spun the gleaming dollar high into the air, deftly picked it out of its arc, and plunked it down on Theresa's desk. Then I saw him slip the Craft girl something on the side, a fifty-cent piece, I think.

"Lunch time," he said. "Right, Mrs. A?"

Mrs. Armstrong consulted her watch and frowned. "We can take our nooning, I suppose."

We ate inside at our desks, and by the time we finished, the snow had let up somewhat. We wanted Prof to stay on, go sliding with us that noon and while away the afternoon. We would get him going on the war; get him to tell us about driving army mules. But while the storm had abated and he had a chance, he wanted to make his way back down the Fiddler's Elbow to the county road. So in a way you could say it was the weather that was to blame for what happened later that afternoon, because if Prof had stayed on with us, the day would have turned out differently. Sooner or later, though, I suppose that something bad would have happened anyway. It would be impossible to throw two persons like Earla Armstrong and Sis LaFlamme together for very long and not have something bad happen.

We got our cardboard sheets off the top of the wood in the woodshed. Except for Theresa and her little sister, Carrie, none of us had sleds. Theresa and Carrie had a Flexible Flyer, a real factory-made sled, varnished slick and shiny with the sled's name painted on it in bright red letters, and the ironwork a fresh, gleaming black. The first couple of times down the hill were slow. We followed Prof's dented chain treads in snow that was already six inches deep. But the Fiddler's Elbow was so steep that by the third time down we had a bobsled ride. Of course we had little control over our cardboard toboggans. Three or four of us would crowd onto one sheet and off we'd go, rarely making it to the elbow halfway down the hill since there was nothing to hold on to but each other. To make the turn itself, you had to lean right, hard. I invariably fell off at the bend, if not before.

Sis slid, too. Nineteen years old, mustache and all, with a dead steer in his dooryard and no apparent way to get through the winter, he got a square of cardboard and slid downhill, whooping and hollering like the rest of us, happy as a clam. "*Bas* da *côte*, by da Jimminy Joe!" he'd shout, and launch himself down the slope on his cardboard, usually falling off after a few yards. But he kept trying, each time yelling "*Bas* da *côte!*"—down the hill.

The sky was still hurricane yellow. I remember how Theresa's blood-red coat stood out against that storm sky as she stood on top of the hill, getting ready to go down once more before noon recess ended. She could not have been more luminous in full, sparkling sunshine. She was beautiful, and I believe that Sis thought so too since I saw him watching her as well. She waved to us and then she was on her way down the steep pitch on her wonderful Flexible Flyer, her little sister sitting between her knees.

When they reached the elbow they leaned hard and squealed, like two girls on a fair ride. They almost made it around the bend. Then the left runner caught in Prof's chain track, and the girls tipped too far in the opposite direction, overcompensating, and were pitched out laughing and squealing. Usually tipping over was the best part of sliding for all of us, including the girls. Pretty and smart as they were, the Dubois sisters were rugged country kids, who worked as hard at home as most of us boys. So I was surprised to see that when Theresa stood up, all snowy and red-cheeked, there was a look of horror on her face. Her hands were in her coat pockets. She yanked them out and pulled off her mittens, plunged her hands into her pockets again, brought them out empty, and burst into tears.

"My dollar's gone," she wailed. "My silver dollar's gone!"

Up the hill, Mrs. Armstrong appeared in the vestibule, ringing her long-handled bell to summon us in from recess. Theresa and Carrie and I pawed frantically in the snow beside the road. But there was no time to search for the dollar. We knew that Mrs. Armstrong would be in an especially bad mood after Prof's visit and we did not dare risk her wrath. All the way up the hill, Theresa wailed like a calf for its mother. Carrie cried because Theresa was crying, and I was almost mad enough to cry myself. I was furiously mad at Mrs. Armstrong for making me afraid to be late and at myself for being afraid.

Mrs. Armstrong stood in the vestibule between the two doors, snapping some of the younger kids in the head with the dead finger as they marched in. Theresa cried all the way by her. "Don't come bawling to me," Mrs. Armstrong said. "If you're going to slide you must expect to be hurt." She said this as though getting hurt was not only inevitable, but somehow desirable.

Theresa continued to cry all the way to her seat. Ordinarily she had a very level head, and I was somewhat surprised by her inconsolable grief. A dollar was a great deal of money to all of us in those days, but I think now that it was more the distinction of the award. To win a silver dollar—then to lose it!

"What ails that girl?" Mrs. Armstrong asked the class. "Did somebody pound her up?"

There was no answer.

Very deliberately, Mrs. Armstrong began to roll up her sleeves.

"She lost her dollar," I said. "Nobody hurt her."

"Lost her dollar!" Mrs. Armstrong said. "What do you mean, lost her dollar? How did she contrive to do such a heedless thing as that?"

"It—it was in my coat, and, and, and now it's gone," Theresa sobbed.

"I see," Mrs. Armstrong said, though it was apparent from what she said next that she did not. "Someone has stolen your dollar."

She picked up her cattle cane and came to the edge of her platform. "Jim Morgan, stand up. Did you steal Theresa Dubois's silver dollar?"

"No, ma'am," Jim said.

She looked at him hard. "Remain standing," she said.

She surveyed the classroom. "Mary Hill, stand up. Did you steal Theresa Dubois's silver dollar?"

Mary Hill was a tall, strapping farm girl of thirteen, Hermie's sister. She was the least afraid of Mrs. Armstrong of any of us, but she faltered slightly when she said, "N—no, ma'am."

"Remain standing, Mary Hill. Austen Kittredge, stand up."

All of a sudden I was sick to death of Earla Armstrong and everything about her. I'd had it with her bullying and her ignorance and her school. I had no intention of standing up. I had no intention of submitting to her arbitrary cruelness for one more moment.

"Nobody stole the dollar," I said. "It fell out of Theresa's coat while we were sliding. It's out there in the snow this minute."

"Fell out sliding!" she said. "What do you mean it fell out sliding? Did it sprout wings and fly out of her pocket?"

"Yes," I said. "Sure. That's what happened."

"Don't you dare put a smart mouth on with me, Kittredge. You aren't too old to feel the arm."

"Nobody stole the dollar," I said. "Ask Theresa."

Just as she whirled around to confront Theresa, Sis LaFlamme burst through the door. He was covered with snow, and snow had gotten down his coat and boots and on his hair, as though he'd been burrowing in a drift. He ran straight to Theresa's desk. "Look me," he yelled. "Look me, I find him."

He was holding the silver dollar.

For once in her life, Mrs. Armstrong looked utterly astonished. But she was not about to bring her inquisition to a close without claiming a victim. She had boiled all morning to see us having fun with Prof, to see him interfere with her prerogatives. No doubt she had drunk her lunch out of her thermos. She had threatened all of us with her green-handled cow cane. Her entire reputation was at stake.

Mrs. Armstrong came bulling down off the teacher's platform, between Sis and Theresa. "Where did you find that coin, LaFlamme?"

"I find him, me!" Sis said excitedly. *"Bas* da *côte."*

"The *coat?"*

"Oui. Bas"—he hesitated to find the English word—*"down* da *côte."*

"Down the coat?" she shouted.

He smiled, nodding rapidly. *"Oui.* I find him down da *côte."*

Mrs. Armstrong had turned the color of Theresa's red coat.

"Down the coat!" she shrieked. "You found the coin down in the pocket of Theresa's coat. Why you sneaking Canuck thief. I'll teach you to reach into other people's coats."

Before any of us knew what was going to happen Earla Armstrong lifted her ugly green cow cane and struck Sis LaFlamme in the left temple. The silver dollar seemed to jump out of his hand. It hit the floor and rolled straight for the Round Oak stove in the center of the room. The dollar bounced off a leg of the stove. It made its way directly back to Theresa's desk and spun drunkenly to rest at her feet. Theresa shied away from it as though it were red-hot. Everyone in the room stared at it, horrified, as though it had been bewitched, like a coin in a fairy tale. But what was happening here in the yellow light of the Lost Nation schoolroom in the winter of 1955 was no fairy tale.

"Down da *côte!"* Sis bellowed out in pain and outrage and humiliation.

He pointed wildly out the window, toward the hill: the *côte,* where he'd found Theresa's dollar in the snow. "Down da goddamn *côte!"*

Mrs. Armstrong, who understood no French, was completely out of control. "I'll teach you to swear at me you good-for-nothing Frog."

She raised the cane again. But Louis-Hippolyte LaFlamme did not intend to be struck a second time. Before she could bring it down he leaped at her. Quick as a mink going for a trout, he wrested the cane out of her hand, broke it in two across his knee and flung the severed halves toward the stove. Then he was on his way out of the schoolroom and across the yard and up the Hollow.

Mrs. Armstrong stood staring after him for a few moments before returning to her desk. Panting hard, she went to her lunch box for the thermos and emptied it in three or four long pulls. Her hands were shaking, but she had a triumphant look on her face.

"He'll be charged for this," she told us. "Don't think he won't, the dirty little louse-ridden Frenchman. I'll have the law on him."

Then in a nearly friendly voice she said, "Shut that door, Kittredge. It's storming out there."

She was right. It had started to snow again, and the room was filled with that yellow light and a preternatural stillness. I got up and shut the door. What else was there to do?

The dollar lay in the aisle by Theresa's desk all the afternoon. When the kids went up to the front of the room to recite, they stepped gingerly out around it, as if it were a bear trap. Just before we recessed for the day, Theresa picked it up, and on her way down the Fiddler's Elbow, in a gesture more dramatic than prudent, she suddenly flung it as far as she could into the woods. Very probably it has remained there to this day, buried under the humus of nearly forty autumns.

There is not much more to tell about the LaFlamme family. I learned from my grandfather that Bumper Stevens charged them five dollars to come out and pick up the bloated Ayrshire steer in his truck. Without telling my grandmother, my grandfather paid Bumper the five dollars himself, but Sis never did return to the Lost Nation Atheneum after the episode with the silver dollar.

One sub-zero day in early December, on our way down the Hollow, my grandfather and I noticed that there was no smoke coming up from the Kerwin place. We left the lumber truck at the foot of the lane and walked up through the snow to check. The milk house was deserted. Even the feedsack curtains were gone from the window. Later that morning Gramp learned from Bumper that the LaFlammes had returned to Canada.

In the spring Bumper put some young stock up in the pasture Sis and his mother had started to clear. He never did find another tenant for the place, and over the next few years, it all grew back up to brush. Along with my early boyhood, the days of the self-sufficient family farm were quickly coming to a close in Kingdom County. The old abandoned homesteads were fast reverting to a state of frontier ruggedness again.

Mrs. Armstrong replaced her cane with a nondescript brown walking stick and blustered her way through the rest of the school year, but the days of her furious rampaging were over. It was as if, along with the thick green cattle cane, Sis LaFlamme had broken her spirit.

Oddly, though our school days from then on were easier, I think we half-missed the old excitement. At times she just sat at her desk and sipped out of her thermos, letting us do pretty much as we pleased. She did not return to the school after I graduated, and I heard nothing of her again for many years.

But Earla Armstrong was not yet to depart from my life altogether. In one of those entirely unpredictable and unaccountable quirks of circumstance that nonetheless, in retrospect, seem somehow inevitable, I heard from her once more. The spring I graduated from the University of Vermont—which I attended free, at the courtesy of the State of Vermont and my Great-Great-Great-Great-Great-Grandfather Sojourner Kittredge, the shrewd old Tory—my graduation picture appeared in the local paper, along with Theresa's and, of all persons, Mary Hill's. A few days later a card came to me in care of my grandparents' address. It was postmarked Pond in the Sky. The handwriting was so scratchy I had trouble making it out. At first I thought it was from an ex-classmate. The writer wondered if I remembered the good old days at Lost Nation Atheneum, and asked me to stop by and visit when I was in her neck of the woods. Not until the last line did I realize who it was from. "I still watch the wrastling," it said. "Fondly, your old teacher, Earla A. Armstrong."

Unfortunately, Mrs. Armstrong died soon afterward. In time, I came to regret not visiting her.

6

UPLAND GAME

During the years that I lived with my grandparents in Lost Nation Hollow, a number of itinerant specialists could be counted on to visit Kingdom County each year. I had no idea where most of these exotic wayfarers hailed from. "Away," most of us called anywhere more than five miles beyond the county line. Or "the other side of the hills." All I knew for certain is that since we could not go to them, the mind readers and barnstorming four-man baseball teams and one-elephant family circuses came to us. Then as abruptly as they'd arrived, they departed, leaving me with a day of desolation on my hands, and maybe a fifteen-cent souvenir: a tattered poster, an autographed snapshot, a handful of spent shells from the Manchester Arms Company sharpshooter, which still gave off a faint and exciting aroma of gunpowder after six months in a dresser drawer.

Of all the itinerants, the sharpshooter was my favorite. Actually, he was an ammunition salesman, a drummer of rifle and shotgun shells, who, as a sideline, put on marksmanship exhibitions at county fairs and rod and gun club suppers and sometimes, on an impromptu basis, out behind the general stores and four-corner filling stations where he sold the company's line. He was a small man of forty-five or fifty, with pale eyes narrowed at the corners from driving into ten thousand suns and squinting over a shotgun barrel at a million clay pigeons. He was slightly hard of hearing, and when he spoke, which wasn't often, it was usually to complain about the weather in what I believed was a mild southern accent. His suit looked as though he'd driven two weeks straight in it, and unlike the other showmen who visited Kingdom County, there was no hoopla about him at all. In fact, he didn't seem to care whether he shot or not, and it was this odd quality, his apparent indifference toward his talent, that appealed to me and annoyed my Uncle Rob, who, by the time he was twenty-one, was considered to be one of the two or three best shots in our neck of the woods himself.

"He's here," Rob said, pulling in behind a dusty gray Pontiac in front of Cousin Clarence Kittredge's general store at the foot of the Hollow.

It was a warm and hazy Saturday morning in early October, and Rob and I had already been out doing a little road hunting in the new Hudson Hornet he'd bought the previous summer with money he'd earned working in the furniture mill in the Common. I was enormously proud to be out riding the roads and hunting with my young uncle. And here, out of the blue, was the Manchester sharpshooter. It was almost too good to be true.

The shooter and Clarence were standing across from one another at the store counter. Clarence was thumbing through an ammunition catalog. The shooter was reading a Socony road map and frowning.

"New line of 16s, I see," Clarence said.

The shooter nodded without looking up from his map.

"Good shell?"

"Fairly accurate upland game shell," the shooter said.

"Wouldn't care to pop a few out back for the boys here?"

The sharpshooter gave Rob and me a quick, aggrieved look. He reached in the inside pocket of his suit jacket and got out a half-full pint bottle of Southern Comfort and unscrewed the cap and took a sip. The whiskey was the color of standing water in a cedar bog. As it went down, the shooter winced. "I got to be up in Memphrema-gog by eleven o'clock," he said. "I might snap off a round or two first if it ain't too cold."

He went out to his Pontiac and unlocked the trunk. It was neat as a pin and contained several cartons of ammunition, a battered leather suitcase with straps and buckles, and three long canvas cases wrapped in a wool overcoat. He handed me two of the cases and took the third himself. It was as warm as a morning in June, but I noticed that he was shivering in his suit jacket. When he shut the trunk lid, the Pontiac shuddered all over, and so did he.

"Big old gas hog," Rob said.

The shooter gave a dyspeptic grin, as though pleased to hear his car disparaged. "She's a guzzler," he agreed. "Burns gas and oil like they was both going out of style. Throw a rod clean through her block one of these days. Brakes ain't the best. Heater's shot. Trade her in five seconds flat if the right deal come along. Lug them around back for me, will you, bub?"

We went around behind the store to Clarence's garden beside the local cow-pasture baseball diamond. Half a dozen men and boys from the store followed us. We laid the cases down on the bench where Clarence sat to shell peas and husk corn.

"Unzip that shorter one," the shooter told me.

Inside was a light single-shot .22.

"All right for a kid starting out," the shooter said.

He stooped over and picked up a Coca-Cola bottle cap. He walked out around the brown cornstalks and frosted Kentucky Won-der pole beans and jammed the bottle cap into a rotten fence post at the base of Tatro's hill. He came back to the bench, put a shell in the .22, and fired without seeming to take aim.

I ran to get the bottle cap. One side was ripped flat, like a penny flattened by a locomotive on the Boston and Montreal tracks. I ran back to the shooter, who looked at the cap and scowled as though he'd missed it entirely.

"You ought to go on Broadway," my uncle said.

"Kid gun," the shooter said, shoving the .22 back in its case. "All right for gray squirrels and such."

"There aren't any gray squirrels up here," Rob said. "Too cold."

"I believe it," said the shooter, and turned up his jacket collar against a warm south breeze. "Man dear, it's chilly."

He unzipped the second case I'd brought around and got out a .30-30 rifle. It was a bolt-action deer-hunting rifle, the kind my grandfather and Uncle Rob used. A couple of men moved up closer.

"You got a fifty-cent piece on you?" the shooter asked Cousin Clarence.

Clarence reached under his apron for his black change purse. He unsnapped it and stared inside for some time. Finally he removed a half dollar.

"I believe," he said slowly, "that it is unlawful to destroy a coin of the realm."

"Trade you Mr. G. Washington's picture for her," the shooter said, going for his back pocket.

"That isn't necessary," Clarence said in a dignified voice. "Heave it up?"

"Not too high. Wouldn't want to miss and pick off some hunter up top the hill."

Two or three of the men chuckled at the thought of picking off a hunter.

"I thought you never missed," Rob said.

"You say?"

"I said, I thought you don't miss."

"Miss quite frequently," the shooter said.

He slid a shell into the gun and rammed home the bolt. "Heave her."

Clarence threw the fifty-cent piece out and up. It spun over and over, flashing against the red sumac and yellow popples on the hillside. The shooter fired, and the coin vanished in thin air.

"Yes, sir," Clarence said with a note of finality.

"Anybody," said my Uncle Rob, "can learn to do that. There's a trick to it, just like shooting a woodcock. You wait until it's at the top of its arc, then you've got a stationary target. All it takes is practice."

"There you have her," said the shooter and shoved the rifle back into its case like a man hanging an old saw up on a nail. "Practice is the main thing, all right."

He took another sip of Southern Comfort. Then he unzipped the third case and slid out the loveliest gun I'd ever seen. It was a sixteen-gauge pump-action shotgun with a rich dark stock and a barrel the color of Lake Memphremagog on an overcast day in duck season, engraved with two pheasants flushing out of a wheat field.

The shooter looked at Clarence. "You got any spoiled hens' eggs on hand?"

"I do not. I don't pass spoiled eggs off on my customers. You want eggs from my store, you'll have to settle for grade-A fresh."

The shooter considered. "All righty. I'll purchase half a dozen grade-A fresh hens' eggs."

Clarence went inside. A minute later he came back with a half carton of brown eggs. The shooter gave him a dollar and Clarence handed him back sixty cents.

"It's on the company," the shooter explained to the men and boys. By now there was a gallery of fifteen or so, lounging against the back wall of the store, hunkered down on the edge of the harvested garden. Among the men I recognized some who were crack shots themselves.

The shooter put six shells into the gun.

"How many eggs?" Clarence said.

"Try three. Three grade-A eggs. Fling them out away. They spatter."

Three brown eggs sailed over the garden at intervals of less than a second. The shooter fired three times. Before the third egg left Clarence's hand, the first two had burst in midair into small, yellow omelettes. The third egg burst, raining yolk and white and fragments of brown shell onto a heap of dead pea vines. I scrambled for the ejected shells, smoking on the ground at the shooter's feet.

Uncle Rob was already haranguing the onlookers, patiently, yet with an argumentative edge to his voice. "What he is, boys, is fast. I don't say he isn't accurate; he's accurate enough for trap and trick shooting. But mainly he's fast. Out in the woods, fast isn't all that important. Accuracy is what counts in the woods."

"I never was much of a hand to hunt in the woods," the shooter said to no one in particular. "Sun never seems to get down between the trees and warm things up good."

He shivered at the thought of the sun not warming things up in the woods. He extended the gun, barrel first, toward my uncle. "Care to try her?"

Rob jumped out of the way like an infielder avoiding a sliding runner. "Watch where you point that thing, mister. It's still loaded."

"Safe's on," the shooter said. "Go ahead."

Rob took the gun, turned it around, and hefted it. "How many shells left in this cannon? Three?"

The shooter nodded. Some of the men squatting on their heels stood up.

"Three eggs," Rob told Clarence, and snapped off the safety.

Clarence sighed. One, two, three eggs sailed into the air. Rob shot three times. A lone egg burst in the air. The others fell back into the garden. One landed intact on the pea vines, and the shooter went over and picked it up.

"Fetch me a glass, will you, bub?"

I went inside the store and got a clean coffee mug from the counter and took it out to him, and he broke the raw egg into it and swallowed it, yolk and white and all in two gulps. "Breakfast," he explained to the crowd. "Only way I could ever get one of these down."

He stuck the shotgun back in its case, and we started for his Pontiac. Singly and in pairs, the spectators came along behind.

"Sharpshooter!" Rob Roy called after him. "I'll bet you my brand-new Hudson Hornet with ten gallons of Flying A gasoline in the tank against that fancy shotgun that I can shoot two birds in the woods for every one of yours."

The shooter kept walking.

Rob ran up and overtook him by his car. "You hear me, mister? My vehicle against your gun I can outshoot you in the woods."

The shooter unlocked the trunk of the gray Pontiac. One by one, he laid the three canvas gun cases on the overcoat. He shut the trunk lid with a puff of dust and turned to look at Rob's Hudson.

"That your rig there?"

"That's my rig. Under four thousand miles on her, radio, doesn't burn a spoonful of oil."

"Heater work good?"

"Mister, that automobile kicks heat like a Round Oak stove in a one-room school."

The shooter walked around to the driver's side and looked in through the open window. The keys dangled in the ignition. He rested his hand on the door. "You mind?"

"No, sir. Go ahead and try her out. Take her for a spin down the country road, open her up wide. Whatever."

The shooter got in and rolled up the driver's window. He leaned across the front seat and cranked the passenger window up tight. He switched on the key and stepped on the starter, and the engine popped right off. He gunned the motor a little. The Hudson idled smoothly.

I expected the shooter to pull away from the store; instead he reached down and turned on the heater. In the packed dirt parking area in front of Clarence's store it was a warm fall day. Inside the Hudson it was getting hotter. Beads of sweat stood out on the shooter's forehead and slid off the tip of his sharp nose. He bent over and turned the heater on full blast and the sweat rolled off his face like water and he gave a small grin like Sam McGee from sunny Tennessee and shut off the engine and got out of the car.

He took a round two-dollar watch out of his pants pocket and frowned at it like a hunter looking at his compass and wondering if he might be lost.

"Be here at two o'clock," he said to Rob.

Evidently the shooter finished his run to Memphremagog early. At one-thirty Uncle Rob and I found him sitting on the porch steps of Clarence's store, drinking from a new pint of Southern Comfort and looking as though he'd just been informed on good authority that he had six months to live.

"Are we still on?" Rob said.

"If you say so," the shooter said unenthusiastically.

My uncle pointed at me. "Austen wants to come too."

"No doubt," the shooter said without looking in my direction. "You boys lead the way. I'll follow along in my old icebox."

Rob drove up the Hollow to my grandparents' place, and up the lane onto the ridge behind Gramp's sugarhouse. When we hit the lane, I looked back and saw the chrome Indian Chief on the Pontiac's hood bucking up and down like the figurehead of a ship in a stormy sea.

We left the cars in the puckerbrush at the upper end of the lane, where it petered out into an old logging trace. The shooter opened his trunk and took out his shotgun. He got a pair of rubbers out of his valise and sat down on the rear bumper and pulled them on over his scuffed brogans.

"The springs in your rig are shot all to hell," I said.

"No call for barbershop talk," he said, yanking at the heel of a rubber. "You was my kid, you'd be cutting a switch about now."

"You ever have any kids?"

"No, praise be."

He stood up and struggled into his overcoat and buttoned it up to the throat.

My uncle stared at him. "Aren't you going to be hot?"

"I hope so," the shooter said. "But I doubt it."

He loaded the shotgun and turned it upside down and shut one eye and squinted down the barrel with the other. I noticed that the safety was off.

"How is it," he said into the gun barrel, "that you ain't off in college? A smart young fella like you."

"I might go next year," Rob said.

"He knows more than most of the professors do already," I said.

The shooter straightened up and gave a sardonic cough.

"Go ahead," I said. "Ask him a question. Any question at all."

"I just did."

"Ask him another one. Baseball. American presidents. Whatever."

The shooter looked off through the fall haze at the hills. "All right," he said. "Where are these so-called birds?"

On the way up through the dying steeplebush and orchard grass, Rob and the shooter agreed on ground rules. As the shooter put it, they would shoot turn and turn about. He would take the first flush,

Rob the second, and so on until one of them had his bag limit of four birds. No one mentioned anything more about two to one odds.

The remnants of an old apple orchard straggled thinly along the fence line between the grown-up field and the woods. The few apples they still produced were wormy and shriveled; nobody bothered to pick them. Here was where my grandfather had first brought me to hunt birds. It was a good spot to see game.

A dark, good-sized partridge flushed out of an ancient Red Astrachan tree a few yards ahead of the shooter. He fired twice after it had already disappeared into some thick softwoods to the left of the trace.

"Man dear," he said. "What in Ned was that?"

"Grouse." Rob grinned at me and winked.

"Why didn't you warn me ahead of time they made such a commotion? Sudden racket like that could give a man a stroke."

We continued up the trace into the woods. It was mixed hardwoods and softwoods, with most of the softwoods sloping off to the left toward a deep ravine and a brook. To our right, maples and birches and beeches spread out over the hillside. Here and there among the tall hardwoods were coverts of barberry, shadblow, hazels, and wild roses with bright orange hips. It was ideal terrain for birds, plenty of feed with heavy cover nearby.

Rob didn't have to wait long for his first shot. Twenty feet in front of us a partridge was dusting itself in the trace. It flew straight out ahead, the easiest wing shot there is; probably he could have gotten it with the shooter's .22.

"One of this year's brood," Rob said when I brought it in. "Poor little dummy. Easy shot compared to yours."

"Don't be second-guessing yourself," the shooter said. "You got him, didn't you?"

He took a drink, stumbled into a swaley depression, stepped over the tops of his rubbers, said "Ned" and "man dear," fired three shots at a bird rocketing out from under a yellow birch into the softwoods and missed all three times. He looked down at his shoes and said with a certain degree of satisfaction, "Sopped through."

"I probably wouldn't even have gotten off a shot," Rob said, grinning at me again.

The shooter was picking stick-me-tights out of his overcoat sleeves. Without looking up he said, "Let's get on with this."

We climbed higher up the ridge. The woods grew denser, the trace fainter.

"Good place to get lost in," the shooter remarked.

"A man can't get lost in this country," Rob said. "You just walk downhill, find a brook, and follow it out to a road."

"Some of us," said the shooter, "might freeze to death before we hit the road. Are we getting up toward the tree line?"

Rob and I had all we could do not to laugh out loud. It was so warm we'd both taken off our jackets and tied them around our waists.

We came into a scattered stand of beech trees. The beechnuts had started to fall, and their prickly brown husks lay open on the leaves around the bases of the smooth gray trunks. Rob stopped on the edge of the grove. I knew he suspected that a bird was nearby, feeding on the nuts. Maybe he'd heard one walking on the dry leaves.

"He calls this being his own pointer," I whispered to the shooter. "If you're perfectly still, they can't stand to wait very long."

"Neither can I," he said. "Winter's drawing closer by the minute."

A bird went up at the far side of the beech trees, a hundred or more yards away. It flew laterally to the trace, appearing in dun-colored flashes between the beech trunks. Rob's gun barrel followed its line of flight. He waited longer than you would suppose even a patient hunter could wait, and finally the partridge veered and came into the opening where the trace ran, and my uncle knocked it cleanly out of the air and into a small copse of fir trees on the edge of the gully.

Rob was ebullient. When I got back with the dead bird, he was saying he'd like to be a sharpshooter too, travel around putting on marksmanship demonstrations and selling ammo. He wondered if the shooter could use an assistant.

The Manchester Arms Company representative looked off in the distance at the red-and-yellow hills. Somewhere he had lost one rubber. His shoes and socks were wringing wet. His pants were splashed with mud up to the fringe of the overcoat, which was bristling with several varieties of burrs. A livid welt zigzagged across his right cheek, where he'd been raked by a blackberry cane.

"Enough's enough, boys," he said, and started back the way we'd come.

Before he'd taken a dozen steps, a partridge flushed out from under a lone wild apple tree we'd walked past not five minutes earlier, and came zooming straight back up the trace at our heads. The shooter took one wild shot, then dropped to the ground. I jumped aside. Rob ducked his head, whirled around, waited until the bird was far enough away for his pattern to spread, and dropped it into the leaves as leisurely as plugging a Campbell's soup can on a stump—turning a nearly impossible shot into a routine one.

"They do that this time of year," he explained to the shooter, who was gulping Southern Comfort. "They get drunk on fermented apples and fly straight at you. Smash into car windshields, house windows, trees even. What do you think about that assistant's position?"

Without a word the shooter headed down the path toward his car.

When we were halfway to the field he stopped suddenly. "What's over yonder?"

"Over where?" Rob said.

"Yonder." The shooter jerked his head toward the ravine.

"Oh, there. A brook runs down through there in the spring. It's mostly dried up this time of year. It's all full of brush."

The shooter veered off the trace toward the gully. He walked purposefully and quickly for a winded and defeated man who had gone through a pint and a half of whiskey since mid-morning, and there was an alarming desperation about the set of his shoulders and the back of his head.

"Watch your step," Rob yelled. "There's a big drop-off over there."

The shooter stopped short at an old barbed-wire fence strung up to keep cows from falling into the ravine years ago when the woods were open pasture. I ran up beside him. We peered over a rusty, single strand of wire embedded inches deep in the trunk of a half-dead maple tree. Far below I could hear the trickle of the diminished brook, but I couldn't see it. It was concealed from bank to bank by softwood slash and brush, and brush trailed down the steep side of the ravine over boulders and stumps and dense berry thickets.

The shooter clicked off the safety of his gun. He put one leg over the fence, caught his overcoat on a barb, and tore a long jagged rent in the lining. He lifted his other leg and momentarily lost his balance. He did a rapid little dance astraddle the fence, waving his gun over his head like a baton. I was afraid he was going to pitch headlong into the ravine or accidentally shoot himself or my uncle or me. Then he was standing on the brink of the gully, looking as unhappy as an aging, wet, and exhausted salesman whose luck had played out at last could possibly look.

He got out his bottle of Southern Comfort and stared at it. There was less than a swallow left in the bottom.

"Story of my life," he said, and flipped the bottle high into the air. It fell into a great pile of brush in the bottom of the ravine.

"Don't take it so—" Rob started to say.

He was cut off by a thunderous roar. The entire gorge seemed to be filled with birds. It was as if someone had tossed a springer spaniel into a covey of eight or ten partridges. In fact, there were only four; but four partridges flushing in four different directions can seem like forty.

I never saw the shooter's gun go up. That's how quick he was. His narrow shoulders swung right and he fired. They swung left and he fired again. He raised the barrel slightly and shot a third time and swung right again and killed the fourth and last bird of his bag limit just as it cleared the opposite bank. The air around us was full of smoke and the scent of gunpowder, and my ears were ringing.

The shooter's voice sounded small and faraway when he said, "Go out around and fetch them birds up, will you, bub? That hollow down there looks colder than Ned's Frigidaire."

When we came back into the meadow where we'd left the cars, it was beginning to get dusky. In the hazy twilight, the bright fall leaves on the hills had faded to a tawny orange. Crickets were singing. It was as warm as an evening in late May.

"All right," Rob said. "How did you know they were there?"

The shooter leaned his gun against the rear bumper of the Pontiac and began to unbutton his overcoat. "Them birds? I watched which way the ones I missed flown. They all flown off toward that quarter."

Rob reached into his pants pocket and got out his keys.

"What's they?"

"You know what they are. You know damn well."

"Oh, them."

The shooter took the keys and unlocked the Hudson's trunk and peered inside. "Needs a good hoeing out, don't she?"

He handed Rob his baseball glove and spikes and two 38-inch Louisville Sluggers. He handed my uncle his three-piece fly rod and fishing basket and toolbox and his rolled-up sleeping bag. He unlocked the trunk of his Pontiac and transferred the cartons of ammunition and his valise to the Hudson. He took off his overcoat, picked out what burrs he could get, spread it lining-up on the floor of the Hudson's trunk, and put the gun cases containing the .22 and .30-30 on top of it. He picked up the shotgun and frowned at it.

"Coming back," he said, frowning at the gun, "it crossed my mind to give this to you. Tell you to practice up, you could maybe be a shooter too."

He put the gun back in its case and put the case on the overcoat and said, "Well, you couldn't."

Rob and I stared at him.

"That's correct," the shooter said in a voice that was almost cheerful. "Like you said earlier, it's ninety percent speed. And you ain't quite quick enough.

"Not quite quick enough," he repeated, and for the first time that day he seemed happy.

He shut the trunk and went around and got into the Hudson. Leaving the driver's door ajar and one foot on the running board, he got a fountain pen and a pad of ammo orders out of his jacket pocket and wrote something on the back of an order blank and handed it and the pen out to Rob.

"Legal bill of transfer," he said. "Sign it."

Rob signed it and gave it and the pen back to the shooter. He did not say a word, but he looked lower than I'd ever seen him look, after losing a ball game in the last inning, or losing a girlfriend, or losing a record trout.

"So," the shooter said, "you ain't getting no nearly new demonstration model pump shotgun to fool yourself with for two, three years until you find out the hard way you ain't quite quick enough for gun club work, county fair work, and have to spend the next thirty years of your life selling shells or clerking in some sporting goods store."

"I could learn," Rob said.

The shooter shook his head. "Quick part can't be learned. Fella has to find what he does best and stick with her. But not this thing. Not for you."

He shut the door and rolled the window partway up and started the engine. Rob turned away.

"You hold on a minute," the shooter said out the top half of the window.

He wrote something on the order pad, tore off the sheet and handed it and the Pontiac keys out to my brother.

"Round one goes to the boot," he said. "Heater's shot. Keep up the Valvoline, she'll get you where you need to go."

He rolled the window all the way up and pulled off the hand brake. Then he unrolled the window six inches. "You might land on your feet yet," he told Rob Roy. "I doubt it. But you might."

He cranked the window back up as far as it would go, leaned over to turn on the Hudson's heater, and drove unhurriedly down the lane and out of sight in the dusk.

The shooter's Pontiac ran all right, on what seemed to me like nearly equal amounts of gas and oil, for the next four years, while Rob was away at the state university. When Rob left Vermont for Alaska, I inherited the car and got another couple of years out of it. Neither of us ever managed to fix the heater so it would work.

The shooter never returned to Kingdom County. His replacement, a young salesman in a white shirt and necktie like any other salesman, knew little about guns. He told Cousin Clarence that our man had requested a transfer to a warmer territory but it was denied and a few months later he'd checked himself into a sanatorium in New Hampshire. The next time the new salesman passed through he said the company had received a burial bill from the sanatorium for two hundred and thirty-five dollars. According to office scuttlebutt, it had been returned unpaid since the company was having financial troubles.

The following fall Manchester Arms stopped sending a representative this far north and Clarence defected to Remington. He was still mad that the company hadn't paid the two hundred and thirty-five dollars, financial difficulties or no; and besides, he told us, Remington shells were eight cents a box cheaper, and probably just as accurate.

7

LOST NATION
CALENDAR

By the early 1950s, my grandparents' way of life in Lost Nation was already long outmoded, even by rural standards elsewhere. With few exceptions farms throughout the rest of Vermont and the nation had already been mechanized for two or three decades, though in Lost Nation we still used horses instead of tractors. For some years after electricity arrived in the Hollow we continued to milk our cows by hand and light the house and barn with kerosene lanterns, and we pumped our washing water by hand throughout my youth on the Farm.

We weren't cut off entirely from the rest of the world; we took our milk to the cheese factory on the edge of the Common three times a week, and our mail was delivered daily to our mailbox just down the Hollow at the end of the lane leading up to my Aunt Maiden Rose's place. But my grandfather's daily paper from St. Johnsbury, forty miles to the south, arrived a day late, so we were usually twenty-four hours behind the news from the rest of the state and nation, as if we lived in an altogether different time zone. Not that it mattered much since most of the natives of Lost Nation and the Kingdom tended to regard themselves as belonging to a separate entity, anyway. Our lives and work were linked much less to Montpelier and Washington than to the harsh yet lovely cycles of the natural world around us.

Spring began each year in Lost Nation with the first strong run of maple sap. Sometime at the end of March or the beginning of April, when the snow still lay deep under my grandfather's eleven hundred maples, there would be two or three sunny days in a row when the temperature would soar into the high thirties, followed by clear, sub-freezing nights. The narrow dirt road connecting us to the outside world thawed into a river of mud. The pond behind the sawmill dam began to thaw, and snowbanks melted, sending dozens of sparkling rivulets rushing down the hillside gullies.

"When the water runs down the hills, the sap runs up the trees," my grandfather would announce. He and I would then pay a visit to his sugar bush, wading up the ridge behind the house through the deep snow to see if the red squirrels had come out to clip off the tender twigs at the ends of the maple branches to drink the new sap. "The squirrels are hanging out their sap buckets, Austen," my grandfather liked to say. This was the sign that it was time for us to tap the maples, and hang our buckets, too.

Like showing our cattle at the fair, maple sugaring more than doubled our regular daily work on the Farm. At the peak of sugaring in the Hollow, school closed for a week or ten days. Everyone helped out. My Big Aunt Maiden Rose, who owned half of the family sugar bush and shared the proceeds with my grandfather, presided over the operation. My little aunts and Uncle Rob helped gather sap. My grandmother's jolly younger sister, my Great Aunt Helen, visited from Boston to help Gram cook for the extra people needing to be fed, including our old cousins, Whiskeyjack and John Wesleyan Kittredge.

Gathering sap was a backbreaking job, and during a big run we gathered all day and sometimes far on into the night. Maiden Rose's matched Morgan team, Henry David and Ralph Waldo, pulled the huge gathering vat on a sledge with wooden runners up and down the steep, snowy slope through the trees. The horses stopped and started on voice commands, but I often had to thrash a hundred yards or more up to my chest in snow to carry the full sap buckets to the vat on the sledge. Snow got down my felt boots, down my wool pants, down my neck. My woolen gloves were sopping wet within an hour. By mid-morning my back ached and by late afternoon my legs felt like lead and I silently cursed the deep snow and the fast-flowing sap and all maple sugaring operations everywhere.

After evening chores and a quick supper, I'd go back to the sugarhouse at the foot of the ridge, where a white plume of steam rose up through the twilit maple branches, and my grandfather and I would hard-boil eggs in the sap and scoop up dippers of snow to eat with fresh hot maple syrup dribbled over it. Then Gramp, who loved sugaring time better than any other part of the year, would tell me stories about the big spring log drives on the Connecticut River of his youth, when he'd run away from Maiden Rose's school to help take one hundred and fifty million feet of logs all the way from the Canadian border to Long Island Sound, and stories about his days as a chainman on crews surveying the American-Canadian Line in the Rocky Mountains, and surveying the border between Labrador and Ungava Quebec.

By degrees, as the days grew warmer, the maple buds began to redden and expand. The syrup darkened into an oily fluid known as blackstrap, good only for shipping in metal drums to the Reynolds Tobacco Company in North Carolina, for sweetening chewing tobacco. One night a warm rain would fall. The ice went out of the river above my grandfather's sawmill in two or three rifle-like reports. In the pasture across from the house a few spring peeper frogs began to sing.

During the next several days we'd pick up our three thousand buckets, rinse them out and stack them inside the sugarhouse. School began again and sugaring was over for another year, though in August my grandfather would bring several big tubs of snow out of his icehouse for sugar-on-snow at the annual Kittredge family reunion, and later that month my grandmother would win another blue ribbon at Kingdom Fair for her maple sugar candies, so blond and delicately sweet that my grandfather never failed to accuse her of lightening them with white cane sugar.

Marly was also Town Meeting month in Lost Nation and throughout Vermont. Town Meeting was held on the first Tuesday of the month at the schoolhouse. My grandfather was among the very few Lost Nation residents who did not attend Town Meeting—the others being shut-ins—but my grandmother and I never missed one, and there was usually still enough hard-packed snow in the road for us to slide down the Hollow to the schoolhouse together on our old travis-sled. No doubt we made an odd sight, my tiny black-clad grandmother sitting in front and steering the sled, and me riding behind her; but there were many odd sights in the Lost Nation of my youth, and I loved gliding fast down the icy road with my grandmother, on our way to Town Meeting.

At the schoolhouse, local government officials were elected: three selectmen, a town road commissioner, a justice of the peace, three school board trustees, a poundkeeper. Proposed budgets were approved or disapproved. Townpersons could and did stand up and say or, as the case often was, shout anything they wanted to. Invariably, Cousin WJ Kittredge delivered a scathing indictment of the rising school costs—$1,348 in 1952, $1,451 in 1953. Several persons rose to their feet and vehemently denounced the state and federal governments. The proposals that Vermont secede from the United States and Kingdom County secede from Vermont were moved and passed, as they had been annually since 1791, when the Green Mountain State first joined the Union. These were the only two measures the people of Lost Nation ever agreed upon unanimously. To me, used to seeing kids squabble every day in the schoolhouse, it was a great treat to see the adults squabble on Town Meeting day. Yet everyone had a say in everything, and anyone with anything to say was listened to. Cousin Clarence Kittredge, in his role as Town Meeting moderator, saw to that.

Always there was a huge noon dinner. Women from up and down the Hollow vied with each other to bring the tastiest casseroles and meat pies. There were fresh rolls, baked beans laced with maple syrup, desserts of all kinds. During the dinner, neighbors who had been at each other's throats all morning chatted and laughed together. A truce was declared until one o'clock, when the meeting resumed. This was the way democracy worked in Lost Nation, and always had.

In the late afternoon some of the men would adjourn to Cousin Whiskeyjack's barn to drink WJ's moonshine whiskey. This too was a long-standing Town Meeting Day tradition. In March of 1950, however, the year I was eight, Cousin John Wesleyan rose at Town Meeting and denounced these drinking sessions in his brother's barn. "The manufacture and consumption of hard spirits is forbidden in this town," the old preacher said angrily. "If the justice of the peace had any grit, this would come to a halt."

Cousin Clarence laid down his moderator's gavel. "Speaking now as town justice," he said, "what a fella makes to consume on his own property has nothing to do with the law, JW. I can't and won't interfere."

As usual, Town Meeting that year ended with no action taken on Cousin WJ's moonshining activities. My grandmother stayed on with some other women to wash dishes and set the schoolroom straight. I headed for home to help my grandfather with barn chores.

A mile north of the schoolhouse, Cousin Whiskeyjack's falling-down old farmhouse sat dark in the late-winter twilight; but a light was on in the barn, and a dozen or so vehicles with chains on their tires sat in the frozen mud of the barnyard. Suddenly an idea occurred to me.

I crept up through the cars and trucks and slipped in through the milk house to WJ's disused milking parlor. Just ahead, in the dim light of a couple of kerosene lanterns, twenty or so shadowy figures were peering down into a large barrel. In the meantime, I'd spotted WJ's big yellow-and-gray rat-fighting cat, Lynx Kittredge, the cat that he'd once informed me was as big as a wheel of cheese. Lynx Kittredge was reclining on a pile of feed sacks on the bow of an old power launch WJ had salvaged from the bottom of Lake Memphremagog years ago. Along the waterline of the launch was a row of neatly-stitched bullet holes, and just below, the words "U.S. BORDER

PATROL,'' written in faded black letters. Lynx Kittredge was staring at the barrel in a way that made me glad that I was not a rat.

I edged up to the rear of the crowd, where the men were talking loudly and exchanging money. Suddenly Bumper Stevens spotted me. Instantly Bumper scooped me up like a young pig. "Looky here what I found, boys. It's old Austen Kittredge's grandboy, come to view the rat fights.''

To me he said, "Look down in that barrel, boy. Ain't that a frightful sight? Count 'em.''

Holding me under my arms, he lifted me over the rim of the barrel. Inside, to my horror, swirling round and round the bottom and leaping partway up the slippery metal sides, were half a dozen huge barn rats with long naked gray tails.

Bumper set me up on a beam above the men, where I could look down into the barrel. "I suppose you think you're a man and a half up there,'' he said good-naturedly. "Witnessing your first rat fight.''

I thought no such thing. At eight I was frightened by the dark barn full of hard-drinking men. Yet I was also deeply interested in what was about to take place, and my fascination was greater than my fear. Below, in the knot of men exchanging money, I recognized Cousin WJ, and the two Kinneson brothers, Resolvèd and Welcome, from the Kingdom Gool, and several other local outlaws.

Bumper took a drink out of a brown bottle someone handed him, and offered me one. "Never mind that,'' Cousin WJ told him. "That boy don't take ardent spirits yet. I've tried him before.''

"Don't take ardent spirits!'' Bumper declared in an outraged voice. "How old be you, boy?''

"Eight,'' I said.

"Eight. And don't take ardent spirits. I suppose,'' he said to WJ, "that he don't swear or smoke or chase after wild women yet, neither.''

"He don't swear or smoke,'' WJ said. "If he chases women, I don't know about it.''

Some of the men laughed.

"You Kittredges up here in the Hollow ain't bringing this boy up right,'' Bumper said. He took a large watch out of his overalls pocket and peered at it and then up at me. "Make a bet, boy. How long will it take WJ's old tom there to dispatch them rats in the barrel? Forty-five seconds? Fifty? Go ahead. Bet. I'll cover it for you."

I had no idea what to say. As an apprentice Methodist, I had been taught by my grandmother never under any circumstances to bet on anything.

"He don't wager, neither. Leave him be," WJ said, to my relief. "Bets are in."

He reached up and grabbed Lynx Kittredge by the back of the double ruff of fur along his thick neck and summarily dropped him into the barrel. Instantly the cat metamorphosed into twenty pounds of pure feline fury. With a great angry hiss and a howl, Lynx Kittredge was on the rats, grabbing them and shaking them and snapping their necks like a terrier dog. From the beam where Bumper had set me I could see everything. The rats squealed and shrieked hideously. Lynx Kittredge hissed like a timber rattler, bayed like his North Woods' namesake. The last surviving rat leaped for him and depended from his notched left ear, and Lynx Kittredge spun over on his back and tore the rat open with his hind claws from neck to tail.

"Thirty-nine seconds," Bumper said. "By Jesus, that's a new record for six rats, boys."

Suddenly the milk house door opened. Everyone turned at once to see who had come in. Outlined against the twilight was a small black-clad figure, holding a lighted lantern.

"Oh, Jesus," WJ said. "It's Mrs. Kittredge."

I was so surprised by the appearance of my grandmother in this most unlikely of places that I scarcely felt alarmed at all. Taking in the scene at a single glance, she set the lantern down just inside the door, and as she did so its dim rays briefly illuminated her sharp features. Her face looked neither angry nor shocked but simply as determined as ever.

"Uh-oh," Bumper said, sweeping me down off the beam. "Here's your boy, Mrs. K. We didn't have nothing to do with how he got here."

My grandmother marched across the barn floor toward the men, many with cash in their hands. She walked by me, stood on her tiptoes, and looked into the barrel. "Ah," she said. She reached down in, seized Lynx Kittredge by his double ruff and drew him out.

"What are you doing, Abiah?" WJ said. "Where are you going with Lynx Kittredge?"

"I'm preventing further cruelty to animals," my grandmother said. "Cats and rats alike. This animal is coming with us. Come along, Tut."

The men stood openmouthed. But no one, even WJ, protested further. Lynx Kittredge was purring loudly. Evidently he recognized an ally in my grandmother. Outside, under the bright March stars, my grandmother set the cat on the travis, and, taking turns, we pulled Lynx Kittredge up the icy road to the Farm in Lost Nation.

WJ never did try to reclaim his cat. Like everyone else in the Hollow, with the possible exception of my Big Aunt Maiden Rose, he was somewhat afraid of my grandmother, who kept Lynx Kittredge for the next five years, renaming him Pharaoh and showering him with all the attention accorded any royal Egyptian cat. My grandfather encouraged him to patrol the barn for rats during the daytime, though he slept most nights in a basket near the stove in the kitchen. When he died of old age, the year I was thirteen, my grandmother had him mounted by a taxidermist in Kingdom Common, and for the rest of her life she kept the mummified remains of Lynx Kittredge, aka Pharaoh, on a shelf in Egypt, where he fit in nicely with her Doomsday Book and other relics.

In late April and well on into May, the Farm was the scene of any number of spring activities: plowing and planting, putting in my grandparents' gardens, mending fences devastated by winter—the list went on and on. Then came June, here before we knew it. June was haying time in Lost Nation. My grandfather waited until a good breeze came out of the northwest, signifying two or three days of clear weather. Then we harnessed up Ralph Waldo and Henry David and cut our fields and Maiden Rose's with a horse-drawn cutter bar, and raked the hay into windrows. The following day we picked it up with Gramp's tall, old-fashioned hayloader. I drove the horses while my grandfather distributed the hay around the wagon with his pitchfork.

Austen Kittredge was a thorough if perpetually disgruntled farmer, and never failed to scythe off by hand the rough places around hedgerows and stone piles where the cutter bar and hay rake couldn't go. Then we'd back the hay wagon up the high drive leading into the big double lofts of the barn. A pair of huge iron hay forks mounted on rails under the barn ceiling dropped down on thick ropes, grabbed big bunches of the hay off the wagon, and hauled them up into the loft. Although they were wonderfully capable horses, Ralph and Henry were skittish around those hooks, which fell from the ceiling onto the load with a great clatter, and they also hated to back up the wagon. My grandfather had to grasp their bridles and walk them up the ramp, coaxing and gentling them along.

Haying was maddeningly hot work. Chaff got down my shirt collar and up under my pants cuffs and in my mouth and nose, causing my eyes to run steadily. The days were as long as they were hot, and there was always the threat of a summer thunderstorm that could spoil a whole field's cutting. Frequently my grandfather's antiquated equipment broke down. Like maple sugaring, haying a hill farm in the pre-mechanized era was a chancy, nerve-wracking job, in which Gramp's patience with me frequently wore thin, and mine with him, and the horses' with both of us. The highlights of the day were the moments when, after helping to unload the wagon, I could run to the milk house cooling tank for the stone jug of switchel, which my grandmother made up each morning and kept full and cool for us there—the traditional northern New England field hands' drink decocted from pure spring water with a touch of vinegar and a touch of molasses.

But by mid-afternoon even the miraculous restorative powers of switchel were not enough to make haying anything but a grueling chore. It was a relief for us all when the bulk-tank law prohibiting the shipping of milk in cans was passed and my grandfather, like many another Vermont hill farmer stranded off on roads no milk truck could possibly negotiate during much of the winter or mud season, sold his milking cows and concentrated his activities on his lumbering operation.

One of the very real perils of haying with horses was that a horse could at any time step in a woodchuck hole and break its leg. Therefore my grandfather shot all woodchucks on sight, and at the age of nine, I began to hunt these otherwise harmless rodents myself with a light .22 Gramp had given me. Right after the first cutting in June was the best time to spot 'chucks; and I loved to go out in the evening after supper and walk the stubbly summer fields with my grandfather, looking for them. Other regular pests and, for me, fair game on the farm included pigeons, which were terribly messy, and which my grandparents encouraged me to pick off the ridge of the barn and the top of the silo with my .22; porcupines, or hedgehogs, as Gramp called them, which would chew their way through a half-inch plank to get into our woodshed, icehouse, and outbuildings; and, worst of all, a plague of white rats, the descendants of an escaped pair of tame ones my little aunts had given me as pets for my tenth birthday: against which, with traps, poison, and a veritable squadron of scrawny barn cats, not to mention the formidable Lynx Kittredge, my grandfather waged a no-holds-barred war; but we could see no diminution in their numbers, which were now beginning to breed with the indigenous population of brown barn rats to be found on all Vermont hill farms, to produce an especially large, bi-colored, prolific, and intelligent hybrid rodent that even Lynx Kittredge had trouble catching.

Finally, in the summer of 1952, my grandfather sent away for a pair of very lively, six-foot-long Kentucky blacksnakes, which he promptly christened Cole and Bob Younger and released in the barn. Not only did the Younger Boys all but eradicate the hybridized rats; they served the unanticipated function of scaring the daylights out of uninvited and unwanted visitors to my grandfather's barn. One of their favorite basking spots was the lintel shelf just inside the milk house door. From here the Boys would casually lower the front third or so of their thick, jet-black bodies, and flick their split tongues inquisitively in the faces of astonished and terror-stricken milk inspectors, tax assessors, border patrol agents searching for illegal aliens, and other undesirable guests, who rarely tarried longer than the time it took them to reach their parked vehicles at a dead run. "They went back down the Hollow quicker than they came up," my grandfather liked to say about these visitors. Of course the introduction of Cole and Bob to the Farm in Lost Nation also enhanced my grandfather's local reputation for misanthropy, though in fact the Younger Boys were perfectly harmless and actually quite amicable—unless, of course, you were a rat.

I, for my part, didn't mind the blacksnakes at all. I don't know that one could call them affectionate; but they were tame enough, and allowed me to lug them around the barn draped over my neck and arms for hours on end. I did notice that the barn cat litters seemed to fall off at about the time of the snakes' arrival, but we never actually saw one of the Boys go after a kitten, and very probably most of the adult cats just exercised the better part of feline valor and moved down the road to another barn.

Now, as my grandfather very well knew at the time he ordered the snakes, my grandmother had a great hatred and loathing for serpents of any stripe. Woe betide the garter snakes—more commonly known in the Kingdom County of my youth as "gardener" snakes—she came across in her flowerbeds or pea patch if her hoe was handy; and she had more than once instructed me, in great seriousness, that when I became a famous archaeologist like Mr. Howard Carter, I must never neglect to wear snake boots when poking around the pyramids. Many times during my boyhood Gram reminded me that it was a poisonous asp with which the love-lorn Egyptian princess Cleopatra had taken her own life; and one of the most horrifying clippings in her Doomsday Book of catastrophic local newspaper accounts described, in lurid detail, the horrible death by snakebite of a young man known as "Lucky" LaPorte, who, while unloading a bunch of green bananas from a freight car in Kingdom Common in 1921, was bitten on the neck and killed nearly instantly by a fer-de-lance hidden in with the fruit.

After the advent on the Farm of the Younger Boys, my grandmother assiduously avoided the barn. During haying time, instead of setting the switchel jug inside the cooling tank in the milk house, she left it outside the door in the shade of her hollyhocks. And when my grandfather teased her one evening, by threatening to bring the

Boys into the kitchen for a fireside chat, she declared that if the blacksnakes ever appeared within one hundred feet of the house, their remaining minutes would be as numbered as Lucky LaPorte's after his sad encounter with the fer-de-lance.

"If those vipers come sashaying in here, Mr. Kittredge, their sashaying days will end on the spot," my grandmother said. "You may inform them I said so."

"Why don't you inform them yourself?" my grandfather said. "That way they'd know you meant it."

My grandmother gave a sigh, and did not reply.

"I guess Grandma's afraid to go down to the barn," my grandfather said.

"Don't call me Grandma," my grandmother said. "I'm a mother and a grandmother. Not a grandma."

But I noticed that she did not deny being afraid of the Kentucky blacksnakes. It was hard for me to believe that my grandmother feared anything on earth; but I understood that some people seemed to be born with an aversion to snakes; perhaps my grandmother was one of these persons.

The next morning when I came around from the hayloft to get the jug of switchel, my grandmother met me in the barnyard. "Tut," she said, "do you think your grandmother is afraid of those reptiles?"

"No," I said doubtfully. "Of course not. You're not afraid of anything, Gram."

"Come," she said, seizing my wrist.

She led me across the barnyard and into the milk house.

Sure enough, one of the Younger Boys—I could never tell Cole from Bob—was reposing on the lintel shelf. With that effortless gliding motion peculiar to snakes when they are unalarmed, he shifted himself and depended over the shelf a couple of feet to examine this new interloper. He flicked out his double tongue and as he did so my grandmother grasped him behind the head. "Get behind me, Satan!" she said, looking him right full in the face from less than a foot away.

She released him unharmed and we returned to the barnyard. Only then did she give a little shudder.

"I knew you weren't scared of those old snakes, Gram," I said with tremendous relief. I couldn't wait to tell my grandfather what had happened.

But again my grandmother reached out and took my wrist. She fixed her dark, kind eyes on me, and with another small shudder she said, "Yes, I am, Tut. I'm terrified half to death by the creatures."

I didn't understand. "But, Gram, you were braver than the milk inspectors, the tax men—any of them."

"Ah," my grandmother said. "Then you've learned an important lesson."

"What lesson, Gram?"

"That being brave has nothing to do with being unafraid," she said, heading up for the house. "Never forget that, Tut."

For three or four weeks each year, in what we called high summer, between the first and second cuttings of hay, my grandfather subcontracted from the International Boundary Commission in Washington, D.C., the job of clearing the sector of the American-Canadian border running between Kingdom County and southern Quebec. The Vista, as the Canadian Line was sometimes called, was a thirty-foot-wide strip of unfenced and unguarded no-man's-land which, in Vermont, happens to coincide with the Forty-fifth Parallel circling the globe exactly halfway between the Equator and the North Pole. For many years, my grandfather had been responsible for clearing the stretch from the Upper Connecticut River separating Vermont's eastern boundary from New Hampshire, all the way to the Green Mountain Range, just north of Jay Peak, to the west: a total distance of about seventy miles. Each summer he cleared a segment of approximately ten miles.

In addition to cutting down the ever-encroaching brush and trees, and repairing any damage to the granite monuments set a mile apart along the Vista, my grandfather sometimes had to resurvey the boundary where it followed a changing streambed or river. Using survey chains and his theodolite, which he referred to as the instrument, and taking most of his sightings several times, he prided himself on registering some of the most precise latitudinal recordings along the entire thirty-five-hundred-mile border from eastern Maine to western Washington.

From my first summer on the Farm, I'd worked with Gramp on this annual project. We'd leave home in the lumber truck each morning as soon as we finished our barn chores and return in time for evening chores and supper, after a long day in the woods. Much of the border country between Vermont and Quebec was still quite wild in those days, accessible only by single-lane, corduroy lumbering traces, and clearing the remote terrain was ideal work for a boy. I liked learning how to use a one-man bucksaw and an ax, and as I grew older, I mastered the technique of reading the theodolite as well. Sometimes, too, under my grandfather's stern direction, I reset missing brass monument plates in the granite obelisks along the Vista.

Over the huge noon dinners my grandmother packed for us, my grandfather told me stories of his travels, and as we looked off along the Vista while eating, I liked thinking that it stretched all the way across the country. It seemed somehow to link me with the fabulous places it bisected: Niagara Falls, the Great Lakes, and the Great High Plains. Someday I would see those places for myself. In the meantime, I was content to work in the Vermont woods with the man I most admired of all the men in the world, my grandfather and namesake, Austen Kittredge.

Not all of the exotic places along the Line were as faraway as the Rockies or even Niagara Falls. There was, for instance, the enclave of collapsing wooden frame buildings just south of the border and less than a mile west of my grandfather's hunting camp known as Fort Kittredge. Fort Kittredge had originally been just that, a tiny stockade where, according to my grandfather, our Loyalist forebears had stockpiled muskets and ammunition in anticipation of that glorious day when the British Red Coats would march south to retake Vermont and the United States. Later, the place had been used as a lumber camp, a hideout for Chinese alien smugglers, and, during Prohibition, a rendezvous for whiskey runners. To me, it was a spooky yet fascinating spot. I liked exploring it—in the daylight, with my grandfather.

Quite frequently, my grandfather hired his two old cousins,

Whiskeyjack Kittredge and his brother, Preacher John Wesleyan Kittredge, to help us with our work. Like my grandfather, who despite his alleged antisocial behavior had the greatest relish for eccentric and unusual characters, I loved to get my two ancient cousins going, as we called it. In fact, this was never very hard to do.

Cousin WJ began each working day like a house afire, hacking away at the encroaching brush like a man possessed. By mid-morning, he invariably ran out of steam and slipped off to fish a nearby brook or nap in the sun with his slouch hat pulled down over his eyes. Still, he was fond of drawing me aside and inveighing against the low wages paid to him by my grandfather. And he filled my head with all kinds of wild, unlikely tales, which I was always ready to listen to.

"Have you ever bedded down two women to once, boy?" he inquired of me one afternoon when I was eight or nine. "I did one time, in a whorehouse up to Montreal." Under Cousin WJ's tutelage I became intimately acquainted by the ripe old age of ten with the delectations of Montreal whorehouses, which he had no doubt learned about from his endless stock of F•U•C•K Books, since my grandfather confided to me that WJ had never been to Montreal in his life.

Preacher John Wesleyan seemed equally determined to enlighten me in matters at the spiritual end of the spectrum. JW refused to work within earshot of WJ and my grandfather, whom he characterized as blasphemers and heretics. This charge seemed especially unfair in the light of my grandfather's very genuine concern for Preacher JW's safety and welfare. At eighty, our sanctimonious old cousin the lay preacher was rather stiff and tottery. Each morning, my grandfather carried JW's ax, saw, and lunch to the section of the Line where he would be working, half a mile or so from the rest of us, blasphemers that we were. As the day progressed, Gramp dispatched me several times to "check up on the pious old son of a bitch and make sure he was all right." But Gramp's charitable solicitude did nothing to soften Cousin John Wesleyan's condemnations of my grandfather's soul to eternal perdition.

"Ain't that a lovely prospect, boy?" JW said to me one noon when I was checking up on him for my grandfather. He pointed off over a typical Kingdom County landscape of distant, dark green mountains, with lighter green farms running up into their foothills. It was as various and beautiful a view, no doubt, as nearly any in the world. But without waiting for me to reply, the preacher declared, "Vermont's beauty is as nothing compared to the splendor of God's Paradise. And do you know what I anticipate most about dwelling there? Do you, boy?

"I'll tell you," he continued. "What I most look forward to in Paradise is the prospect of being there alone, without my scofflaw brother or your grandfather to trouble me."

"Where will they be, Cousin JW?"

"Oh, we won't talk about that now," he said in a merry voice, crinkling up his eyes with glee. "We won't ruin our day by going into that, boy."

Quite often, the black flies and mosquitoes along the Line were fierce, and their numbers legion. In places the brush we cut was so thick that you couldn't have fallen down if you had tried. I did not always relish being the butt of Whiskeyjack's ribald jokes and John Wesleyan's tirades. Still, I learned things working up in the woods on the border with those hard old men that I would not have been apt to learn anywhere else; and I am nearly as grateful for that experience as I am for my free education at the state university. For I think that the likes of Cousin Whiskeyjack, Cousin John Wesleyan, and my Grandfather Austen Kittredge himself will not soon be seen again, in Vermont or elsewhere.

In the middle of September, the hills of Kingdom County shone gloriously red and yellow and gold. Then at the peak of the fall foliage season, my grandfather began going to the woods again, now to cut timber for his sawmill. On weekends I accompanied him.

As I grew older, my job was to skid the logs down to the mill with Maiden Rose's horses, Henry David and Ralph Waldo, which my grandfather used in exchange for helping Rose with her maple sugaring and haying. Later on in the fall, I worked Saturdays and after school sweeping up sawdust or tailing one of the saws in Gramp's mill below the pond.

The sawmill, with its big whirling log-saw, its several razor-sharp smaller saws and its shrieking planer, was a dangerous and fascinating place. What I liked best about it was my grandfather's cramped office, jutting out over the penstock. Gramp's office contained a pot-belly stove, a rolltop desk, and two or three straightback chairs. It was cluttered with bills and order forms, antique saw-files, worn-out gears, wooden boxes full of drill bits and nails of all sizes, chalklines and measuring tapes. Best of all was an ancient, battery-operated Stromberg Carlson radio as large as a big bread-box, on which my grandfather listened to the news and weather from Montreal.

On certain clear fall and winter evenings, when the reception was good, my grandfather and I convened around the pot-belly stove in his sawmill office to listen to our favorite programs. We especially loved Lowell Thomas's travelogues. Two programs my grandfather heartily despised yet rarely missed were *Sergeant Preston of the Yukon* and *Our Miss Brooks*. Gramp regarded Sergeant Preston as a bold-faced imposter, a deep-voiced charlatan who knew nothing about the Far North. And he disliked *Miss Brooks* for the singular reason that in it, Eve Arden played the part of a schoolteacher.

Gramp loved Jack Benny and detested a detective thriller called *The Shadow*. Many times he declared that if Lamont Cranston, aka the Shadow, ever came slinking around the Farm in Lost Nation with his wild laugh, he'd be a shadow, all right—a shadow of his former self.

I loved listening to the Stromberg Carlson with my grandfather. The big red and green tubes winked and flashed like Christmas lights. My grandfather scowled. And I sat enthralled by the crackling old radio, magically bringing the outside world up over the rugged hills and mountains to Lost Nation Hollow, where electricity was still years away.

My grandfather was one of the few remaining hunters in Kingdom County who, each November, still ventured up to the high hardwood ridges, far from roads and road hunters, and shot one big buck each year. And although he refused to shoot a bear, which, he pointed out, after it has been skinned has an uncanny resemblance to a human being, Austen Kittredge was a lightning-quick wing-shot with his old double-barreled twelve-gauge. Frequently when I got home from school on October afternoons we went up to the overgrown apple orchard behind the house and Gramp filled the game pocket of his red-and-black wool hunting jacket with a limit of four partridges. And he was pure hell on ducks and geese, though you'd never catch Austen Kittredge holed up in a heated duck blind with a steaming jug of coffee. Instead, my grandfather loved to walk the marshy riverbanks below his sawmill on sleeting gray fall mornings and jump-shoot male mallards with their brilliant emerald heads and big black ducks with blue epaulets on their wings, not to mention the little wood ducks, colorful as tropical parrots—though he wouldn't shoot a merganser, or allow me to shoot one after I started to hunt ducks with him, because mergansers tasted fishy, like their diet, and my grandfather did not hold with shooting any game that he did not intend to eat.

Of course my Uncle Rob Roy and my father were both expert hunters, and fishermen, too, having been taught at a very early age by my grandfather, who, for all his prejudices against schools and schoolteaching, was himself a superb instructor.

"Cast short and straight," he'd say, showing me how to cast a wet fly with his limber bamboo rod, as we stood by the sawmill pond after supper. "I won't fish with a fancy-dan caster, Austen."

"Don't ever be in a hurry in the woods. Take one step and look around. That way you'll always have seen something, whether you get anything or not."

Again it is October of my sixth year. It is late afternoon, and my grandfather and I are sitting on his homemade deer-stand platform, fifteen feet up in a butternut tree on the Canadian Line a mile west of Labrador. Although deer season is still a month away, and I am still several years away from the time when I will be ready to handle a rifle myself, my grandfather wants me to see a deer from the stand. He wants me to have that experience with him. So we sit waiting, as the fall evening fast descends, hoping that one will appear to feed on the grass in the Vista. Suddenly, as if from nowhere, a great horned owl flies into the butternut tree and alights on a nearby branch. He

cranes his head down at the fallen butternuts below, no doubt looking for mice, then spots us. In total silence he swoops off the limb
and into the woods. No deer comes that evening, but over the years
that moment when my grandfather and I and the huge owl all sat
silently in the tree together will become a nearly mystical memory
for me.

Four years pass. By now I have seen plenty of deer from my
grandfather's stand in the butternut tree, and other remarkable
things as well. Together my grandfather and I sat on the platform
and watched a bobcat stalk a porcupine. We've seen a flock of angry
crows mob a barred owl, sitting imperturbable in the top of a big
black spruce as they dive-bomb it. We've watched a full-grown bull
moose saunter unconcerned straight down the middle of the Line.

Today is a chilly November dawn in deer season, my first season
to hunt from the stand alone. I know that my grandfather and
Cousin Clarence and Rob Roy and my father are hunting along the
ridge somewhere to the south of where I am waiting. Cousins WJ
and JW are hunting the ridge to the west. All of them are trying to
push a buck my way, though if one crosses their sights they will of
course shoot it themselves.

Shortly after dawn I hear the short bark of Rob's .30-30, once,
from the big beaver swamp behind Maiden Rose's Home Place, and
I am quite certain that he has killed his deer. My grandfather has
taught me that a single shot in deer season usually means a clean
kill. A couple of hours later, I hear three louder shots—probably
Cousin WJ's .30-06. This is a maybe. Maybe he got his deer on the
second or third shot, maybe not. Near noon, another single shot.
This sounds like my father's .278, from a couple of miles to the
west. So I know that regardless of whether I get my deer today, by
evening there will very probably be at least two bucks hanging from
the beam extending out from the woodshed attached to the side of
Labrador. I sit in the stand all afternoon, hearing one more shot,
another .30-30 from far off in the mountains. No deer comes out
onto the Line. At dusk my grandfather appears to walk back to the
camp with me, where three big deer are hanging from the beam.

The following November I shoot my first buck from the stand, a
six-pointer. Back at Labrador, I eat some of the liver, broiled over

hardwood coals in the camp stove, and don't like it but don't say so. From now on I will shoot a deer each fall during my boyhood in Lost Nation including a ten-pointer weighing two hundred and thirty pounds, which Cousin Clarence will photograph with me standing beside it. Clarence tacks the snapshot up on the camp wall beside a couple of dozen others of my grandfather and Rob and Dad and my other uncles and cousins, with their trophy deer, where the snapshot remains to this day.

Much of December on the Farm in Lost Nation was devoted to Christmas. Although my grandmother accused my grandfather of not keeping Christmas at all, this was not precisely the case. Always, Gramp cut the Christmas tree, taking me along with him. He picked a big, handsome, blue-green balsam fir, which he'd usually selected two or three years earlier, pruning it carefully and keeping it clear of other encroaching trees and brush. At six, seven, and eight years old, I rode the tree home, like a horse, while my grandfather skidded it along over the snow. When I was too big to ride the Christmas tree I helped my grandfather pull it.

My grandmother put the tall fir in the best parlor. Without electricity, we had no Christmas lights, and Gram wouldn't dream of using candles because of the fire hazard. Instead we trimmed the tree with gold and silver tinsel and lovely colored glass balls, some as large as baseballs and more than one hundred years old.

With the exception of my grandfather, the whole family convened at the Farm on Christmas Eve, including my strict old Big Aunt Maiden Rose, the ex-schoolteacher; my grandmother's younger sister from Boston, my Great Aunt Helen, who made fun of everyone and everything; my father and little aunts; Rob Roy—even my old cousins, Whiskeyjack and John Wesleyan. Gramp, for his part, repaired to Labrador immediately after Christmas Eve evening chores. His absence hung over me like a snow cloud as we opened our presents Christmas morning and ate our festive meal at noon; but after dinner I was allowed to take a big plateful of turkey and trimmings up to the camp, and to keep Christmas there with him for the rest of the day.

"You and your grandfather are as like as two peas in a pod," my grandmother said with a sigh. And it is true that I would much rather be off at Labrador with Gramp than socializing with the family below.

"What's this?" he invariably demanded when I handed him the heaping platter, which he set aside on a shelf. Then he'd fry us a big slab of venison smothered with onions, lace it with plenty of salt and pepper, and we'd eat the deer steak together at the camp table with the greatest satisfaction in the world.

When we finished the venison my grandfather got down the pint of cherry brandy he kept on a shelf below his maps of Labrador and the Far North and poured himself a generous Christmas cordial in his tin tea mug.

"Well," he said, "what are the rest of them up to down below, Austen?"

"Eating, mainly. After breakfast we exchanged Christmas presents."

"I never exchanged presents with anybody in my life," my grandfather said. He fixed his pale blue eyes on me. "Do you think I did?"

I did not, and said so, though I knew that my grandfather was in no way an ungenerous man. It was just that one of his many peculiarities was his inability to receive a gift of any kind.

"Have they been talking about me? Hashing over my shortcomings?"

"No," I said. "They wouldn't dare."

He frowned and looked somewhat disappointed.

"Last night we read Christmas stories out of the Bible," I ventured.

My grandfather snorted and poured himself another jolt of brandy. "I'll read them something if they aren't cleared out of the house by morning. And it won't be a Christmas story."

My grandfather turned down the lantern on the table, and blew it out. He got into his lined sheep coat, opened the camp door and we stepped out into the cold December dusk. "Chore time," he said.

Then he looked at me in the fading light of the holiday afternoon, and in a voice so harshly ironic it was nearly cheery, he said, "Merry Christmas, Austen."

8

FAMILY REUNION

Among the hundreds of old photographs in the albums stashed away in my grandparents' farmhouse attic, my favorites were a series of formal ensembles from Kittredge family reunions. They covered a span of many decades, dating back to some ancient tintypes of family gatherings in the 1850s. That, according to my little aunts, is when Kittredges started to range out from Lost Nation Hollow to other parts of the country, and the tradition of the annual family reunion first began.

To me, there was also a spooky quality about these photographs. It was always a trifle unsettling to come face to face with the likenesses of my older relatives when they were young. My grandfather at twelve bore an uncanny resemblance to Rob Roy at about the same age in a reunion photo taken thirty years later. And here in several pictures was my father, tall for his age and athletic-looking, his expression studious and rather impatient, as though waiting for that moment when he could leave the Farm for the university. My grandmother, for her part, was instantly recognizable by her tiny stature, black dress, and stern visage. In fact, she looked almost totally unchanged over nearly half a century of reunions; that, at least, was reassuring.

The Kittredge family reunion photographs were usually taken in the dooryard of the Home Place, as my Big Aunt Maiden Rose's farm a quarter mile down the Hollow from my grandparents' place was called. Family members arrayed themselves on and in front of the porch, some standing, some leaning against the four wooden porch posts, some sitting in canvas camp chairs. The kids were sprawled on the grass or perched on the porch railing. It was disconcerting to me to note, however, the photographs of some of these same kids laid out in state in coffins in a special section in my grandmother's Doomsday Book.

Of course the further back toward the turn of the century the reunion photographs went, the fewer people I recognized. At the same time, the pre-twentieth-century reunions were much larger. A typical tintype from 1885 showed one hundred and ten Kittredges and in-laws. By the late 1940s, when I first began appearing in the photographs, we were down to a mere thirty-five.

My little aunts, Klee and Freddi, were as interested in the family reunion photographs as I was. Right up to my early teens, they loved nothing better than to whisk me off to the big, square, multi-windowed cupola atop the farmhouse, where for hours on end they brushed one another's gorgeous long hair in the sunlight and conducted lengthy genealogical explanations of who was who in the old photographs, always laying the strongest emphasis on the unpleasant secrets of our more unusual Kittredge forebears. In fact, Freddi and Klee seemed hell-bent to divulge every family horror imaginable during our Sunday School lessons in the cupola.

"Here's your Great-Grandpa Gleason Kittredge again, Austen. Grandpa Gleason was the gentleman farmer of the family. He sat around the house for fifty years in a white shirt and necktie, and carried that swirly-colored glass cane you've seen down at the Home Place in the parlor, and never did a tap of work in his life. This was taken about a year before he went mad and tried to blow up the farmhouse and had to be confined in the cedar-pole cage in Maiden Rose's attic."

"Here's our Great-Uncle Cy. Great-Grandpa Gleason's brother. He taught classics at the state university until he went round the bend. We called him Cyrus the Great, remember, Klee? That's who he thought he was those last years of his life."

On they went, in hushed and delighted tones. My grandfather's first appearance in a reunion photograph—a toddler in one of the odd white dresses children of both sexes wore in those days—reminded my little aunts of yet another family scandal. In fact, it was Freddi and Klee, during one of our Sunday School lessons, who first revealed to me my grandfather's mysterious origin as a foundling, and the true significance of the ritual in which he informed me that the meanest old bastard in Kingdom County lived on our farm, never failing to enjoin me to remember that I had *heard it first from him*. According to my little aunts, my grandfather had been discovered as a newborn baby on the farmhouse porch of Maiden Rose's Home Place in a California orange crate. The crate was lined with an old coat, my aunts said, to which was pinned a note consisting of the following two lines:

> *"Take me in and treat me well*
> *For within this house doth my parent dwell."*

Hence the ironical piquancy of my grandfather's frequent meanest-old-bastard declaration to me; and my little aunts' conspiratorial intimation that since Maiden Rose had immediately come home from college to care for my foundling grandfather, she might actually be that unnamed parent in the note found with the baby. "It would certainly account for Aunt Rose's harsh treatment of him," Klee said.

Nor, during our perusals of the family reunion photographs, did my melodramatic little aunts neglect to point out my Big Aunt Maiden Rose Kittredge's ex-student at the Lost Nation Atheneum, and dear friend and bosom companion, April Mae Swanson. After losing both parents while she was still in school, April Mae had lived with Maiden Rose on the Home Place for twenty years, until her own early death in 1920. Long before I had the faintest glimmering what the term implied, my aunts gleefully whispered to me that April Mae had also been Maiden Rose's lover. "If you're going to be heard from, Austen," they frequently told me in order to justify such unusual disclosures to an eight-, nine-, and ten-year-old, "you must know *all* the family history."

As I entered my teenage years and enrolled at the Kingdom Common Academy, continuing to stay with my grandparents in Lost Nation, I visited my Big Aunt Maiden Rose frequently, helping her get in firewood and shoveling out her dooryard in the winter, though far less from the goodness of my heart than because my grandparents insisted that I do so. After Maiden Rose's eyesight began to fail in her eighties, I stopped by two or three evenings a week to read aloud to her. She especially liked Shakespeare; and sometimes as I sat under her critical pale blue gaze at the beautiful applewood table in her kitchen, reading the wonderful old plays to her, she'd get out a shoebox of letters April Mae had written to her from Boston, where April had attended college for a year.

In the reunion pictures, April always looked like a student, smallish with a pretty face. She was buried in the Kittredge family graveyard above the Home Place, and each fall when Gramp and I cut balsam boughs to bank the outside foundation of our farmhouse and Maiden Rose's, we cut an extra load for Rose to weave into a thick evergreen grave-blanket to put over April's plot for winter.

"Maiden Rose never fully recovered from April Mae's death," my little aunts told me. "It was a tragic blow to her, Austen. You must take that into account when she seems bad-tempered to you."

"Daughters!" my grandmother called sharply up the cupola stairs from the attic below. "You, Cleopatra and Nefertiti! What are you filling Tut's head with up there?"

"Just a little Sunday School lesson, Mom," my little aunts would call back down; and as soon as Gram's footsteps retreated, they'd launch into yet another sensational saga.

"Who's this?" I asked one afternoon when I was about seven. I pointed at a long-haired, handsome young woman astride one of my Big Aunt Maiden Rose's matched team of Morgan horses, Henry David and Ralph Waldo. The young woman on the horse was partway up the hillside pasture behind Rose's place, in the background of a reunion photograph.

"We've been waiting for you to ask us about her, Austen." Freddi said. "That's Great-Aunt Liz."

She and Klee exchanged a deeply significant look, then nodded. "The bank robber!" they said almost in unison.

Over the next several years, I heard many wonderful stories about my Great-Aunt Liz. Liz was my grandfather's and Maiden Rose's younger sister by my Great-Grandfather Gleason's second wife. She'd been married four times—four times that Klee and Freddi knew of, that is. She was a celebrated practical joker, an expert horsewoman and markswoman, and, since the age of sixteen, when she'd run away from home for the first time, she had conducted a passionate love affair with the American West.

Of all my independent-minded relatives, Aunt Liz was universally agreed upon to be the most so. She had even refused to have her picture taken from the age of four, covering her face or running away from the camera. And from her boldly-curious expression in the single extant snapshot we owned of her as an adult, sitting on the Morgan in the far background of the family reunion assemblage, it seemed that she had no earthly idea that she, too, would appear in that photograph.

As I grew older, I learned to take some of Freddi and Klee's tales with a grain of salt. Not that they told me any outright untruths in our Sunday School lessons. But both of my little aunts were inveterate embellishers who knew all about how to make a good story better in the telling. Yet when it came to Aunt Liz and the bank robbery, most of the other grownups I knew would tell me exactly the same story. On May 13, 1941, around noon, a single masked bandit of about Liz's build, wielding a pearl-handled revolver, had held up the First Farmers' and Lumberers' Bank of Kingdom Common, and gotten away scot-free with slightly over forty-two thousand dollars. My little aunts professed to believe that Liz had buried the loot somewhere on Maiden Rose's or my grandparents' farm before going West again the next year, intending to return for it at some point in the future. The fact that she had not done so in almost fifteen years somehow enhanced the story. As for Liz herself, she was already something of a myth, at least in Kingdom County, even before the supposed robbery. Year after year, my fondest hope was that she would someday return to the Hollow in a blaze of glory, so that I could meet this family legend face to face.

After I moved up to Lost Nation to live with my grandparents, I began to make my own appearance in the annual reunion photographs. By the late 1940s the reunions had become peripatetic affairs, stretching out over the entire length of the Hollow, like medieval fairs. They officially began around ten in the morning with the solemn ritual of visiting and cleaning the small family graveyard on the hill above the Home Place, followed by the big noon picnic at my grandparents'. In mid-afternoon, activities shifted to the ball diamond behind Cousin Clarence's store at the foot of the Hollow, for the family baseball game. We reconvened around seven at the Home Place for Rose's traditional Elizabethan festival, in which my scholarly great-aunt produced, directed, and starred in an abridged version of a different Shakespeare play each year. The reunions ended with a corn roast and sugar-on-snow party and dance at the schoolhouse. Throughout the day, some of the men relatives slipped down to Cousin Whiskeyjack Kittredge's barn to sample his latest batch of white mule moonshine; and any kids who wanted to were welcome to visit my grandfather, who, characteristically, spent the day working at his sawmill or up in the woods.

The family reunion was always slated for the second Saturday of August. Invitations were sent out by Maiden Rose, who also dispatched a hundred or so special summonses to her ex-students and other interested community members, to attend the Shakespeare play and the party afterward. In the summer of 1957, however, the summer I turned fifteen, the future of the annual family reunion was uncertain. At eighty-four, beset by near blindness and rheumatoid arthritis, Maiden Rose was bowed over almost into a hoop. She now required two canes to walk; and while there was no outright talk about canceling future reunions, there were telling hints.

The play Maiden Rose had selected for presentation that summer was *The Tempest*. Naturally my great-aunt cast herself in the role of the ancient magician Prospero, and at the auditions in mid-July, Little Aunt Freddi tearfully told Klee and me that when Prospero put aside his book of spells at the end of the play, it would signify the finality of both Maiden Rose's reign on the Home Place as the dowager empress of the Kittredge family, and of the tradition of the family reunions themselves.

As far as the Elizabethan festival went, I could only hope that Freddi was right. For although I had nothing much against the reunions themselves, I despised being dragooned into acting in those plays. I knew, however, that there was no way of weaseling out of this onerous family obligation, and only prayed that I would not have to act the part of a girl or woman. As the '57 reunion approached, I was somewhat encouraged to discover that there was only one female part in *The Tempest*. But at the audition I had a few very bad moments, fearing I might be tapped for Ariel, which I instantly recognized as the sort of sexually ambiguous role that some malign fate would delight in reserving for a boy of fifteen. Two summers ago I'd been forced to prance around as Puck in *A Midsummer Night's Dream;* as a result, I have looked unkindly on that lark of a play ever since.

Fortunately, Ariel was snapped right up by Klee, whose beauty was still quite boyish. Miranda went to lovely, brown-eyed Freddi; young Ferdinand to Jim Kinneson from Kingdom Common; and the monster Caliban, whose lines Maiden Rose had cut to a few manageable surly rejoinders, to our moonshining Cousin Whiskeyjack. I got off lightly with the Boatswain's part.

The rehearsals proceeded smoothly. Three or four times a week we convened after supper at the high drive behind Maiden Rose's hay barn, where the Home Place pastures sloped up sharply on three sides to form a natural amphitheater. Rose's shortened version of the play took about forty-five minutes to perform; and under her exacting direction, there was no doubt that, as Editor Charles Kinneson invariably put it in his review of her productions in *The Kingdom County Monitor*, Maiden Rose Kittredge would once again present "the most spirited summer Shakespeare in all Lost Nation Hollow."

A few days before the reunion, I helped Maiden Rose convert the high drive and entryway of the hay barn into a makeshift stage for the play. Also I let her use me as a tailor's dummy while she put the finishing touches on this year's costumes, including her own fantastical magician's cloak. And although nothing I did, then or ever, was quite right so far as my elderly aunt was concerned, we somehow got through that week together without a blowup.

Then on the evening before the big event something happened to put the 1957 reunion in an entirely different light. It was the totally unanticipated and unannounced arrival in Kingdom Common, on the seven-ten p.m. passenger train from Montreal and points west, of my Great-Aunt Liz, the alleged bank robber.

I was the only one at home when she called the Farm to say she'd arrived and needed a ride out to Maiden Rose's. My grandfather was up at Labrador, my grandmother was blackberrying in the cut-over woods upriver in Idaho, my little aunts, who by then were living in New York, had not arrived yet, and Uncle Rob, having graduated from college at last, was off in Alaska working for a newspaper.

"Who's this?" Liz demanded, and her voice was very sharp and very good-humored. "You don't sound at all like my brother Austen."

"This is Austen's grandson, Austen."

"Well, Austen's grandson, Austen. How old are you?"

"Fifteen."

"Can you drive?"

Of course I could drive. Every farm boy in Kingdom Country could drive long before he turned fifteen.

"Then leave a note on the kitchen table and come fetch me home, Austen's grandson," my great-aunt said. "I'd hitchhike, but I've got too much baggage. Don't hurry. I'll be right here when you arrive, and you won't mistake me for anyone else. I seem to be the only accused bank robber in town this evening."

Although I'd never done it alone before, I had no trouble driving the truck into the Common. I expected, I suppose, a slender cowgirl, maybe looking boldly curious as she had in the single picture I'd seen of her. But although at fifty-five my Great-Aunt Liz Kittredge looked scarcely forty, it was an older-appearing, stronger-featured, and stockier woman I found waiting for me in the village, with long straight auburn-red hair, long legs like a cowboy, an outdoors complexion, and the same pale blue, assessing eyes of my Big Aunt Maiden Rose and my grandfather. She was wearing jeans and cowboy boots, a fringed leather jacket over a sky-blue western-style shirt and an off-tan-colored cowboy hat. Next to her in the station waiting room were several worn, old-fashioned carpetbags with wooden handles, and two expensive-looking leather saddles. So my first impression of my Great-Aunt Liz was that she was definitely a woman of the West, of open spaces and horses and cowboys.

"Now throw a saddle over your shoulder, and grab two or three of these sorry excuses for valises and let's get out in the country," Aunt Liz said. "You've heard the old saw: God made the country, man made the city, and the devil made small towns. It's true, Austen's grandson, Austen. Let's vamoose."

Meeting Aunt Liz was like encountering a fresh gust of wind right off the high plains of Montana, a sage-laden, invigorating blast of the frontier. I was all the more delighted, and a little awe-stricken too, when as we left the station with her luggage I saw the unmistakable pearly-white handle of a revolver sticking out of her jacket pocket.

Something about my great-aunt's wonderfully assured manner inspired a latent boldness in me. As we headed out into the summer dusk, I surprised myself by saying, "Did you really rob the bank, Aunt Liz?"

"Well," she said thoughtfully, "to tell you the honest truth, I considered doing so more than once."

"So the loot isn't buried up in the Hollow?"

"Austen," she said, heaving one of the saddles up into the back of the truck, "you put me in mind of myself at your age. Back before I learned that the best way to find out what I wanted to know was not to ask too many questions. For the time being I'll tell you just this and no more. I've come back to get something I left here a long time ago. Now I've got a question for you. How's Maiden Rose?"

"She's pretty crippled up," I said, starting the truck and heading out toward the county road. "But you know Aunt Rose. She's tough."

"Yes, she is," Liz said soberly. "You drive very well, by the way."

"I don't have my license yet."

"Neither do I," Liz laughed. "And I've driven all over the country without one. You and I have a lot in common, Austen. We're going to be close compadres, my boy."

Reunion day dawned clear as a bell, a beautiful blue summer morning in the hills of northern Vermont. My grandmother had been up since long before dawn, working in the summer kitchen preparing for the huge midday picnic after the family grave-cleaning. Klee, Freddi, and my grandmother's jovial younger sister from Boston, my Great-Aunt Helen, were helping Gram and laughing at Aunt Helen's irreverent jokes. My grandfather, for his part, had gone to the woods immediately after barn chores, as he did on all family holidays.

Right after breakfast my grandmother sent me down to the Home Place to ask Maiden Rose if one o'clock was a good time for the picnic dinner, and whether she needed any help from my little aunts or me. When I arrived, Rose was transplanting some purple pansies growing in the center of the big millstone that served as her porch step. She was bent down so low she didn't need to stoop to dig up the flowers. I was actually afraid that she might topple over onto the millstone face-first, and offered to help, but she shooed me away.

"One o'clock is fine," she said. "No, I don't want the nieces here yet. They'd just be in the way. Have you seen Liz this morning? She seems to have sneaked off someplace."

I hadn't.

"Do you know your lines for the play tonight?"

I said I believed I did.

"I hope so," Rose said. "It wouldn't do to forget them in front of half the county. Your father never forgot his lines. I could trust him with a substantial part by the time he was your age."

"Well," I said.

"What did Liz say about me yesterday evening when you fetched her up from the village?"

"Nothing. We talked about Montana."

"Your Great-Aunt Maiden Rose knows better than that, Austen. What did she say about me? About the family? Is she going to stay on?"

"I hope so," I said. "I like her a lot. Maybe it would be nice for you, too."

My aunt picked up her two canes and straightened up as far as she could. "You don't know much about loneliness, do you, Austen? Not yet. I hope you never have to find out."

"Are you lonely, Aunt?"

"Yes," she said without a speck of self-pity, indeed with a certain terrible, grim satisfaction. "Since April Mae Swanson died I've not had an unlonely hour in my life. Oh, I hold no brief for myself. I've been a hard woman, and I know it. But not unlonely. Now I don't even know whether I can drag myself up to clean April's grave this morning."

"I'll do that for you, Aunt."

"Don't you touch it!" she said. "Don't you lay a finger on it."

"I'm sorry you're lonely, Aunt. I'll help you up to the graveyard."

"You needn't trouble yourself about it," she said. "You needn't condescend to feel sorry for *me*, boy. I won't have it."

Then why did you say you were lonely? I wanted to shout. But I didn't.

"Aunt, would you not be lonely if Liz stayed on in Lost Nation?"

"It wouldn't matter in the least one way or the other."

Rose returned to her pansies, and I returned to the Farm, uneasy about what my great-aunt had told me. How, I wondered, could she manage to get through another winter, even with my help? I could cut and stack her wood and fill her woodbox morning and night, as I had for two or three years. But in her condition could she even fetch a stick from the woodbox to the stove? Get to the outhouse? I didn't know.

By nine o'clock, family members had begun to arrive. Dad appeared around nine-thirty, and he and I immediately set up the horseshoe stakes behind the barn. Cousin Clarence, armed with his camera, set up a two-o'clock family reunion picture and a two-thirty ball game. From his store, Clarence had brought up boxes of hot dogs, big trays of hamburger, cartons of rolls and potato chips and soda. Cousin Whiskeyjack appeared in a clean pair of denim overalls. Preacher John Wesleyan arrived in his black Sunday suit.

"Where's your grandfather, boy?" Preacher JW demanded.

"Working up in the woods."

"Aye," John Wesleyan said. "He may be a blasphemer and he may be a nonbeliever, but he's a hard worker. I'll say that for him. In the end, though, hard work is just another vanity."

"I'm surprised you're willing to participate in all this frivolity today, Preacher JW," my Great-Aunt Helen said with a look at me. "Aren't family reunions just another vanity?"

"Nay, nay," JW said with a good-natured grin. "I like to say grace at the noon and evening meals, ma'am. And I like the vittles!"

Lately John Wesleyan had become so stiff from his own battle with arthritis that my grandfather had to carry his saw and ax both to and from the woods for him, and the work he did there amounted to scarcely anything. More than once JW had confided to me that Gramp was as good-hearted an old devil as any he'd ever met. But then he'd shake his head and chuckle and announce that no man could be saved by good works alone.

What about Cousin Whiskeyjack, Aunt Helen wondered with great innocence, rolling her eyes at me. Did Preacher JW hope for a glorious salvation for his moonshining brother? Not by a long shot, JW said with grim pleasure.

How about Aunt Liz, I asked, trying to go Aunt Helen one better. Did she have a chance at the Great Beyond?

Preacher John Wesleyan's eyes twinkled. "Liz will take heaven by storm with her pearl-handled revolver," he said unexpectedly. "Or trick St. Peter into looking the other way whilst she slips past unnoticed. Liz is all right, boy. She's all right."

By ten o'clock most of the family had assembled. Armed with trowels and grass clippers and sickles, and with Preacher JW brandishing a great old scythe like the Grim Reaper himself, we all filed up to the Kittredge family graveyard on the knoll above Maiden Rose's Home Place for the annual reunion-morning grave-cleaning.

To my great relief, Maiden Rose was there ahead of us. Greetings were exchanged in somber tones. "Cousin. Aunt. Brother."

It was not a large cemetery. In all, there were one hundred and twenty-two stones, most matching the names in the old family Bible in the attic. Here lay almost all the Kittredges who had not died Away, on the other side of the hills, and I could feel their presence, grim and disapproving and eternal. The stones were granite or slate, and some were weathered so faint you could hardly read the inscriptions.

We began with Preacher JW offering up a short prayer asking that our grave-cleaning efforts be blessed, and praying for the souls of the departed. With the entire family working, it took no more than an hour to clean the graveyard and burn up the debris, and for the grown-ups, it was a surprisingly lighthearted task. No doubt the annual grave-cleaning expanded the scope of the reunion by temporarily reuniting us living family members—so few now—with our bygone ancestors. Relatives who hadn't seen each other for a year chatted pleasantly as they grubbed up encroaching sumac and sapling chokecherries and gray birches, clipped and raked, picked up dead limbs from the row of big maples at the back of the graveyard, where Maiden Rose's sugar bush began. As we worked, Preacher John Wesleyan led us in a few solemn old hymns: "Rock of Ages," "Onward, Christian Soldiers," and so forth; and I thought what a strange sight we would have been for a stranger to come upon, singing together as we moved slowly through the remote little cemetery from the graves to the smoky bonfire, as intent upon our hundred-year-old ritual as ancient Druids.

A few of the more recent graves still had faded evergreen grave blankets on them from the past winter. These we removed and burned, leaving the graveyard once again neatly clipped and cared for, our visible link with the past. I offered to help Maiden Rose trim the grass on April's grave, but she waved me away with her clippers. She did let me drag away the balsam blanket she'd woven last fall to protect the grave from the fierce winter storms. Then she transplanted her purple pansies into the border. Rose's name and birthday were inscribed below April's on the same stone. Only the date of Rose's death had been left blank. Below their names was the simple legend, "Together at Last."

While Rose was working on the grave she would someday share with April, no one else ventured close. The ultimate privacy of their love for one another, whatever its exact nature, was respected and honored, like the misanthropy of my grandfather and my grandmother's unaccountable fixation with all matters Egyptian, and Liz's wild ways. "Liz is who she is. Maiden Rose is who she is. Old Austen is who he is." The names were interchangeable, but I must have heard the sentiment expressed a hundred times during my boyhood in the Nation.

I was commissioned to stay on for a few minutes to make sure the bonfire was completely out. As the rest of the family members moved singly and in pairs and small groups back down the hill, Rose creeping along in the rear on her two canes, solitary in her impenetrable loneliness, a figure on horseback burst out of the woods above the sugar bush. A figure in cowboy boots, a fringed vest, and a western hat. It was Liz, on Henry David, and when she reached the gate of the graveyard, she leaped off the horse, threw the reins over the iron pickets, and began to shout, her eyes blazing.

"Just as I expected. The only grave that hasn't been properly tended up here is the only one that matters to me. Damn that sister of mine for neglecting it and damn the rest of the family for not having the grit to stand up to her."

She was pointing at a leaning slate stone near the rear fence of the cemetery. This was the stone of her fourth husband, Foster James, who had died in Lost Nation just before Liz had gone West in 1941, sixteen years ago.

"I ought to get out my pearl-handled sidekick and hurry these so-called family members on their way," Liz hollered, starting for the saddlebags on Henry David. She was really roaring now, and the departing relatives were looking apprehensively back over their shoulders at her—all but Maiden Rose, who continued down toward the Home Farm, one small step at a time, bent over into a cramped letter "C" on her canes.

Liz came striding up toward me. "Come, Austen," she said,

grabbing a pair of clippers. "You and I will hoe out old Foster's grave ourselves."

As she passed me, she winked and said, under her breath, "Diversion."

Then she was roaring again, which she continued to do until we reached her fourth husband's grave. What under the sun was going on, I wondered. Foster James's grave seemed as neatly trimmed as any of the others. But Aunt Liz set to work with the clippers, meticulously cutting and pulling any slip of grass that had escaped the other cleaners, and as she worked, she talked steadily. "Husbands!" she said. "Number one I married at sixteen, shortly after I arrived in Montana the first time. His name was Hartley Stone, which was what his heart was made of, I reckon. And that's odd, because he was the only one of the bunch I ever really loved, even though he turned out to be a skirt chaser. Off to the cathouses in Butte and Helena every time I turned my back, and then he blamed me because we didn't have any kids. Wanted sons, he said. Well, mister man, I've had four sons since, all big strong capable smart fellas at that, like all the Kittredge men. So I reckon old Stony had that part of it wrong."

Liz gave a vicious yank on a half-hidden clump of witchgrass rooted in under her fourth husband's slate marker. "As I was saying, I'd had it with Stony. I put up with his catting longer than I should have but after three years of it, I walked out. I'd accumulated some animals, which I loaded onto a boxcar. I had a pregnant Morgan riding horse, several steers, a couple of hogs, some chickens, a goat, two mated geese, two turkeys. I lugged 'em right back to Vermont with me on that boxcar. Arrived in the middle of the night during a January blizzard.

" 'Sister, I hope you've learned your lesson.' That was how Rose greeted me when I arrived.

" 'What lesson?' I said.

" 'About men,' Rose said. Never welcomed me home or spoke any kind word. Just told me she hoped I'd learned my lesson about men, damn her spinster tongue."

Liz stood up and surveyed her fourth husband's grave critically. "Well, obviously I hadn't. I was pretty sure old Hartley Stone would write and beg for me to come back, and for several weeks I swore when he did I wouldn't, and then I softened and said I would. But the son of a bitch never did write, Austen. I was heartbroken. So I went out and married number two, on the rebound. He was a good-looking and thoroughly good-for-nothing fella from Pond in the Sky. He was the laziest man I ever met. Born lazy and had a relapse, I used to say. One day I told him to make himself useful and take a broom out to the barn and brush down the cobwebs. That was the last I ever saw of him. So far as I know, number two's still down at the barn, brushing cobwebs."

Liz chuckled. "Left Vermont again. Worked as a cook at a lumber camp, nurse assistant in a hospital for the insane, housekeeper on a big estate in Connecticut. Drifted West a second time. Had my first two boys and acquired a third husband, in that order. Number three was a harmless-enough fella. Nice guy, actually. But I was leasing a small horse ranch and he was terribly afraid of horses. Finally a horse kicked him in the head and killed him on the spot. Had two more kids by then, and along waltzes husband number four, Mr. Foster James—the great-grandson of Frank James, Jesse's brother, or so Foster claimed."

Frank James's great-grandson—this was almost as good as Liz robbing the bank.

"Was he really Frank James's great-grandson?" I asked.

"Who knows? He said he was. That's all I can tell you. That, and that he was a slick, smart customer. A gambler from over in Great Falls, somewhat older than me, with a history of trouble with the law himself. Wore a necktie every day of his life, Austen, just like my father over there, the gentleman farmer." Liz gestured at Grampa Gleason's tall pink granite stone on the far side of the family graveyard. "Anyway, I brought Foster East with me the last time I came, sixteen years ago, and I don't know but what the hoorah over the bank robbery a week later was too much for him. All those F.B.I. agents swarming out here to pester me, every day, every day. Foster just keeled over in the barnyard one afternoon. That was that. That and that Rose insisted we plant him off here in the back away from her precious family like some sort of outcast.

"So," Liz said as we started back toward the horse, "I guess you could fairly say, Austen, that I have not had good luck with husbands. I truly loved just one of the four and he was that catting son of a bitch I never heard from again. Two are dead. Two are missing and might as well be. No, sir, I haven't had good luck with men in general, or they with me."

She stopped by Miss April Swanson's grave, and chuckled. "Maybe my sister had the right idea. She avoided men altogether and married a woman."

"Did you know Miss April, Liz?"

"Oh, yes. She was a harmless little fluff of a thing. Rose rode roughshod over her, same as she tried to the rest of us. There was all kinds of talk in the village, of course, about their living arrangements, but I never made any judgments about that and neither so far as I know did the rest of the family. We figured how they lived was their business, long's they weren't hurting anyone else, which they weren't. I've already told you who created villages."

Liz unwound Henry David's reins from the gate, and glanced briefly out over the hills. She shook her head. "Too many hills and not enough mountains in these parts, Austen. When I was growing up here, I used to feel closed in, hanker after bigger spaces. Narrow valleys, narrow rivers, narrow people, come to think of it. Out West they might shoot you if you cross 'em. They're much less apt to gossip about you."

She glanced back once more at Foster James's grave, shook her head, gave me a wry grin. "Let's you and me go on a ride together after the picnic dinner, Austen. I'll meet you at Maiden Rose's barn at two-thirty sharp."

By the time I returned to my grandparents' place, the big picnic dinner was ready. Planks from my grandfather's mill had been set up across sawhorses, and were laden with the traditional reunion fare: potato salad, new potatoes with peas and salt pork, baked beans, mincemeat pies with home-canned venison, Cousin Clarence's hot dogs and hamburgers. There was food enough to feed a Kittredge family reunion from fifty years ago.

After the picnic came the photography session. This was followed by foot races, games of horseshoes and flies and grounders, and wrestling. Then the venue shifted to Clarence's baseball diamond. And although I hated to miss the big game, I was greatly looking forward to the horseback ride with Liz. A little before two-thirty, she and I started out on Henry David and Ralph. This time, however, instead of saddlebags, Henry was carrying a good-sized packbasket.

I had no idea where we were headed. Liz led the way, up a grown-up lumbering trace behind the Home Place toward the border. As we rode she continued to talk about the Kittredge family, Kingdom County, the West, and her own life. Her mirthful observations struck me as remarkably generous-minded. I thought that she must be the wisest person I'd ever known. She was opinionated without being censorious, and as curious about herself as about everyone else. "I'm as unpredictable as the old lady who had to hear what she said to find out what she thought," Liz told me, laughing. Never in my life had I met anyone like her. She stood conventional wisdom on its head at every twist in the old military road.

"We aren't what we do, Austen. We're what we hope to do. We're our dreams."

"Be careful what you want, Austen's grandson, Austen. It'll probably come true. And be careful whose bed you put your shoes under."

"Be careful what you do. Be more careful what you say. Careless words hurt a great deal longer than a quick blow."

"Klee has a sharp tongue sometimes," I said.

"Yes, and she gets it from Maiden Rose. It was that as much as anything else that drove your grandfather away as a boy, and later drove me away."

"What makes her so mean? Is it being all crippled up and in pain?"

"Why, Austen. I'm surprised by you, man. Maiden Rose isn't mean. She doesn't have a mean bone in her body."

I looked at Aunt Liz to see if she was kidding. She didn't seem to be. "But you just said she drove Gramp away when he was a kid, and you, too, later."

"She did. But that's not the same as saying she's mean. Stubborn, yes. Stubborn, and ruthless too, if ruthlessness was called for. Being ruthless is how she kept the family together as long as she did. But Rose was never mean or low . . . There's Fort Kittredge. We'll leave the horses here."

Ranged along the cleared strip through the woods that marked the border, all that was left of the old fort built by our Tory ancestors was a hodgepodge of shacks. Around the turn of the century, the fort had been briefly rebuilt as a tiny hamlet for a granite quarry. But the granite sheds were now just windowless hulks overrun by wild raspberry bushes. The air of desuetude about the place made it spooky, even in broad daylight.

One of the ghost hamlet's few remaining recognizable structures was a windmill once used to pump up drinking water from a well. Most of the huge wooden blades had been shot to pieces, and even in a high wind, it no longer turned. Nonetheless, it loomed up above the second- and third-growth woods in a way I did not at all care for. Neither, for all her Wild West bravado, did Liz. "That mechanism makes my flesh creep, Austen. Always has. I used to bring my boyfriends up here after dark to scare 'em. Come over here, and watch your footing."

Lugging the packbasket she'd brought along, Liz thrashed her way through the raspberries to the old well at the foot of the windmill. Together we heaved off the rotting wooden cover, and peered inside. She dropped a stone down and listened for the splash, but there wasn't any. "She's dry as a bone, down there, Austen. I won't get my hopes up yet, but so far so good."

From her packbasket Liz got out a bucket, a coil of clothesline rope, a short-handled shovel used to remove ashes from a woodstove, an ax and a lantern. She handed me the ax and instructed me to cut her a limber spruce pole about ten feet long. I did, and she began to probe down the mouth of the well with it. "Just as I thought," she said. "It isn't all that deep. Eight feet at most. Now, sir. Are you afraid of tight, dark places?"

"No," I lied, feeling my heart start to beat faster. "Of course not."

"Good. Some years ago I could have shinnied down there like a monkey, but I've added a few pounds since then. I'll light this lantern and lower it on the rope, and you go down the pole. Don't worry, it's stout enough to hold two of you. When you get down there I'll lower the bucket on another rope. I want you to fill it with leaves and dirt and such for me to pull up.''

I looked doubtfully down the shallow well. "Now don't fret," Liz said. "There's no skeleton down there and it's too dank for serpents. We'll attach the rope to your waist and not let you get stuck in the muck. See here, we'll lower the lantern first, test if the air's still good. If the lamp goes out, we'll strike for home and forget this whole harebrained enterprise.''

What had I gotten myself into, I wondered. But the lantern stayed lit, and down the spruce pole I went, into that dark hole, sure that this was where Liz had hidden the loot from the long-ago bank robbery. I was so excited to be helping her recover it that after a minute I forgot to be afraid.

I don't know how long I dug around in the leaves and clay at the bottom of the old well. Maybe fifteen minutes, though it seemed much longer. As my aunt pulled up bucket after bucket of debris, the footing in the well started to grow mucky. I began to wonder whether we were on a fool's errand after all.

When I'd nearly given up hope, Liz shouted, "Eureka! Here he is, Austen. We've found him. Skin back up that pole, man, and rejoice. We've done it.''

Found who? Done what? I certainly hadn't unearthed any forty-two thousand dollars. Seconds later I was back up in the warm, fresh, green-leaf-scented summery air, and Liz was holding out her hand to show me what she'd discovered. Nestled in her palm was a thin gold ring set with a single tiny diamond. I looked from the ring to my aunt's radiant face and back to the ring again.

"It's my wedding band from my first marriage, Austen," Liz said with the greatest delight. "Don't you see?"

I saw, all right. But I didn't understand.

"Look, man," she said, wedging it onto the ring finger of her left hand. "It's a tight squeeze but it still fits. Hartley Stone, my first husband, gave me this little ring when we got married. When I left him to come home to Vermont, I was going to leave it on the bedtable for him to find. But at the last minute I said to myself, no you don't, girl, take it along with you. For as I've told you, Austen, I fully expected he'd come East for me in a few weeks or write begging me to come back West to him. Then it ran along a number of months, and there was no word, no word, no word, and I got madder and madder. And more and more heartbroken, too, if you want the truth, because love Stony I did. I made myself half-crazy with worry, but I was too proud to go back to him on my own. Finally one day I couldn't stand any more. I came up here with another fella who shall remain unnamed and I took off my ring and threw it down this well. That was my mistake. I should have written to Hartley myself, you know. At least told him why I'd left. Well, I lost him. I lost the only man I ever really loved. Don't you tell anyone, but we never did get divorced. Legally speaking, if he's alive, we're still yoked together. I thank you for your assistance, Austen. Now we can go back to the reunion.''

"What about the loot, Aunt Liz? From the bank robbery?''

"What about it?'' Liz said. "All we can say, Austen's grandson, Austen, is that it still hasn't seemed to have turned up.''

On our way back to Maiden Rose's, I felt sharply disappointed by the outcome of our expedition; but Liz was as happy as a schoolgirl. It was almost as if she'd reclaimed Hartley Stone himself and her first marriage, along with the thin little ring with the tiny inset diamond.

"It's going to be a grand evening for Maiden Rose's play,'' Liz said as we approached the Home Place. "That's curious. We've got early visitors, and it isn't yet five o'clock.''

Below in the dooryard was a dark sedan. As we drew nearer, a tall young stranger in a suit and tie got out of the driver's side. "Mrs. Kittredge?''

"Good evening, sir. And you are?''

"Agent Jordan Sanders, of the Federal Bureau of Investigation. I'd like to ask you a few questions.''

Liz shot me a delighted look. "Why, of course,'' she said. "I'd be honored to answer your questions. First, though, let me ask you one. You've heard of something called the statute of limitations?''

"Sure,'' Agent Jordan Sanders said. "I'm quite familiar with it. Only one problem about that, Mrs. Kittredge. It doesn't apply to federal offenses.''

"Like bank robbery?"

"Like bank robbery," Agent Sanders said. "Shall we sit in the car?"

"Oh, no," Liz said. "Let's go inside the kitchen, have some coffee. My sister will want to hear this, I'm sure. I suppose you haven't ruled her out as a suspect anyway. And"—Liz shot me another look—"she may just want to recruit you for her play."

"Can I come in, too?" I said.

"You may not," Maiden Rose's harsh voice said from the porch. "Feed and water Henry and Ralph, Austen, and then go straight home. There's no need for you to hear any of this."

"So you've been out riding all day?" I heard Agent Sanders say as he and Liz headed into the kitchen.

"Yes, sir," Liz said. Adding loudly, for my benefit I was sure, "Looking for hidden treasure."

"Any luck?"

"You bet," Liz said, holding out her left hand. "Look here on my ring finger. Ain't that just about the prettiest sight you ever saw?"

I was terrifically excited about the appearance in Lost Nation of the F.B.I.; but now preparations were in full swing for the play, to be followed by the party at the schoolhouse. Before I knew it, I'd been recruited by my grandmother to pick several bushels of early Golden Bantam from her garden for the corn-roast.

As the sun lowered toward the Green Mountains and Jay Peak, cars began to drive up the Hollow from the county road. They belonged to spectators for Maiden Rose's play. As they pulled into the Home Place lane, I recognized many people from the village. Zack Barrows, my grandmother's lawyer, had come with his girl-friend, Julia Hefner. Sheriff Mason White was on hand in full uniform. Judge Allen had driven up with Mr. Roger Whitington, president of the First Farmers' and Lumberers' Bank. Prof Newton Chadburn, Kingdom County's superintendent of schools, and Editor Kinneson of *The Kingdom County Monitor*, had come in one car with their wives.

The F.B.I. agent had evidently finished with Liz, or vice versa.

Laughing and joking, she came outside onto the porch of the Home Place with him, and the instant she clapped eyes on Roger Whitington she smiled her big smile and guided the agent by his suit-jacket elbow over to him. "I presume you two gentlemen have met?" she said. "Roger, it's good to see you again."

"It's good to see you, Liz. I'd heard you were back East."

"Evidently you weren't the only one," Liz said, nodding at Agent Sanders.

I was afraid the bank president and the F.B.I. agent might gang up on my great-aunt, but Mr. Whitington seemed genuinely surprised by the agent's presence. He was very friendly, and wanted to know all about Liz's kids. More cars arrived and people began to move around to the natural amphitheater behind Rose's barn. Everyone seemed to be reminiscing about old times.

"This good-looking young man thinks I was up at Fort Kittredge digging up the bank robbery boodle this afternoon," Liz told Roger as they headed toward the rear of the barn. "I haven't entirely disabused him of the notion, but he has yet to pin me down and prove it."

"Liz is tough to pin down," Roger Whitington said. "But I don't think she robbed any banks. Not around here at least."

"There was a time when you might have pinned me down, in a manner of speaking, Roger," Liz said. "You were one good-looking boy, I tell you true."

"And you, Liz, are still one good-looking woman," Roger said gallantly.

"I don't understand this place at all," Agent Sanders said to nobody in particular, shaking his head.

The impromptu stage occupied the entire mouth of Rose's hay barn, at the top of the high-drive ramp leading up to the big open double doors. It was illuminated by battery-operated tractor lights. The hundred or so spectators ranged themselves around the pasture hillside, in the natural bowl above the barn, sitting in the purple shadows of the high ridge.

An expectant hush fell over the countryside, and the play began with Preacher John Wesleyan's booming baritone narration. "On a ship at sea: a tempestuous noise of thunder and lightning heard."

From the depths of the empty old hay barn came a crashing of milk cans rolling together to simulate thunder. In a few short moments, the playgoers had been transported from an end-of-the-road Vermont hill farm to Prospero's magical island. Once again the old Home Place began to ring with poetry, and people from throughout the Kingdom sat rapt on the disused cow pasture, swept up in the age-old themes of love and pride and vengeance and reconciliation. The most spirited summer Shakespeare in Lost Nation Hollow was off and running.

Out onto the high-drive I tore in the sailorly garb of the Boatswain. "Yare, yare!" I roared, and I did not know then, nor do I now, what under the sun "yare" meant. Arrayed in her gauzy white dress, Freddi, as beautiful Miranda, pleaded with her father to allay the troubled waters. Maiden Rose was magnificent in the role of the exiled old magician, ancient and bent-over though she was. Her dark gown was embellished with silver stars and golden moons and suns. For a magic wand she used Great-Grandpa Gleason's multicolored glass walking stick, a family heirloom dating back one hundred years. Cousin Whiskeyjack came slinking up from under the high drive as a backwoods Caliban, all slouch hat and whiskers and ratty old lumber jacket; and to this day, my Little Aunt Klee remains the most acrobatic and winning Ariel I have ever seen.

As always, though, the premier performance was Rose's. When her Prospero announced his intention to "retire to Milan, where every third thought shall be my grave," she paused and stared out over the audience, up toward the dark family burying ground and beyond, as if into some private realm she would soon share with her beloved April. On her face was an expression both tragic and hopeful. And with no warning she lifted my great-grandfather's colored glass walking stick to her waist and brought it sharply down on the plank floor of the high-drive, showering the air with flying bits of brilliant glass.

There was a stunned pause. Then one by one the spectators ranged around the dark pasture stood in a prolonged ovation.

Talking in hushed tones, the crowd began to head for their cars, to remove to the schoolhouse for the corn-roast, sugar-on-snow party, and dance. I tagged along beside Liz.

"Well, Austen," she said, "that was very fine. Very fine indeed."

The F.B.I. agent and Mr. Roger Whitington were right behind us. "I wouldn't have believed all this if I hadn't seen it," Agent Sanders said quietly to Mr. Whitington. "I'm going back to Boston. These people didn't rob any banks."

Liz laughed and turned around. "Well, sir, it's been a pleasure to meet you, and now I'll bid you good night. Unless you'd like me to save you a dance down at the schoolhouse."

By the time Liz and I got out in the barnyard the agent was gone, along with many of the relatives and play spectators. It was quiet after all the bustle of the play. I wanted to get right down to the schoolhouse party myself, but Liz glanced through the kitchen window and saw Maiden Rose sitting alone at the table, still dressed in Prospero's cloak, her long gray hair unpinned and flowing down on her shoulders. "I don't like to leave Rose alone here like this, Austen. She's alone enough of the time as is. Let's get her to come along to the dance with us."

I did not at all want to go inside and try to persuade Maiden Rose to come to the schoolhouse party. In a few minutes Cousin Clarence would be tuning up his fiddle while his wife banged away at the old black upright school piano. I wanted to dance with Theresa Dubois, taste the delicious cold sweetness of maple syrup on snow that had been preserved in my grandfather's icehouse from last winter, eat half a dozen of my grandmother's donuts. Maybe later I'd sneak up to Cousin Whiskeyjack's to watch the men drink white mule moonshine.

"Come," Liz said.

At the applewood kitchen table, Maiden Rose was riffling through her long shoebox of old letters from April Mae Swanson. Liz and I sat down at the table, around which Maiden Rose had grilled and drilled three generations of Kittredges, including me, in grammar, arithmetic, spelling. Liz shot a warning glance at me out from under the cowboy hat. She'd spotted April's return address on the envelopes, too.

"Sister," Rose said wearily, "this is not one of your Wild West cafes. I'm obliged to ask you to check your firearm before you join me here.''

Liz grinned and took her pearl-handled revolver out of her jacket pocket and placed it on a shelf behind the stove.

"Well, sister," Rose said, "where did you find your old bauble?" She was looking at Liz's wedding ring from Hartley Stone.

Again Liz darted a glance at me. "I and Austen here found it where I lost it, many years ago. Up at Fort Kittredge."

"Better by far that it had stayed there. Surely you don't intend to wear it again?''

"Of course I intend to wear it. As a token of what Hartley and I once had between us, if nothing else."

"As a token of your mistreatment at the hand of that good-for-nothing, you mean." Rose's eyes snapped angrily. Despite Prospero's astrological gown she now looked just exactly like Maiden Rose again.

"He's still my husband," Liz said. "I intend to wear it. Why shouldn't I?''

"Why?" Maiden Rose said. "Because he was cruel to you. Because he was a faithless drunkard. Have you forgotten? Your memory's far too short, sister."

"Yours is too long. All that happened years ago. Times change."

"Times may. People do not."

"Maybe not. What difference does it make? I loved him, and still do today. You of all people ought to understand that. You too have loved, sister."

"Yes. A pure love fully requited, tenderly repaid a thousand thousand times. My love has endured for fifty years and more, even beyond the grave."

"I don't know anything about that," Liz said, and abruptly stood up.

"Where are you going, sister?" Maiden Rose sounded alarmed.

"To Hartley," Liz said. "If he's alive, I intend to find him. You've yourself to thank for helping me make up my mind."

"He'll break your heart again," Maiden Rose said, rising and holding the table for support. "All your men were weak, miserable. He was the worst. You're betraying yourself."

Now Liz no longer looked angry. She just looked determined, as she must have looked forty years ago, a girl of sixteen, heading West with her cardboard suitcase. "Maybe I am, sister. I'll admit that I'm doing this against my better judgment. But if I'd relied on that all my life, where would I be? A retired schoolteacher in Lost Nation, maybe. Look here. Come with me. Or join me in the West, whether I find Hartley or no. We'll make a life for ourselves."

Maiden Rose shook her head. "You know I can't do that. This is beyond stubbornness."

"Who are you, Maiden Rose, to read me a lecture on stubbornness? Austen, fetch your grandfather's truck down here. I want you to take me to the railroad station straightaway."

By the time I'd left a note on the table up at my grandparents' farmhouse saying where I'd be, and gotten back with the truck, Liz was waiting on the porch with her carpetbags. This time she had only one saddle. "The other's yours, Austen," she said. "It's in the harness room. Take good care of it."

I was astonished, nearly overcome by her generosity. But she waved off my thanks, already talking, talking, talking, the perpetual commentary on her life and times unfolding as we headed down the Hollow road.

"You'll note that I neither said good-bye to my sister nor looked back, not that there's that much to see," Liz said. "No, Austen, the Home Place is as empty now as the old wizard's island in Rose's play. There's nothing to detain me any longer, if there ever was. I figure I've got just enough vigor left to find that old son of a bitch Hartley, assuming he's still in the land of the living."

I hated to see Liz go. For me this had been by far the most memorable reunion ever. Then we were driving by the lighted schoolhouse where the sugar-on-snow party was going on. I could hear Cousin Clarence's fiddle and the deep *thum-thum-thum* of his wife playing chords on the old piano. I caught a glimpse of Theresa Dubois's bright blond head through the windows; but I felt proud to be with my aunt. There would be other schoolhouse junkets, other dances.

Liz launched into more stories, and before I knew it we were in the Common, unloading her carpetbags and saddle at the station.

It was nearly twelve o'clock now. According to Percy Fennel, the old stationmaster, the Midnight Flyer to Montreal and points west was on schedule. There wasn't much time for good-byes, even if Liz had believed in them.

"Where will you look for Hartley, Aunt?" I said as we waited together on the dark platform.

"The same place I looked for his ring, of course."

I was puzzled. "At Fort Kittredge?"

"No. Where I lost him. Back in Butte. If he ain't there, I'll trace him on to the next town. He was a drifter, old Stony, but he had people in Butte. If he's alive, I'll run him down."

From a mile south of town, the Flyer hooted, and Liz shook her head. "Human nature is a strange commodity, Austen. Here stand I on a railway platform, excited to be boarding the train and heading West, yet already missing Lost Nation and the Home Place and, yes, missing Maiden Rose, too. Not so much as I've missed that sneaking coyote Hartley, though. This time if he goes to catting on me, he'll deal with my— Damn, Austen!"

"What's wrong?"

"My revolver's back on the shelf behind Rose's stove. I feel downright naked without it. Well, it can't be helped. Have your grandfather unload it and pack it in excelsior and ship it to me in Butte, general delivery. That's where I'll land first. Will you remember to do that straightaway when you get home?"

I said I would. She held out her hand and we shook hands on the station platform and she clapped me on the back. "Now, Austen. Instead of good-bye, I'll say visit me out West when you can. I've enjoyed our time together, short though it was. Good luck to you."

"Good luck to you, Aunt. With your—"

"First and fifth husband, I reckon we'd call him," she said as the train pulled in.

Liz was as good as her word. Once she and her carpetbags were aboard the Flyer, she never looked out the window at me. I watched the train pull out the way, years ago, I'd stood on the platform with my grandfather and watched the departing train that had brought me to Kingdom County for the first time. This time, though, I half-wished I were on it, too, headed West with my aunt to search for Hartley Stone. I hoped she'd find him, and wondered what she'd do with him if she did.

There was a great deal to think about on the way home, but after the big day I was too tired to concentrate on anything but my driving. The schoolhouse was dark as I approached it. A faint glimmer of lantern light appeared in Maiden Rose's window. I imagined her poring over April's letters at the old applewood table and was tempted to stop and reassure her that Gramp and I would help her through the coming winter. But I was tired, and I knew she'd be harsh with me, as she always had been; as she had been with Liz, driving her away from Lord Hollow as she had Gramp. So I continued on up the road to the Farm, where, to my surprise, I found both my grandparents waiting up for me with coffee and cookies left over from the reunion picnic.

"Well, Tut," Gram said, "did you get your Aunt Liz off?"

"Yes. She wants me to visit her when she gets settled in."

"Perhaps someday," my grandmother said. "At fifteen, you don't need to be sashaying off around the country."

"I wonder what Maiden Rose'll do now? All alone, bent over the way she is."

"You can't predict the future, Tut," Gram said. "But Rose will get along. She always has."

My grandfather looked up from his book, a nineteenth-century account of Sir John Franklin's lost expedition to Hudson Bay. "Rose is who she is," he said. "Like Liz. Times change, but my sisters never will."

"For once, Mr. Kittredge, we agree," my grandmother said. "Well, it's been a long day and a wonderful reunion—for those of us who troubled ourselves to attend. I'm going to read in Egypt for a few minutes. Then I'm going to bed. Tap on my door and say good night to me before you go up, Tut."

The moment my grandmother went into Egypt, I asked my grandfather what it was like to grow up with Maiden Rose. "Well," he said, "she rode pretty tight herd on me, Austen. At home and at school. There wasn't much hunting and fishing done, I'll tell you that."

"Liz said Aunt Rose drove you away from school and home."

My grandfather thought for a moment. "Rose was harder on me than on the other scholars, and hard enough on them. I never abided school a day in my life and she was part of the reason but only part. The plain truth is that I could have had the easiest teacher in all Vermont and still wanted to be off in the woods. I liked to read, and the other schoolwork wasn't hard for me, but I belonged in the woods and still do. That's as certain as the sun coming up in the morning over the White Mountains of New Hampshire and going down at night behind the Green Mountains of Vermont. And on that note, Austen, I'm going to bed myself."

A heavy layer of fog lay over Lost Nation when my grandfather rousted me out at dawn the next morning. Day after the family reunion or not, there were still chores to do. While Gramp grained and watered his young stock, I cleaned the barn gutters, and fed my grandmother's hens. Then I headed down the Hollow road toward Maiden Rose's to get Liz's pearl-handled revolver. The fog above the small east branch of the Upper Kingdom River was very thick. It felt more like fall than midsummer, and the mist enhanced the silence of the Hollow after the bustle of the reunion the day before. It reminded me of the fairgrounds the day after the fair closed, or Cousin Clarence's empty baseball diamond a few hours after a big game.

Usually Maiden Rose was up and around when I arrived for morning chores. Frequently I encountered her weeding her flowers or patrolling her dooryard or lane, bent over on her two canes like a witch in a fairy tale. Today there was no sign of her, just a wisp of woodsmoke from her kitchen chimney to tell me she was all right and had made her usual morning fire to take the chill off the air and boil her tea kettle.

She was sitting at the applewood table, exactly where Liz and I had left her the night before. She was still wearing her magician's gown, and I had no idea whether she had gone to bed the night before or not. Before her on the table the shoebox of April's letters sat in exactly the same spot. Beside it lay Liz's revolver, the pearly handle gleaming softly in the thin, misty light.

"Sit down, Austen," Rose said in a voice devoid of everything but a kind of weary determination. "No doubt you've come for that."

She looked at Liz's revolver, and I nodded.

"So, Austen," Rose said, her voice still weary yet now also fierce and certain, "no doubt you pity your great-aunt. An old woman scarcely able to creep up to visit a grave. Do you pity me?"

"No, Aunt," I lied.

She seemed scarcely to hear what I said. "You've never known utter loneliness, Austen. I hope you never will. You can't imagine it." Suddenly Rose looked straight at me. "Did you ever hear a wild goose that's lost its mate? I have. I've heard it circle and circle in the night, calling in vain. I've seen the survivor of my father's team of Morgans after its harness-mate of twenty years died, heard it nicker for its companion morning and night. The poor dumb beast wasn't even aware of what it missed, only of the missing, the loneliness, the desolation. The utter desolation."

She was quiet for a moment and so was I. But then in some instinctive moment of understanding beyond my years, I said, "Then how can you blame Liz for going back to her first husband?"

And Maiden Rose looked at me across the table, and nodded grimly, as she had sometimes done when, after an especially trying lesson in grammar or long division, I had finally mastered a hard concept. And in a haunted flat voice devoid of all pity and self-pity, she said, "I don't."

Of course, neither Maiden Rose's nor Liz's story ended with the last Kittredge family reunion. To everyone's astonishment but her own, Rose seemed to undergo a personal renaissance. She auctioned off her farm implements and much of her furniture, rented a small house in the village that had admired yet secretly censured her for fifty years, and dwelt there well on into her eighties. Bent over almost into a full circle, she nonetheless volunteered several afternoons a week at the village library, tutored kids after school in every subject from first-grade reading through high-school Latin and algebra, and wrote a series of scathing broadsides for the American

Shakespeare Society's quarterly publication, roundly denouncing the pernicious theory, then just beginning to come into vogue, that Edward de Vere, the Sixteenth Earl of Oxford, had secretly written the great bard's plays. She visited the Home Place only to tend April's grave. The fields continued to grow back up to brush. The empty house sagged on its foundation. The barn leaned off away from the hillside, the way my great-aunt herself was leaning off toward the earth. She died at ninety, during my last year in college, and was buried beside her beloved companion in the family grave-yard overlooking the abandoned old farm. "Together at Last."

Over the years I have come to admire greatly this unyielding woman, who led a hard, lonely, useful life and accommodated change only enough ultimately to achieve her private triumph over it, through her great, lasting love.

Of course it was my grandfather who regularly checked on Rose after she moved to the village, and brought her out to visit April's grave. For a foundling and a misanthrope, he had, it seemed to me, as much staying power as any other member of the family, including my grandmother and Maiden Rose herself—though his true origin before appearing in the California orange crate on the stoop of the Home Place remained as much a mystery to me as my grand-mother's preoccupation with all matters Egyptian. If, as my little aunts had speculated, Maiden Rose knew more about the orange crate than she'd ever acknowledged, it was a secret she took to her mutual grave with April, where it lies buried with her to this day.

"Who lives here?" my grandfather continued to say to me each time we approached the Farm dooryard.

"Who does?"

"The meanest old bastard in Lost Nation Hollow," he replied, and his harsh, ironical pleasure in our ritual and in contemplating his status as an interloper in the Kittredge family never dwindled.

Surprisingly enough, Great-Aunt Liz did scout up old Hartley, her first husband and one true love, and yoke back up with him. They bought a small horse ranch in northwestern Montana, where they lived together for fifteen years. I don't think that they were particularly happy. I visited Liz there when I was in college, and though she hadn't changed at all, Hartley seemed as much of a millstone to her then as ever. He was a small, rail-thin, dissatisfied, sour, sharp-tongued character, who, though he no longer visited the cathouses, drank a pint of cheap blackberry brandy a day, and seemed not to appreciate any of Liz's many wonderful qualities, yet was all too ready to point out her shortcomings. Even so, she continued to wear the ring he'd given her, then and for the rest of her life, and obviously loved him straight through to the bad end Maiden Rose had predicted for him, in the lunatic asylum where he spent the final year of his life in a state of complete dementia.

Liz never visited Lost Nation or Vermont again. Up and down the Hollow, the abandoned farms grew back to puckerbrush. The fields reverted to woods, the woods to something akin to original wilderness. In 1972 the Home Place collapsed under a heavy March snowstorm. The barn where Rose had performed her Shakespeare plays went down the following winter. But Liz didn't want to hear about any of it.

The last time I visited her, on her eightieth birthday in 1982, she was living near two of her sons, in a sort of old-age boarding home in Butte, and a great favorite with everyone there. As she did each year on her birthday, she got out her pearl-handled revolver and put on an impressive marksmanship exhibit.

"So," I said to her when it was time for me to leave, "I know you don't like questions. Will you answer just one for me?"

"It depends which one, how I feel about it at the moment, and how you put it. If it's about your grandfather's true origin, I simply don't know. If it's about Maiden Rose and April, we both already know the answer, and now let the dead bury their dead. If your question's about me, I might answer it."

"It's about you. Did you rob the bank?"

"Listen to what you hear, Austen. What did I tell you the evening I first met you?"

"You told me you'd considered it."

"What did I tell you the next day? About Foster. My fourth husband."

"Foster James?"

"No other. What did I say about him?"

I wracked my mind. Then it came to me. "That he was Frank

James's great-grandson and that he'd been in some trouble with the law."

"Exactly. You never asked what the nature of the trouble was, Austen. Listen to what you hear, and ask the right question."

"What was the nature of the trouble?"

"Why, he'd just gotten out of federal prison, man. Where he'd spent the better part of the past fifteen years. You tell me what for."

I began to laugh. "Bank robbery," I said. "But where did he bury the boodle before his heart attack? If not up at Fort Kittredge?"

"What makes you think he didn't bury it there? Say under the windmill?"

I looked at Liz and she smiled and her pale blue eyes flashed triumphantly. "What," she said, "do you suppose I was out doing that morning of the reunion, before I rode up to the graveyard with full saddlebags and caused that hollering diversion about the condition of Foster's grave? And what did you suppose that old coyote Hartley and I used to support ourselves with on our horse ranch? Recovering the boodle was the whole point of my venturing back to the family reunion, man. By then I figured enough time had gone by so I could get away with it. Listen to what you hear, Austen's grandson, Austen. Listen to what you hear, and then you'll be heard from. Now go catch your plane. And don't say good-bye, and don't look back to wave because I'm going inside, and won't be here anyway."

And when, contrary to Liz's injunction, I did glance up at the porch, once, quickly, she wasn't.

When I first set out to record these recollections of growing up with my grandparents and our extended family in Lost Nation, I wanted to discover for myself what was important enough to me from those times to have stayed fresh and clear in my mind down through the years. What was special about Lost Nation in the late 1940s and 1950s? The answer, of course, is the people who lived there, then and earlier, their lives and loves and secret mysteries, most of which, like my grandfather's origin, will remain mysteries for all time to come.

Strangely enough, it is Rose's plays, so hateful to me at the time, that I seem to remember most frequently and clearly from the annual Kittredge family reunions. Not, heaven knows, that there wasn't drama enough in the ongoing saga of the family itself, and high and low comedy and tragedy and noble sacrifice as well. But somehow it all seemed to be encapsulated in the most spirited summer Shakespeare in Lost Nation Hollow.

Here Rose is again, now raging as Lear, now boasting as Falstaff, now agonizing over the bitter ironies of human existence as Hamlet. And once again I see her as Prospero, shattering the swirly-colored glass walking stick, while a hundred people sit silent as ghosts in the natural amphitheater, spellbound by the magical make-believe world fleetingly created despite all of the hardship and loss and despair on that remote, soon-to-be-abandoned farm in northern Vermont, which held its own secret dramas of the heart, overseen by the ever-changing yet unchanged granite hills and the graveyard, where for nearly two centuries Kittredges had been laid to rest in the final family reunion, together at last.

9

THE SEASON OF THE
CLUSTER FLIES

In August of my seventeenth year, at the height of the prolonged drought and unprecedented heat wave in Kingdom County that we would later come to call the season of the cluster flies, my Grandmother Kittredge suffered a heart attack. As heart attacks go, it did not seem to be a very severe one. But there was no doubt in Gram's mind, or mine, or that of my Great-Aunt Helen, Gram's younger sister visiting from Boston, about what was happening.

I ran for the phone to call the local ambulance in Kingdom Common. Old Josie, my grandmother's new housekeeper, ran out of the kitchen wringing her apron and calling upon the divine intervention of Jesus, Joseph, and Mary. Aunt Helen started to run to the door to call for my grandfather, who had just left for the woods and might still be within hailing distance. But my stricken grandmother called for my great-aunt to come back inside instantly and unlace her corset stays so that she could breathe easier while sustaining the attack.

There was, however, a problem. The strings of my grand-mother's corset turned out to be bound so tightly that Aunt Helen, who I doubt ever wore a corset in her life, couldn't get them unfastened.

"Austen!" my great-aunt cried. "Quick! Fetch your grand-mother's sewing shears."

The sewing shears were in Egypt, and I hoped against hope I could locate them there. I had never been good at locating things my grandmother and my various great and little aunts sent me to fetch, beginning with my grandfather, and I was desperately afraid that before I could lay my hand on the shears, my grandmother would expire.

Fortunately, I immediately spotted the shiny handles sticking out of Gram's sewing basket. When I rushed back into the kitchen with them, my grandmother calmly reminded me not to run with a pair of scissors in my hand, then in the same steady voice enjoined my frantic aunt not to destroy the corset by cutting the strings.

"There's no need to spoil a perfectly serviceable corset, Helen," Gram said. "Take your time and unlace the strings properly."

Unlace the strings properly! For all we knew to the contrary, my thrifty-minded grandmother was expending her last breath to issue this measured edict.

Abiah Kittredge was no easy woman to defy. But this might very well be a matter of life and death, and for once, my Great-Aunt Helen was not about to cave in to her strong-willed older sister.

"Don't move a muscle, Ab," Aunt Helen said. "You haven't any need for a corset in the first place and you know it."

Whereupon, with great resoluteness, my aunt cut away the back of my grandmother's black blouse and slit the corset strings with half a dozen rapid snips while Gram shook her head in dismay.

Later my great-aunt claimed that what my grandmother actually said just before the fateful action with the sewing shears was, "Helen, there's no need to spoil an *eight-dollar* corset." Regardless, the corset strings were cut; my grandmother did seem able to breathe easier; and the ambulance arrived as quickly as could be expected, considering that we lived fifteen miles from the village over winding steep roads, the last five miles of which still consisted of a one-lane dirt trace no better in 1959 than in 1948, when I'd first come to Lost Nation to live with my grandparents.

"Helen, you stay here and keep an eye on her," my grandmother said as the two attendants carried her out of the house on a stretcher. She meant Old Josie, who continued to wring her apron and invoke the assistance of the Holy Family on behalf of my grandmother. So while my great-aunt baby-sat Josie, I rode to the hospital in the back of the speeding ambulance with Gram and the volunteer fireman from the village who was administering oxygen to her.

At the hairpin bend partway down the Fiddler's Elbow, where years ago Theresa Dubois had lost her silver dollar in a snowbank, my grandmother grasped my wrist.

With her other hand she lifted the oxygen mask. "Tell the driver to slow down, Tut. There's no need to kill us all."

The ambulance driver, a man with dark jowls and a put-upon expression, cranked his head around for a fraction of a second. "What'd she say?"

"Step on it," I told him. "She said step on it."

He nodded and slued the ambulance out of the switchback at the foot of the Elbow. On the flats approaching the Currier farm I looked over his shoulder at the speedometer. The red needle was vibrating just under one hundred. Out the window, Ben Currier came chugging down his roadside hayfield on his ancient green Allis-Chalmers tractor. As we went screaming past him he started to lift one gloved hand, then dropped it to the tractor steering wheel again, as though unsure about the protocol of waving to an ambulance carrying one of his neighbors to the hospital.

Now we were shrieking along the edge of the central green in Kingdom Common; now racing up U.S. Route Five toward Memphremagog at a flat one hundred and ten miles per hour. Shimmering heat mirages danced on the highway ahead of us, imparting an air of unreality to the morning and the ambulance ride. How could any of this be happening to my indomitable grandmother? I felt as though I'd stumbled into another dimension, one from which I might never return.

In a matter of minutes we skidded up to the emergency entrance of the Hospital of Mary, Blessed Queen of the Border Country: the hospital my Little Aunt Klee had selected for my grandmother a year ago, after Gram had sustained a gall bladder attack. But today my grandmother was having none of the Blessed Border Queen. Looking out of the ambulance window and seeing the serene, blue-robed plaster statue over the emergency door, arms extended in benign welcome, she brushed the oxygen mask aside again and said distinctly, "County." Meaning that she was to be taken to the county hospital on the other side of town.

And that is pretty much the way the relentlessly hot and arid summer of 1959 had gone for the Kittredge family.

Back in June, when my grandmother's gall bladder threatened to act up again, my Little Aunt Klee arrived from New York where she and Freddi were pursuing their Off-Broadway acting careers by working as counter girls in various Off-Broadway cafeterias. Immediately the entire household had been thrown into the state of tumultuous disarray that inevitably accompanied Klee's visits. In 1959, besides a nearly round-the-clock regimen of papering and painting several remote upper bedchambers that no one had slept in regularly for twenty-five or thirty years, Klee fought tooth and nail to get Gram to allow electricity to be installed at the house as a labor-saving device to prevent her from working herself into the ground, as Klee put it. Of course my grandmother refused even to consider such an innovation. In the first place, she had worked herself into the ground all her life and was not about to stop now. Moreover, she harbored a deep fear of burning up in her bed in a fire caused by faulty wiring, and had not one good word to say about either electricity or any electrical appliances. In desperation my little aunt paid for the wiring herself, but my grandmother had the last word after all by refusing to allow anyone to use it after it was hooked up.

My grandfather, in the meantime, was retreating further each week into the isolation of his work in the woods. Once again this summer he and I were cutting brush off the clearing marking the American-Canadian Line along the northern border of Kingdom

County. After Klee's arrival he stayed overnight in Labrador more often than not.

Not that Gram didn't have plenty of help at home if only she could be persuaded to avail herself of it. My Great-Aunt Helen, whose husband had died the previous year, had more or less moved in that summer. Dad faithfully drove up from White River Junction once a week, and of course there was always Old Josie.

Old Josie, for the record, was the most recent of a succession of housekeepers hired by Dad and my two little aunts since Gram's first gall bladder trouble. I remember them now as a featureless string of widowed and maiden women in their fifties and sixties, smelling faintly of sweat and strong yellow soap, with names as drab and sad as their personal histories: Mrs. Brown, Mrs. Gray, Mrs. Quick—here was a misnomer if one ever existed—and Old Josie, whose last name I don't believe I ever did know. They were supposed to prevent my grandmother from working herself into the ground, but didn't, for the simple reason that she refused to allow them to do a tap of housework.

"Whatever else she may be or may not be, Old Josie is no housekeeper," my grandmother had said with a heavy sigh several times a week since Josie's arrival. "She is thoroughly incompetent."

How Gram knew this was beyond me, though, since she continued to insist on doing every last stroke of housework herself. Yet in the end, I have no doubt that, more than any other factor, it was the onslaught of the cluster flies that resulted in her heart attack.

First singly, next by the dozens, finally in vast legions, a veritable plague of them came swarming out of the walls of the old house, starting in early August, soon after Little Aunt Klee's return to New York. Slightly smaller than an ordinary housefly and slightly darker, they began to emerge about eight o'clock in the morning. By noon you could hear their maddening buzz from any place in the house. They congregated by the thousands on the inside windowsills and along the wide baseboards; even after my grandmother had swept up the last invaders of the day, around six in the evening, we could hear their incessant humming from somewhere deep within the walls of the farmhouse, like an alarm clock someone had forgotten to shut off in some faraway upper chamber.

To repel this scourge, my grandmother resorted to every conceivable stratagem. She stopped up the cracks in the window casings and along the baseboards with pliable felt weather stripping, which proved to be no deterrent to the flies at all. From the hardware store in the Common she purchased a bright green, pump-handled bug sprayer, which Aunt Helen promptly dubbed the Bomb. The Bomb held three full quarts of a popular DDT solution. Armed with this virulent infusion, my grandmother saturated the windowsills and baseboards with the dispassionate ruthlessness of a veteran crop duster. She retraced her path of destruction with broom and dustpan, sweeping up thousands of victims, whose tiny corpses she consigned to the outside burning barrel. Yet invariably, by the time she completed bombing the farthest-back bedroom, fresh reinforcements of cluster flies were overrunning the kitchen. For weeks on end the entire house reeked of the sweetish, lethal odor of DDT, but the flies kept coming, numberless as the hordes of Genghis Khan.

Not that my grandmother was ever less than a formidable adversary, her gall bladder troubles notwithstanding. Some years earlier she had waged war with glorious results against an army of shiny black carpenter ants that had filed in endless procession out of the woodshed, across the kitchen floor, and under the door of Egypt, only to disappear there beneath the floorboards. Equipped with a treacherous homemade decoction of rose water laced with arsenic, which the Borgias themselves might have coveted, my grandmother quickly thinned down the ranks of the ants to a few stunned survivors.

Over the decade that I had lived with her and my grandfather, Gram had also put to rout a dynasty of white-footed field mice, several swarms of irascible blue hornets, and an untidy colony of little brown bats, not to mention half a dozen wintering red squirrels that had taken up residence in the attic some years ago.

No matter. Unimpressed, the cluster flies just kept coming. I suppose it was ironical, if you could only look at it that way. Here was my grandmother, unvanquished by the Depression and its interminable aftermath in Kingdom County, unvanquished by the border country's notorious seven-month winters, unvanquished by the ongoing ordeals of alternately nurturing and chivvying her family through every imaginable vicissitude of rural life and by forty years of unabated rivalry with the meanest old bastard in Kingdom County, about to be brought to her knees at last by a swarm of little flies.

"To win is all, Tut," my grandmother had told me many times. Now she seemed on the brink of losing one of the great battles of her life.

Apparently the cluster flies had been there in the walls of the farmhouse all along, biding their time like seventeen-year locusts. It was as though they had been waiting, like the instruments of some malevolent and unfathomable design, until my grandmother was at her weakest, worn down by the years and by her troublesome gall bladder, by Little Aunt Klee's recent visit, by Old Josie, the house-keeper whom she refused to allow to keep house, by the unprecedented three-month hot spell in which the fields turned brown in June, the river dwindled to a small stream by July, and the spring that supplied water to both the house and barn was now threatening to run dry for the first time since Sojourner Kittredge discovered it in the summer of 1775. Only then did the flies issue forth, rarely flying anywhere at all but rather reclining on their backs with their legs in the air and buzzing like swarming bees until we imagined that we could hear them not only all day but all night as well, whether we actually did or not.

After the failure of the felt weather stripping and the Bomb, Aunt Helen somehow prevailed upon Gram to avail herself of the electrical outlets my Little Aunt Klee had caused to be installed earlier in the summer, and the Hoover vacuum cleaner my little aunts and my father had purchased for her soon after the arrival of the flies. The Hoover, as we called it, was a gigantic old-fashioned floor model with a heavy canvas dust bag the size of a tackling dummy. Gram had not used it once, of course, any more than she had used a lamp or toaster or any other appliance powered by the invisible current she believed would inevitably result in a fire that would burn up the house and us in our beds along with it. Now, in desperation, she turned to the Hoover as a last resort.

Seventy years old, weighing no more than ninety pounds, still

recovering from her latest bout with her gall bladder, my grandmother charged through the house with the vacuum cleaner, from
downstairs to upstairs and back downstairs again, in relentless pur-
suit of her tiny adversaries. Overnight, to Hoover-up became a common verb in our family. All day long my grandmother Hoovered-up
flies. The infernal machine weighed a ton, and although I lugged it
up and down the stairs for Gram when I was around, I all but had to
wrest it out of her hands to do so.

Please, could I Hoover-up the flies? Hardly. I had my sashaying
grandfather to keep track of. Couldn't Aunt Helen? Preposterous.
Aunt Helen, though younger than my grandmother and in excellent
health, was getting on in years. The heat of the dog days might do
for her; how would we feel then?

Well, what about Old Josie? Old Josie, her quaint cognomen
notwithstanding, was scarcely fifty, and as strong as most men.
Wasn't housecleaning what Gram had hired her to do? Out of the
question, Tut. For whatever else she might or might not be, Old
Josie was no housekeeper. Old Josie was thoroughly incompetent
and everyone knew it. Even Old Josie herself seemed to be in no
doubt at all about her unmitigated incompetence, since each time
my grandmother made this declaration, Josie wrung her apron and
nodded her head in sad concurrence.

To this day I can see the four of us. My grandmother in the
vanguard, manhandling the Hoover along with its business end roaring like some horrendous implement of war. Next comes Old Josie,
kerchiefed and aproned—Why? My grandmother never permitted
her to so much as boil water for coffee or swab out a frying pan—
trailing along in the Hoover's wake, fingering a string of rosary beads
of a sickly-pink hue. Here I am, bearing yards of extension cord,
since there were no outlets upstairs. And finally my merry great-
aunt, rolling her eyes and inclining her head at the same time that
she was scared to death that my grandmother was about to have a
heart attack.

"For God's sake, Mom, can't you ease up?" my father said one
afternoon when he arrived from White River in time to witness this
memorable procession returning to the kitchen from a futile
Hoovering-up expedition.

"No, I cannot ease up," Gram said. "Not until every last cluster fly is eradicated from this house."

This, then, is how matters stood on the steamy August morning when my grandfather and I got back from the village with a new chain saw blade and I went inside for a glass of water before I headed back to the woods with him, and met my grandmother hell-bent for election on her way out of the kitchen with the Hoover. According to Aunt Helen, who told me the whole story afterward, Gram had been in the summer kitchen slicing corn off the cob for canning when, in a horrible moment of epiphany, she had somehow or other divined that the perpetual night-and-day buzzing of the flies must be coming from the farmhouse attic.

The attic! Without hesitation she lugged the Hoover through the house and upstairs. One step at a time, she heaved that behemoth of a vacuum cleaner up the winding attic staircase, with me un-winding the extension cords behind her, and Old Josie hovering at the foot of the stairs next to Aunt Helen with her hands over her eyes, beseeching the Holy Family for protection. My grandmother took one quick look at the high attic windows under the east and west peaks of the roof. The panes were blackened with cluster flies and the floor beneath was crawling with them.

She switched on the Hoover and made straight for the nearer, west window. Past the ruined horsehair sofas and heaps of disabled wooden chairs and tables. Past the antiquated foot warmers and bed warmers and the porcelain washbasins and pitchers and the vast old chamber pots my grandfather insisted on calling thunder mugs. Past the boxes of children's books I now considered myself too grown-up to read, until, just a few feet from the window, my grandmother stopped short and, unaccountably, turned back.

Without the Hoover this time, she retraced her steps, by me, by Aunt Helen at the head of the attic stairs, by Old Josie with her apron now flung over her head, and down to the first floor of the farmhouse. My grandmother proceeded to the kitchen. She got a glass of water from the sink pump and drank two or three swallows and frowned at me slightly. Only then did she say, "Call the ambulance in the Common, Tut. I believe my heart's flar-ing up."

When at last Gram was ensconced in the hospital—the county hospital—in an oxygen tent, she seemed quite herself again. In other words, in charge. "You can go back to the village with the ambulance people, Tut. Phone the Tatros or the Curriers when you get there and they'll come in and run you home."

She reached out from under the plastic tent and took my wrist, and her grip was very firm. "Sweep up the flies at least twice a day. Don't bother with that Hoover anymore, except to make sure I shut it off before I left the attic. I don't want to lie here worrying about the rest of the family burning up in their beds."

She paused. "Keep track of your grandfather. He's not to be allowed to sashay off somewhere behind my back while I'm indisposed. I'll be home tomorrow or the next day at the latest. This is just a little flare-up."

She released my wrist and nodded for me to go. But before I reached the door she called me back again.

"Tell your Aunt Helen not to let Old Josie go rummaging in my cupboards, Tut. Whatever else she is or is not, Josie is no housekeeper."

For once, however, it appeared as though my grandmother's sheer will alone might not be enough to keep her going. Dad arrived from White River early that afternoon, and Dr. Perry Harrison told him flatly that Gram's heart was running down like one of her old winding clocks for which the key had been lost. My little aunts were summoned home from New York. Doc Harrison met with all three of them the following morning and told them that the only encouraging news was that Gram was in fighting spirits. "She's mad at you, Cleopatra, for installing electricity in the house. And she's mad at all of you for going in together on that vacuum cleaner. That's what she's blaming her heart attack on. The Hoover."

My grandfather, in the meantime, registered only grim silence and a perpetual scowl. Except at chore time, he did not even come down to the house from Labrador, much less visit my grandmother in the hospital.

The one happy turn of events was that against my grandmother's express orders, Old Josie and I, armed with the Hoover, invaded the attic on the day after Gram went into the hospital and made such a successful inroad in the cluster flies' population that for the rest of the day only a fraction of their usual number appeared on the downstairs windowsills. Early the next morning we returned to the attic yet again and, despite Josie's thorough and self-acknowledged incompetence, we wreaked such vengeance upon the flies that by noon the humming in the walls had ceased altogether for the first time in two weeks.

That evening Aunt Helen and I drove up to the hospital in Gramp's lumber truck. We arrived around dusk, a few minutes after Dad and my little aunts had left for the Farm. To cheer Gram up, and partly as a small joke, I'd brought along Lyle, the stuffed pink crocodile my grandfather had won many years ago at Kingdom Fair.

My grandmother's face lit up the moment she saw him. "Put him on the foot of the bed, Tut. Where I can see him when I wake up in the night."

I was glad to see that Gram was out of the oxygen tent, though she looked very pale, and a tube in the side of her mouth made it difficult for her to speak distinctly. "How's Lord Ra?" she said, meaning the hawk-headed wooden god at home in Egypt.

"He's fine."

"Oh, yes," Aunt Helen said, cutting her eyes at me. "Lord Ra's right as rain."

"Be serious, Helen," Gram said. "Sarcasm doesn't become a woman of your years."

For a time no one spoke. Except for a dim night light by the door, the hospital room was dark. The August heat was stifling. Outside the open window, stretching off into the night through the far Canadian mountains, Lake Memphremagog was lower than the oldest people in Kingdom County could remember. Wells and springs were running dry all over the border country as the drought held on, day after day, week after week.

"How are you coming against the flies?" my grandmother asked, enunciating each word as precisely as possible because of the impeding tube.

"Fine," I said. "Josie and I got five cleaner bags of them out of the attic. That noise has stopped."

My grandmother frowned.

After a minute she said, "I'll see for myself soon enough. I intend to go home tomorrow."

"What did Dr. Harrison say?" Aunt Helen said.

"I didn't consult Dr. Harrison. This is my decision."

"Oh?" Aunt Helen said, looking at me.

"I'll expect your grandfather to call for me at eight a.m. sharp," my grandmother said.

I could hardly believe I'd heard her correctly, and said I'd relay her wishes to Dad and my little aunts as soon as I got home.

My grandmother reached out and gripped my wrist. "You'll do no such thing, Tut. You'll tell your grandfather, and only your grandfather, that I want to come home at eight o'clock tomorrow morning. Do you understand that?"

I did. But it seemed exceedingly unlikely to me, as Aunt Helen and I headed back to Lost Nation that night, that my grandfather, of all persons, would be of any help at all in assisting his wife and implacable adversary to return to the Farm.

"Your grandmother is a strong woman, Austen," my great-aunt said a few minutes later as we jounced along the heaved concrete through the deep woods between Memphremagog and the Common.

"I know," I said.

"Do you know how strong?"

I glanced over at my aunt. As nearly as I could tell, her face in the faint illumination of the truck dashlights looked totally serious.

"She's the strongest person I've ever known," Aunt Helen said quietly; and then, with none of the mischievous irony for which she was renowned, she told me a story I had previously heard only fragments of: the story of how she and my grandmother had come to North America, nearly sixty years ago, as Home Children.

Now when I think of my grandmother's girlhood odyssey, I envision a picture. It is a picture never painted, yet I can see it as clearly as if it had been shown to me many times from my earliest years. It presents itself to my imagination in dark tones, and depicts my grandmother and her sister standing on a Halifax dock, with many other children, in a driving sleet storm. My grandmother is thirteen years old. Beside her Aunt Helen, at eleven, is already by several inches the taller of the two. Both girls are wearing severe black bonnets and black woolen coats and my grandmother is holding fiercely to my great-aunt's wrist, taking no chance that they might be separated. Looming in the harbor background through the pelting sleet is the black steamship in which they left Liverpool eighteen days ago, as part of the exodus of nearly one hundred thousand orphaned and impoverished Home Children shipped from the British Isles to Canada during the late nineteenth and early twentieth centuries, to work as hired hands and household servants.

As my great-aunt explained, the steamship that had brought them to America was to have a significant influence on the rest of my grandmother's life. The orphan ship was a battered, leaky, ancient, British-owned hulk commissioned out of Cairo. And stacked in the hold just adjacent to the cramped, airless barracks in the bowels of the ship where the orphans were quartered were thousands of Egyptian mummies. At the ages of thirteen and eleven, my grandmother and great-aunt had never before in their lives beheld such a phenomenon as a mummy. Yet my aunt told me that from the moment my grandmother laid eyes on these odd relics, which for a time in the late nineteenth and early twentieth centuries were exhumed from Egyptian common burial grounds by the millions and burned with coal to fire the boilers of North African ships and steam locomotives, she was consumed by an awe that would grow into a deep, lifelong interest in all matters Egyptian. Aunt Helen confided to me that she herself found the mummies at first frightening and then ludicrous; she could never in any way connect them in her mind with living people. To my young grandmother, however, there was about them an air of aloof serenity and wisdom as though, besides resins and plant fibers and desiccated bone, they contained some wholly spiritual essence rendering them invulnerable to the very worst that mortals could do to them, including wrenching them out of the ground and using them to stoke the smoldering coal in the furnaces of orphan ships.

But the most vivid images in this picture are not the black orphan ship in Halifax harbor, the teeming dock, or the fierce expression of my girl-grandmother as she clasps her younger sister's wrist. The most vivid images, as described by my great-aunt more than half a century later on our truck ride home from that tiny North Woods hospital, and reconstituted now in my memory after yet another thirty years, are the large placards fastened around the girls' necks on strings, bearing not their own names but that of the backcountry Cape Breton sheep farmer whose wretchedly poor forty acres was their destination. There they stand, the two of them, linked hand to wrist and waiting in the storm with their fading placards, fixed in my mind forever.

My grandmother and Aunt Helen stayed less than a month on the sheep farm. My great-aunt told me that they fled the place in the dead of the night with just the clothes on their back and a short length of rope tying them wrist to wrist so they wouldn't wander apart in the thick coastal fog. Somehow the two girls made their way on foot down to the Nova Scotia mainland and on into New Brunswick. They worked at whatever odd jobs they could find: stacking firewood, flaking codfish to dry on long seaside racks, cleaning out lumber camp horse hovels. When no work was available they simply appeared at a farmer's back stoop. Not asking, mind you. Aunt Helen emphasized that my grandmother never asked, and she always insisted on chopping up some stove wood or sweeping the dooryard or doing a load of wash in exchange for whatever food they were given. If they were allowed to sleep in the barn, my grandmother took care that they were up and gone long before dawn, in case the farmer or his wife tried to detain them and find out where they belonged.

In fact, they belonged nowhere except together, two young girls, attached to one another by a frayed rope, now ghosting barefooted —their shoes had fallen to pieces weeks ago—through the raw, turn-of-the-century terrain along the northern New England border with Canada.

"Adrift in the wilderness, Austen," my great-aunt said with uncharacteristic somberness. "Your grandmother and I were adrift in the wilderness. We were Home Children with no home."

Where were they headed? Only away from their past. They had

no other destination. Just away. Away from being shunted from one distant relative to another in Scotland after their parents had died of smallpox when the girls were five and three, away from the Glasgow orphanage where they were finally selected to go to Canada as Home Children, away from the brutal Cape Breton sheep farmer.

One day they were chased through the woods by two tramps. They escaped into a swamp, where they hid all night behind a beaver lodge. After that they traveled mainly by dark, dodging the lumber camps and hobo jungles and junction hamlets, and foraging their food from the countryside.

It was late summer when they came to the paper mill on the Upper Connecticut River, on the remote eastern boundary of Kingdom County. They could smell the mill for the better part of a morning before they arrived, the way horses in arid terrain can scent water a great distance off, except that the paper mill redolence was sulfurous and rank, and when they arrived and looked down onto it from a completely denuded ridge through the hazy reeking cloud of effluvia belched out of the mill's three smokestacks, the place resembled a mirage more than a real town. Only the fact that they were now close to starving kept my grandmother from immediately giving the place a wide berth.

"Come, sister," she told Aunt Helen, "we have to find something to eat. We have to find work."

The mill was hiring, and for the next year my grandmother and aunt worked there nights sorting the rags and old linen used for high-grade writing paper. They lived with several dozen other mill girls in a vast riverside tenement known as the Beehive, to which, on Sundays, the young men who worked at the mill and in the surrounding woods came sniffing around in their cheap cloth caps, their newly-shaved necks swelling out their tight collars like the lust-swollen necks of buck deer in the rut. Then my outraged and frightened grandmother locked herself and her sister inside their room, where they remained barricaded until the following morning.

Late one spring afternoon soon after the ice had gone out of the river, as my aunt and grandmother were walking to work from the Beehive, they looked upstream and perceived in the slant, thinning light of the lowering sun, a single figure profiled above the white water. He was riding a log in the vanguard of the vast log drive that passed the mill for two weeks each May from the big woods and lakes upriver along the Canadian border. He was steering the log casually with his long pick pole, guiding the bouncing thirty-two-foot length of spruce trunk down the roaring spring rapids as comfortably as a man might lean on an ax handle on the packed smooth dirt of his farm dooryard. He wore a checked red shirt, green wool pants stagged off at the top of his high caulked boots, and a dark, wide-brimmed woodsman's hat, which he suddenly lifted to the two mill girls on the bank. As he swept off the hat to reveal his dark hair and light eyes, he nodded gravely. Then he set the hat back on his head again and passed around the bend below the mill, out of sight in the setting sun.

Other 'jacks came down with the drive that evening, and for the next two weeks the paper mill hamlet was a roaring carnival of brawling rivermen, while hundreds of thousands of logs swept past from the huge woods upriver. But no one else rode a log through the white water, much less tipped his hat to my grandmother.

That fall a spectacular conflagration destroyed both the mill and the Beehive. Fortunately, it broke out during the night, when my grandmother and aunt were at work, but the sight of their tinder-dry tenement bursting into an inferno so impressed my grandmother that throughout her subsequent life at the Farm she kept two brimming buckets of water in every last room in the house in case of fire. Five hours later the entire town was gone. All that remained were the fire-twisted rails of the spur line up which the old rags and linen had come in freight cars, and down which the newsprint and stationery had gone.

Next my grandmother and Aunt Helen landed in the Kingdom County railroad and lumbering town of Pond in the Sky, where they found work cleaning out passenger coaches on the Grand Trunk Line from Montreal to Portland. And though you might suppose that my grandmother's aversion to my grandfather's sashaying habits originated during her transatlantic crossing in the orphan ship, or from her hand-to-mouth odyssey along the Canadian frontier, hitched wrist to wrist to my aunt by a hank of frayed rope, Aunt Helen intimated to me that Gram's strange antipathy to traveling developed from that job swabbing out spittoons and brushing off sooty seats on the passenger coaches, while ignoring the ribald blandishments of the traveling dry goods drummers and cattle and lumber buyers and soldiers who regularly rode the Grand Trunk. There is no doubt that she was more than willing, after two months of these indignities, to answer my Great-Grandfather Gleason Kittredge's ad in *The Kingdom County Monitor* for a live-in housekeeper to take care of his home and his ailing wife on the Farm in Lost Nation Township, just south of the Canadian border.

Yet it was much more than the opportunity to get away from the Grand Trunk riffraff that influenced my grandmother to accept a housekeeping job in a place only slightly less remote and wild-appearing than the sheep farmer's outpost on Cape Breton. It was the photograph in my great-grandfather's parlor of the bare-headed young man in a checked shirt and lumberman's wool pants, looking soberly down into the camera from the top of a twenty-foot-high rollway of logs waiting to be broken out into the spring river just north of the Farm—leaning easily and confidently on his peavey exactly the way he had leaned back on his pick pole to steer that log through the white water above the paper mill eight months ago.

"I know that man," my grandmother said, pointing at the photograph. "He lifted his hat to me."

"I'm glad to hear it," my Great-Grandfather Gleason said. "I wasn't aware that he'd learned any manners. He certainly hasn't learned much else. He left school at twelve to go on a log drive, and never went back."

"Where is he now?" my grandmother said, staring at the picture.

"Out West someplace on a surveying crew. Instead of attending college, where he could go free if he wanted."

"I'll take that housekeeping job if my sister can come live here with me," my grandmother said abruptly.

"And that," my great-aunt told me as we turned off the county road and started up into Lost Nation Hollow on our way back from the hospital, "is when Abiah most certainly set her cap for your grandfather."

The night was very dark, and by the summer of 1959, the Hollow was a Lost Nation in more than just its name. Where there had been farms and lantern lights in farmhouse windows eleven years ago, when I'd first come to live with my grandparents, there was now darkness, and the dark bulks of deserted buildings already starting to collapse into cellar holes darker still.

"So," I said, "Gram fell in love with him. When she saw him in the picture. Or even back riding the log down the rapids. That's what you're telling me."

"Oh, my, no," Aunt Helen said with a short laugh. "Nothing of the sort, Austen. I'm sure falling in love had nothing to do with it. You see, your grandmother mistakenly thought that by lifting his hat, your grandfather was paying tribute to her. That's why she set her cap for him. Then it was just a matter of outwaiting him. Every time he got back from one of his sashayings, she was there waiting. In the end, she wore him down through sheer persistence."

When Aunt Helen and I got back to the Farm that night, I said nothing to Dad and my little aunts about Gram's plans to come home the next day. Well before sunrise the following morning, I hurried up the ridge to Labrador, where I found my grandfather boiling coffee in a fire-blackened saucepan. As I came through the door he threw in another handful of coffee without speaking. He was already dressed in his work boots and hat.

I grinned at him. "What do you do, sleep in your hat?"

"What I do or don't do here is my concern."

"I'm going to tell Gram you've been sleeping in your hat."

"Tell away."

"I guess taking it off at the wrong time fifty years ago got you into a peck of trouble."

My grandfather looked at me sharply.

"I saw Gram last night," I told him. "She wants you to drive up to the hospital and bring her home."

"Does she now?"

The smell of boiling coffee filled the camp as my grandfather poured us each a scalding mug of the powerful stuff. Camp coffee, we called it. We sat at the plank table and sipped it. From time to time he looked across the table at me, but said nothing. Mainly he stared broodingly at the map of Labrador on the wall with its large blank white spaces labeled "terra incognita."

To my surprise, however, my grandfather did not go to the woods that morning. He returned to the farmhouse, put on his town clothes, and told me we were going to Memphremagog.

Scheduled morning visiting hours at the hospital did not begin until ten o'clock. My grandfather and I arrived before eight, just as Doc Harrison was coming out of Gram's room. When my grandfather asked how she was, Doc walked a few steps down the hall away from Gram's door and said bluntly, "Old. She's old and tired, Austen. Worn down like the rest of us. Only more so from putting up with a devil like you all these years."

My grandfather looked at Doc Harrison as though to assess what he had really said. "Evidently she wants to go home. She doesn't find this as much of a holiday as she expected," Gramp finally said.

"If you spring her out of here and cart her up to that so-called farm of yours, I wouldn't guarantee she'd live a week," Doc said.

"And if she stays here?"

Doc sighed. "Frankly, I can't guarantee much either way."

My grandfather walked past Doc Harrison and on down the hall and into Gram's room, with me behind him. The first thing I noticed was that the tube was still in the side of her mouth. In the daylight, it made her look helpless, a way I'd never seen her before, though her dark eyes were as alert as ever.

"Do you want to go home?" my grandfather said louder than necessary.

My grandmother started to say something, then lifted her hand and touched the tube.

"Yes or no?" my grandfather said. "Speak up."

"She can't speak up," I said. "They've got something in her mouth."

My grandfather left the room. Almost immediately he returned with a nurse. "This woman can't talk with that apparatus down her gullet," he said. "Snake it out."

"She needs it, Mr. Kittredge. To eat."

"No, she doesn't," my grandfather said. "She's going home. She can eat there the same way she always has."

I was half-fearful and half-hoping that Dad and my little aunts would show up and prevent my grandmother from returning to the Farm. They didn't, though. The nurse wheeled her to the door, clutching Lyle the Pink Crocodile, and my grandfather carried her out to the truck and lifted her up into the cab. She sat by the passenger's window, grim-faced and silent, still clutching Lyle.

"I think she sets more store by that reptile fella than she does by me," my grandfather said as we went around to get in the driver's door.

I nodded, sure that she did.

Oddly, neither Dad nor my little aunts protested much when my grandfather and I appeared at the Farm with my grandmother. For her own part, Gram seemed greatly relieved to be home and to see for herself that the cluster flies were gone. Old Josie went around wringing her apron and thanking Jesus, Joseph, and Mary for my grandmother's deliverance. Freddi cried and wanted to hug everybody. Klee tried to get Gram to drink a tall glass of a vile-tasting homeopathic cure-all called Tiger's Milk, but my grandmother was not about to be prayed over by Old Josie, squeezed half to death by Freddi, or physicked by Klee. She instructed my grandfather to carry her into Egypt, and there she spent the next few days subsisting on tea and a little toast, and dozing or sleeping much of the time.

During Gram's waking moments she was perfectly alert but even more silent than usual. A tense quietude had settled over the entire house. All of us, including Gram herself, seemed to be holding our breaths to see whether she would regain her strength. During those days I divided my time between working up on the Canadian Line with my grandfather, who now that he had fetched my grandmother home from the hospital seemed to feel he had fulfilled all his responsibilities to her, and reading to Gram or just sitting with her in Egypt.

"I'm going back to White River in the morning, Austen," my father told me one night. "With school starting next week, I have to begin getting ready. Can you hold down the fort here for a while?"

I assured him that I could.

In the meantime, Gram seemed to stay about the same. She ate very little and slept a great deal, as though to make up for all those years of sleeping only four or five hours a night.

Evening after evening, I sat by her daybed, reading aloud her beloved passages on the Egyptians in the Book of Genesis and in Herodotus's *History of the Ancient World*, and the catastrophic articles from the Doomsday Book, as well as the dog-eared old magazine articles on the discovery of King Tut's tomb. " 'What do you see?' Carter's awe-stricken assistant asked as the eternally hopeful archaeologist played his electric torch on the innermost chamber of Tutankhamen's final resting place.

"Carter paused for a long moment. Then in hushed tones he replied, 'Wonderful things. I see wonderful things.' "

As I read on into those hot late-summer nights in the farmhouse at the end of Lost Nation Hollow, the great Sphinx and hawk-headed Lord Ra looked on in the yellow-white lantern light as though they too were deeply attentive to the marvels of Tutankhamen's tomb. Except for Lyle the Pink Crocodile, reposing incongruously next to my grandmother on the counterpane she'd quilted of the Four Colorful Ramses guarding the temple of Abu Simbel, we might have been thousands of miles away, reading by lantern light in the antechamber to a pharaoh's burial chamber in the Valley of the Kings.

"How many books have you read this summer, Tut?" my grandmother said suddenly one night in a clear, sharp voice. It was very late, well after midnight. I had just finished reading the old *Life* article on Howard Carter again. I'd supposed that my grandmother had at last fallen asleep, and when she spoke, I started.

"Well, well," she said before I could reply. "Never mind. The exact number isn't important. You still like to read and study, don't you?"

"Yes," I told her.

"I'm glad you do. Very glad. No one can ever take a book you've read away from you. And you're going to be heard from, you know. Like Mr. Howard Carter. You'll see great sights and you'll be heard from."

My grandmother reached out and took my wrist, the way she

had on the day I first arrived at the Farm with my grandfather and again on the afternoon when she first saw the huge snow owl and on our way to the hospital with the rescue unit and so many other times over the past eleven years. "Your grandmother is going on a long sojourn herself, Tut."

"Where, Gram?" I said, alarmed. "Where are you going?"

"To Egypt," she said in a strong and steady voice. "See it?"

With her free hand she made a short, encompassing gesture, and I too saw Egypt. I saw Egypt everywhere I looked in Gram's sitting room.

With great effort, gripping my wrist as fiercely as hawk-headed Ra ever gripped a sacrificial victim, my grandmother rose partway off her pillows and extended her free hand toward the opposite wall. "I see them!" she exclaimed.

"See what, Gram? What do you see?"

My grandmother lay back, her face triumphant and composed. "Wonderful things," she said. "I see wonderful things, Tut."

Then she let out her breath quite easily, though her fingers remained as firm as ever on my wrist until, some time later, I detached them myself and went up to Labrador, crying the entire way, to notify my grandfather that my grandmother had departed on her long sojourn at last.

M y grandfather could hardly have been surprised by the sad news I had to report, yet it seemed to make him very angry.

"What do you expect me to do about it?" he said. "I can't bring her back."

He did return to the house with me, but instead of looking in on my grandmother, he went directly to his sawmill. A few minutes later I heard the whine of the big log saw starting up, though dawn was still hours away.

"Grief, Austen!" Freddi said through a shuddering sob. "Does he know?"

I nodded.

Aunt Helen went back into the sitting room with Old Josie, who had resolutely refused to leave my grandmother's remains, to get the body ready to be viewed. My aunts had called Dad in White River, and he was on his way up. Unfortunately Uncle Rob was off in the wilds of Alaska that summer and couldn't be reached by phone.

Klee, in the meantime, continued to work on an elaborate stencil pattern of fleur-de-lys around the top border of the dining room wallpaper. "Your grandmother never left a job unfinished once she started it, Austen," she told me from the top of her stepladder. "I'm sure she won't rest comfortably until this job is finished."

I was in a daze. The full impact of my grandmother's death had not hit me yet. I still couldn't seem to accept the fact that she was gone. Teary-eyed and out of touch with my surroundings, I wandered here and there around the Farm. Everywhere I went I was aware of both her absence and her strong lingering presence. Several times a desperate intimation of ultimate finality swept over me, a certainty that my life and the lives of the rest of the family had come to a kind of close along with my grandmother's. Each time the desolation passed and again I'd just feel detached from the morning and the Farm and myself. My wrist still tingled from my grandmother's grip, or at least I imagined that it did. I was only vaguely aware of my grandfather's screaming log saw.

Dad arrived about seven o'clock. He glanced toward the sawmill, where my grandfather was now operating the higher-pitched ripsaw, and looked at me questioningly. I shrugged.

Little Aunt Freddi was most helpful to me. While Dad called Lawyer Zack Barrows, in accordance with some private instructions Gram had evidently given him, I confided to Freddi my sense that Gram was still here, yet not here. Freddi listened sympathetically and said that I would always have that sense, and I always have, though along with the death of my mother, the loss of my grandmother when I was seventeen years old remains to this day the most difficult memory of my youth.

About ten o'clock Lawyer Barrows appeared in the shiny bottle-green suit jacket he'd worn to court the day my grandmother hauled my grandfather up in front of Judge Allen to prevent him from flooding her orchard. With Zack was his crony Sheriff Mason White, who was also the local undertaker. They drove up in Mason's hearse.

Dad and Freddi and my Great-Aunt Helen watched from the kitchen as the old lawyer and the sheriff solemnly approached the house, not without a few wary looks over their shoulder in the direction of my grandfather's sawmill. Zack was carrying a large briefcase.

"No doubt Mom's laughing up her sleeve at all this," Freddi said, "wherever she is."

"Wherever she is, Mom is not laughing," Klee called in from the dining room, where she was still working on the stenciling. "The dead, you know, always act entirely in character."

"We're terribly sorry about your loss, folks," Zack said after shaking hands all around. "Terribly sorry."

"Yes," Mason White said in his most unctuous undertaker's tones. He put a comforting hand on Freddi's shoulder. "We want to express our deepest condolences."

Freddi pulled away from the undertaker's hand. "We know very well why you're here, Mason. There's no need for you at all. Mom wants to be buried here at home in the family plot."

Mason gave a sad and knowing little smile, as though well-accustomed to the vagaries of the suddenly bereaved.

"How's Mr. Kittredge taking it?" Lawyer Barrows said.

"Fine," Dad said. "Can't you hear him?" He jerked his head toward the mill, where my grandfather was hard at it with the rip saw.

Zack cleared his throat. "I'm afraid," he said, "that he's going to have to be here for this."

"I'll get him," Freddi said.

Aunt Helen looked at me, but today I was in no frame of mind for our usual conspiratorial glances. I simply could not accept the fact that a person as fiercely alive as my grandmother, a person whose guidance and good opinion I had depended on daily for eleven years, could be dead.

Zack Barrows sat down at the kitchen table and began rummaging through his briefcase. At last he produced a long, official-looking, buff-colored envelope containing a typed document. He cleared his throat. "Now, folks," the lawyer said in his most pompous courtroom manner, "usually, as I'm sure you're well aware, the reading of the last will and testament comes after the funeral service. In this case, since the will stipulates certain conditions for that service—"

The door opened and Freddi reappeared, followed immediately by my grandfather.

"Austen," Zack said, half-rising.

Mason held out his hand toward my grandfather. "We want to express our—"

"Get on with your business," my grandfather said to Zack. "I don't have all morning."

He ignored Mason's hand entirely. The last time he and Mason had officially met was up at Labrador some years ago, when my grandfather had tossed him a stick of lighted dynamite.

Again Zack cleared his throat. Then he read aloud in the farmhouse kitchen that I had never thought of, and never afterward would think of, as belonging to anyone but my grandmother, that Abiah Kittredge, being sound of mind—"*very* sound of mind," Zack added—willed all her real estate and other property and assets to her husband, Austen Gleason Kittredge, with the exception of my college spending-money fund and her collection of Egyptian memorabilia. Along with her remains, her Egyptian artifacts were to be disposed of according to the stipulations in a private letter to her husband, to be found in the top drawer of her worktable in Egypt.

Everyone looked at my grandfather.

"Are you acquainted with the contents of the letter in question, Austen?" Zack asked.

Without answering, my grandfather took three or four long strides through the dining room hallway into Egypt, where Old Josie was still sitting next to my grandmother's bed, crying and fingering her rosary. The room was very dim; someone had drawn the curtains across the single window. At the appearance of my grandfather, Old Josie gave a gasp and rose from her chair, her rosary beads dripping out of her trembling hands.

Before anyone knew what he was going to do, my grandfather yanked open the curtains. In the flood of morning sunlight my grandmother lay on the daybed, where my aunts had arranged her in her best black dress. Lyle the Crocodile still reposed at her side.

My grandfather glanced at his deceased wife for a moment. "I can't say I detect any great change," he said.

Someone gave a shocked gasp. At the same time I heard the kitchen door slam as Dad headed out of the house.

In the cheery sunshine, neither Egypt nor my grandmother struck me as particularly otherworldly. The picture of the extinct Sphinx looked like any other picture of a Sphinx. The carved wooden figure of Lord Ra looked downright ordinary. Everything had a mundane, homespun aspect, including the tiny body of my grandmother, her eyes closed, her hands folded across her still, dark-clad breast.

My grandfather jerked open the top drawer of the bedside table and got out an envelope. Inside were two sheets of instructions in my grandmother's close, neat hand. My grandfather took his reading glasses out of his shirt pocket and scanned the letter rapidly.

"What's it say?" Lawyer Barrows asked from the doorway. "Read it to us, Austen."

"It says 'Private, for My Husband Only' right here across the top. You read us the will, Barrows. The will said a private letter."

My grandfather put the letter back in the envelope, which he stuck in his rear pants pocket. Abruptly, he whipped the curtains closed and said, "Clear out of here now, all of you."

"Don't you want me to transport Mrs. K's remains into the undertaking parlor, Austen?"

"No, Mason, I don't want you to transport Mrs. K's remains to the undertaking parlor. Or anywhere else. The service will be held here at this house, in Mrs. K's own parlor, tomorrow afternoon at one o'clock sharp. She'll be buried in the family plot according to her wishes. You and Zack clear out of here now. You've done what you came to do. I'll handle the rest."

"But what about the casket? You can't just—"

Mason faltered as my grandfather continued to stare at him.

"I'll handle matters from here on," my grandfather said. "You boys shove along."

The cluster flies were nearly gone, with only a few hapless stragglers left to be swept up and disposed of. But the late-summer heat was as intense as ever. Plainly, it was essential to get my grandmother's body into the ground as soon as decently possible. Dad put some left-over blocks of ice from the icehouse in maple sugar pans and cream pans and set them on the daybed beside Gram. My grandfather had returned to the sawmill.

Around noon I went down to the mill to offer to help. "This is tamarack, Austen," my grandfather said when he finished running a stack of freshly-cut boards through the shrieking planer. "Tamarack makes good durable stable flooring. It made very sound foundation posts for the old log-driving dams. It's quite the old bitch to work with, but it stands up well to the elements."

My grandfather shook his head. "Even so I wish we had six months to let these boards season. I'll double-cleat them all around with square nails and that's the best I can do. If they warp, they warp. She'll have to take her chances."

My grandfather allowed me to wait on him off and on for the rest of the day. I brought him a sandwich and kept his water bucket full of fresh cold drinking water from the river. Despite all of my grandparents' feuding, I felt much less cut off from my grandmother when I was near him. In the middle of the afternoon he told me to go up to the woods and cut a load of cedar and balsam brush. "Just small stuff," he said. "Nothing bigger than what you'd put in a Christmas wreath."

"You want some flowers too? Late-blooming roses?"

He shook his head. "Just the brush."

All afternoon, as the news of my grandmother's death spread through the county, cars and farm trucks came up the Hollow road and parked in the dooryard and barnyard and people stopped by to deliver food and pay their respects. A few visitors ventured down to the mill but did not stay long. On my grandfather worked, straight through the supper hour into the evening. Old Josie kept an unbroken vigil over my grandmother's body. Freddi and Dad and Aunt Helen congregated in the kitchen, now overflowing with baked beans and homemade bread and rolls and casseroles and soups and ten different kinds of pies and cakes, and Klee finished her stenciling.

As the night wore on, the heat was too oppressive to talk much. Every two or three hours Dad emptied the meltwater out of the pans on the daybed and replenished them with fresh blocks of ice. We were all worried about the heat.

Sometime around midnight I couldn't keep my eyes open any longer and had to go to bed. To my surprise, I fell asleep immediately and didn't wake up until after eight the next morning.

Evidently my grandmother's remains had been moved to the parlor, because the door to Egypt was open and Old Josie was bustling around in the kitchen, trying to make a pot of coffee and getting in everyone's way. Aunt Helen shot me a glance and mouthed the words "No housekeeper." What on earth would become of Josie now, I wondered. What would become of my grandfather and me?

This morning the turmoil of the past twenty-four hours finally seemed to have caught up with me. I'd be fine for a few minutes, until I thought of something my grandmother and I had done together, or some simple chore I'd done for her and now had to do alone, and that would set me off teary-eyed all over again. For a seventeen-year-old, I wasn't handling this well at all.

Soon after my grandmother's clocks struck eleven, my grandfather appeared from the parlor. For the first time I could ever remember, he needed a shave. His short white hair was flecked with sawdust and his pale eyes looked haggard. "You people can go in and see her now if you want," he said.

I was exceedingly nervous about what might greet us in the parlor. I held my breath in apprehension as we trooped in.

What we beheld there remains to this day one of the strangest sights of my life. On two sawhorses sat a large coffin. No. Not a coffin. A sarcophagus. A wooden sarcophagus, in the unmistakable shape of a mummified Egyptian figure. It was painted antique green and blue with the stenciling paint Little Aunt Klee had used for the dining room fleur-de-lys pattern; and inside, on a bed of woven cedar and balsam fir boughs that filled the room with a woodsy fragrance, lay my minuscule grandmother.

Stenciled in bright gold lettering on the side of the sarcophagus was the word "Egypt." But there was more, much more. The sarcophagus itself was commodious enough for a large man, and inside it, propped on the fragrant evergreen boughs all around my grandmother, were her most treasured Egyptian artifacts. There for everyone to view were the hawk-headed carved wooden figure of Lord Ra, the framed picture of the extinct Sphinx, Lyle the Pink Crocodile, her stereopticon and Egyptian slides, and her treasured old copies of *Life* and the *National Geographic*, open to the articles on the discovery of King Tut's tomb; and my grandmother was covered from her folded hands downward with the quilt of the Four Colorful Ramses guarding the Temple of Abu Simbel.

At her feet, crouching in the interwoven cedar and balsam boughs, were the mummified remains of the rat-fighting cat Lynx Kittredge, whom my grandmother had renamed Pharaoh, its fierce yellow eyes staring out over the room as though defying us to so much as smile. Which, of course, no one dreamed of doing. Even my Great-Aunt Helen was awe-stricken by my grandfather's handiwork. This, we all realized, was exactly the way my grandmother should be laid to rest. Here, indeed, was Egypt.

At the service that afternoon, while my grandfather finished digging the grave in the family cemetery above Maiden Rose's place, our ancient lay-preacher cousin, John Wesleyan Kittredge, read my grandmother's favorite passages from the Bible: Joseph's run-in with Potiphar's wife; the discovery of the infant Moses in the bullrushes by Pharaoh's daughter; the great plagues and afflictions visited on the venerable and undeserving population of Egypt, no doubt as a result of some sort of black magic practiced by that same meddling Israelite. Otherwise, the service was conventional enough, as my grandmother's own firm religious convictions were conventional enough apart from all matters in the Bible touching upon her unimpeachable Egyptians.

Freddi played a thumping version of Gram's three favorite numbers on the wheezing old parlor pump organ: "Bringing in the Sheaves," "Rock of Ages," and "The Noon Bazaar at Cairo." And at the end of the service my good-hearted little aunt slipped the photograph of my eighteen-year-old grandfather, standing on top of the log rollway, into the sarcophagus beneath Gram's folded hands. Only then did I see my Great-Aunt Helen swipe at her eyes with her handkerchief.

After the service my grandfather came down to the house and

nailed on the sarcophagus's lid, and then he and Dad and I carried it up to the family graveyard. During the short committal service I stood back on the edge of the gathering with my grandfather, my mind swirling with the images of Egypt inside the tomb-like painted box Gramp had made. Once, when Preacher John Wesleyan paused for breath, and I found myself wiping my eyes with the back of my wrist, my grandfather took hold of my arm and whispered, "Tamarack, Austen. Very water-resistant."

A minute later he leaned over toward me again and said, seriously, "She's all right. I double-cleated the lid down."

We lowered the tamarack sarcophagus with the double-cleated lid into the grave and then my grandfather told us to clear out, he'd finish the job himself. On my way down to the house I looked back once and saw him shoveling dirt fast, angry and desolate in the fierce August sun.

I sympathized deeply with my father later that day. We all did because it had fallen to him to return Old Josie to her people in New Hampshire. Without my grandmother to bully her and do all of her work for her, Josie had gone completely to smash in the past two days. She'd cried constantly and wrung her apron up to the size of a dish towel, and Dad said that she cried all the way over to Groveton, too. The last thing she said to him was, "Missus was dead right, young Mr. Kittredge. Whatever else I may be, I am no housekeeper."

No serious consideration was ever given to my leaving the Farm or my grandfather. I don't believe that the possibility was even discussed. It was simply understood by the entire family that I would stay on, and my grandfather and I would look after each other, at least until I graduated from high school.

"You can't predict the future, Tut," my grandmother had told me many times. How frequently, over the next several weeks, her words would come back to me. It had been taken for granted in our family that my grandfather would die first, before my grandmother. Isn't that what hill farmers with bad tickers nearly always did? My grandmother would then remain at the Farm until she became too frail to manage alone, at which point she would move in with Aunt Helen or Dad or one of my little aunts. I am sure Gram herself had assumed as much. Then came the cluster flies and her untimely departure, combined with my grandfather's stubborn disinclination to cooperate by dying first. So he and I seemed to have been thrown together on our own resources by default, as it were.

I have mentioned that on that fateful ride to the hospital with my grandmother I felt as though I was in another dimension. It was a sensation I never entirely lost during the coming fall, and I now believe that this is, in fact, exactly what had happened to me. I had entered the dimension of our lives called adulthood, which is often no more than an awareness of those things we were not entirely aware of as children. I had become aware of the inexorableness of death.

"Who lives there, Old Man?" I said to my grandfather late in the afternoon on the day after my grandmother's funeral. We were walking down toward the house from the woods, where once again we were clearing brush off the Canadian Line. Except for the lumber truck, the dooryard was empty now. The last of the family had left that morning.

My grandfather frowned slightly, and said nothing.

"Who lives there?" I said again.

"Who does? You tell me."

"The meanest old bastard in Kingdom County. I heard it first from you."

My grandfather's creased face, tanned as dark as the leather tops of his high work boots, remained abstracted; and I believe that at that moment, coming down the ridge toward the empty house, the full force of my grandmother's absence hit him. It was as if, now that my grandmother was gone, being the meanest old bastard in the county was a hollow designation.

Still, my grandfather was not about to give up on life, then or any other time. Nor, for all his fabled misanthropy, did he intend to stop being a grandfather to me. That evening he suddenly looked up from *The Lure of the Labrador Wild*, from which he had just read aloud to me the passage in which the starving explorer Leonidas Hubbard was unable to shoot a goose that might well have saved his life because he had heedlessly failed to bring a shotgun on his fateful trip.

"How old are you, Austen?" my grandfather demanded when he reached the end of this chapter.

"You know how old I am."

"You're what, seventeen? In a year you'll be eighteen. That's the summer we'll go to Labrador. You and I and a canoe, with no one to stop us."

"By then you'll be too old to go."

"Yes, sir. And you still won't be able to paddle with me or fish with me or keep up with me on the portages."

"We'll see."

"We will." He looked at me sharply. "We'll take a shotgun. Unlike Christly Leonidas Hubbard. And," he added, with unmistakable irony, "we'll see wonderful things."

10

NORTHERN BORDERS

From my earliest days in Lost Nation, I thought of my grandfather in connection with deep woods and well-oiled shotguns, bamboo fly rods with bright red guide wrappings, and leather fly books full of marvelous feathered creations that were brighter still: big, battered, old-fashioned wet flies and streamers with exotic names evocative of the North Woods, like Adirondack, Queen of the Waters, Labrador Belle. Also I connected my grandfather with old photographs of men surveying faraway places, and men with trophy bucks and enormous trout. And invariably, when I thought of my grandfather, I thought of maps.

For Austen Kittredge loved maps of all kinds. His hunting camp, Labrador, was full of them. The plank walls were festooned with topographical maps of Kingdom County, maps of the remote stretches of the American-Canadian border he'd helped survey in his youth, maps painstakingly razored out of old travel books of

Africa and Asia and, especially, the Far North, some of which still contained sizable blank white spaces across which were printed the stirring words *terra incognita*.

Near the south window of my grandfather's camp hung one such map from his 1914 World Atlas and Geographical Gazetteer, depicting that little-known northernmost peninsula of mainland Canada consisting of Labrador and the Ungava Barrens. Nearly half of the interior of this vast land was still designated as *terra incognita*, though my grandfather had carefully inked onto it the farthest point reached by the 1910 government survey party on which he had worked as a chainman. The official line of demarcation between Labrador and Quebec ran along a natural height of land known as the Snow Chain Mountains, and ended where the partially-completed survey had ended—out of good weather and supplies and funds—on a peak called No Name Mountain. Here the Snow Chain range veered sharply northeast in a configuration known to my grandfather and a few other old Labrador hands as the Great Lost Corner.

According to my grandfather, the Great Lost Corner and the surrounding wilderness contained countless unexplored white-water rivers connecting huge lakes frozen nine months of the year. The country was home to numberless caribou, gigantic brook trout as colorful as a subarctic sunset, and, until not so very many years ago, a handful of nomadic Indians with whom Gramp had stayed for a time after the survey ended. This was the place he'd promised to take me when I turned eighteen.

"You and I and a canoe, Austen," he'd told me a hundred times. "Just you and I and a canoe, for a summer of fishing and exploring. Then we'll see what sort of man I've made out of you. We'll see what sort of fella you are to go down the river with."

Still, for many years our trip seemed far-off in the misty future, and impossible to imagine in very specific terms—just as growing up and leaving Lost Nation, or the death of either of my grandparents, was impossible to imagine. When my grandmother did die, suddenly and unexpectedly, in the summer between my junior and senior years of high school, my grandfather fell into a prolonged brooding, which not even deer season seemed to jolt him out of; and for many months afterward he didn't mention our Labrador trip to me at all.

One evening in May of 1960, less than a month before my high school graduation, my grandfather and I were listening to the CBC news from Montreal on his old battery-operated Stromberg Carlson radio. The broadcaster had just announced in his precise, British-sounding accent that plans had been set in motion to construct a gigantic hydroelectric dam deep in the interior of Labrador. He went on to report that the dam would create the largest man-made lake in the world, a veritable freshwater inland sea covering millions of square acres of wilderness, some of which had never been mapped or thoroughly explored.

Without a word, my grandfather switched off the radio and disappeared for more than three hours. I knew better than to question him when he returned. I assumed he'd been up at his camp looking at his maps of Labrador, and knew he'd tell me anything he wanted to tell me in his own good time. Over the next few days, he seemed more abstracted and withdrawn than usual. On several occasions, when I asked him a question or made some remark about the weather or school or our work at home, he nearly snapped my head off. At the time, however, I didn't think much about it. Without my grandmother to contend with, Gramp had not been entirely himself for nearly a year. And with graduation coming up, and college just around the corner, I had important considerations of my own.

For these reasons, what happened a couple of weeks later hit me like a thunderbolt. It began with an early-morning phone call from the railway freight agent in Kingdom Common, to say that a long wooden crate had just arrived for my grandfather.

"How long?" I asked.

"Long," he said. "Bring your truck."

Characteristically, my grandfather refused to tell me what he'd ordered. Something for his sawmill, I supposed. The planer had been acting up recently. Possibly he was replacing it.

In fact, the mystery crate turned out to have come from

Oldtown, Maine, and to contain a brand-new eighteen-foot Oldtown canoe, painted a rich forest-green.

"The canoe's mine," my grandfather informed me when I brought it home from school in the back of the truck. "The trip's your graduation present."

I looked at him, my face as blank as those empty white spaces on his map of Labrador. "What trip?"

"Our trip north," my grandfather said. "You and I and that canoe, Austen. Just like I've always told you. We'll leave the day after you graduate."

Over the next several days my grandfather assembled what seemed like a ton of camping equipment. A collapsible sheet-metal stove arrived from someplace in Wisconsin. From L. L. Bean came a two-man waterproofed canvas tent, two lightweight insulated sleeping bags, a pair of Maine Guide hiking boots for each of us and two pairs of bear paw snowshoes for crossing the Snow Chain Mountains. My grandfather made several trips to the hardware store in the Common for towing line, a Coleman lantern, a new bucksaw and ax. And he bought boxes, more boxes, and more boxes still of rifle and shotgun shells. "Leonidas Hubbard died of starvation up in that territory for want of a shotgun, Austen. You can bet no such thing is going to happen to us."

As our departure date drew nearer, I grew more and more excited by the prospect of a summer with my grandfather in some of the last unexplored terrain on the face of the earth. Yet I must admit that I felt more than a twinge of apprehension, both of the desolate land itself and of the responsibility of seeing that no harm came to us while we were there. Not that Gramp was by any stretch of the imagination over the hill. At seventy-two, he was still about as tough as any man in Kingdom County, which is to say as tough as anyone anywhere. Yet since the CBC announcement about the dam, he'd seemed not only more abstracted than usual, but strangely agitated as well. Not himself—in a way I could not quite put my finger on but strongly sensed whenever I was in his presence.

Graduation took place in mid-June. Nearly all I can recall from the event itself is that Theresa Dubois had beaten me out for top class honors by a couple of percentage points, thereby earning the privilege of delivering the valedictory address, during which I all but heard my grandmother tell me sternly, "To win is all, Tut."

Yet it occurred to me that Gram's displeasure with my class standing would have been very mild compared to her horror over my impending excursion with Gramp to the Far North. Talk about sashaying!

"You can't predict the future, Tut." Never had Gram's observation seemed truer; and never, if I'd had a hundred years to try, could I have guessed exactly how unpredictable the summer of 1960 would turn out to be.

"Nobody lives forever," my grandfather declared as we pulled out of Sept-Îles, Quebec, on the weekly bush train north. "But they say living in the bush adds twenty years to your life."

We'd driven the five hundred miles from Kingdom County to Sept-Îles in twenty-four hours, arriving just in time to load our canoe and gear on the train for the day-long trip to Schefferville, a tiny mining outpost three hundred miles to the north, and our jumping-off place for the Labrador bush. Our plan, as my grandfather had finally divulged to me on the drive up, was to canoe the major river systems and lakes destined to be flooded by the great dam, exploring and mapping the countryside as we proceeded. If all went well, we'd arrive at the Great Corner and No Name Mountain in late August. A week before Labor Day, a bush pilot whom we'd hire in Schefferville before heading into the interior would pick us up on No Name Lake, up in the Barrens.

All my life, from my first great journey up to Lost Nation at the age of six on the Montreal Flyer, I have found traveling north to be an exhilarating experience. Now as our ancient Canadian National passenger coach crowded with miners, fishermen, and Montagnais Indian hunters and guides rattled up into the vast taiga of the Canadian Shield, I realized that I was entering an altogether different land from any I'd ever imagined, a land of deep woods and mountains stretching for hundreds of miles and broken only by glacial lakes and wild white-water rivers. My grandfather, however, regarded the magnificent scenery with a frown.

Directly across the wooden aisle from us sat a youngish-looking man in jeans and a bulky blue sweater embroidered with a bright silver salmon, a polar bear, an eagle with a gleaming white head, and a caribou. His hair was coal-black and very thick, he had sad, almond-shaped eyes, and on his face, when he glanced at me, was the most sorrowful expression I'd ever seen. Half an hour out of Sept-Îles my grandfather offered him a White Owl and fired up one for himself, whereupon the man with the lugubrious countenance began to talk a blue streak. He told us that his name was Donny Snowball, and he was an Inuit guide and trapper from Ungava Bay. He'd been to Quebec City to visit his sister for a couple of weeks. That was all he could stand of any city at one time, he assured us. And where, if he might inquire, were we headed?

When my grandfather explained that we were going up into the Barrens beyond the Snow Chain Mountains, Mr. Snowball shook his head and looked more somber still.

"What's the matter?" Gramp asked.

"Nothing," Mr. Donny Snowball said. "You'll probably die up there, is all."

"Die up there! What are you talking about?"

"That's what usually happens when white men go out in the bush alone without a guide who knows the country," Mr. Snowball said, taking a satisfied puff at his cigar. "They die."

"Do they now?" My grandfather nudged me. "How do they usually die?"

"They drown in the rapids," Mr. Snowball said more cheerfully. "Just last summer five white fishermen went down the George River without a guide. That can be a bad river, the George. Full of white water. Three of them drowned. That was really too bad."

"What happened to the other two men?"

"What other two?"

"The two that didn't drown. You said there were five and three drowned. That leaves two."

"That's so," Mr. Snowball said, brightening up a little more. "The blackflies got to them and they went bush-crazy."

"We've got plenty of bug dope," my grandfather said. "You wouldn't be trying to scare this young fella here, would you?"

"Oh, no," Mr. Snowball said matter-of-factly. "What good

would being scared do him? Either he'll drown or go bush-crazy or he won't. Being scared won't help. What you fellas need is a good experienced guide. Without one I wouldn't think you'd last a week. This is a good cigar."

"Have you been up there?" my grandfather asked. "In the Great Corner?"

"Hardly nobody's ever been up there," Mr. Snowball said. "That's a bad country. Rivers too rocky to canoe. Witch mirages. Then you got the tall white Indian ghosts."

"The ghosts?" my grandfather said.

"Sure. The Great Corner, that's where the ghosts of the tall white Indians live. They'll kill you if they catch you. Even the Montagnais don't go there. A few did, long time ago. The tall white Indian ghosts got them. Better not to go there at all. Rivers up there are worse than the George."

"These ghosts," I said. "Ghosts of who?"

"I guess we won't be canoeing any rivers quite as big as the George," my grandfather said. "We're going up the Tree Line River. Are you familiar with that one?"

"Yes," Mr. Snowball said. "A nice young man from Toronto and his bride of two months went up to the Tree Line two summers ago. That's a much smaller river than the George. It looks very innocent. But they lost their canoe in the white water. Then the husband caught pneumonia. A few days later he died."

"What happened to his wife?" I asked.

"Well, she tried to keep going on foot. Hoped to come to something, maybe a fishing camp? But it was terrible walking and she didn't understand the bush at all and there aren't no fishing camps up there. So she wrote what happened to her husband on some cliffs by the river. With a lipstick? Later a rescue party found the writing. Never the woman, though. I wonder what she wanted a lipstick for in the bush, anyway?

"Then you've always got lightning fires," he went on in a downright gleeful vein, though his face was as sorrowful as ever. "Last summer half western Labrador took fire. Three uranium prospectors, educated gentlemen from the States, took refuge from the flames on a big island. Fire jumped a mile to the island on the wind and got them anyway. Not to mention starvation and exposure, like what happened to Mr. Leonidas Hubbard. You've got to watch out for late-summer blizzards, too. Catch you out unprepared and kill you in a few short hours. Do you know about late-summer blizzards?"

"Yes, yes, yes," my grandfather said. "You can't best this fella, Austen. He's got a catastrophe for every occasion."

"Oh, sure," Mr. Donny Snowball said. "That's generally what happens to white men alone in the Far North. They meet with catastrophe."

I was alarmed by Mr. Snowball's grim prophecies. But my grandfather said it cheered him up beyond measure to meet a man this gloomy. He added that if he ever needed a guide, he knew where to find a good one.

"Not for the Great Lost Corner, though," Mr. Snowball said, and he appeared to be totally serious. "That's all going to be flooded out anyway, and when it is, nobody in the Labrador's going to shed no tears. I don't want to talk about it anymore now for a while. It makes my skin creep all over just to think about the Great Lost Corner."

Farther north, the scenery became still wilder, with long ranges of hills on which nothing seemed to flourish but granite outcroppings and gray caribou moss. In the middle of the afternoon it began to snow. Soon afterward I fell asleep. When I woke up my grandfather was leaning across the aisle, deep in conversation with Mr. Snowball, who was studying one of Gramp's maps with great interest. I had the vague impression that they were calculating how far north the inland sea from the hydro dam would spread, but almost immediately I drifted off again, and this time when I woke, Mr. Donny Snowball was asleep and my grandfather was staring out the window at a huge lake still partly frozen, with the same brooding scowl I'd first noticed a month ago at home in Lost Nation, as if he were withdrawing into the untamed land itself.

The electric blue and silver currents shot up and down the night sky from horizon to zenith until I felt connected to all Labrador by them. Although it was past eleven p.m., the brief subarctic night had just set in. Soon flaring pinks and greens and yellows mingled with the silver and blue. I sat by our campfire transfixed, temporarily forgetting all about my aching shoulders, the fiery pains in my back, and my blistered hands.

For the past seven days, from the first gray light of dawn until twilight, my grandfather and I had been on the water or portaging around unnavigable rapids. We'd passed through spectacularly wild country, encountered scores of fishing ospreys and eagles, several remarkably large and unafraid black bears, numerous small groups of woodland caribou. The trout fishing, what little we'd done of it, had been phenomenal. But as we pushed on into the Labrador interior, stopping only long enough for my grandfather to make rough measurements with his surveying transit and notes for the maps he drew before turning in each night, his face hardened into a somber, determined cast, and he seemed more haunted by his private brooding than ever.

My grandfather's nearly obsessive determination to map every last feature we passed perplexed me. He thought nothing of pushing up small, incredibly swampy or rocky tributaries to discover a new lake, spending half a day hiking to a ridge offering a panoramic view of the surrounding territory, and working on his maps by firelight for two or three hours after I'd turned in for the night, so that he often slept no more than a couple of hours.

"What's the point of it?" I finally asked him. "I can understand exploring the country. Seeing it for a last time. But every last lake and stream and island and river and esker you're drawing will be under water in a year or two. What's the sense of mapping them?"

"Because they've never been mapped, and that's what a surveyor and a cartographer does, Austen. There needs to be a record of all this wild country, goddamn it. There needs to be a record of what it was like before it disappeared."

"What practical use are your maps going to be to anybody? Once it's gone?"

"That's a shortsighted question. There doesn't have to be any practical use to a map to make it worthwhile. Besides, they'll be useful to you and me. We'll know where we've been. Maybe some places no one else ever went before."

"Or ever will again," I said.

Obviously, nothing was going to deter my grandfather from his self-appointed mission. Yet more than once it crossed my mind that Gramp might be making the maps so that if he collapsed on a portage or while tracking the canoe up a bad stretch of river, I could find my way out alone.

"Well, Austen," he said suddenly as we watched the spectacle of the northern lights, "now you know why the early explorers called Labrador the land God gave to Cain."

For the first time in days I laughed. "Who else but Cain would want it?"

"You've got a point there. But remember, old Cain was a hunter. He'd have been right at home up here."

I was bone-tired and ready to turn in. But as the fire began to die down, my grandfather picked up a stick and drew an oval in the sand near the embers. "This is Tree Line Lake, Austen. It's about another three weeks from here. A month at the most, by my calculations."

Leading out of the top of the lake, he scratched a crooked line a couple of feet long. "This is the Rivière de la Mort. Up here, near where it rises, is No Name Mountain and the Great Lost Corner. And here, about halfway up the river, was the base camp of the Indians I stayed with when the 1910 survey ended. That's our first destination."

Suddenly I was keenly interested in what my grandfather was telling me. This was the first time he'd mentioned an old Indian camp. I wondered if these were the same tall white Indians whose ghosts Mr. Donny Snowball had mentioned to us back on the bush train. Might they still be lurking in the vicinity, waiting for two unsuspecting explorers who didn't know the country?

My grandfather shook his head. "I don't think the white Indians or anyone else has been up that way for years, Austen. Decades maybe."

"You mean there really were white Indians? I thought Mr. Snowball was just trying to scare us."

"No doubt he was. But there actually were white Indians. The Indians I stayed with were white Indians. There were probably never more than a few hundred of them to start out with. By the time I got to know them, there were no more than a dozen or so. They were the last ones so far as I know, and I imagine they've long since died out entirely."

"You never told me these were white Indians," I said. "What's a white Indian anyway?"

"Just what young Snowball said. Except they weren't ghosts. Blue-eyed Indians, white Indians, Beothuks. All names for the same tribe. They were lighter than the local Montagnais, and quite a bit taller, though the Montagnais are a tall people themselves, like the Sioux. Most of the Beothuk men were well over six feet and so were a number of the women. One tale I heard is that they were descended in part from Viking settlers. Originally they were from Newfoundland, but the early settlers up there, the whalers and fishermen, hunted them down for sport, the bloodthirsty sons of bitches. A few survivors escaped across the straits to Labrador and took refuge way up here in the interior, where nobody could get at 'em. The rest were just annihilated, I presume."

"Did they really have blue eyes, Gramp?"

My grandfather paused. Then he said, "Some of them did. Gray-blue, anyway. The old fella that called himself their chief had gray-blue eyes, and so did a couple of his kids. Whether they really traced back to the Vikings I have no idea. I suppose it's possible. Or more likely they got thrown in with a few old blue-eyed Hudson Bay Post traders. The whole point of this is I want to see that old camp again before it's flooded out. I want you to see it, too."

Abruptly, before I had a chance to ask more questions, my grandfather stood up and kicked sand over the fire. "Time to turn in, Austen," he said. "There'll be light in the sky by three. We'll be on the water soon afterward."

Fatigued as I was, I did not fall asleep immediately that night. I was far too excited over my grandfather's revelations about the white Indians. Why, I wondered, hadn't he ever mentioned their light color and blue eyes to me before? Were they, in fact, the descendants of Vikings? In his own good time, my grandfather might tell me more. Meanwhile, I was terrifically eager to reach the old encampment. For me too, now, our journey had suddenly become something of a mission.

For the next three weeks my grandfather toiled across that trackless country like a driven man. I no longer asked if we could stop to fish, though everywhere trout rose in great numbers to natural flies. We continued to map the main land features, and to name the lakes and rivers, doomed though they were. Mount Sojourner, for my great-great-great-great-great-grandfather, Sojourner Kittredge. Lake Whiskeyjack for our old reprobate cousin. The Little Abiah River, in honor of my grandmother, not to mention Fiddler's Elbow Falls, Lake Kingdom, Upper Lost Nation Stream and Lower Lost Nation Stream, and a host of other designations reminiscent of the topography of Kingdom County, a thousand miles to the south. My grandfather kept his maps and notebooks in a flat steel case in our big wooden grub box, along with our flour and sugar and tea, a couple of dozen of his most precious travel books, and his transit and theodolite, which he used mainly for gauging the length and width of the lakes we crossed—paddling and portaging from dawn to dusk, as though the floodwaters from the big dam were lapping at our heels.

We reached Tree Line Lake on the twenty-sixth of July, and the following morning we started up the dreaded Rivière de la Mort. At first it wasn't too bad. But a day north of Tree Line, the river ran through a series of deep gorges full of swooping white-water cascades, and we spent most of the next week portaging around the rapids. More than once I thought of Mr. Snowball's macabre story of the Toronto woman who'd lost her husband and scrawled his fate on the rocks with her lipstick before vanishing herself, like my grandfather's blue-eyed Beothuks.

One sunny afternoon as we were paddling across a rare stretch of quiet water, I saw an island covered with black spruce trees hanging in the blue Labrador sky, a mile or so away. As we approached it, it appeared and vanished several times before eventually resolving itself into an ordinary ground-level island like any other. For the remainder of that day and the next, we traveled through a land of amazing illusions, caused, my grandfather explained, by heat waves reflected off moisture in the rarefied northern sky. Distant waterfalls lifted majestically into the air, lakes tilted themselves on edge and floated across the horizon, violently-colored rainbows covered half the firmament. At dawn and dusk, when the air was clearest, an upside-down snowy peak hovered in the sky far off to the north.

"What in the hell is that?" I wondered.

"No Name Mountain," my grandfather said. "Its mirage, anyway. Drink your tea, Austen. That's real."

My grandfather took each new illusion in stride. He had seen Labrador's witch mirages before, and his mind was elsewhere, as it had been for weeks. I, for my part, felt more strongly than ever that, day by day, I was entering a different realm from any I had ever dreamed of.

"What I'm going to tell you now is between you and me, no one else," my grandfather said. "When I'm gone, you can inform anyone you please. Do you understand that?"

"Yes," I said. "Of course."

It was full dark, and we had just zipped ourselves up inside our tent, near a well-worn caribou crossing on the Rivière de la Mort where, decades ago, the small band of Indians my grandfather traveled with had established their base camp. We'd arrived just before dusk and, to my sharp disappointment, found no trace at all that anyone had ever been here before us, though my grandfather had assured me that this was the right spot.

Now as we lay side by side in our sleeping bags near the age-old caribou ford, a hundred miles and more from the nearest human settlement, my grandfather's voice sounded strangely remote. It was almost as if he were speaking not just about the long-ago past, but from it.

"There was a girl," he began. "The oldest daughter of the blue-eyed chief. She was a year or two younger than me, maybe nineteen or twenty. Her Indian name was impossible to get your tongue around unless you were Beothuk, but it meant "mirage." So that was what I came to call her—Mira.

"This Mira was a very handsome girl, Austen. She had the same blue-gray eyes as her father and hair so dark it glinted blue in the sunlight. She could stand in her moccasins and look me right straight in the eye, and I'm six feet, one-and-a-half-inches tall, or was then. She didn't speak more than a few words of English. None of the tribe did. But she was as smart as a whip, and as good-natured as she was headstrong, and as headstrong as she was good-natured, and from the moment I first laid eyes on her I knew that this was the gal for me. Do you understand?"

"Yes."

"We lived together like man and wife for the better part of a year," my grandfather said in that remote voice, as if he were speaking more to himself now than to me. "She's the reason I stayed here with the Indians after the rest of the survey party went home."

I waited for him to continue but he did not. His story seemed to have ended as abruptly as it had begun. A minute or two passed. Finally I couldn't bear the silence any longer. "So what happened, Gramp? What happened between you and Mira?"

But except for the deep, rasping breathing of my grandfather, and the murmur of the river at the ancient animal ford, the night was silent.

I woke up smelling campfire coffee and frying trout, which my grandfather had caught minutes earlier. Although he said little as we ate, and his face seemed as determined as ever, he seemed somehow more reposed now that he had at last told me about the Beothuk girl. Immediately after we finished eating he got our collapsible shovel and a large waterproofed canvas sack from the canoe and told me to follow him.

As the Labrador sun came up, huge and red through the mist, we climbed a ridge overlooking the country to the north and west. Near the top we came to a beautiful spruce glade ankle-deep in bright gray, green, and orange mosses. Far below us the Rivière de la Mort lay blue and innocent-looking. In the distance the inverted peak of No Name Mountain glowed pink in the sunrise, like Jay Peak at home in Vermont on a clear January dawn. Here, after a brief search, my grandfather located a stone cairn about eight feet long and three feet high.

I was terrifically excited. This was the first sign of any kind that the Beothuks or anyone else had ever been here before us.

"What is it, Gramp? Some sort of monument? A lookout?"

My grandfather was staring off at the distant mountains, now right-side up again, and fading quickly from pink to white. He did not reply. But just as I was about to climb up on the cairn to admire the view, I saw something that I had never seen before and would never see again. I saw that my grandfather's eyes were wet. And although here in the moss glade at dawn was where I, too, felt fully the impending tragic loss of the immense and lovely wilderness I had come to think of as my grandfather's personal domain, I knew instantly that he was not weeping for the doomed terrain spread out in all its fresh morning glory below us.

"What happened to her, Gramp?" I asked quietly. "Mira?"

"She died," he said. "This is where I buried her."

Then in a voice devoid of everything but a terrible, angry determination, my grandfather said, "I can't and won't leave her here to be buried under all that water, Austen. I can't and I won't. I promised I'd lay her to rest where her spirit could come and see the country she was born in. The lakes and the river and the mountains. The mirages her people named her for."

My grandfather took a long breath. His eyes were dry now, his gaze the same pale, bleakly-assessing gaze as always. His face was set in the hard, unalterable lines of a man doing a hard thing he neither expected nor particularly wished for anyone else to understand, though in fact I thought I did.

"You go back down to the canoe now," he said. "I'll be along shortly."

At last I understood my grandfather's abstract moods and his driven, agitated behavior over the past weeks. Yet it was a conundrum to me, an inexplicable wonderment of human nature, that a man as studiously aloof and ironic as Austen Kittredge, a confirmed and self-styled misanthrope, had evidently once been pas-

sionately in love. That he might still be in love with Mira, nearly
fifty years after her death, was more astonishing still.

Soon enough, however, I had no more leisure to consider this
revelation. As my grandfather and I pushed on upstream, the Rivière de la Mort, that lovely blue ribbon that had looked so serene
from the high ridge where Mira's cairn stood, transformed itself into
an unnavigable torrent. For hour after hour, day after day, we
hauled the canoe upriver on tracking ropes, wading chest-deep in
icy, rushing water. It was a punishing ordeal for me at eighteen, near
the peak of my physical capacities. For a man of seventy-two, even a
lifelong woodsman with enormous endurance, it must have been a
hellish odyssey, though my grandfather's face remained as stony and
inexpressive as the primordial granite outcroppings surrounding us.

We no longer stopped even to catch trout for supper, but sub-
sisted on cold hardtack and boiled beans, washed down with mugs
of tea. I fell asleep the moment I was inside our tent, though my
grandfather still labored on into the night over his maps. Twenty
times a day when a rock rolled under my feet or I scraped my leg on
a jagged underwater ledge or towed the canoe around the bend out
of a mile-long stretch of crashing white water only to confront another identical rapids, I silently cursed my grandfather and his relentless stubbornness.

Our way grew worse instead of better. We entered a boreal bad-
lands of violently upthrust ridges divided by tumultuous streams,
some sterile of all life, and bare tundra. I understood why the
Montagnais Indians had avoided this territory. The weird mirages
were not the only reason. The terrain itself was deeply inhospitable
to people. My grandfather said it was harder to map because it all
looked the same: terrible.

A week above the old Beothuk encampment we came to a dark
gorge out of which the Rivière de la Mort poured in a solid, thundering cataract. We spent the morning reconnoitering. Many deep
and treacherous side ravines cut into the chasm upriver, with no
way to portage out around them. Having no idea what we might
encounter, we set out up the gorge that afternoon, tracking the
canoe behind us on tow ropes. We had lashed down everything we
could possibly secure in the canoe, including the wooden grub box,

inside which my grandfather had packed the canvas sack with Mira's remains.

In the gorge the de la Mort was frigid as a glacial river. Sunlight played on the cliff walls high above us while we forged our way through a perpetual greenish gloom. There was no bankside vegetation to build a fire. In places there were no banks. When the river became too cold to endure any longer, we had to take turns wringing out our clothes while the other held the canoe on the tracking line. It tugged like an enormous fish, eager to escape and leave us stranded without food and shelter, to die in the bush like the feckless expeditionaries in Mr. Donny Snowball's grisly tales. To make ourselves heard over the rapids, we had to shout at the top of our lungs. Soon we stopped speaking altogether.

Once, while I was handling the stern rope, I slipped on a loaf-shaped rock, went entirely under, and lost my grip on the line. Instantly the stern of the canoe swung out at a precarious slant to the torrential current. My grandfather had all he could do to keep it upright, and the weight of the rushing water against the side of the heavily-loaded canoe began to drag him downstream.

"Get the grub box if she swamps!" he shouted. "Get the grub box!"

Whether he was more concerned about losing our food or Mira's bones, I had no idea. As he approached me, struggling to stay on his feet like a man being dragged along by a runaway horse, I grabbed him around the waist. Together we somehow managed to work ourselves and the canoe back into the slack water off the current, where I could grab the stern rope. My grandfather glared at me angrily, but I was not about to apologize for the accident.

"This is crazy!" I shouted at him. "You're going to drown us both."

"Nobody's going to drown," he shouted back, and as soon as he caught his breath we started off upriver again.

That evening we camped on a ledge no more than six feet wide. There was no room to set up a tent, no brush for a fire. Even so my grandfather got out his compass, mechanical pencil, and ruler, and spent the last hour of daylight sketching a map of the section of the river we'd come up that day. Fortunately, the night was quite warm.

Except for an occasional lethal-looking glint of heat lightning high overhead, the gorge was as dark as a cavern.

Toward dawn a terrific thunderstorm struck. Lightning bolts seemed to crash off the cliff walls all up and down the gorge. Sheets of rain poured down onto us with a frightening intensity. By daylight, when we set out towing the canoe, the river had already risen a foot.

Ahead through the driving rain the canyon walls sheered straight out of the water. But any thought of canoeing back through the gorge to safety, even if my grandfather had been willing to consider a retreat, was out of the question. No canoe would have survived sixty seconds in that thundering rock-filled maelstrom.

Just when it seemed impossible to proceed, a house-sized boulder that had long ago broken off the cliff overhead loomed up in the rain ahead of us. Between the boulder and the rock wall of the gorge lay a churning backwater about thirty feet in diameter, and somewhat sheltered from the furious main current by the huge rock. In the face of the cliff ten or twelve feet above the surface of the big whirlpool was a fissure, a broken seam where a few stunted black spruces had managed to establish a toehold. Using the stern and bow tracking ropes, my grandfather managed to snub the canoe to two of these small trees.

"We're all right," he shouted. "We aren't going anyplace." His hand was on the grub box lashed in the stern, and I had the feeling that he was reassuring Mira as much as me, though I knew that if the ropes holding us to those little spruces broke, or the trees were pulled out by their roots, we would certainly be swept out to drown in the rapids.

Sometime during the afternoon the rain ended. By evening the river had started to go down. But it was noon of the following day before we could proceed, and two more days before we emerged from the gorge, battered and more fatigued than I could ever remember being in my life. I couldn't decide whether I was more angry with my grandfather for jeopardizing our lives for a bagful of bones, or relieved to be out of that hellhole.

The first thing we did after our deliverance was to build a roaring fire. Except to fetch more wood, we didn't move away from its blessed warmth until the following morning.

Above the gorge were more impassable rapids, connecting a long chain of wave-swept, north-to-south-running lakes that left us wind-bound on shore for days on end. The mirages, which I thought we'd left behind us, were stranger than ever. Illusory Niagaras hundreds of feet high hovered in the middle distance, so real-looking I imagined I could hear them. Whole ranges of snow-covered mountains, Himalayan in magnitude, reared up along the horizons. One morning an oceanic strait jammed with opalescent ice packs rose into view, stately as a great work of art. My grandfather shook his head and said that Ungava Bay, the nearest arm of the sea, lay a hundred miles away, across the Snow Chain Mountains and the Barrens.

July had come and gone. And still we pushed up the apparently unending Rivière de la Mort into the Great Lost Corner. The brook trout were turning bright red for spawning time. The nights were lengthening out noticeably. The lower slopes of the mountains shone purple where the blueberry bushes had been touched by early frosts. In the glades between the scattered enclaves of stunted spruce, bake-apple berries were turning from pink to a luscious ripe orange.

One day in the middle of August we woke up to the earth vibrating beneath our sleeping bags. Just upriver, thousands of migrating caribou were passing from east to west. The next morning a dusting of snow covered the ground. My grandfather pushed harder, stopping now only to map the major features of the Great Corner. He didn't say so, but I was quite sure that he was hurrying to reach No Name Mountain before the first big late-summer snowstorm.

One night I woke up smelling smoke. I jumped up and unzipped the tent flaps. Outside, the entire horizon to the south and southeast was an iridescent rose. "Wake up," I called to my grandfather. "The country's on fire!"

He came out of the tent, coughing in the smoky air. The wind was gusting out of the southeast, pushing the fire straight in our direction.

"Now what do you intend to do?" I said angrily.

"I intend to get out of this place and up into the mountains before that fire gets here. It'll be light enough to travel in half an hour. Get the tent and gear in the canoe while I boil up water. We'll have a quick mug of tea and get the hell out of here.''

As soon as we could see a few feet in front of our faces we set off, tracking the canoe up yet another rapids by the tow ropes, feeling for our footing beneath the rushing dark water. The shock of that first icy immersion of the day was something I had never grown accustomed to, but today I hardly noticed. The advancing flames frightened me far more than the narrow-gauged gorge at the height of the flood.

The sun was a lurid scarlet disk through the smoky air. A glaring incandescence had seeped out across the entire southern and eastern horizons. By mid-morning the fire was only a few miles away.

Suspended in the haze ahead of us hung a good-sized lake. I hoped against hope that this was no illusion, though I well remembered Mr. Donny Snowball's horror story about the prospectors who took refuge on an island only to burn to a crisp when the inferno jumped out to them.

The fire appeared to be less than a mile behind us when we reached the lake, which to our great good fortune turned out to be a real lake, not a mirage. We rushed the canoe into the water and began to paddle frantically. The wind was fiery hot on our necks and backs. Flakes of fire as large as the palms of our hands spiraled down onto the surface all around us. Several fell into the canoe and we had to beat them out with our paddles. Waves kept creeping over the stern and spilling into my grandfather's lap. Soon the bottom of the canoe under our feet was awash, but there was no time to stop and bail. Suddenly dozens of closely-spaced explosions went off behind us. I glanced over my shoulder and saw that the fire had reached a belt of pitch-soaked young trees on the southern margin of the lake, which were detonating like fireworks.

"Paddle!" my grandfather shouted.

Outside our tent, the wind howled like the northbound freight to Canada at home in Kingdom County. We were camped partway up No Name Mountain, where, just hours after escaping the wildfire, we'd been overtaken by one of the fierce August blizzards Donny Snowball had warned us about. We'd just had time to lash the canoe to the base of a jagged boulder, throw up the tent, weight it down with rocks, and get into our sleeping bags before total darkness and the full strength of the storm descended on us simultaneously. Inside with us were our snowshoes and the grub box containing Mira's remains. Everything else was beneath the canoe, itself no doubt already buried under many inches of snow.

For some time we were both silent. But just when I was sure he'd fallen asleep, my grandfather spoke.

"There were things between us, Austen. There were things between this girl and myself that come between a man and woman just once in a lifetime. For one thing, we thought a great deal alike. We always picked the same spots to stop and fish. We set traps the same places. Admired the same prospects when we were on the move. I didn't know any of her lingo at first. But more than half the time I understood what she was about to say before she said it and she seemed to read my thoughts, too. Some days when we were tracking up the river, or snowshoeing a trap line in the winter, we'd go along for hours on end without speaking. But that didn't seem to matter. One always seemed to know what the other was thinking. Look off in a new direction we wanted to explore, or at a likely place to camp for the night, look at each other, and nod."

My grandfather paused. Outside, the wind continued to howl. I didn't say a word. "We were never married, of course. We met in the fall of the year when I was on my way back down the Rivière de la Mort with the survey party. There wasn't any way to be married out in the bush like that. I suppose we eventually would have gone out to Chimo or Nain or somewhere and gotten hitched up by a missionary. At the time, what did it matter? As far as she and I were concerned, we were man and wife. Do you understand that?"

"Yes."

"I thought you would," my grandfather said, to my gratification. "So you won't be too surprised to hear that when winter came, she was pregnant. That was fine with her and with me. But in the summer, when the time came for her to have the baby, it all went wrong. Why, I don't know. A strong young woman like her, who could run thirty miles a day on snowshoes, paddle a canoe like a man, Viking blood in her veins for all I knew. It just didn't turn out right, wasn't meant to be, I guess, and not a goddamn Christly thing her mother or her father or I could do about it. The baby was born dead and a day later she died. And she never made a sound or spoke more than one word. Not when the baby was born or when she went. She just looked off at that ridge where I buried her, and I looked at her and nodded to show I understood, and then she said the name she'd taken to calling me. That and no more, and then she went. Quick. Before I quite knew what had happened. Just like that.

"It was a boy, Austen. A boy baby. I buried them together, up where she'd looked off at, where we liked to go together to look out at the country and see the mirages she was named for. Then I set out in a canoe and came home to Vermont. A few months later I married your grandmother. That's all. That's where the story ends."

"Did Gram know anything about all this? About Mira and the baby?"

"She knew everything about it. Until now, she was the only one I ever told about it."

"And she wasn't mad?"

"Of course she was mad. She was mad about everything I did before I met her as well as after. But I'll tell you one thing about your grandmother and me, Austen. We abided each other. We agreed on very little. And she wasn't Mira, not by a long shot, and I reckon I wasn't the fella she thought I was the day she first clapped eyes on me, riding that log down the Horserace on the Upper Connecticut. But your old grandmother and I abided each other for nearly fifty years and that's more than a lot of married folks can say, and now that's the end of all of this. In the morning, or whenever this storm blows over, we'll bury them up on the top of this mountain, where they can look off at the Barrens and be content. Then it'll all be over with, and you and I will both go ahead with our affairs. Now, good night."

But I couldn't let it rest there. I just couldn't.

"Gramp?"

He said nothing, so I nudged him. "Gramp? What was it Mira called you? What was the name she gave you? The one she said just before she . . . went?"

He heard me. He wasn't sleeping yet, and I knew he heard me. But for a long time he said nothing. Then when I had almost drifted off myself he made that hoarse click in his throat and said, "I could never get my tongue around the word in Beothuk, Austen. But as nearly as I could figure, it meant something like 'The Fella Who Never Smiles Except When He Looks at Me.' "

Even before I came fully awake, I knew that something about the world was different. An instant later I realized that the wind was no longer blowing. Outside, the August sun was shining brightly. My grandfather had already dug the canoe out of an eight-foot drift, and the sunshine on the two feet of new snow was dazzling to look at. The dark green canoe looked incongruous against the white mountainside.

Ten minutes later we had taken down the tent and were hauling the loaded canoe up the slope by its tow ropes. The snow was already melting fast; it stuck to the bottom of the canoe and to our snowshoes. Every dozen steps we had to scrape it off with the paddles, but soon we reached the crest of the mountain, where most of the snow had blown away in the big wind the night before.

From the top of No Name, the view was spectacular in all directions. Off to the south, the terrain we had fought through flood and fire to traverse looked as peaceful as a summer calendar scene. Beyond us to the north, the Snow Chain range dog-legged sharply east to form the Great Lost Corner. To the west lay the fabled Barrens, where the waterways drained north into Ungava Bay. No Name Lake, a huge body of water many miles long, gleamed invitingly in the sunshine.

"Is it about the way you remembered it?" I asked.

"No," my grandfather said. "It's exactly the way I remembered it. Now help me find our last survey benchmark, Austen. If I remember correctly, it ought to be right here, someplace."

My grandfather scraped some moss off a massive rectangular rock. Sure enough, there was the old brass plate, screwed tightly into the granite. The weathered inscription read: 1910 ROYAL CANADIAN SURVEY EXPEDITION. UNGAVA-LABRADOR BOUNDARY. ELEVATION + − 2,134.

"I doubt anyone's laid eyes on this marker since we set it here half a century ago, Austen." My grandfather looked around again at the magnificent view. "This is as good a place as any I know of to put them to rest. That inland sea won't reach up here, I reckon. And it's a lovely prospect of the Barrens out there to the west. She and I had planned to go over there with the baby at the end of the summer, maybe spend part of the winter trapping that country."

"I'll help you, Gramp."

My grandfather shook his head. "I'll manage. You head in the direction of that big lake with the canoe. I'll catch up with you before you run out of snow."

"Gramp—"

He held up one mittened hand. "I'll tend to matters here myself. This is between them and me, Austen."

With no further talk, I left him with the shovel and the canvas sack containing the bones and trudged down the west slope of the mountain, hauling the canoe behind me like a great green toboggan. Soon I came to a crease in the mountainside full of rushing snow runoff. At the foot of the mountain it widened into a negotiable stream leading out through the Barrens toward No Name Lake; and here, on the fringe of the snow line, I waited for my grandfather to finish the job he had begun fifty years ago.

That night we camped partway down the stream to No Name Lake. We'd paddled almost until dusk, since the bush pilot out of Schefferville was scheduled to pick us up at the north end of the lake just five days later. The following morning we canoed out to the big body of water and started up toward our rendezvous point. We camped three nights on the shores of No Name, each time where wild-looking streams poured in from the west. For three days we paddled up the huge lake through the Barrens, which were both bleaker and lovelier than any of the country we'd traveled through yet. This was a terrain of violently-folded parallel ridges, long eskers, numberless rocks, moss of every imaginable bright color, riotously gorgeous sunsets and trout more brilliant still. There was no sign that anyone had ever been here before us. It was a land of bare granite, icy water, and wide vistas, and it filled me with a deep awe. At the same time, my grandfather seemed much more himself again, taking an hour in the evenings to fish, joking with me in his harsh way—"You might yet turn out to be a good fella to go down the river with, Austen"—and looking around and appearing to enjoy the country for the ruggedly beautiful place it was.

Midway through our fourth morning on the lake, I heard the steady hush of distant rapids. The mirage of No Name's outlet lifted into sight, high over the north end of the lake. Soon the river itself materialized. At its exit from the lake, it was divided by a good-sized island thickly forested with spruce, though most of the surrounding terrain was treeless.

As we made for the island between the split rapids, I said over my shoulder to my grandfather, "How far are we from other people? A hundred miles? Two hundred?"

He shook his head. "About half a mile."

Thinking I must have misheard him, I turned back around to see a lone man standing at the edge of the woods on the island, where a moment ago there had been no one. His hand was raised in greeting, and behind him in a clearing in the spruce trees I spotted a small trapper's cabin, resembling my grandfather's camp at home in Lost Nation. The cabin was so new the peeled logs still shone with fresh sap. For seventy-five days I had seen not one other person besides my grandfather. Now I could scarcely have been more astonished by an apparition.

But no apparition could have duplicated the lugubrious, ironical expression of Mr. Donny Snowball as he waded out into the lake to help pull the canoe to shore. "Good to see you boys," he said in the most sorrowful voice imaginable. He handed a wooden box to my grandfather. "Here, I bought you some cigars. White Owls. Then I thought I'd have to smoke them all myself. When you didn't show up last week, I thought you'd drowned down on the Rivière de la Mort. Or burned up in the wildfire. I saw a lot of smoke over across the mountains a few days ago, figured I'd have to go dispose of your charred remains."

"This must be quite a setback for you," my grandfather said, getting out of the canoe and stretching with his hands in the small of his back. "You seem to have been greatly looking forward to disposing of our remains."

Mr. Snowball gave me a wan smile. "Your grandfather has a pretty good sense of humor," he said. "We ought to get along fine up here, him and me. I've got a sense of humor too."

To Gramp he said, "Did you find the old chief's camp you told me about on the train?"

"We did," Gramp said. "And very nearly killed ourselves a dozen times over coming up that godforsaken river. They can flood it off the face of the earth now so far as we're concerned. Right, Austen?"

I nodded, remembering the night in the gorge, the towering flames from the forest fire.

"Is that your cabin?" I asked Donny.

"Mine and your grandfather's," he said. "Didn't he tell you?"

"Tell me what?"

"That we're going partners on a trapline up here."

I whirled around and stared at my grandfather, who just turned to Mr. Snowball and said casually, "The fur sign looked good on our way up the lake. The pilot find it all right?"

Mr. Snowball nodded. "No problem. That map you drew me and him was right on the money. But I don't think anyone's ever been here before us. All kinds of animal sign. Otter. White wolf. Marten. Some wolverine. We ought to do all right if we don't go through the ice and drown. An American fella named Brewer went up to the English River to trap back four, five winters ago—"

"Tell us about Brewer later," my grandfather said. "The plane's due in to pick up Austen tomorrow, and he wants to go fishing now."

"Down off the bottom tip of the island," Mr. Snowball said sadly. "Best I've ever seen."

"That's a shame," my grandfather said. "Unlimber your fly rod, Austen. You and I are going brook trout fishing."

I was stunned by my grandfather's disclosure that he planned to stay on in the Barrens with Mr. Snowball. He refused to discuss the matter, however, until we'd had our trout fishing, which turned out to be the finest afternoon and evening of fishing I have ever experienced, before or since. Brook trout weighing up to six pounds were congregated in enormous numbers in the rapids and the gravel riffles off the foot of the island, and over the next several hours my grandfather and Donny Snowball and I caught and released hundreds. At last the trout wore me out. My casting arm ached from playing them, and as the sun lowered over the Barren Lands in a great wash of crimson and gold, I sat down on a boulder beside Mr. Snowball.

After a while he motioned toward my grandfather, who was still fishing, and, in the gathering dusk, had seemed to become more and more a part of the river and the wilderness.

"He belongs up here, eh?" Donny Snowball said.

"You don't think he'll fall through the ice and drown? Or burn up in a forest fire?"

"Oh, maybe. Very possibly, in fact. But he belongs here anyway. I don't know why he ever left the first time."

"I do," I said, and Mr. Snowball looked at me curiously but didn't say anything else and neither did I. My grandfather could tell him about Mira in his own time, or not tell him. I wasn't about to breathe a word of what I knew.

We kept just three medium-sized trout to eat that night, and after we'd finished them and Mr. Snowball had gone inside the new cabin to go to bed, my grandfather and I had a final mug of tea together while he smoked one of Mr. Snowball's cigars. I had not asked him anything else about his decision to stay in Labrador. But there wasn't much time left. The plane taking me out would be here in the morning.

Although we'd had a spell of Indian summer after the big blizzard on No Name Mountain, the late-August evenings had turned very chilly. My grandfather threw another chunk of spruce on the fire. Then he rummaged in the old wooden grub box for his pocketbook, from which he handed me three hundred dollars.

"Your summer wages," he said.

Next he handed me a carbon copy of a typed document. By the firelight I saw that it was the deed to the Farm in Lost Nation, signed over to his four children. Attached was a separate, shorter document deeding his hunting camp, Labrador, to me. "The taxes on everything are paid for the next four years, Austen. Zack Barrows has a copy of the deeds in his office. I mailed your father and Rob and your aunts theirs the day before we left to come North."

I looked at my grandfather in the firelight, and his face seemed at repose. I thought of Mr. Snowball's observation. "He belongs up here." And although I knew that Donny Snowball was right, I could not seem to reconcile myself to the idea.

"So you really aren't coming back?"

"No," Gramp said. "There's nothing to go back to."

"Who's going to farm the place? Who's going to farm the Farm in Lost Nation?"

My grandfather made that rasping click in his throat. "There isn't any more Farm in Lost Nation, Austen. There hasn't been since I quit shipping milk. It was just barely a farm for years before that. The sawmill's played out too. There aren't ten acres of usable timber left on the entire place."

My grandfather threw his tea leaves into the fire, in a gesture dismissive of the Farm. "Lost Nation Hollow is a bygone place. I watched it pass into history and so did you, though at the time you were too young to know what was happening. The farms are all gone. The big woods are gone. The best of the hunting and fishing is gone. The kids, including all four of mine, have grown up and gone away and not come back. What is there for them to come back to? What is there for any of us to come back to?

"Now, Austen, they say living in the bush adds twenty years to your life. I don't know about that but I intend to find out. Not sit around the stove on a gone-by farm and dry up and fade away. And I'll tell you something else. Lost Nation is no place for you to live now, either. Use the camp for a hunting camp if you can find anything left to hunt. But don't go back there to live. What would you do there, even with a college education? Go to schoolmastering like your father? That would be a fine thing for a smart young fella like you that's supposed to be heard from. The world is bigger than Lost Nation, boy. That's what I'm saying to you."

Suddenly I was very angry with my grandfather—angrier than I'd been when he had insisted that we put in eighteen-hour days mapping the territory we'd crossed, angrier than when he'd led me on the forced march up the flooded gorge and on through the fire-ravaged country into the blizzard. I was angry because he and I had been inseparable for twelve years and now his decision to stay here seemed like a rejection of me.

"Fine," I said. "Then I'm staying too. You and Mr. Snowball and I can all run the trapline together."

"You'll do no such thing, mister," my grandfather said.

"Then where the hell else do you think I should be? I can't stay here with you. Lost Nation's dead and gone. I can't go back there. Where should I be?"

"In college," he said. "I promised your grandmother I'd see you through your schooling, Austen. By my calculations, you've got four more years to go. In the meantime, you can come up here and work for me summers. I can pay you some from my trapping proceeds. I'll need a man to help me map these Barrens, no doubt. There's a lot of them."

Again my grandfather began to rummage in the grub box. "These are for you, Austen. Take proper care of them because someday, despite what you think now, you'll come to value them."

He'd taken out the flat metal case containing the maps he'd drawn over the summer of the Great Lost Corner of Labrador. The only maps in existence of that vast tract of wilderness, soon to be inundated by an inland sea.

I didn't know what to say. The maps were undoubtedly the greatest gift my grandfather could possibly have given me. But he just threw his cigar butt into the fire after his tea leaves and said, "This meeting is adjourned for the evening. Douse the fire before you come to bed."

When he reached the entrance of the cabin my grandfather turned back. "Austen," he said out into the darkness, "you did all right this summer. You're a good fella to go down the river with."

My grandfather was both right and wrong about life in the Far North. Living in the bush did not add twenty years to his life, but it very well may have helped to add ten. For a full and happy decade, he dwelt on No Name Lake with his trapping partner and friend, Donny Snowball, and I spent some of the happiest summers of my life visiting him there.

In the late fall of 1970, when the caribou began returning from their summer migration to the big hidden lake beyond the Snow Chain Mountains, my grandfather, then eighty-two though looking scarcely sixty, went through the ice on No Name's outlet and took a bad chill. He and Donny had been on their way into the Barrens for the fall trapping, and Donny told him flatly that they should return immediately to their cabin and wait there for Gramp to regain his strength. "You stay out in the bush now, you'll catch pneumonia and die sure as shooting," Donny warned him.

"When I can't stay out in the bush anymore I don't give a good goddamn if I do die," my grandfather said, and insisted on pushing on.

Four days later, Austen Kittredge died of pneumonia. Donny towed his body back across the ice on a hand-sledge and buried him under a cairn on the top of No Name Mountain, next to Mira, though how he managed this, alone in the Ungava winter, I have no idea. It was a great act of loyalty, after which Donny ran their trapline alone for another two or three winters, before establishing a fly-in hunting and fishing lodge on the outlet of No Name, which today is a lucrative business. "Things change, Tut. You can't predict the future."

The Farm in Lost Nation Hollow? I stay there summers with my family, though of course the true hill country of my youth and the hill people who lived there then long ago passed into history. There has been no farming in the Hollow now for decades.

Recently I have found myself dreaming of family pictures, most never taken. I see my grandmother and my great-aunt, two young girls standing on a Halifax dock, looking gravely through the sleet into the camera of my imagination.

And my grandfather at seventy-two, with the best decade of his life still ahead of him, standing on the shore of the island at the outlet of No Name Lake as the floatplane I am riding in wheels and banks and whines off over the wilderness toward Schefferville.

Here I am at six, standing next to my grandfather beside his millpond, learning to use a fly rod. "Cast short and straight, Austen," he says harshly. "I won't fish with a fancy-Dan caster."

In stark tones of black and white, I see my sable-clad grandmother against Lost Nation's wintery hills, drawing a bead on the great white snow owl. And I see her rising off the pillows of her deathbed, fierce and exultant in her vision of Egypt, and lying in state in the tamarack sarcophagus my grandfather built for her, surrounded by her strange and wonderful Egyptian artifacts.

They come at night, unbidden, just before I fall asleep and on nights when sleep comes slowly. They are photographs, sepia-tinted. Most are of my grandfather and grandmother, who throughout my boyhood were at the center of everything for me. They remain at the center of my memories today, frozen in those recollections of my youth in Lost Nation, along with all their ancestors and mine back to my Great-Great-Great-Great-Great-Grandfather Sojourner Kittredge. They are a lost nation themselves now, existing in my memory, and on these pages, and nowhere else.

Mosher, Howard F.
Northern borders